Caleb Anthrop was born in Lafayette, Indiana, and raised in West Point, Indiana. He joined the United States Marines Corps in December 2006 and served until December 2014, receiving an Honorable Discharge. A veteran of both Operation Iraqi Freedom, 2009, and Operation Enduring Freedom, 2010, he later attended Ball State University in Muncie, Indiana, acquiring a Bachelor's of Science in Graphic Arts Management.

To Jackie Anthrop and Mary Hendrickson, for inspiring a love of the written word that persists to this day.

To the Men and Women of the United States Marine Corps. Semper Fidelis.

Caleb Anthrop

HUNTER IN THE STORM

The Minutemen Saga

AUSTIN MACAULEY PUBLISHERS™
LONDON * CAMBRIDGE * NEW YORK * SHARJAH

Ordering Information
Quantity sales: Special discounts are available on quantity purchases by corporations, associations, and others. For details, contact the publisher at the address below.

Publisher's Cataloging-in-Publication data
Anthrop, Caleb
Hunter in the Storm

ISBN 9781638296713 (Paperback)
ISBN 9781638296720 (ePub e-book)

www.austinmacauley.com/us

Library of Congress Control Number: 2022923948

First Published 2023
Austin Macauley Publishers LLC
40 Wall Street, 33rd Floor, Suite 3302
New York, NY 10005
USA

mail-usa@austinmacauley.com
+1 (646) 5125767

To my brothers and sisters in uniform: Semper Fidelis Marines.

To the men and women of Detcomm Co Indianapolis and Cincinnati, for the inspiration of so many characters.

To my grandmothers, Mary Hendrickson and Jackie Anthrop, who sparked a literary fire in my soul that has yet to diminish.

Thanks to Mara Semon for the cover.

The snow was coming down in heavy, fat flakes, adding to the three feet already on the ground. It would most likely add another two feet before the sun broke upon the horizon. Colonel Huang Xu Lin of the New Imperial Asian army looked once more to the sky and cursed silently. He hated this godless country. He had been fighting here for the last three years and had yet to see the eastern side of these mountains. Three years of trying to bring a glorious new civilization to these barbarians. Things had started off so well. First the surprise invasion of all the western states. Hawaii was cut off and conquered within a day. San Diego, Los Angeles, San Francisco, Seattle, and Portland were all sights of the invasion forces.

The surprise attack of these major cities had left the American scrambling to the defense. The armies pushed as deep as they could before a concentrated resistance rose up. Once they realized that they had already lost the coast, the Americans order all forces to fall back to the eastern side of the Rocky Mountains and set up a line of defense. Like so many other great conquerors throughout history, it was a line that the imperial army was having an impossible time breaking through.

Hundreds of flights had been sent in pursuit of the retreating American forces, hoping to cripple any bases in the Midwest before the ground assault made its way through the mountains.

Every flight was surprised when an invincible line of anti-aircraft weapons opened fire the second the flights cleared the range. Every flight since had failed as well. To slow the empire down further, the treacherous Americans had destroyed every major road and rail way through the mountains, forcing the empire's forces to blaze trails through. The generals were hoping to clear the ranges within a month. Then the worst snow storm in over a century rolled in, covering the entire range in a heavy blanket of snow and ice. Avalanches and fallen trees were common.

Huang looked up the trail, past the line of armored vehicles idling in the snow and slush, their exhausts creating a hanging screen of steam in the air. A recent avalanche had blocked the path ahead with very large trees and rocks, further delaying the battalion from their rendezvous with the rest of the division. As Huang watched several of his engineers move between the block and the convoy, he heard the muted crunch of boots approaching from behind him. It signaled the return of one of his reconnaissance squads. He had sent several on ahead to get the lay of the land.

"Report," Huang ordered.

"Sir, advanced reconnaissance shows no signs of American forces within five miles of our position," a male voice said from behind Huang. "There is, however, a small farm eight miles to the northeast. Three structures: a two-story house, a large barn, and a smaller outbuilding. Three occupants were observed: two males and one female. We can easily slip by them without ever exposing the battalion."

Huang allowed the report to circle his mind before setting upon a course of action. "Kill them. Take another squad and kill the family. Search the buildings and the home, take anything of value and any weapons you find. Once that is complete, burn it all," Huang ordered. He could sense the officer behind him stiffen with hesitation.

"Sir, they are harmless to us. They do not know we are here," the officer said. "Why is it necessary to kill those who pose us no harm?"

"Are you refusing to follow my orders, lieutenant?" Huang asked. "Shall I remind you what happens to officers that question the orders of their betters?"

"No, sir. Your will shall be done," the officer replied dejectedly. Huang heard the officer turn and begin to walk away. He turned slightly to watch the white and gray-clad troops disappear within the flying snow. A set of muted explosions signaled that the way ahead was clear. The vehicles of his convoy throttled their engines like the roars of many bloodthirsty war beasts. Huang looked toward the east, envisioning his enemies huddling in their bases, hiding from the cold. Further east, he could see his ultimate victory shining upon the horizon. He could see his name in the history books now, hear it sung from the Forbidden City itself.

The clearing was wide, flat, and calm, the snow had lightened slightly, allowing one to see the entire spans. Nothing seemed to move amongst the many trees that encircled it. Almost nothing. A small puff of steam rose from the southern section of trees as an older buck moved cautiously toward the edge of the line. Its ears flipped back and forth, trying to pick up the smallest of sounds that did not belong. Its nose twitched as it sniffed out the barest scents. It stood immobile for ten more minutes, before deciding that it was safe to venture forth. It strode forward, still looking for signs of danger. It moved thirty meters out into the center of the clearing before stopping. It gazed around at its surroundings once more before looking down at the ground. It pawed at the snow, looking for any scrubs of grass that survived the snow. Its hoof finally found what it was searching for and the deer lowered its head to eat, completely unaware of the mortal threat that lingered nearby.

The crosshairs settled on the shoulder of the deer and rested there. The eye behind the scope stared unblinkingly.

Johnny had been lying in the same spot on the western side of the clearing just inside the tree line all morning, waiting for the perfect prize to come along. He had been reflecting upon the last few years and how twisted his life had become. At five feet eleven inches tall, his time on his family's ranch had honed his body and strengthened his muscles. He was the star linebacker of his high school and was a starter for his freshman and sophomore year at Purdue University where he was studying physics and chemistry. Then the invasion had come. He had been home on summer vacation when American forces abandoned the west coast and turned the mountains his family had lived in for generations into a giant wall.

For the last year, he and his parents and brother had survived in the same way his ancestors had, by hunting and growing their food. They also scavenged parts and supplies from nearby areas that had been abandoned during the retreat. Now at twenty four, he was lying under a snow bank that had covered him in the hours of waiting, trying to help his family survive the harshest winter anyone had ever known.

Johnny incrementally moved the forefinger of his left hand to the trigger of his Winchester rifle and let it sit there for a few moments as he gauged the wind and distance. He began to apply pressure to the trigger, squeezing it back. Just before it reached its terminus, Johnny let some pressure off as the buck took a couple of steps forward. He readjusted his aim and began to put the pressure back on the trigger. He brought it back to the terminus and paused. His father had taught him to fire between heartbeats. Just as he timed the shot, the buck's head snapped up, its ears alert and searching. Johnny took his finger away from the trigger, hoping the buck would again calm down.

That's when he heard it. The distinct rattle and pops of gunfire being brought upon the wind to his ears. Instinctually, his ears located the sound to the southwest toward his home. Johnny burst from his position in an explosion of snow and ice, causing the buck to panic and cry out as it tore off toward the safety of the north woods. Johnny took a quick second to stretch his extremities and sling his rifle over his shoulder before taking off at a sprint toward his home. Using the skills taught to him over the course of his life, Johnny was able to distinguish between thick snow and the recently covered trail. The sounds of gunfire increased as he closed the distance. He was still a half mile out when the concussion of an explosion rattled the air.

Johnny tried to will his legs to move faster as panic began to set in. He crested the final ridge separating his home from the valley he was hunting in. He slid to a stop at the edge of the tree line and gazed in horror at the scene below him.

Smoke rose from a charred hole in what used to be the second-story window of his parents' bedroom. He looked out into the yard and spotted over a dozen camouflaged men moving steadily from the southern tree line across the front yard toward the house. He spotted at least two bodies lying in the snow close to the trees. Johnny could see and hear them firing controlled bursts at the house. As he watched, one of the assaulting troopers was flung backward, as though he had been struck by and invisible force, blood and bits of bone shot out and stained the snow behind the fallen man. The intense boom of his father's 7 mm rifle followed shortly after. Another seemed to go into convulsions as multiple rounds peppered his body. Johnny figured it was his brother's AR-15 finding its mark. Johnny unslung his rifle and began to look for a way to assist his family, when a sudden flash of movement behind the barn caught his attention.

Johnny dropped to the ground and brought his rifle to his shoulder. He centered his eye in the scope and swung his gaze over to the barn. Once settled, he spotted several men moving silently around the back of the barn. He counted ten of them. If he didn't slow them down, they would slip around behind the house and attack his family from the rear. The line of flanking soldiers moved along a split rail fence that ran from the barn to the shed. Johnny couldn't help but grin. If they had been on the opposite side of the fence, the soldiers would have seen the thousands of impact craters and nicks in the wood from years of target practice he and his brother had performed. Johnny swept his crosshairs forward to the end of the fence and waited.

Just as the first soldier entered his scope, Johnny squeezed the trigger. He felt the rifle bounce against his left shoulder as the .338 Lapua solid copper round left his rifle and sped away, covering the three hundred yards in a matter of microseconds. It slammed into the soldiers head at over three thousand pounds of force. The hydrostatic energy blew the soldier's head apart, spraying it over the ground to his side. The soldier's body simply dropped where it was. The rest of the soldiers stopped and tried to take cover as much as they could.

Johnny quickly swept his aim to the last guy in the line. He rested the crosshairs on the man's chest and squeezed the trigger. The soldier was thrown sideways into the snow. The troops were now in a complete panic as they tried to get any exposed extremities out of the line of sight of the unknown sniper.

Johnny smiled to himself as he began to work his way down the line: a shoulder, two knees, an elbow, the top of one's head, and a thigh. He worked his way through the line and his magazine. He was methodical and patient. As he cycled the bolt of his rifle, his internal count told him the magazine was empty. He quickly reached for his spare magazine, when something in the yard caught his eye.

One of the soldiers had stopped in the yard and begun to shoulder a long black tube.

An icy hand gripped his heart as he realized what the tube was. Johnny switched out the dry magazine for the fresh one as quickly as he could and cycled the first round into the chamber. He brought the crosshairs to bear on to the soldier with the launcher. He went to squeeze the trigger when a great gust of wind blew up a wall of flying snow in front of him. Panicked, Johnny pulled the trigger and then cursed, knowing the shot was off. What he didn't know was that the round passed in front of the rocket trooper, giving away his position. Still panicking, Johnny fired off every round in his magazine, hoping one would take out his target. Because of the flying snow, he never saw one of the rounds hitting the rocket trooper in the upper arm, nor the trooper's comrades turning toward Johnny's position and opening fire into the trees above him. Johnny heard the rounds impact into the branches above him. There was a terrific snap and just before Johnny lost consciousness, he heard an explosion.

Lieutenant Lau Ping looked upon the battlefield with disgust and sorrow. What was supposed to have been a simple mission to kill three civilians, instead had turned into the massacre of his unit. He had begun the assault with twenty-six of the best soldiers he had ever known. He looked at the twelve wrapped bodies of those who would not be going home. The assault went wrong the minute they emerged from the tree line. The woman had been the first to spot them. She had run into the home shouting. A few seconds later, Sergeant Wu fell into the snow, his blood beginning to stain the area around him. The roar of a rifle reached their ears a split second later. Corporal Shang was the next to fall. A perfect head shot from a smaller caliber rifle. Ping decided to split his forces and sent ten of his men around the side of the barn to flank the civilians. He lost two more men to accurate fire from the house. His hopes for a quick resolution began to wither the longer the battle was drawn out.

Once they reached one hundred yards from the house, Ping ordered Sergeant Xi to fire a rocket into the home. Xi was getting set up when a round missed his face by a couple of inches. Xi called out to the rest of the unit. Ping and the others turned and fired into the trees at the unseen sniper.

Xi still took a round into his upper arm as he fired the rocket. Ping turned his gaze to the four men he sent to look for the sniper. They were returning back down the small rise, two of them dragging a limp body between them. The thought of a single person causing so much damage to his unit was startling. When the battle had ceased, Ping had sent a runner to his flanking team. The runner discovered seven of the ten dead in a line along the fence. Two others were trying to stabilize and dress a wound to a third survivor's knee. Ping was certain Private Liu would not survive the trip back to the main convoy. Xi was also going to most likely lose his arm.

Ping watched as Corporal Yin tended to Xi's arm as his men dragged the sniper over and dropped the body into the snow beside the bodies of the civilians. Private Chow walked up to Ping and handed him a Winchester bolt action rifle. Ping took the rifle and pulled the bolt back, catching the chambered round as it was ejected. Ping held the round up before his eyes. Chow whistled in amazement.

"Lapua round, .338, one hell of a round," Chow commented. Ping nodded, then looked down on the body of the sniper. He wore a coat made from some kind of skin, most likely elk or deer. His pants were simple hunting camouflage from one of dozens of hunting stores Americans loved to shop at. He also wore hiking boots and thick leather gloves. A simple black balaclava covered his face. Ping reached down and pulled the face cover up over the sniper's face. He was as young as most of Ping's own men, had a life full of dreams ahead of him before this war had started.

Now he was just another casualty in a war of pride and arrogance. Ping looked once more at the rifle in his hand. He had a sudden flash back to his grandfather. The old man had been a soldier in his youth. He had told Ping once that the weapons of a warrior should lay at rest with the warrior. Ping nodded to himself before laying the rifle down next to the sniper. This was one weapon he no longer wanted to see. He straightened himself back up and took a look around at his troops, at least those that were still alive. His two wounded were sitting as calmly as they could while Corporal Yin tried to stop them from bleeding to death and get them ready for the extremely long hike back through insanely tough terrain to the battalion. He felt a pang of guilt and sorrow as he realized that Liu wouldn't make it. His leg had nearly been severed by the sniper's round. Yin was trying to do his best to stabilize Liu, but it was a futile attempt.

Ping shook off his sorrow and guilt, then steeled himself for what was to come. "Listen up! We move out in fifteen minutes," Ping ordered. "Chow, take Hon and Ngyen and cover up our fallen. Mark the site on GPS for the recovery teams and follow up units." Ping watched his people get into action. Chow and the other two began to unfurl tarps and field blankets, while the others reloaded magazines and helped Yin with Xi and Liu. Ping observed them as they did what they were supposed to do. After fifteen minutes, Ping called for his men to collect their gear and move out. Chow walked up to him as he took one last look upon the farm that had cost so many lives to take.

"Ready, sir?" Chow asked.

"Yes, Chow, I am ready. I fear though, that this battle is just the beginning."

"Beginning, sir?"

"Yes. If it took the lives of fourteen of our finest to take a simple farm, how many is it going to take to conquer this entire country?" Ping asked. "Think upon that, Chow. I do not think we have seen the full might this land has to throw at us, despite what our superiors claim." Ping looked at Chow and nodded to the young soldier. "Come, it will be nightfall before we return to the battalion."

The two soldiers turned and began walking back toward the woods.

Dreams always come in weird and random intervals for Johnny. He had had more than a few of those dreams after hard hits from football and twice from getting thrown from his horse. This dream was no exception. Johnny stood in the middle of the clearing he was hunting in that very morning. He looked down at his hands, at the rifle he had been using. The wind whipped around him, moaning like a bad horror movie. Snow obscured his sight, only allowing him to see a few feet in any direction. Johnny looked around as a new sound emerged, the sounds of battle, the sounds of screams and explosions. His hands suddenly felt slick against his rifle. He looked down and saw his hands covered in blood. The snow around him began to turn red, flowing toward him from the flying snow.

As soon as the blood reached his boots, there was a violent gust of wind, pushing the flying snow out away from him. Johnny looked around in horror. There were hundreds of bodies lying twisted in the snow. Some were simply lying there, others were blown apart, and still more were staring into the sky with lifeless eyes. Johnny felt fear creeping into his heart the more he looked upon the carnage. The sound of boots crunching in the snow approached him from behind at a quickened pace. Johnny spun around to see a man rushing at him, a long knife in the attacker's hand.

Johnny responded instinctively, bringing his rifle to bear, up into his shoulder, barrel swinging into position. Johnny squeezed the trigger without a second's hesitation. The heavy round leapt from the barrel and lanced straight at the attacker. It slammed into the man's chest, causing his back to explode outward in a spray of blood and bone. The attacker fell on his face and slid a few feet in the snow, coming to a stop a few inches from Johnny's foot. Johnny stared down at the corpse, the wound still smoking, matching the smoke still exiting the barrel of his rifle.

Johnny stared as the blood oozed from the body and into the snow. What had he done?

You did what was necessary, what was needed to survive. The voice seemed to come from nowhere and everywhere at once. Johnny spun around, looking for the source, his rifle at the ready.

Stay calm, young warrior. You are in no danger here. "Where is here?" Johnny asked.

The place where you learn of your future. Johnny heard the crunch of snow once again and spun around, preparing for another attack. Instead, he came face to face with a very large timber wolf. The creature stood four feet at the shoulder. Its calm and intelligent brown eyes stared into Johnny as though it were staring into his soul, judging the man it saw there. The wind had begun to pick up once again, the edges of the clearing began to disappear as snow began to fall and get whipped about by the wind.

The land is under siege once more. It will fall upon the few to inspire the many to take up arms in defense of their homes. It will fall upon ones like you, you who have lost all.

"How?" Johnny asked. The wolf tilted its head to the side, as though confused by the question. Johnny asked again, adding more clarity. "How am I supposed to inspire and defend my home?"

You are a hunter, no? You have spent your life learning to become one with the environment and nature. Use the skills that come naturally and the rest shall fall in line. The wolf looked at him with more determination in its eyes. First, however, you must release the hatred and vengeance that is burning in your heart. Flashes of the attack on his home ran through his mind. Hunt down those that took your life from you and end their existence. The wolf nodded to Johnny and then turned to leave. We will speak again, once you have secured the mountains.

The wolf walked away, disappearing into the encroaching snow. The wind picked up in ferocity again, whipping the snow about him in a blinding haze. It rushed at him from all sides, soon enveloping him in a white out blizzard.

Johnny groaned as he began to regain consciousness. His head felt like it was too big for his skull. He then felt cold in his extremities. It took him a few moments to realize that he was lying on his back in the snow. He slowly wiggled his fingers and his toes, making sure that they worked and he could feel them. He then moved his hands and feet. Finally, he opened his eyes.

He could see the cold gray and white of the snow heavy clouds in the sky. A few light flakes were falling slowly toward him. He brought his arms up to visually inspect his hands. Everything seemed to be working just fine. Slowly Johnny rolled himself over on to his side, and came face to face with the cold dead eyes of his brother. Johnny jerked away in fright, coming to his feet in a hurry. His brother's body was already turning blue as it froze in the snow. Johnny saw blood freezing and drying on his shirt from wounds in his chest.

Johnny began to shake as he reached down to close his brother's eyes. Eyes that were once so full of life and passion for everything wild. He remembered how his brother wanted to become a zoologist and spend time in the wilds of every continent. Johnny looked past his brother and saw his mother lying face down in the snow, her blond hair splayed out around her head. A tear began to form in the corner of his eye as he realized he would never hear her laugh or her sardonic sense of humor. He stood back up and spotted his father's body beside his mother. It hurt to see the man who had taught Johnny everything he knew about the forest, about hunting, about survival, lying in a broken heap on the land his ancestors had settled before him.

Johnny looked up toward the house and his heart sank. There was the hole in his parent's bedroom. A second hole was blasted into the wall of the dining room, causing the whole second floor to sag on that side. Johnny took a step forward toward the house. It was broken, but still standing. He shook his head to clear it, then turned to head toward the barn. He needed to find a shovel, he needed to bury his family. He walked slowly, as though he was in a trance. The pounding in his head had begun to subside as he made it to the door of the barn. He paused to take a look at the fence that ran along its side. Several pools of frozen blood marked the locations where the men he killed had fallen.

Johnny continued into the barn, trying to shake the images of blood and brain matter from his thoughts. He made his way to the back of the building where his family had kept all of their tools. He stopped for a moment to admire what he had always taken for granted. Every tool had its place, each place marked the tool's purpose. Clean, organized, now to be forgotten.

Johnny slowly reached for one of the spades, when something caught his eye. A simple flash of light, a reflection of the bare bulb above him off the handle to the armory safe. Johnny stared at the solid black door his father had installed when his parents had moved in. A veteran of several conflicts, Johnny's father was a staunch believer in home protection, as well as practice and training make perfect.

The internal fight then began as two sides of Johnny's personality vied for control of his actions. Remorseful and mourning, Johnny wanted nothing more than to pick up the shovel off the wall, go outside and bury his parents and brother. To lay them to rest in the very earth they had loved and tended for decades. It was what they deserved, what was expected.

On the other hand, vengeful Johnny blazed for control. It wanted nothing more than to hunt down the survivors of the unit that had slaughtered his family and make them pay tenfold. It wanted blood and wanted it now. The fire of hatred and rage were building up inside Johnny at an alarming pace. Soon, Johnny didn't want revenge just on the ones that performed the actual assault, but he wanted to take revenge on their friends and their comrades, on their officers and their homes. And then it happened, vengeful Johnny overpowered and consumed his remorse in a hellfire of rage. Johnny lowered his arm and turned toward the armory door. He walked calmly, but the fire behind his eyes blazed. He quickly put in the combination his father had taught him years ago. The date when his father and mother had met.

The internal computer recognized the code and the sound of tumblers falling into place signaled that the door was unlocked. Johnny gripped the handle and paused as his conscious tried once more to regain control.

What would be gained by hunting those men down? It asked. What would your parents say if they could see what you are about to do?

For a moment, it looked as though Johnny's conscious was getting through to his rage. Then his mind flashed to a memory of his family out on their yearly camping trip and he knew that such activities were never going to happen again. Fueled by the image, his rage flared once more and Johnny yanked the door to the armory open with all his strength.

He stood there for a moment to take in the sight. Rows upon rows of weapons met his gaze. Rifles, shotguns, and pistols of varying sizes and makes were at his disposal. Johnny went down the row of rifles, trying to decide which one to use, when he stopped before a glass case. Inside was a rifle very much like the one he was using this morning. A .338 Lapua bolt action rifle. Only this one was much older. His father had told him it belonged to his great grandfather. The great grandfather that spent a lifetime in the United States

Marine Corps. Johnny knew it still functioned as well now as it did when his great grandfather that used it at the beginning of this century, his father had made sure to keep it maintained and oiled.

Johnny thought it fitting that the weapon that first brought his family down the military path would be used to avenge them. Johnny opened the case and reverently took the rifle from it. It weighed slightly more than what he was used to, but it wasn't going to be an issue. Johnny walked to the back of the armory where a table had been set up for maintenance and cleaning purposes. Johnny extended the attached bipod and set the rifle down on the table. He then moved down the pistol aisle. He stopped and pulled two pistols from their built in holsters.

Presents from his grandfather, the pistols were .45 caliber Berretta customs. The grips had been form fitted for his hands. His grandfather had them add extended barrels and compensators to each, as well as built in laser sights that activated when Johnny held them. He took the pistols to the table, picking up his leg holsters as he went. He laid the pistols down next to the rifle and turned to the ammo cabinets. He yanked them open and began to pull boxes of ammo and magazines from the cabinet. He laid them all out in a line and began to work. He loaded fifteen magazines of .338 Lapua solids, ten rounds to each magazine. He then moved to the pistols. Ten magazines for each pistol, each magazine holding twelve rounds. He set the last magazine down and went to the tactical closet, as his father used to call it.

He searched for and quickly found his father's jacket and load-bearing vest. The jacket was a custom build for his father by an old military friend. The jacket had pouches for several magazines of all sizes, plus loops for shotgun shells and grenades. As a bonus, his father's friend added a drop down slide for extra pistol magazines. The slide was concealed inside the back of the coat and merely required a tug on what was disguised as a simple tag near the right hand. Johnny brought both to the table and began to load up the magazines.

He quickly shed the jacket he had been wearing and donned the black jacket instead. He secured the leg holsters to the bottom of the jacket and then to his legs. Johnny picked up his pistols one at a time, sliding a full magazine in place with a satisfactory snap, then pulling the slides back to chamber the first rounds. Johnny made sure each was on safe and then placed them in their respective holsters. He picked up the rifle and pulled the bolt back. He inserted one of the magazines into its well and gave it a tug to make sure it was seated properly, then he pushed the bolt forward, chambering the first round. He collapsed the bipod and slipped the sling over his shoulder, adjusting it so he could quickly bring the rifle around, but not so loose that it would swing wildly as he ran.

He went back to the closet and pulled a balaclava from the drawer of winter gear and slipped it over his head. He looked around, trying to think of anything else he should take, when his gaze fell upon a shotgun. His first shotgun, a side by side double barreled break breach weapon, Johnny had cut the barrels down.

He quickly strode over and picked it up. He opened the breach and then moved to the ammo cabinet. He found the shells for it quickly and inserted two. He closed the breach and then slid the weapon into a built in sling on the jacket's lower back built originally for a launcher tube. Johnny adjusted the straps and made sure he could quickly and easily retrieve and store the weapon. He then pulled two handfuls of shells from the cabinet and put a dozen in the loops on the jacket and the rest in one of pockets. He turned on his heel and marched out of the armory. He now had a purpose, and it was time to get to work.

He left the barn at a trot, making his way back to the line of the dead. He noticed that the sun had begun its crest in the sky and a light snow was beginning to fall once again. He came to a stop and began to search the snow for tracks and clues. He saw a few cigarette butts and some dropped ammo before he found the trail. They were not cautious, Johnny mused. They were spread out, instead of being in a single file line. He followed the trail to the edge of the woods and stopped to take a look back at his home. The smoke from the missile curled into the sky, marking where death had come to a peaceful home. Johnny turned back to the trail and began his hunt, knowing that by nightfall, more would die by his hand.

Lieutenant Ping walked slowly at the center of the formation. His eyes scanning the trees for any sign of trouble. What was left of his unit was spread out in a lopsided arrow formation. He knew they should be traveling in a single file, but he was confident they were not going to be followed anytime soon. His gaze swept over the trees to his right and as it did, he saw Sergeant Liu. Liu was limping along as best as he could after that round had nearly severed his leg at the knee.

His thoughts drifted back to the assault on the farm. It had gone all wrong from the start. He had wanted to avoid the farm, keep their presence this deep into the mountains a secret, but his commander had overruled him. And now a full half of his men were dead, and another may yet join them. The civilians' defense of their home had been amazing, Ping begrudgingly thought. Their fire had been constant and accurate from the home. Then when the sniper had added his own fire to the defense, the real toll had been tallied. Ten shots, ten hits, nine kills. Amazing.

Ping wondered if all mountain people fought with such ferocity. He remembered stories his grandfather used to tell him and his cousins. His grandfather told him that the dwellers of mountains the world round spent their lives contending with the beasts and spirits that also inhabited their mountains. Born and bred to be more beast than man, a wise person would avoid all conflicts with them. If conflict could not be avoided, then it would be best to wipe them out to a man, woman, and child. Survivors would bring the full weight of the natural and supernatural world down upon those that violated the sanctity of their mountain home.

This led Ping's thoughts to drift to the stories of ghosts and monsters that would inhabit the ancient forests of the world, like the one he and his men were in, looking to pounce upon unwary travelers, dragging them off. Never to be seen again. The hairs on the back of Ping's neck and he quickly brought his head around to view his surroundings. His eyes were wide as his unspoken fear expected to see yetis and yerrens hiding amongst the trees. He gave himself a little shake and then internally berated himself for indulging such fantasies. He was an officer in the strongest military in the world, he had no time to allow such childhood nightmares affect himself nor his men.

He gazed skyward and for the first time noticed how dark it actually was in this forest.

He could just spot the weepy sun through the clouds above him. He then looked down at his watch, they had been moving for almost three hours, and they still had several more to go before they returned to the convoy. He looked ahead of the unit, up the trail, and spotted the rock outcropping they used as a trail marker.

He looked around, looking for his radio man. He spotted Private Chu slightly back from him and a dozen feet to his left. He might as well radio the convoy of their position and eta. He contemplated reporting the outcome of the assault, to let command know of his failure to protect his men from four civilians. To let them know of his shame. He ultimately decided not to, it would be better if he made his report in person. He would also accept any punishment they decided to hand down.

"Private Chu!" Ping barked, waving the young man over. Chu trudged his way through the deep snow to catch up to him. As soon as Chu fell in step with Ping, he unclipped the radio handset and handed it to Ping. "Command Net."

"Yes sir," Chu responded. He began to press keys on the wrist computer on his left arm.

Ping brought the handset to his ear and had just pressed the talk button, when there was a sudden splash of warm liquid against the side of his head. Ping looked over just as Chu's body began to fall, a massive bloody wound in his chest. Ping hesitated a split second, his mind still trying to register what had just happened, before he dove to the ground. That split second was enough time for Sergeant Liu to join his ancestors as a second round ripped through his chest. Ping rolled to his left and looked for more substantial cover as yet another round blazed from the shadows of the forest and through the neck of yet another one of Ping's dwindling forces. Ping spotted a large cluster of boulders ten meters to his right and began to judge how fast he could cover that space. He tensed his muscles, preparing to fire all of them at the same time to get to cover as quickly as possible. He paused for half a heartbeat and then jumped to his feet. He moved as though death were at his heels, and for all he knew, it was. He covered the ten meters in seconds and slid behind the boulders, just as a round split the air above him with a wicked hiss.

His slide was stopped short by the body of his unit medic, Corporal Yin, who had had the same idea. Yin, startled by the sudden appearance of his commanding officer, whipped his pistol around to meet whatever threat was there. Ping used a free hand to knock the pistol from the frightened Corporal's hand. The weapon fell into the snow as Yin finally recognized Ping.

"S-sir? Where is it coming from?" Yin asked. Ping took a deep breath.

"I do not know. Not yet." Ping replied. He readjusted himself and peered around the boulder. He spotted several of his men taking cover near a fallen tree, more behind individual trees. As he was watching, one of his men leaned out to take a look up the trail. Before Ping could warn him, the soldier's head snapped backward as the large caliber round tore through his head. He watched the body fall backward into the snow. Three of the surviving troops took their chances to move to more sufficient cover behind another pile of large builders. Only two of them made it, as the third was caught in the chest mid-run, corkscrewing the body into the snow. Ping then heard the crack of the passing round. He looked up the trail, hoping against hope to locate the sniper.

Sniper? Ping thought, his mind briefly flashing to the fallen young man back at the farm.

He shook the thought from his mind. They had made sure that the young man was dead. This was most likely an American commando or Marine keeping them pinned down until the rest of the sniper's unit could flank them. Ping continued to search for the sniper as another shot rang through the forest, impacting a tree covering one of his men. Ping followed the impact into the tree up into the forest. He spotted a hanging cliff nearly two hundred yards up the trail at his two o'clock. If he were positioning a sniper, that's where he would put him.

"Suppressive fire, my two o'clock," Ping shouted to his men. He put the barrel of his rifle over the top of his cover and squeezed off a short burst. He had reloaded after the assault on the farm, meaning the first two rounds in the fresh magazine were tracer rounds. He watched as the tracers bit into the bottom of the cliff above where he suspected the sniper to be. The survivors of his unit began to pop randomly out of their cover to squeeze off short bursts of fire, hoping to keep the sniper pinned, as they worked out their next move. Unfortunately, their enemy was not as skittish as they had hoped. Another round tore through Ping's only surviving marksman as he leaned out from his cover. The round took the marksman in the throat, and even from a dozen feet away, Ping could hear the gurgle of the man's dying breath.

Another round took the last of his heavy weapons specialists in the chest as the man tried to lay down a sustained burst from his squad suppression weapon. The man's muscles clamped down on the trigger of his weapon, which began firing at a cyclic rate, burning through the belt loaded into its receiver. As he fell, the torque of the weapon caused him to twist. Unfortunately, the movement sent more than four dozen rounds into the cover position of two of his comrades. The rounds tore through them as if they were simple paper targets. The weapon finally ran dry, but not before turning the two unfortunate soldiers into a bloodied puddle. Ping looked around to see just how many of his men were still alive and felt the blood drain from his body. The engagement had been going for only a couple of minutes, and already, his remaining forces had been cut in half. Ping spotted his men that were still alive and tried to formulate a plan to get them all out alive. His thoughts were interrupted as another of his men took a round through his neck.

He tried to send out orders to the last four of his men, but found his voice unable to articulate anything other than strangled cries. He saw one of his men dart between trees, trying to get closer to Ping and Yin. The man's tactics seemed to be working as he covered more than half the distance without a problem. He stopped behind a large oak to catch his breath and look to see how much further he had to go. He was less than ten feet from Ping and Yin, a very quick dash could get him to safety. He took a deep breath and spun from his cover. Ping saw the look of triumph in the young man's eyes turn to panic as the round punched through his thigh. He fell to the ground and slid a couple of feet as blood sprayed from the wound. Ping saw the panic turn to despair and then to resignation, just before a second round impacted his back, just above his heart. Ping saw the light fade from the man's eyes and then a panicked thought crossed his mind: They were all going to die.

Ping heard another shot and knew, without having to look, that his last man was dead.

Ping then hear nothing. To him, the silence was not only deafening, but more terrifying. Steeling his resolve, Ping turned and peeked over the cover he was using. He saw all of his men, lying in red stained snow, unmoving. He saw no other movement, nor did he hear any more shots ringing through the forest.

As the silence dragged on, Ping began to believe that they had a chance to escape. If they could get deeper into the forest, then they could evade any pursuer long enough to get help.

"Yin. Yin," Ping whispered. He looked down to ensure he had Yin's attention. "We are going to move out in a few moments. If we can get further down the trail, then we can get into the deeper parts of the forest. With the falling snow to cover our tracks, we may survive this. You ready?" Yin nodded in response. "Ok, let's map out our—"Ping began as he turned around, stopping mid-sentence as his brain tried to register what he was seeing. Yin, too, turned around and gasped in surprise.

Standing a few feet behind them on the trail was a man, pointing a double-barreled side-by-side shotgun at them. He was like a statue, unmoving, cold, and silent. He was dressed in a black tactical jacket and woodland camouflage pants. His hands were in black gloves, his face and head covered by a black balaclava. Ping saw the barrel of a rifle sticking up over his shoulder and two pistols in hip holsters. His chest was covered with magazines and a handful of shotgun shells. A serious looking knife was strapped to the upper right side of his chest. Ping, Yin, and the man just stared at each other for what seemed like minutes, waiting for someone to make the first move.

Ping's eyes locked onto the man's, and recognized something…familiar in them. They sized each other up for a few moments. Then something unexpected happened: The man began to lower the shotgun. As he did, Ping sensed a slight movement next to him. Yin had begun to move his hand, very imperceptibly, toward his pistol, still lying in the snow. Ping made a soft negative noise, hoping to get Yin to stop moving. The man finished lowering his shotgun and had begun to turn away, when Yin lunged at the pistol. His fingers had just begun to close around the grip, when there was a deafening blast. Yin was thrown backward into the boulder behind him, as Ping was sprayed with something wet and warm, Yin's blood. It took a few seconds to process what had happened. Somehow, whether by some sixth sense or enhanced perception, the man had known when Yin was going to make his move, turned back toward Ping and Yin, raising the shotgun and firing both barrels at the same time into Yin's chest. The large shot rounds ripped through Yin's body armor without a problem. Ping sat there, stunned, unable to move or think as the shooter lowered the shotgun once more, turned and began walking down the trail back toward the way Ping and his men had come.

Ping watched him walk away as the snow began to fall faster, the flakes were getting thicker. Ping exhaled a breath he hadn't realized he had been holding and relaxed his grip on his rifle. Then the rage took over. This man killed his men and now he was going to walk away?

Ping looked up the trail and saw that the shooter was now at least twenty to thirty feet away. Ping brought his weapon to his shoulder and aimed down the sights, bringing them to bear on...nothing. Just as Ping brought the sights to his eye, the wind kicked up the snow between Ping and the shooter, whiting out Ping's vision. As his eyes widened in disbelief, he felt a sharp impact to his forehead, causing him to fall back against the boulder. His rifle fell from his hands as his strength abandoned him. He felt a warm trickle down his face. His eyes were having trouble keeping focus as he used the last of his strength to lift his hand to his face and touch whatever was dripping down his face. His hand followed the trail up to his forehead and felt the hole. He brought his hand to his eyes and saw it covered in blood.

His grandfather had been right all along: Never desecrate the homes of the mountain people, nothing good ever comes of it. Ping's thoughts began to fade from his mind as he lamented the fact that his men and he would be left to wander these mountains as yet more lost souls. Then a final thought entered his mind.

That was an impossible shot.

Johnny held his pistol up a few more seconds, watching the smoke and steam from the shot drift and disappear into the frigid, winter air. Thirty-four feet in front of him, he saw the last soldier fall back against the rocks behind him. His rifle lay forgotten in the snow as the soldier reached up and touched his blood covered face. He watched the hand fall back down and the soldier stopped moving. Johnny flipped the safety back to the on position of the pistol before replacing it in the holster on his left leg. He then brought the shotgun up and flipped the barrel catch, opening the breach and allowing the two spent shells to pop out of the barrels and into the snow. He reached up and pulled two fresh shells from his jacket and inserted them into the barrels. He snapped the breach closed and ensured the hammers were not in the cocked position.

He replaced the shotgun in the holster on his back and then looked back over the field of death he caused. Fourteen more bodies to add to his tally. As he stared at all of the bodies, he had a sudden inspiration. His grandfather had always told stories of how native tribes the world over would mark sites of ambushes and victories with personal designs of the tribe. Johnny walked over to the largest tree on the battlefield. He drew his knife from its shoulder sheathe and got to work. It took nearly twenty minutes to carve out the design. He chose one particular to his own family, an opened eye, then added a personal touch of a slash through the center going from upper right to lower left. He then went to the last of the fallen soldiers, the only one with the markings of what appeared to be an officer.

He searched the body until he found the man's own combat knife. He then found the man's identification tags around his neck. He pulled the tags off the body and the knife out of sheathe on the fallen man's belt. He straightened up and took one last look at the two men leaning against the boulders. Strangely, he felt no remorse nor shame at killing them, nor at killing any of the men he had killed so far. Johnny walked back over to the tree and stabbed it with enough force to bury the blade a few inches into the bark, enough to keep it secure. He aimed the strike so that the blade was piercing the tree in the center of the eye. Johnny finished by hanging the identification tags from the blade of the knife.

He stepped back to survey his handiwork. It was as best as he could make it. Johnny turned his back on the carving and began the trek back to his home. He still had a responsibility there. He had gone no more than ten feet, before the crunching sound of footsteps on snow to his right caught his attention. Reacting without any thought, Johnny spun toward the sound, pulling both pistols at the same time. It was a smooth move that should have taken years of practice. For Johnny, it was all instinct and natural muscle movement. Finishing the spin, Johnny came face to face with a wolf, both pistols brought to bear, the laser dots holding steady between its eyes.

It was the largest one he had ever seen, with fur as white as the snow around them. It stood there silent and still, its icy blue eyes, staring straight into Johnny's emerald ones. There was almost a look of familiarity between the two of them. It cocked its head to the side as it sized Johnny up. Johnny, for his part, straightened back up and went to replace the pistols in their holsters, when more movement behind the white wolf caused him to tense up. More wolves calmly walked out of the snow and forest, materializing like ghosts. Johnny began to back away, apprehension beginning to take hold. One of the younger wolves snarled at him, baring its maw of deadly teeth. It took a step toward Johnny, who reacted by stopping his movements and shifting one of the pistols to aim at the young wolf.

It took one more step toward Johnny, when the white wolf, obviously the alpha, barked at the younger one, who, after taking a quick look at the alpha, stepped back in line. Johnny shifted his aim back at the alpha. The two of them stared at each other once again, until the alpha nodded his head at Johnny. It was as if it was telling him it would be fine for Johnny to take his leave of the area. Johnny backed further down the trail, the pack of wolves, all fifteen of them Johnny counted, spread out and stayed in step with Johnny until he was at least forty feet from the battle zone. They stopped and watched as Johnny continued to back away. He was nearly a hundred feet away, the whole time keeping his eyes one the pack, when he felt safe enough to finally turn his back on them. He place the pistols back in their holsters and picked up his pace. The sun had begun to set below the mountain range, it was going to be a race to see if he would make it back before the sun had fully set.

He had been walking for nearly an hour by his watch, making it a little more than halfway back to his home. The whole way, he had been lost in his own thoughts, going over all the actions that had transpired since he had left that morning to go hunting. He knew he should feel something, anything. Remorse, shame, sad, angry…anything but the cold he was currently feeling. He knew, however, that the temperature around him wasn't causing the feeling currently enveloping his being. He barely felt the snow nor the wind. It was though he was already dead. The only time he felt that rush of being alive was when he was hunting and killing those soldiers. He knew he should not feel that way, he had been taught that taking human life was wrong, both morally and legally. However, he had also read that, historically, the law of the land over rode the laws of civilization when the crimes of human greed threatened a person's home and life.

Johnny felt an internal argument begin to boil as he went through what he was feeling, or supposed to be feeling, and whether what he did was right or wrong. He stopped moving and took a look up at the sky. It had begun to go from warm orange to blue as the sun set further down. For a moment he thought he could see the stars beyond the clouds and changing sky. He wished he could see them now. His father used to say that no matter where he was in the world, he could always look at the stars and know that, at that precise moment that his loved ones were looking at those very same stars. He was hoping that he would feel something, anything, by looking up at the stars. Nothing. No feelings of any kind registered within him. It was then that he knew he was truly alone in this world now. He had nothing left. Nothing but revenge, he realized. The flames that had burned inside his heart while he hunted down the soldiers that killed his family blazed once more as he saw his destiny ahead of him. There were more soldiers out there killing more families, all receiving orders from officers who saw innocent civilians as little more than insects. Johnny knew then what his path was. He was a hunter. Like all hunters throughout history, he needed prey. And now he had it.

He began to plan out how he would achieve his new goals. First he would need to get more supplies. His family's home had enough supplies to last a good long while if he hunted smartly.

What little warmth left in his eyes turned to cold steel as he looked down the trail ahead of him, it was time to get to work. He began walking down the trail once more, the wind howling around him as it blew through the trees. He walked in silence for another twenty minutes, before some innate sixth sense alerted him to danger. It was nothing overt as he halted mid-step. More like a branch swinging back into place and the sudden stop of all surrounding animal noises. Johnny slowly lowered his foot back into the snow as his ears tried to pick up any sounds not natural to the forest. His hands moved slowly toward his pistols when he heard it. A slight sound of a strap being put under stress to his right, completely unnoticeable to anyone not listening for it.

Johnny pinpointed the sound to a stand of trees a few meters to his right. Johnny quickly pulled both pistols and spun toward the trees. He approached them slowly, trying to determine where the threat truly was. He immediately eliminated all the trees too small to hold a full grown person without causing the branches to visibly bend. That left two trees to choose from. Something drew him toward a larger oak tree to his right. He looked at it without turning his head, trying to see anything out of place. There. A slight glint of metal about eight feet up, hidden behind the snow covered branches. Johnny was prepared to shift his aim at the person in the tree, when the snow to his left shifted. It wasn't a large shift, but it was in an opposite direction to the wind.

He took a deep breath, coordinated his movements in his mind, and then moved swiftly.

He shifted the aim of both weapons toward the location of the metal and the shifting snow. Once the move was complete, Jonny kept his eyes moving between the two spots so as to ensure he wasn't jumped.

"You have five seconds to show yourselves," Johnny said with an even voice. He pulled the hammers back on the pistols to make his point. He then began to mentally count. His count was interrupted by a distinct crunch of snow immediately behind him, signaling that someone had approached without his noticing. He heard the safety of a weapon click off. Slowly, Johnny removed his fingers from the triggers of his pistols.

"Easy now, Son. Lower the weapons. Nice and easy," a deep, slightly accented voice ordered. Johnny was beginning to calculate his chances of taking down all three of the men when more movement around him alerted his senses that he was well and truly surrounded. A figured lowered itself from exactly where Johnny had been aiming. Once on the ground, the man pointed his rifle at Johnny. It was marksman's rifle, judging by the scope attached to the top rail. Unlike the one Johnny carried, this one was a semiautomatic, medium caliber, most likely a 6.95 NATO round. Johnny slowly raised both

31

of his pistols into the air, making a deliberate show of ensuring that he was no longer a threat.

A man rose from the snow bank he had also chosen as a threat. This one was armed with a standard MR26 battle rifle, chambered to 5.75 NATO round. It, too, had a scope attached to the top rail, this one was shorter, more of an ACOG variant than the distance scope attached to the marksman's rifle. The new man stepped forward and reached up to take hold of Johnny's left handed pistol, removing it from Johnny's grip. Someone standing behind him also gripped his right handed pistol and tugged it from Johnny's hand. He felt more hands pull his rifle and shotgun from their holsters and finally his knife. Once he had been disarmed, Johnny heard several footsteps retreat from him a couple of paces.

"Slowly turn around, keep your hands up and in sight," The voice ordered. Johnny slowly turned around to face his captors. He kept his facial expression blank so that they wouldn't see his surprise. He had expected maybe five men, going from the number of footsteps he had heard. Instead, he was staring down the barrels of a dozen weapons. Thirteen, counting the marksman now behind him. They were dressed in standard U.S. military winter fatigues, a combination of whites and grays and blacks. Their faces were hidden behind gray and white balaclavas, their eyes behind combat goggles. They varied in size from the small framed soldier holding Johnny's shotgun, to the massive figure on Johnny's right hefting a large, belt fed weapon, most likely a M290 variant.

The leader of the group lowered his rifle and approached Johnny. He was slightly taller than Johnny was. He looked at Johnny in the eyes, trying to size him up. Johnny stared straight back, giving nothing away. The leader grunted as he reached up and pulled Johnny's balaclava down under his chin.

"What's your name?" The leader asked. Johnny looked at him and slightly narrowed his eyes, but kept silent. He didn't know who these men were, so until he did, he had nothing to say to them. The leader narrowed his eyes. "You part of some partisan or militia group?"

Again Johnny said nothing, but he did lower his hands. The soldiers around him tightened their grips on their weapons, but Johnny knew they were not going to fire, besides...his arms were tired. He continued to stare down the leader as the other soldiers began to relax again.

"Where are you coming from?" The leader asked. Again, Johnny kept silent.

"I'm guessing he was out to ruin someone's day, judging by the firepower and ammo," the soldier holding his shotgun said. He opened the breach and pulled the two shells from the barrels and slipped them into his pocket. The other soldiers also unloaded his weapons, pocketing the magazines and loose shells. The leader held up Johnny's hunting knife.

"Or he was just out hunting?" The leader queried. Johnny's eyes narrowed slightly at the question. A motion caught by the leader. He nodded slightly, coming to a decision. "Johnson, Teddy, Malik, keep heading up the trail, I want to know where he was coming from. The rest of us will head back to the rally point. Peters, take point, Rat and Bull have the six. Doran and O'Malley, keep our new friend under your watchful eyes. Let's move out."

The soldiers he called out went to work immediately. The three that were ordered up the trail toward the battle zone, all turned and moved out at a brisk pace. The rest stowed Johnny's weapons into a bag on the soldier named Bull's back. The leader lifted his rifle and motioned for everyone to move down the trail toward Johnny's home. Johnny pulled his balaclava back up over his face to keep it safe from the cold. The soldiers were moving in a staggered line, keeping ten feet between them, all except Johnny and his two new friends. They kept Johnny three feet ahead of them, their rifles not pointed directly at, but enough toward Johnny to let him know that any wrong move and a half a second later Johnny would be a pile of bullet ridden meat lying in the snow.

They were moving at a steady pace, trying to keep ahead of the setting sun behind them. Johnny spotted signs of the Imperial unit in the snow, but those signs were quickly being obliterated by the newly fallen snow. Johnny knew that if they were to look thirty meters off to the side, they may find signs of Johnny's path when he was tracking them.

It took another hour of travel before they came to the final rise separating the valley of Johnny's home from the valley they were currently in. He hadn't realized how far he had tracked the Imperial unit, but it had been more than ten miles. Johnny suddenly felt a pang of fear and anguish at what he would see. The fear and anguish were smothered by the rage and vengeance that still burned in his heart. He followed the soldiers to the top of the rise and took a look into the valley at his home. His old, broken home he reminded himself. The house was still there, a gaping hole in the second story where his parents' bedroom used to be. The roof was threatening to cave in, leaning heavily into the hole. The smoke and fire had been put out at some point. A large, twin rotor helicopter, Johnny recognized as a UH-515 Colossus transport, was sitting in the yard, its blades unmoving, and its rear ramp down. A large American flag was painted on the side, along with foot high letters spelling out MARINES.

He could see dozens of people moving around the house and the helicopter. The barn was wide open, a few more people were coming out of it. The one thing Johnny didn't see was the line of corpses that had been there when Johnny had awoken. The line began moving again, this time toward the helicopter. Johnny began to wonder what was going to happen next.

Captain Jacob Emmis, United States Marine Corps, First Raider Battalion, Alpha Company, First Platoon, had been trying to get a line on their prisoner since they had encountered him in the forest. He had yet to say a word, yet his movements and body language spoke volumes.

The hardness in his eyes spoke of extreme hatred and loss, but it was the slight eye movement during Jacob's initial questioning that told him what he needed to know. This young man was extremely dangerous. He then thought about what had brought them to this point.

They had been moving toward the insertion point for their current mission, when the pilots had spotted a large column of smoke coming through the trees. At the insistence of command, the chopper had been redirected to investigate the smoke column. Command wanted to know if it was an advanced Imperial camp or civilians trying to keep out of the conflict. The pilots had alerted them to the scene as soon as they had seen it. They had done an initial flyover before they flared out for a landing. Captain Emmis and his unit fell out to secure the area. Once secured, they found the line of corpses in the snow. All but three were dressed as Imperial Recon troops, the other three were clearly civilian.

As the pilots coordinated the other unit of Marines on the helicopter, Emmis's scout, Corporal Kenneth "Owl" Orteg, found the tracks of a large number of people leaving the scene to the northwest. Their medic Doran found a single set of tracks leading from the line of corpses to the barn and then off in the same direction as the larger group. A quick check with Command had Emmis and his men following the tracks of both to figure out what was going on. They had been on the trail for only two hours when the sounds of the firefight reached them. They quickly ascertained that the fight was further up the mountain trail and not toward them, before setting out at a faster pace. The fight only lasted a few minutes before it seemed to stop. They paused to see if there were any other sounds. A few seconds passed before the boom of a large weapon reverberated through the trees, then the loud crack of a single shot.

All went quiet again. This time the silence dragged on. They waited another ten minutes, before they moved again, this time at a slower, more cautious pace, and trying to follow the quickly disappearing tracks. They had been moving for nearly an hour when Owl stopped the unit and pointed up the trail. Emmis spotted the figure moving amongst the trees, heading in their direction. Emmis quickly spread his people out to cover and concealment positions along the trail. He posted Owl in the tree to get a bird's eye view of the figure, which he relayed to the others. As the figure got closer, Emmis could make out more details, like the large rifle and pair of pistols the figure was armed with. Emmis gripped his weapon a little tighter and waited. His plan was to wait until the figure moved past them, and then ambush him when they had the advantage.

The plan went to hell almost as soon as the figure moved into the ambush sight. For whatever reason, the figured stopped and turned toward the positions Owl and Rat were placed. The man moved closer to them and stopped. He stood there, unmoving in the wind and snow. Then he moved with such speed and intensity that it caught them all off guard, and if Emmis didn't know any better, with supernatural speed.

After their standoff, Emmis gave his orders and then they moved out back to the rally point. The whole way there, the man was silent, as though he were preparing for something. Emmis was fearful that the man would do something rash, and if he managed to slip away, he would disappear into the encroaching darkness. But he made no moves to escape. When they came to top of the rise leading to the farm, Emmis saw a slight movement of the man's shoulders. He had some connection to the place, Emmis just wasn't sure what.

They moved down to the chopper, exchanging greetings with other Marines moving about the property. Jacob waved to Doran and O'Malley to bring their prisoner into the helicopter with Emmis. He pointed to spots around the helicopter, indicating to the others they need to take up guard positions. Jacob walked halfway down the belly of the chopper, stepping around crates and gear, before stopping and pointing to a seat.

"Take a seat. Go ahead and remove the head gear, Son, there are a few questions you are going to answer." Jacob told the young man. He watched as the man pulled the balaclava over and off his head. He stuffed the headgear into a cargo pocket as he used his other hand to brush through his hair. He had strong, set features, with a slightly crooked nose, signaling that it had been broken at least once. The man's eyes locked on Jacob's as he removed his combat glasses. There was that steel he saw in them the first time, but this time he also saw a brilliant fire behind them. Jacob turned to his men and nodded toward the rear of the bird. They nodded and moved off, leaving the young man sitting by himself. Jacob took one last look at the kid and went into the cockpit.

Lieutenant Colonel Adam Bredan and Major Abigail Louis were sitting in their flight seats going over maps and timetables, arguing over their next flight path and the next drop point for Jacob's unit once their mission got back on track. They both looked up as Jacob knocked on the cockpit door.

"Sir, got someone you may want to talk to," Jacob reported. Colonel Bredan nodded. "Anything else?" He asked.

"Yes sir, he was coming from the direct of the gun fire. He was also armed to the teeth and looked like he could use them proficiently," Jacob reported.

"What did he have to say about why he was out there and armed as he was?" Major Louis asked.

"He hasn't actually said a word. He's been silent since we found him. I sent three men to check out the battle zone, they should be back shortly. Bull's been lugging the kid's weapons since we apprehended him." Jacobs replied.

"Any idea what connection he has to this place, Captain?" The colonel asked.

"Not for certain, sir, but if I had to take a guess: He lived here," Jacob answered honestly. The hurried thuds of boots upon the chopper's deck signaled the approach of one of the Marines. Jacob turned around to see who it was. Teddy, one of the Marines Emmis sent to scout the battle zone, came running up behind Emmis. He slid to a stop and doubled over to catch his breath. Emmis was sure the man had ran the whole way back to the helo. "Easy, Son. Take a deep breath and calm down."

Teddy took several deep breaths and then looked at the trio of officers. Emmis could see whatever he had to say was not going to be easy for him. Emmis nodded to the young man as soon as his breathing returned to normal.

"Now tell us what you found," Emmis ordered. Teddy looked at him and Emmis could see the fear in his eyes.

Johnny sat there, still silent as the grave, observing the movements of the Marines around him. Several had moved to enter the helicopter via the ramp, only to be turned away by two of the Marines that had escorted him in. The leader if the group had moved toward the cockpit after having Johnny sit. Though they were only a dozen feet or so from him, Johnny couldn't hear what was going on. He looked around himself, boredom beginning to set in after sitting there for ten minutes or so. He spotted a pack sitting on a crate to his left that was partially opened. Taking a look to the ramp and again toward the cockpit to ensure he wouldn't be spotted, Johnny reached into the pack and withdrew the first object he found. At first he thought it was the barrel of a dismantled weapon, but once he pulled it fully out, he saw that it was, in fact, a suppressor designed for a large caliber rifle. He estimated that it would fit over the barrel of his own rifle. The sounds of running feet approaching the ramp caused Johnny to quickly stuff the suppressor inside a cargo pocket.

One of the Marines the leader had sent to check out the battle sight came rushing up the ramp and moved quickly down the helicopter to the cockpit. As he passed, Johnny could hear the labored breathing of a man who had run a long distance. He looked back at the ramp and saw the other two talking animatedly to their comrades standing guard at the bottom of the ramp. A few times, they motioned toward Johnny, causing the two guards to steal glances in his direction. Johnny smirked at the thought of what they were being told. Movement from near the cabin caused him to turn his attention to it. The out of breath Marine, the leader of the group, and two others dressed in flight suits moved into the helicopter's cargo bay. The first pilot was an older man, the lines on his face and graying hair told the story of his age and a life of stress and hard living. The second was a younger woman, not nearly as tall as her fellow pilot, but she held herself up regally, her auburn hair pulled into a tight bun. Her face showed none of the same lines as the older pilot, telling Johnny that she was the junior officer of the two.

The out of breath Marine moved passed Johnny to join his friends at the bottom of the ramp. Johnny heard him shout to the one known as Bull. His attention was drawn back to the trio as the older pilot took a seat directly across from Johnny, his younger companion moved the pack from the crate to an empty seat behind her, then sat down on the crate. The leader of the group that captured him stood a few paces to his right, his battle rifle at rest in his hand, not quite pointed at Johnny, his finger not quite on the trigger. Johnny took the opportunity as they all settled into their places to take a closer look at the two pilots. They were both armed with pistols holstered in shoulder holsters, judging by the end of the grip and magazine, Johnny suspected they were Colt M47s. Large bore pistols, magazine capacity of twenty, semiautomatic, but could be fired at a rapid rate. Guessing from their placement on their bodies, the older pilot was a left handed pistoleer, while his co-pilot was a right hander. Their flight patches depicted an open mouthed skull surrounded by fire and read "Primam Fugam ad Inferos," which meant First Flight to Hell. The insignia on the older one was silver oak leaf, signifying the rank of Lieutenant Colonel, whilst she had the bronze oak leaf of a Major. Her brilliant blue eyes were boring into Johnny as though she were trying to figure out what he was, while the Lieutenant Colonel's deep brown eyes were sizing Johnny up, trying to guess what Johnny was capable of.

Movement at the rear of the aircraft drew Johnny's attention to the massive figure of Bull, as the giant made his way to them. His bulk was almost comical in the confined space of the helicopter's cargo bay. Bull stopped behind the leader of his unit and removed the pack on his back containing Johnny's weapons. Johnny watches as bull handed the pack to the Colonel, who began to unload its contents onto a crate next to him. Though he kept his facial expressions blank, his eyes showed amusement at the looks of confusion and then bewilderment that played across the faces of the two pilots as his arsenal was laid out for all to see. Once the pack was empty, the colonel took a long look at Johnny, who tilted his head slightly.

"I understand the good captain here was unable to get much out of you when you met in the forest. That's fine, he really didn't need to know who you are, but I do. I want you to understand that if you refuse to answer my questions, I will have you arrested and held as a possible enemy combatant and transferred to the nearest detainment facility as soon as possible," The colonel said. His voice was deep and gravely, with the slight bur of a New England accent. "Conversely, you can answer my questions, honestly, and then we will determine what we can do to get you back to American civilization without too much of a fuss. Now the choice is yours, what do you say?"

Johnny stared at the colonel for a few moments, trying to gauge the sincerity of his words. He stole a glance at both the copilot and the captain who had brought him in. Both were watching him closely, and with the captain and his men on alert at the back of the helicopter, Johnny knew his chances of causing a distraction and slipping away were now well and truly zero. He took a deep breath and let out a weary sigh as he looked back at the Colonel.

"What do you want to know?" Johnny asked, looking the Colonel straight in the eyes. The colonel's mouth showed a slight grin as he leaned forward slightly.

"Let's start with a name."

"Johnny."

"Just Johnny? What about a last name?" The copilot asked in a light Midwestern accent. "No last name anymore." Johnny replied, looking at her, his eyes betraying him to show the sadness behind them.

"Do you know what happened here, Johnny?" The colonel asked. Johnny's eyes hardened once more as he looked back at the Colonel, all the memories of that morning rushing back to the forefront of his mind.

"Yes."

"Care to tell us?" The colonel asked softly, seeing the fire and hardness in Johnny's eyes. "My home was destroyed."

Johnny heard a light gasp from the copilot as she realized the implications of his words. "So the civilians that were killed were…" She began.

"My mother, father, and brother." Johnny finished. Images of their lifeless, broken bodies lying in the snow flashed before his eyes.

"Do you know why the Imperial Army would attack you and your family?" The colonel asked. Johnny shook his head. He had no clue, nor did he care any longer, all he wanted was his revenge.

"How did the attack begin?" The captain asked, his voice still riddled with suspicion. "I don't know," Johnny answered truthfully. "I wasn't here when it began."

"Then explain what happened from your perspective." The colonel requested. Johnny took a deep breath and began his tale.

"I was out hunting, left before sunrise. I was two miles to the Northeast, there is a clearing there where deer and elk can still find some sparse grass, when I heard the gunfire begin. I ran back here as fast as I could and stopped at the tree line. There were a dozen or so soldiers moving toward the house, firing randomly. I heard return fire from the first floor, mostly likely my brother and father. I watched a couple of the soldiers go down in the snow." Johnny paused to take a breath. "That's when I saw the second group of soldiers, ten or so, across the valley, moving behind the barn, trying to flank the house. I took aim and began firing. Killed most of them too."

"You killed ten Imperial Recon soldiers? With a hunting rifle? From across the valley?" The copilot asked incredulously. "That has to be what? Three hundred yards?"

"Three hundred and fifteen yards from my firing position to the fence they took cover behind. The same fence we would practice on whenever we got the chance." Johnny retorted.

"This rifle?" The colonel asked. Johnny shook his head. "No. I was using a Winchester. Same caliber though." The captain nodded as two points now connected for him.

"We found a .338 Lapua in the snow near the line of bodies. Its barrel was bent and the action had been broken off." The captain added. Johnny nodded.

"Please continue," The colonel said.

"I took care of the flanking soldiers pretty quickly. Then I shifted my aim at the ones out in the yard. Before I could start firing, however, I saw one of them lift a tube to his shoulder. I..." Johnny paused to take a breath before continuing to the hardest part of his story. "I missed the first time. Then the wind kicked up and I couldn't see him anymore, so I fired as fast as I could. They must have spotted me, because the next thing I knew, rounds were tearing into the trees and branches above my head. I heard something crack above me and then it was lights out." Johnny finished.

"We found your shooting position. We wondered why there were so many broken branches there, now we know." The colonel said. "Then what happened?"

"I don't know how long I was out, couldn't have been long, but I woke up lying in the snow. As soon as I was able to I sat up and then I saw them. The dead soldiers had been covered with tarps, but my family had just been laid out next to me. The house looked like it was on fire. It was just too surreal to be true." Johnny went on, the images playing out in his head like a bad movie. "I went into the barn to get a shovel, so I could bury them, when I saw the armory door. I loaded up instead and went after the survivors."

"And where are they?" The colonel asked. Johnny's face split into a malevolent grin and his eyes took on a terrifying glow as he replied.

"Which pieces?" He asked, his voice tinged with pride and malevolent joy, as he envisioned what the wolves would have done to the bodies by then. He settled down and continued. "I tracked them up the mountain, got in front of them and then hunted them. The radio guy was the first to go, then the two injured, then the rest. I hunted them down and killed each and every one of them. I left them for the wolves and mountain to consume."

Johnny felt a little better now that his tale had been told. He looked up at the three around him. The woman had a look of fear mingled with disgust at how much enjoyment Johnny took from hunting down and slaughtering other humans. The Captain was nodding his approval of the events that unfolded. The colonel just stared at Johnny, their eyes connecting as he deciphered the truth.

"We can corroborate what you have told us about the attack on your home. The blood stains and shell patterns are a match. I can also tell you that our corpsman were able to confirm that your family died instantly from the concussion of the rocket blast, they didn't suffer." The colonel told him.

"The rest has been confirm by my boys," The captain said. "They couldn't go too far into the zone, there were wolves all over the corpses. They found his firing position up the trail. The one thing they couldn't rectify was the carving and knife." He looked at Johnny to supply the answer.

"My grandfather told me stories of native tribes throughout the world that would signify ambush points or calls to war with carvings into trees. The call to war was a weapon, buried into a sacred tree or pole. One at the ambush site, or one at the warriors' home or village. I was putting the Imperial Army on notice." Johnny explained.

"What notice?" The Colonel asked.

"They brought war to my home, now I am going to bring war to them." Johnny said, his eyes shining with a ferocity that scared those around him. There was silence for a few moments as everyone processed the information they were given. Johnny leaned back in his chair and waited. The colonel looked from his copilot to the captain, who nodded.

"Ok, you are coming with us, at least until we get back to base. The brass hats there can figure out what to do with you." The colonel said, coming to a decision. "We are going to be wheels up in forty minutes, should give us night cover. You have until then to gather anything from the house or barn you need or want."

Johnny nodded his thanks and stood up. He held out his hand to the colonel who shook it. Johnny gave a lopsided grin to the copilot and then turned to the captain, who motioned Johnny to follow. They made their way to the ramp, where the captain stopped and turned to Johnny.

"They may not appreciate what you went through, nor the skill it took to track that unit and wipe them out, but I do. That was a helluva story. Teddy and Marco will be your escorts while you get your things together." The captain said.

"Still suspicious?" Johnny asked, knowing the answer.

"Not as such, but I now know your capabilities. You would take the first chance you had to slip away into the forest, wait until we left, gear back up and hunt down more Imperial units," The captain replied.

"And that's a bad thing?" Johnny asked.

"No, it's not a bad idea. But you could do more with better equipment and more support than you could do on your own. The only way you get that is if you stick around with us," The captain explained. "Be a shame if your skills and talents went down in a blaze of fire before you find out just how much you could accomplish, wouldn't it?"

Johnny nodded as he took the captain's words and began to think on them. The moved down the ramp into the snow, the rest of the captain's unit looking expectantly at the two.

"Teddy, grab one of the crew, you and he are going to keep an eye on our new friend as he collects his things," The captain ordered. Teddy nodded and ran off a short distance to grab another marine that was standing under one of the wings, smoking. The two jogged back to Johnny's position as the captain waved the rest of the unit into the helicopter.

"Where to first?" Teddy asked, his thick Georgian accent slurring his words. Johnny shook his head and walked toward the house. He saw what was left of the front door, hanging from a single hinge, opened wide into the front hall. Johnny walked in and took a look at the mess. Pictures of happier times were hanging crooked on the wall, some had fallen to the floor from the blast.

Johnny stopped by the door to the living room and took a look inside. There was a bloodstain near the window and dozens of discarded, empty rifle shells. From the size of them, they had come from his father's rifle. Johnny gave his head an almost imperceptible shake and moved on toward the kitchen. The sink was still full of water and dirty plates, the table still had the remains of a breakfast and his father's coffee cup upon it. Cabinets were open and a few broken dishes and cups were scattered across the floor.

Johnny moved past these reminders of a past that was now a bitter, painful memory, to the door to the basement. He descended the stairs into the furnished game room his family and friends had used for decades. The TV had been thrown to the floor from the blast, his brother's controller and game chair sat in the same spot he had abandoned them. Johnny quickly crossed the room to a door on the opposite side, trying to stay ahead of the memories that wanted to rush him. He was determined to keep them buried forever. He crossed the threshold into his room, still in the exact same condition he had left it. He looked on bemusedly at his unmade bed and dirty clothes just haphazardly tossed at his hamper. He moved to his closet and searched for a particular bag.

It had been a gift from his grandfather when Johnny had joined a competitive shooting team and a woodland group. It was small, designed to carry a few days' worth of clothes. He found the bag tucked away in the corner and retrieved it. He set it on his bed opened and began to gather a few clothes. He packed what he needed, closing the bag as Teddy and the other Marine walked in. The unnamed Marine let out as whistle as he took a look around. He wasn't much older than Johnny was, with a shock of red hair.

"Nice room. Beats the hell out of the barracks." He commented. Johnny nodded absent mindedly as he grabbed his buckskin coat. It was the first one he had made from the deer and elk he had hunted, having always been told that such things were irreplaceable. He swung the jacket one and spotted his wallet sitting on top of the dresser. He looked at it for a few moments before picking it up. He looked at the license inside. The face that stared back was a stranger now, no longer capable of the joyous smile that he once was. He contemplated taking the wallet, but decided not to. Jonathan Allan Wolfe was dead. He had died when his family had. He placed the wallet back on the dresser and picked up the necklace next to it. A family heirloom that had been passed down for generations. It had a simple bronze medallion with an opened eye etched into it. The story went that his ancestors had been part of a secret mercenary group and the only way they distinguished themselves from other mercenaries was by the medallion they all wore. Johnny never believed it, but it was interesting story none the less. He moved to his bed, picked up his bag, and, as an afterthought, reached behind his headboard and pulled another family heirloom from its hiding spot.

This one was an antique tomahawk that supposedly was gifted to an ancestor before the outbreak of the revolution. It too had been handed down through the generations. This time, it was Teddy who whistled in admiration of the weapon.

"That's cool. Where'd you get it?" Teddy asked.

"It's been in the family for generations," Johnny answered. Carrying the weapon, he made his way through the basement and up to the kitchen. He was about to turn to the front door, when something out in the backyard caught his eye. He walked out the backdoor and spotted freshly turned earth at the base of a very large, very old oak tree. The tree was over a century old if it was a day. It had been the center of the yard since his parents had moved in. In the bark, carved years ago, were the names of the Wolfe family. Under each name was the date of their birth. New carvings under three of the names were new dates. Dates of Death.

"We figured that this was the best place for them," the unnamed Marine said, standing a few feet behind Johnny. He nodded his thanks as he stared at the tree he used to climb as a child. Johnny moved to the tree and, with a shaking hand, brushed his fingers over the carvings. He felt a tear form in the corner of his eye as the rage that had been burning in his soul swelled to an inferno, mixed with the feeling of an incredible loss. As his fingers brushed over his own name, an unearthly bestial roar erupted from his throat as he drew his arm back, the blade of the tomahawk catching the dying light of day. With unnatural strength, he swung his arm forward, the blade of the weapon biting and sticking into the bark, bisecting his name.

Johnny stood there, motionless for a moment as adrenaline and rage boiled in his blood. He finally took a step back, releasing his grip on the tomahawk.

His breath was ragged as he began to calm down. He took one final deep breath as he eyes beheld what he had done. He had buried the blade of his weapon to nearly the hilt into the bark of the tree. He reach for it, thinking about pulling it free, when the words he had spoken to the colonel hit him. He paused, hand in the air, as he contemplated those words. Coming to a conclusion, he nodded once and let his hand drop to his side. The blade would stay where it was, at least until he had finished his mission and the war was over. He took a last long look at the names on the tree and then turned away, heading for the barn. He entered through the same door he had this morning, side stepping Marines as they carried out things they could use. He made his way to the armory door and stopped as he caught sight of five of them trying to get through the door to the armory. One of them was kneeling next to the lock, sparking a cutting torch. The spark finally caught and he adjusted the spitting flame so it was a hissing blue shade.

He walked up to the one who seemed to be in charge and grabbed his arm, pulling the angry torch away from the door.

"What the—?" The man began, he spun to his feet as Johnny tossed the torch to the ground, where its flame guttered and died. The Marine came face to face with Johnny, who had a murderously angry look in his eyes.

"Not this one," Johnny said, a dangerous calm in his soft voice. The Marine looked as though he were going to argue with him, when Teddy stepped forward.

"It's okay Corporal, take a smoke break," Teddy said. The Corporal took a look at Teddy, and then one last look at Johnny, before shrugging.

"Ok. Take a break guys, smoke 'em if you got 'em," he said as he stepped around Johnny and led his group out of the barn. Johnny watched them leave, before turning back to the armory door.

"Wait here," Johnny said, as he punched the code into the lock. "We were told to stick with you," Teddy answered.

"This is the only way in or out, I'll be right back," Johnny said. The locks on the door clunked open and Johnny tugged it open enough to step inside. He made sure to close it quickly enough to keep his two watchers from getting a good look inside. Johnny quickly moved down the racks and rows of weapons as his pulled magazines and ammo from lockers. He also pulled a battle rifle similar to the one the Marines were carrying from a rack. This one had been modified with a shorter barrel and collapsible stock. He quickly loaded ten magazines for the rifle and stuffed it and the loaded mags into the bag with his clothes. He also loaded ten more magazines for the other weapons he had and placed those appropriately on his body, the excess going into the bag. He added two dozen more shotgun shells to the ammo he was carrying. He then moved to the cabinet that held all of the bladed weapons his family owned. He opened

46

the cabinet and pulled his set of throwing knives. Perfectly balanced, he placed the twenty knives in quick release sheathes on his arms and the sides of his torso. He pulled a second hunting blade, this one a Bowie style, from the cabinet and slid it and it's sheathe on his right leg, securing it with a set of straps. The last things he pulled from the cabinet were a pair of hatchets, much like the tomahawk he imbedded into the tree, these were lighter, easier to throw, but sharper as well. The each also had a climbing pick on the back. Johnny secured them to his back, ensuring he could pull them even with his rifle and shot gun back there.

He grabbed a one point sling for the battle rifle as he moved back to the door, pausing to switch the gloves he was wearing out for a pair of his competitive shooting gloves. He opened the door to the armory as he was stuffing the sling into his pocket. Teddy and the other Marine were leaning against opposing stalls, chatting as Johnny exited the armory and closed the door, engaging the locks.

"Got everything?" Teddy asked. Johnny nodded as he walked past them, pushing the sling further into his pocket. Teddy and the other Marine fell in step a few feet behind Johnny, continuing their conversation where they had left off. Johnny made his way to the door, noticing that the outdoor lights had kicked on. He left the barn and looked out over the valley. Night had truly fallen, casting an eerie twilight on everything. The moon was full and bright, the clouds having retreated, allowing the stars to make their presence known. Johnny again got the sense that no matter how hard he stared at those stars, his answers and his family were not up there. He sighed silently and returned his gaze back to earth. He started walking toward the helicopter, his feet making almost no sound in the snow compared the thick crunches of footsteps behind him. He led the way to the helicopter ramp. He headed up the ramp, while the other two broke off toward the smoking area under the wing.

Johnny walked up the ramp and then headed further into the helicopter, making his way to his gear. He spotted the captain, the two pilots, and a pair of the captain's marines standing in a cluster around a crate arguing. As he got closer, he saw maps and charts on the crate. He finally made to his weapons and looked down at them. His weapons and the ammo taken from them had been placed in a neat row while he had been gone. He unslung the backpack and laid in on the seat beside the crate. He went to pick up one of his pistols, when he overheard what the group was arguing about.

"Intel is telling us that the next flyby is in eighteen hours. If we continue as planned, we are not going to make it to the insertion point for another twelve hours. From there it's a ten hour forced march to the jump point," One of the captain's marines said. "That means, if we stick to the current plan, we are going to miss the fly by and our window by four hours, at which point the intel is useless."

"I'm all ears for a new plan," The colonel replied.

"What about a straight shot from our old trajectory? Shaves six hours off the round trip," The other marine asked.

"Not possible," The Major responded. "Why not?" The captain asked.

"If we tried to take a straight shot from our old flight path, it will put us in direct line with the bomber flights they send over the mountains, as well as put us in range of their AA emplacements." The Colonel explained. "While we might be able to dodge one or two of their bomber flights, we cannot outrun, nor out maneuver their antiaircraft fire. Not without using our chafe. And if we do that, the mission is over at that point."

"Ok, what about heading further west, try to swing around behind their lines? It will cut travel time in half," The captain asked.

"No. I am not going to risk this bird trying that. We do not have any stealth systems installed, we would have to try to keep our flight down to the tree level," The colonel said. "Without accurate topographical maps, we'd slam into one of these mountain faces. Or we would get spotted by a patrol, and then we would be in real trouble. We wouldn't be able to outrun any of the craft they would send our way. Keep trying."

"What if we moved out from here on foot?" The captain asked. "It's only forty miles to our jump point from here overland." The Colonel looked at the map for a few moments before speaking.

"Can't do it. We do not have any intel about this area. None of the sats have done a flyby to this area. You may end up walking straight into the arms of an Imperial division. Without any way of knowing you can get through safely, I can't allow you to take the risk." The colonel replied. Johnny was continuing the motion to pick up his pistol when he heard the captain mention their target was only forty miles out. He racked his brain to figure out what they could be looking for within forty miles of his home. Then it hit him. There was a small town almost exactly forty miles from the farm. Johnny and his dad stopped heading there for supplies when they spotted troops in the town over a month ago. He straightened up and looked at the group.

"Are you guys heading to Silverton?" Johnny asked. They all stopped talking and looked at Johnny as though just noticing him.

"And if we are?" The captain asked, his eyes narrowing slightly.

Johnny shrugged. "I could take you there. Take us no more than twelve hours." Johnny replied. The group had a mixed look of disbelief and skepticism.

"You can point out at safe route that will get the team where they need to go?" The colonel asked.

"No. I said I can take them there. Not point them." Johnny replied. "We can't allow you to go," The colonel said.

"Why not?" Johnny asked. The major looked at him as if his question was ludicrous. "One, you're a civilian. We cannot allow you to take on the risk of leading these troops through enemy held territory, nor can we expect to unit to spread themselves thin trying to protect you." The major explained. "The second is that this mission is classified." Johnny thought about what she said for a few moments. He contemplated how he was going to word his position. Once he had his thoughts in order, he spoke again. He looked straight at the captain.

"Captain? How many of your men have gone up against a grizzly, brown, or Kodiak bear?" Johnny asked. The captain looked confused for a moment, then understood what Johnny was getting at.

"None," He replied.

"How about wolves? Or Mountain lions?" Johnny asked again.

"Again, none."

"Do they know how to tell the difference between grizzly or Kodiak signs? Or if a mountain lion was stalking the area? If a pack of wolves are near enough to jump you?" Johnny asked.

"Nope. But you know, don't you?" The captain asked, a sly grin on his face. "Yes, I do," Johnny replied.

"Wait...Aren't bears supposed to be hibernating by now?" one of the marines asked.

Johnny nodded, causing a self-satisfied and superior grin to appear on his face. A grin that was quickly dashed by Johnny's next statement.

"Yes, normally. Unfortunately, their habitat has been flipped upside down," Johnny began. "The war has disrupted the migration, feeding, and ranging patterns. This disruption caused the predators who normally consume enough to go into hibernation to starve. These animals were then forced to range further and further for food. They even began to go after large groups of people and even into towns." Johnny paused to take a breath while he let his words sink in. "Now, yes, it is true that I could point out the path that will take the captain and his men to their 'jump point,' but I wouldn't be able to tell them if there were predators around them, hunting them, or if they were about to walk into a waiting pack of wolves." Johnny looked meaningfully at the captain. "If you want any guarantee that you will all make it there alive by your deadline, then I have to go with you."

Johnny looked at each and everyone in the group, seeing that most of them were one the edge of allowing Johnny to go along. They just needed that last push over the edge.

"Besides, if you truly wanted this to stay classified, you wouldn't have been arguing so loudly," Johnny added. The captain and his two men grinned, the look of shock came over the major, and the colonel stared at Johnny straight in the eyes. He was trying to gauge how much of the truth was behind Johnny's words.

"How do you know how these animals act?" the colonel asked. Johnny looked right into the colonel's eyes.

"Because that has been my life since the war started. Every time we went hunting, or went for supplies, or looked for help, we had to compete with every predator out there." Johnny replied. "I've had to learn quickly how to survive in a place where having a gun just meant that you could even the playing field against a stalking predator. I've hunted and scouted every inch of these mountains, I know how to get through safely."

Again, the colonel stared at him for a few moments. Johnny could almost see the arguments dancing around in his mind. It appeared that he may have been leaning toward denying Johnny's request, when he nodded.

"Very well. He goes. Staff Sergeant, get him a comm unit, get it set and wired for him," The colonel ordered. The staff sergeant, the marine that brought up the hibernation issue, nodded and moved toward the rear of the helicopter to retrieve and program the communications gear the colonel ordered him to get. The colonel looked back at Johnny. "You understand that by going along you agree to terms of combat: the captain and his men do not have the resources to protect you if shit goes sideways. I am agreeing to you carrying a live weapon."

Johnny nodded. "I understand."

"Good. You leave in ten minutes." The colonel stated. He stood up and turned toward the cockpit. The Major and captain followed him. The other Marine stood straight and turned toward Johnny, who turned back to his weapons. Johnny closed the distance to them and reached down. He picked up one of his pistols and reinserted the magazine, pulling the slide back and watching it slam forward, seating the first round into the chamber. He double checked to ensure the safety was on. He placed the pistol in his right thigh holster. He picked up the second pistol and reinserted its magazine, allowing the slide to rush forward home. He checked the safety, then placed it into the left hip holster. He picked up his shotgun and put two fresh rounds in the barrels. He closed the breach and made sure it was secure. He slid it into the make shift holster on his back. He picked up his hunting knife and slid it into the sheathe on his shoulder. He finally picked up his rifle. He pulled the bolt back, opening the chamber to ensure that it was empty. He picked up the magazine and ran his thumb along the first round. He slid the magazine into the well until he felt the click, letting him know it was secure. He slid the bolt forward, watching it push that first round into the chamber. He secured the bolt with a second satisfying click.

For the first time that day, he felt whole and complete. He slid the rifle into its holster on his back. He picked up his back and slung it over his shoulder, adjusting the strap so it did not interfere with any of the weapons on his back, nor the ammo on his chest. He shrugged his shoulders a few times to get used to the new weight of the bag and extra weapons. After months of dragging deer through the woods, the new weight was almost nothing to him. He heard the sounds of footfalls approaching him. He turned toward the sound and spotted the staff sergeant walking up to him. He held a small headset and wrist band.

"Hold out your non-firing arm," The staff sergeant said. Johnny held out his right arm and stood still as the staff sergeant secured it to his arm. The strap auto adjusted to his arm as the staff sergeant explained the device. He then placed the bud in Johnny's right ear and extended the wire down to his throat. "This is the whisper comm. No need to talk loudly, just whisper and we'll hear you. The wrist band had an interface on it that will allow you to see who is on the same freq as you are. Pressing a name will allow private comm between you and whoever you chose. Range is eight miles by line of sight to a drone in low orbit. If the satellite is in line of sight, then the range is worldwide. There ya go, try not to get us killed please." He stepped back and grinned. Johnny nodded to him, accepting the jab for the joke it was. The staff sergeant moved back to the rear of the chopper as the captain came out of the cockpit.

"Let's go," He said. Johnny nodded and pulled his balaclava from his pocket. He walked to the ramp and looked out toward the mountains. A new hunt was on, time to get to work. He pulled the balaclava over his face, essentially replacing his former self with the new animal he had become. He looked at the marines around him. He nodded to them and then headed off toward the trail in silence. The captain was right: Time to get to work.

Johnny had first set a brisk pace to move to the trail. It started out as the same path he used to hunt down the Imperial soldiers. They covered the distance quickly, coming to the ambush point in less than half the time it took for them to originally walk back to the farm. About halfway to the trail break, Johnny heard the turbines on the helicopter reach full spin. He paused long enough to see it rise above the trees and bank to the southeast. Now that their only vehicle was gone, the Marines put their entire trust and lives into Johnny's hands. Johnny turned his attention back to the trail, keeping his eyes open for the break off point. He spotted it thirty yards from where the captain and his marines had ambushed him. He started down the trail, signaling with his right hand for the group to follow him. He only made it sixty yards down the trail, when movement to his left caused him to stop and take a knee.

The Marines following him took his lead and also stopped, each shouldering their rifles and scanning for trouble. The soft crunch of snow alerted Johnny to the approach of one of the Marines. Johnny scanned the snow where he first noticed the movement. He moved just his eyes at first, using an old hunting and tracking technique his father taught him as a child.

"Whatcha got?" a soft voice asked in his ear. Johnny slowly put his finger against his lips, signaling silence. He then moved his hand incrementally toward a set of his throwing knives on his arm. His fingers barely touched the end of the first one when a small hop alerted him to the creature he was waiting for. In a flash, Johnny whipped the throwing knife from its sheathe, sending it spinning toward the movement. It covered the twelve feet in a matter of seconds, the force of the throw burying the blade into the side of the unfortunate rabbit. Tracking his throw, the Marines took aim at the rabbit. As they began to register what they were seeing, they lowered their weapons and began to stand. Johnny pulled a small string from his pocket as he stood and moved toward his kill.

He sent a silent apology at the dead hare as he squatted down next to its body. He pulled the blade from it and then used the knife to begin field dressing the carcass. The marines watched silently for a while as Johnny worked. He finished halfway through the process by tying the string around the hind legs of the carcass and then picking it up. He cast his gaze for a suitable spot to hang it from. He found a good branch just off the trail to his right. He moved over to it and tied the other end of the string around the branch just above his head. He let it go and watched for a moment as the carcass swung back and forth with the light wind, blood dripping from it to pool and freeze in the snow. Johnny nodded, satisfied with his work, knelt and used snow to clean the blade of his knife. Captain Emmis walked over to him as Johnny slid the knife back into its sheathe on his upper arm.

"And this is for?" He asked, confused as he looked at the morbid scene in front of him. "Distraction," Johnny replied as he turned back toward the trail.

"Distraction?" One of the other Marines asked as Johnny began to move. "Distraction for what?"

Johnny stopped and looked off the trail to the left.

"Them." He indicated with a nod of his head as he pulled his rifle from its holster on his back. The marines followed Johnny's indication and fear began to grip them. Staring out of the shadows of the trees, over a dozen eyes gleaming in the winter moonlight watched the group. "They have been tracking us since we left the farm. I figured I would give them something else to occupy them for a while. Should allow us to get a fair distance down the trail before they follow again." He moved another dozen steps before noticing that the Marines were still watching the wolves. "Unless you want to stay here and try to deal with them now."

His words seemed to shake the marines out of their haze. They began to move out again. They were nearly three hundred yards down the trail when the snarls and howls began, signaling that they were trying to get Johnny's bait. Johnny grinned to himself, wondering what was going through the minds of the marines behind him. He then set his features and brought his thoughts to the task at hand. He had thirty eight miles worth of snow covered mountains and forests to lead these Marines through, and all of it concealed hidden predators and other dangers.

Emmis followed Johnny's path, staying fifteen feet behind his man, Owl, who was walking ahead of him and behind Johnny. He was still amazed at what the young man was becoming. He hoped he made the right decision, he put the lives of his men and many others into Johnny's hands, but his gut told him it was the right thing to do. Johnny had pointed out the hidden dangers of the land around them, and, then to put a point on it, showed them the real life versions of his warnings.

Something told him that there was more Johnny could do to help, he just needed to find his path. Emmis couldn't imagine what the kid was going through, but knew it was going to make him stronger, more capable. He had been a hunter before, but now he was something truly different. At times Emmis could see almost an animal like fury in Johnny's eyes, at others he could see the cold determination of an assassin. It was almost scary to watch the two personalities struggle for domination. Emmis knew, out of all of it, he didn't want to be on the receiving end of Johnny's fury. He wondered if they could use Johnny on this current mission further down the line. Emmis began to realize, as his mind worked through the arguments, that he may not have much of a say in whether Johnny gets involved or not.

The timer on Emmis's wrist unit ticked off another hour, marking three since they left the valley. His GPS unit showed that they were ahead of the original schedule set by Johnny before they left. Johnny was moving at a steady and quick pace, making the Marines of Emmis's unit struggle slightly to keep up. They were nearing their first rest point in five miles. The first fifteen having gone by in what seemed like a blur. Johnny's movements through the passes and up and down short cliffs, his ability to dodge around troubled areas by simply seeing minute differences on the trail or the bark of trees. Twice Johnny had stopped the group to observe the forest around them. And twice the Marines had spotted the flash of fur moving through the shadows. The Marines were a bit on edge after each sighting, but Johnny seemed to shrug it off both times and keep moving.

Emmis took a look up at the sky, the moon had reached its crest and begun its fall back toward the horizon. The stars kept their dance of the ages around the edges of its twilight. He mused on the fact that he had never seen the sky so clear, when a coughing roar rattled his train of thought. He looked back down and to his right, the location of the roar, and came eye to eye with a mountain lion crouching atop of a small rock out cropping ten feet from him. Emmis reacted quickly and brought his rifle up to his shoulder. The rest of the unit all spun to back up their captain. They stood there, waiting for the next move. Emmis put his finger on the trigger of his rifle and began to squeeze, his eyes focused down the sight at the lion, its haunches up and fangs bared. His finger was at the terminus point, preparing to release the bolt and firing pin, when a hand pushed his rifle down. Emmis instantly released the pressure on the trigger and he swung his gaze to the person who just interrupted him. Johnny's green eyes stared back at him. He gave Emmis a slight shake of his head and pressed a fore finger over his lips.

"Back away slowly," Johnny said, no more than a whisper. "Keep your eyes on her and do not make sudden movements. Now go. Five feet back, then move up the trail, I'll catch up."

Emmis looked back at the lion, then took a step backward, his boots crunching in the snow. He kept his firing hand on his rifle and used his other hand to wave his men to follow his example. The unit moved slowly, their eyes never truly leaving the lion. Johnny was the only one who wasn't moving. After Emmis had begun to move, Johnny turned toward the lion and stood there. At some point, he had pulled the large knife from his shoulder sheathe and one of the hatchets from the small of his back. He was facing the lion head on, unmoving. Emmis and the unit were now nearly eighty yards down the trail, moving a little faster at this point. They reached a bend in the trail that dipped into a frozen creek bed, causing them to lose sight of Johnny and the lion. Emmis finally felt safe enough to turn to his men. They looked at him quizzically.

"Let's keep moving. He said he will catch up shortly," Emmis said. "Owl, take point, Bull, you have the six." His men nodded and formed back up. They set out again at a somewhat slower pace than before, each casting a worrying glance back down the trail. Each thinking that they had just left that young man to die in the forest alone.

It took nearly the full hour and a half to get to their rest point. The point was at the edge of a large, frozen river. On the opposite bank, Emmis could see the next rise they would have to go over. The plan called for them to rest for twenty minutes before continuing. Emmis had decided to wait longer if necessary, his guilt causing him to extend their rest period.

"Sir?" a voice called him out of his stupor. He turned to the man who had been trying to talk to him.

"Sorry, Teddy, what did you need?" Emmis shook his head to clear it as he addressed the marine.

"We were wondering if a couple of us should head back to the kid?" Teddy asked. Emmis was about to answer, gathering his thoughts to make the hard call, when another voice broke the silence.

"Why would you head back down the trail? Seems kinda counterproductive." The marines all whipped their rifles up and spun toward the voice, realizing seconds later who was speaking. Leaning against a large conifer, arms crossed, with an amused look in his eyes was Johnny. He appeared to be unharmed, and slightly bored. "Took you guys longer to get here than I thought."

The Marines lowered their weapons and relaxed again. A few began to chuckle. Emmis lowered his rifle and stepped up to the young man as he straightened up. The shook hands like old friends.

"Well we didn't have our guide to lead us," Emmis replied. "Good to see you in one piece." Johnny nodded his thanks.

Johnny looked into Emmis's eyes as he applied pressure to the top of the latter's rifle. He had spotted markings and signs along the last three hundred yards of the trail indicating a lion was in the area, but he figured they could move through quickly enough not to disturb it. He had been wrong. Now he and the others were staring down the fanged visage of a fully grown female mountain lion. Johnny knew they could easily shoot the creature and keep moving, but something told him that this particular lion didn't want to attack them, it was in a defensive posture.

Johnny whispered to Emmis to move down the trail slowly and he would catch up. Johnny waited until Emmis was a couple of feet back before stepping around to face the lion head on. He slowly drew his knife from his shoulder sheathe and reached back and tugged one of his hatchets free. He held the knife, blade up, and the hatchet, blade down and slightly back. He could hear the huffs coming from the lion as they stared each other down, waiting for one side to make the wrong move. He could almost read what the lion was thinking in its glaring amber eyes.

He took the chance to slide his right foot back, trying to distance himself from the lion. He made it a couple of feet, when a new sound caught his attention. It was a softer mewling, almost lost in the sounds of the forest. Movement coming around the side of the rock outcropping caught Johnny's attention. He shifted his stance in response to face both the lion and the new threat. The lion tensed, readying itself. Johnny pulled the hatchet back to prepare to throw it at the new threat, stopping himself at the last second. With a tiny growl, a small kitten launched itself into the snow at the foot of the outcropping, quickly followed by its twin. The lion, ever watching Johnny for any aggressive movements, hopped down, putting herself between her cubs and the potential threat that Johnny posed. Johnny finally understood.

He nodded to the lioness, and then began to slowly step backward away from the trio. The lioness watched him, relaxing slightly, as he put his knife back into the sheathe. He waited until he was a hundred yards down the trail before replacing the hatchet in the sheathe on his lower back. He could still feel the eyes of the lioness on him. They would remain focused on him until he was further away. He finally turned and reoriented himself on the trail. The unit had a nearly thirty minute head start on him. He had to hurry. As soon as he was reoriented, he turned slightly left and launched himself into a sprint, pulling the straps of his back holsters tighter to keep them from bouncing around on his back. Trees began to blur around him as he dodged around and under trees and branches.

The sound of rushing steps to his right caused him to look over. He saw several elk, spooked by Johnny, began to run away in parallel to him before breaking away to the north.

He jumped a fallen, snow covered tree and then swore as he hit the embankment on the other side and managed to drop into a slide. Snow was kicked up around him as he slid down. He finally reached the bottom and rolled himself back to his feet. He quickly shook the collected snow off and resumed his running. He estimated that he had at least drawn parallel to the unit by then.

His lungs began to burn with the frigid air, and he could feel sweat form on his neck and back. He felt exhilarated as he ran through the forest. It was as though he was in his natural element. He leapt over a scrub bush and landed in a particularly deep snow bank in an explosion of snow. He worked his way out and surveyed his surroundings.

He was standing on the bank of a frozen river. He looked up and down the bank, trying to spot the geographical landmarks he pointed out on the map to the unit. He was beginning to fear that he was really far off course when he spotted a downed tree that marked their crossing point two hundred yards downstream from where he was standing. He turned and started to make his was toward it, careful to avoid ice patches and particularly deep snow banks. He kept glancing at the ice covering the river, trying to gauge its thickness. He was hoping that the ice had built up enough during the winter that it would hold their weight. He did spot debris and ice chunks here and there floating under the ice, signaling thin spots.

He was about fifty yards from the rest point when the light wind picked up and brought the sounds of soft conversation to his ears. At first he tensed up, thinking that an imperial patrol had decided to camp out at the river. He went to pull his pistols, but stopped. As he got closer, the voices became clear enough for Johnny to pick up English words and varying accents. He moved around the clearing to ensure that they were alone. He spotted the unit at the river bank, most relaxing slightly after the rough hike through the mountains. Johnny found an opening in the tree line and stepped up to a large conifer. His ears caught several conversations about the mission thus far and how much help Johnny had been or could be for the remainder of the mission. He decided to wait and see how far the conversations would go, crossing his arms and leaning against the tree. The moon was reflecting off the ice over the river, casting the unit in eerie shadows.

He only spoke after the marine named Teddy asked the unit's captain if they should head back to find Johnny. Johnny answered their questions as they came, stepping by Emmis as he did. The unit was becoming more relaxed around Johnny, accepting him more as one of their own. He stared at the ice, watching the reflections of the moon and stars dance across it. He judged that they would have to go one at time, trying to keep as much weight off the ice as possible, when new sounds in the wind caught his attention. He turned his head slightly to pick the sounds up better. It was soft, but steady. The crunching beat of feet in snow. Then the huffs came through, the labored breathing of running creatures. They were getting closer. Making a decision, Johnny turned to the unit and looked for the best candidate. His gaze fell on Owl, the unit's marksman. He tried to judge how fast he and Owl could get across the river versus how quickly the approaching pack would reach the unit. It would be too close for comfort.

"Captain, spread your men out in a defensive pattern," Johnny said. "Why?" Emmis asked. He looked at Johnny, confusion evident in his eyes.

"You may have to defend yourselves while Owl and I cross the river," Johnny responded. He took a look behind him into the forest as he heard the first of the growls. He knew the unit heard it too as they turned away from the river. Emmis took one last look at Johnny, nodding to him once, then launched into giving orders.

"Spread out, by twos, defensive postures. Bull, make sure you have the widest angle of fire. Short bursts, stagger reloads. Only fire if you have too," Emmis ordered. The unit spread out in a half circle, charging handles being pulled back, safeties being clicked off. Johnny turned to Owl.

"We are going to cross as quickly, and safely, as we can," Johnny began. Owl nodded. "Watch for white or clear spots in the ice, means the ice is thin.

Once we get to the other side, we are going to set up to cover the others as they cross."

Owl nodded his understanding. Johnny looked once more into the forest, the growls and barks of the wolf pack now evident and echoing through the trees. He turned back toward the river and carefully put a foot on the ice. He felt and heard it creak under his boot as he put weight on it. Confident it would hold, he added his full weight and then added his other foot.

He began to move across the river, more sliding his feet than lifting and walking normally. He heard Owl copying his movements just behind him. The river was sixty yards across, but it felt more like a hundred. Johnny was beginning to feel as though he was moving at a snail's pace. The intensity of the howls and growls emanating from the forest behind them seemed to intensify as he and Owl made it to the fallen tree. They had less than ten yards left until they were back on solid ground.

Johnny had hoped that the tree would cause the ice to build up more than the open river.

His hopes had proven true as he saw the ice change color, showing it to be thicker than what they had been walking on. Johnny chanced a short sprint to finish their trek. As soon as his boots touched the far bank, Johnny moved with more intensity. He slid to a stop behind a set of river rocks and unslung his rifle. He went to set up, when Owl tapped him on the shoulder. Johnny looked up. Owl was holding out a small barrel attachment Johnny recognized as a sound and flash suppressor.

"This should fit your barrel. Let's keep this as quiet as possible," Owl said. His Boston accent coming through nice and thick. Johnny nodded and accepted the suppressor. He quickly threaded it to the end of his rifle's barrel, giving it a solid twist to ensure it was seated properly. He carefully set the barrel against the top of the large rock in front of him.

"Let's bracket the crossing," Johnny said. "Set up on the other side of the tree. It will give us the widest angle."

"Good thinking." Owl moved off to set up. As soon as Johnny saw him get set, he looked at his the device on his right arm and pressed Emmis's name, opening up a private channel to the captain.

"We're set. We'll cover you as you cross." Johnny said.

"Copy." Emmis responded. The channel opened to team wide. "Teddy, Vincent, move." Johnny settled behind his rifle and peered through the scope.

He saw Teddy and the marine named Vincent stand and turn. They had been set up beside Bull and another marine, ensuring that the defensive line did not suddenly develop a hole the pack could exploit. The two marines made it to the edge and carefully test the ice before putting their full weight on it. They tried to move with purpose, but caution. Johnny watched them for the first third of their crossing, then shifted his aim back to the rest of the unit. He focused on the forest just beyond the unit and spotted shadows flitting between trees. It seemed to take forever for Teddy and Vincent to make the crossing. Johnny estimated that they were a little more than three quarters of the way across when Emmis spoke again.

"Malik, Johnson, your turn." Two more marines stood and made their way onto the ice. They also started out slowly and cautiously, but picked up speed as they gained confidence. Johnny kept his focus on the forest, trying to determine how bold the pack was getting. They were still moving between the trees, trying to keep the unit distracted.

"We're across," Teddy said over the radio. He spoke again a few seconds later. "We're set, back to back." Johnny took his eye from the scope for a moment to clear up his confusion into Teddy's words. He looked over to his right and spotted Teddy and Vincent, kneeling halfway between Johnny and Owl. Teddy was aiming back across the ice, Vincent had his weapon oriented to the forest behind them. Johnny put his eye back to his scope, just in time to see a shadow stalking toward the unit. The other shadows were still darting between trees, keeping the unit focused on them. Johnny adjusted his aim to a tree just in front of the stalking shadow. He squeezed the trigger and felt his rifle bucked against his shoulder. The normal crack of the rifle was muted to nearly a whispered pop. He kept the sight on the shadow and the tree as the bullet traveled. It shot between two of the Marines seconds after he fired, causing them to jump slightly. It impacted the tree, chewing a chunk of the bark off, a split second after that, the shadow having just gotten parallel to the tree. The shadow tore off back into the forest in fear.

"Sorry about that," Johnny said into his comm unit. "Didn't have time to send out a warning."

"No worries, just gave us a startle," a voice answered. Johnny pulled the bolt on his rifle back, causing the spent round to fly out of the chamber and go spinning off into the snow. He pushed the bolt back forward, chambering the next round. He swept his sight over the forest, looking for more stalking shadows. He wasn't able to see any more shadows stalking forward, but he also didn't see any reduction in the number of shadows darting between trees.

"Rat, Doran, move," Emmis ordered. Johnny spotted the two stand and move toward the ice, now a pair of holes appeared in the line. "Bull, tighten up." Bull slid to his left until he was a couple of feet from Emmis. Rat and Doran moved faster than the others once they hit the ice.

"Malik and Johnson are across. Take up positions behind Johnny and Owl." Teddy ordered.

Johnny heard the crunch of ice and snow beneath boots approach his position. They stopped shortly behind him.

"I got your six," a voice quietly said. He had no accent to speak of, so Johnny couldn't quite tell where he was from.

"You are?" Johnny asked. "Malik."

"Gotcha," Johnny replied. He refocused his attention on the forest beyond Emmis and Bull. His blood turned cold as he realized what he saw. The shadows were no longer darting back and forth, they were all standing, silent, preparing their next move. "Emmis, Bull, you are not going to be able to wait. Move now. Owl, watch for flank attacks out of the forest."

"Copy."

"Copy, let's go Bull." Emmis ordered. Johnny watched as they stood and moved to the ice. Johnny shifted he aim back toward the forest and saw the shadows begin to stalk forward. He steadied his aim and started to apply pressure to the trigger.

"You all need to move faster. Do not look back. Owl, you seeing this?" Johnny asked. "Yep. I'll take the far side and work my way in," Owl replied.

"Hold fire until they step onto the ice, we may still be able to convince them to leave us be." Johnny said. Emmis and Bull were fifteen yards into their crossing when the first of the wolves stepped out of the shadows of the trees and onto the moonlit bank. Johnny put his crosshairs on the creature, willing it to stop. It stalked forward until its paws were inches from the ice. It dropped into a crouch, its teeth bares, eyes focused on the marines on the ice. Several more wolves joined the first on the bank, some growling, some howling, the rest just staring. Johnny swept his sights back and forth, trying to determine which would attack first. His sweep stopped upon a male wolf, its fur still showing signs of adolescence. Johnny again tried to will the young wolf to stay where it was. A few more yards and the Marines on the ice would be clear and out of danger from the wolves. The young wolf snarled and lunged forward a bit, only to stop at the snapping jaws of an older one. It looked slightly chastised, but still determined. It looked back and forth between the marines on the ice and the elder that snapped at it.

Johnny could see that it wouldn't be able to hold back much longer. He kept his sights on it as he opened his other eye to get a wider view of the river. Rat and Doran were nearly to the other bank, while Bull and Emmis were still less than halfway. He closed his eye once more and refocused on the wolf. Its impatience finally overrode its fear of the elder wolf and it launched itself onto the ice in a sudden burst of speed. The sudden movement caught Johnny by surprise for a split second. He quickly adjusted his aim and squeezed the trigger. His rifle once again bucked against his shoulder. The round travelled quickly, covering the distance in a couple seconds. It punched into the wolf's chest at over a thousand feet per second, killing the young creature before it knew what hit it. The force of the round caused its body to spin on the ice several times as its forward momentum allowed it to slide another dozen feet. Johnny kept his sights on the body of the wolf as he cycled the bolt to chamber a fresh round.

After a few seconds, he shifted his aim once again to the rest of the pack on the bank. They were still there, standing silently, watching the scene play out. Johnny scanned the bank once again, looking for any other wolves preparing to attack. None of the others were eager to try their luck. He opened his right eye to see how far Emmis and Bull had to go. He was pleased to see that they were within twenty yards of the bank. Johnny closed his eye and focused on the opposite bank. The wolves were beginning to disperse back into the forest. Johnny began to relax, when he spotted something hiding in the shadows. It was only a flash, but Johnny could have sworn he saw white fur disappearing back into the shadows. Johnny scanned the forest once more, but no longer saw the movement. He released his finger from the trigger of his rifle, sliding it out of the trigger guard. He lifted his eye from the scope and took a last look at the opposite bank before standing. He engaged the safety on his rifle and then place it back in the holster on his back.

The Marines were gathering around Emmis and Bull, already talking about the amazing shot Johnny had made. Johnny looked at them and then turned to look up the trail they had to follow. He narrowed his eyes while looking into the trees. The moon had reached its half way mark in its decent behind the mountains, causing the shadows of the forest to elongate. Johnny grinned as he likened the shadows to skeletal fingers reaching toward them. His grin faded as he spotted a sign he had been looking for. Four scratches marred the bark of a maple tree not far from him. Now he knew why the wolves were not eager to continue their pursuit of Johnny and the Marines.

"Hear you pulled off an impossible shot," Emmis said, Johnny had not heard his approach while he had been lost in thought.

"Not impossible, just a bit unlikely," Johnny responded.

"You have my thanks anyway." Emmis said. He stepped up to stand next to Johnny, looking into the forest in same direction as Johnny. "Now, you want to tell me why you knew the wolves wouldn't follow us to this side of the river?"

Johnny took a deep breath and then turned to look at Emmis. He saw that the other Marines were gathered around them.

"Because from this point forward, we don't have to worry about wolves," Johnny replied. "What do we have to worry about?" Teddy asked.

"Bears." Johnny looked at each marine as his explanation sunk in. "The trail from here on out is all bear territory. Mostly grizzlies, but also some Kodiaks, browns, and blacks. The blacks will avoid us if we get close. Kodiaks and grizzlies will charge us if we encroach. Brown bears will go at us if they are starving. Keep your fingers on the triggers, and we stay tight. I know you want to follow your training and keep spread out, but in this case it would be a lethal mistake."

"We are going to pick up the pace, try to move through as quickly as possible. Should only be about ten miles." He paused to allow the explanation to register. "We will rest for a few minutes once we are clear."

"Alright, you heard the man, check your gear and lock down anything loose. Owl, you are going to stick with Johnny. Bull and I will bring up the rear. Heads on swivel people. Things just got real." Emmis ordered. Johnny turned back toward the trail and pulled his shotgun from its holster. He opened the breach to check the shells, then closed it with a definitive click. He stepped off onto the trail and quickly set the pace. Owl fell in step with him and they led the unit into the forest.

Johnny kept his ears attuned to the sounds of the forest and wind, trying to pick out the unnatural sounds. He could feel the tension of the Marines around him as they shifted their gazes from one shadow to the next. He could almost feel the eyes of the predators around them. Twice he thought he saw a lumbering form between the trees off the trail. As their trek carried them higher into the mountains, the air in his lungs began to burn from the exertion.

He could hear the labored breathing of the Marines as they too felt the strain. It took them a little over three hours to make the ten miles. By then they were all exhausted and ready for that rest point. Johnny was the first to reach the top of ridge that marked the ten mile mark. It overlooked the scenic valley that Silverton was nestled in. The moon was still just above the opposite mountain range, casting its light into the valley.

Johnny had been to Silverton hundreds of times in his life, it use to be an amazing tiny town, where everyone knew everyone else. The economy relied heavily on the winter wonder seekers, snow boarders, and seasonal residents. He looked down at the town, whose lights should have been bright and shining like a beacon, now dark and foreboding. It had been abandoned just after the Imperial army had begun their bombing runs on the other side of the range. He and his father had gone to Silverton to scavenge things they needed. Johnny had always felt guilty about it, but his father had left notes to the store owners with a tally of what was taken and owed to them. They had always meant to repay them, and now it would never happen. Off to the west of the town, however, was the harsh glow of hundreds of bright lights. Johnny couldn't see their origin, but he knew their location: a small park where the locals had gathered for town events. It was tucked away in a bowl shaped valley. He also knew that whatever those lights surrounded was the target of the Marines' mission.

"We are going to rest here," Johnny said. He put his shotgun back in its holster and moved to an old tree stump. He sat down and pulled a canteen of water from his backpack. He lowered the facemask of his balaclava and took a long drink from it. He decided to wait for Emmis to explain what their mission was. He heard the crunch of snow as the Marines spread out around the clearing and relaxed. They talked quietly amongst themselves while Johnny sat quietly and stared at the valley below them. He heard the crunch of boots approach and looked up as Emmis stopped next to him. Johnny pulled his facemask back up and held out his canteen. Emmis took it with a grunt of thanks. Johnny turned his gaze back to the valley and waited.

"You've probably guessed that those lights are part of our mission," Emmis began. "I gathered as much once I saw them."

"I guess it's time to fill you in." Emmis continued. "Gather round gents." Emmis put the cap back on the canteen and handed it back to Johnny. Johnny took the canteen and put it back into his bag. He turned away from the valley and looked at Emmis as the Marines settled in around them. "You all know the mission, but it's time to fill Johnny in. Next to Silverton is Huan Zhi Lo prison camp. According to the last intelligence flyby, there are one hundred and forty three members of the Imperial military under the command of one Colonel Jerun Quai, four forty sixth imperial assault regiment. They are guarding fifty six members of the United States military captured in various engagements throughout Colorado, the Dakotas, and Minnesota. One of those members is in fact an intelligent asset that had been working to get more information on the units moving through the northern United States. Our priority one is the asset. However, we will not leave those men and women to rot. We will be waiting for the next flyby to get better information on the camp and guard positions. We will also be getting more information on our extraction point on the fly by." He took a breath and looked around to ensure that they were all getting the information. "Our initial guess at infiltration is through the northern portion of the perimeter. There is a pond that freezes over, but it makes it difficult to place a fence or proper barrier. Once we know the guard rotation, we go in. Once we are in, first priority is to split into two teams. Team one will set whisper charges on the main power generators. Team two will locate the asset and the other POWs. Once team one is complete, they will rendezvous with team two and the prisoners. Once we are together again, we will set the charges off. Once the charges go off, we will make our way to the nearest perimeter fence, which would be the eastern fence, and make our way into the forest. Our flights will meet us eight miles from the camp. We load up and leave. First rounds will be on me back at base."

"Where do you want me?" Johnny asked. He knew their plans didn't include him originally and knew that he would be more of a hindrance if he were to go into the camp with them. He would do more good outside the camp than inside.

"I want you on the exfil trail. You know the area best, you would know how to get us to the point faster and hopefully leaving as few tracks as possible. We want to keep you out of any engagement if we can." Emmis said. Johnny nodded and turned to the valley.

"The spot you guys want to go in at is eleven miles in that direction." Pointing to indicate the direction. "The trail is easier once we get down this ridge and into the valley proper. More roads and driveways, a couple of creeks we can take advantage of, and the pipe."

"Pipe?" Bull asked.

"It's a drainage pipe the county set up to mitigate the thaw. Keeps the area from flooding, most of the time. The pipe actually runs through the valley you want to go to. It will put you inside the camp without having to go through the fence." Johnny explained.

"Does it have an access point inside the park area?" Emmis asked, surprised by the new information.

"Yes. There is a pump house on the southwest side of the park. There is a grate in the back on the floor, it leads to a short shaft that connects to a similar grate in the pipe."

"And no one would expect it to be an entrance point?" Owl asked.

"Not unless they went down it themselves. The grate has two bolts holding it in place in the pump house and a single pin and hinge in the pipe. We can go through the pipe to get to your insertion point to check to see if they had found and plugged it." Johnny recommended. He turned and looked at Emmis. Emmis was staring into the valley, trying to come to a decision.

"Flyby is when?" He asked.

"Eight A.M." Vincent replied immediately.

"How long would it take us to get to the pipe and then to the insert point?"

"Two and a half hours to the pipe if we move quickly. Twenty minutes through the pipe to the grate. At least ten minutes to check its viability. Then another thirty to insertion point in time for the flyby link." Johnny said.

"Gives us three hours to dig in and wait." Bull calculated. Emmis nodded, coming to a decision.

"We leave in ten. Johnny is going to lead us to this pipe he described and we will check it out. If it's a better insertion point than our primary, we go for it." Emmis said.

Johnny nodded and looked into the valley. He began to wonder how he could use his skills to help other than being the guide. The ten minutes went by quickly. He stood and shook out the kinks in his legs. He looked down the backside of the ridge, mapping out their route, when Owl approached him. He held out a pair of goggles, their lenses tinged with a light green.

"These should help." Owl said. Johnny took the goggles and slipped them over his head. As soon as he settled them over his eyes, they activated, bathing everything in an eerie green. He looked around, marveling at the detail the goggles gave. He looked over toward the lights and watched as the goggles automatically adjusted to the light. He nodded his approval.

"Thanks." Johnny said. He pointed to the trail he chose. "This leads to a creek bed covered by trees. Should keep the snow shallow. It'll allow us to run more or less. Three miles down, the creek runs under a back road. Take the back road four miles to a wash. The wash is two hundred yards long leading to the pipe, it's rocky, so we need to watch for ice. The pipe is two miles long. It's then a mile to the insertion point." He looked at Owl, then to the other marines. "Ready?"

They all hefted their weapons and nodded, each one now wearing a set of goggles. Johnny grinned behind his balaclava. They were all faceless ghosts now. He turned back to the trail, unslung his rifle and set off at a quick pace. His feet were sure as they slipped and slid down the trail to the creek. He could hear the Marines sliding along behind him. Once in the creek bed, Johnny waited for Rat to finish his slide, then he turned and began to run down the bed toward the road he pointed out. He was glad to see he had been right about the trees keeping most of the snow out of the bed, it was mostly gravel and made it easier for them to run at almost full speed. The Marines, used to runs like this, were able to keep up easily. A little over twenty minutes later, they came to the road Johnny mentioned. They took two minutes to catch their breaths, before Johnny led them up onto the road. Here, the Marines' training kicked in and, once they were all on the road and moving, the spread out, five to each side, fifteen feet between each person and staggered.

While they were still able to move at nearly a run, the snow was a bit deeper on the road and ice patches dotted their path. They moved silently, no more than phantoms amongst the shadows. The moon had fully set behind the mountain range, leaving them with only the stars as their source of external light. Johnny kept his ears open for any sign of noises outside the wind and swaying branches. Nothing was sending up red flags as they got near the wash and the valley currently inhabited by the Imperial army. They kept their pace steady, eating the miles in just over a half an hour. Johnny slid to a stop as he spotted the wash, signaling the others to stop as well. He climbed down the steep ditch to the wash and began to pick a route that would keep them all from twisting their ankles. He moved up the wash with all best speed, spotting the end of the pipe. He went to move to its entrance, when he spotted something in the snow. He stopped and took a closer look. The tracks were jumbled and confused. He was just beginning to make sense of them, when Owl moved to the entrances of the pipe.

"Wait!" Johnny said. He rushed forward and tackled Owl out of the way, just as a larger brown blur came flying out of the pipe. It hit the rocks at an odd angle, rolling to its feet and spinning to face Johnny and the Marines. The Marines instantly brought their weapons up, but Johnny scrambled to his feet and jumped into their line of sight. Johnny stared down at the lion as it bared its fangs at him. Without taking his eyes off it, he slung his rifle. He was reaching for his knife and a hatchet when the lion took the opportunity to lunge at him. Johnny spun to the outside of its swipe, drawing his knife and slashing its leg in one fluid move. He stopped his spin, drawing his hatchet out of its sheathe. The lion screamed in surprise and shock at the sudden pain in its leg. It looked at the wound, which began to well up with blood. Johnny stood in a defensive posture, his hatchet slightly back and his knife blade out.

The two began to circle each other, the marines standing witness to the primal struggle.

Johnny was calm as he watched the lion's movements. It feinted in and out, gauging Johnny's reaction. Johnny shifted his stance each time the lion took a swipe at him. Johnny's eyes narrowed as he recognized the feral look in its eyes. It was starving and sick, but it was also full grown and determined to kill him. It feinted another attack at Johnny, who went to sidestep the swing. Instead, his boot slipped on an icy rock, causing him to stumble. The lion, seeing the stumble, let out a deafening roar and launched itself at Johnny, claws and fangs bared for the fatal strike. Johnny managed to recover his footing in time to see the leap, but not in time to dodge it. He knew in the split second it took for the lion to cover the distance separating the two that he only had one chance to survive. If he were to try to back away or spin to either side, those claws would make short work of him. That left only one option.

As the lion's feet left the earth, Johnny launched himself forward. The two collided, hard. The lion's superior weight and power should have been enough to force Johnny to the ground, where its powerful jaws and razor sharp fangs would end his life. Instead, Johnny's angle of approach and leverage gave him the advantage as he drove his knife into the lion's chest, using the creature's forward momentum to bury the blade to the hilt. It screamed in pain and rage as the two of them fell to the ground and rolled toward the bottom of the wash.

Johnny felt sudden and sharp pain in his left arm, causing him to lose hold of his hatchet. The fall was a tumble of fur, snow, and rocks in his perspective. He felt the hits from each and every rock. A sudden jolt to the side of his head dazed him, causing stars to explode in his eyes. He came to a sudden stop, the weight of the lion pressing down on him. He laid there for a few moments, trying to stop his head from spinning, before pushing against the unmoving body on top of him. He stopped when pain lanced through his arm and shoulder. He heard running feet and loose rocks rolling down the wash toward him, the sounds of people calling out his name.

The weight of the lion was suddenly lifted off him as several pairs of hands pulled the two apart. Johnny's vision suddenly cleared as his goggles adjusted to the night.

Several more hands pulled him up into a sitting position. Several voices were arguing about helping him, when one broke through.

"Get him into the pipe. Doran could look at his arm there. We need to get out of sight," Emmis ordered. "Bull, bring the cat. Teddy, find his hatchet. Move people." Johnny felt his arms being lift and set across the shoulders of two separate people, his feet dragging along the ground as they half dragged him back up the wash. His vision kept washing in and out, the pain in his head and arms causing his eyes to cross every now and then. They made it back to the entrance of the pipe, this time stopping long enough for one of the Marines to turn on a flashlight and check to see if the pipe was safe.

"All clear," Vincent said, moving into the pipe first. The two carrying Johnny followed Vincent in, taking him a hundred yards into the pipe before setting him down. Someone turned on a flashlight, causing his goggles to try and compensate, but washing his vision out in a white haze. Someone then pulled the goggles off his face, quickly followed by his balaclava. His vision began to return slowly as someone pressed a thumb to his left eye and held it open as they shined a pen light into it.

"Johnny? Keep your eyes open for me pal. That's it," Doran said, moving to his right eye. Seeming to be satisfied with Johnny's ocular response, he turned off the light and shifted his position to his arm. Johnny heard and felt his sleeve being torn as his vision became accustomed to his surroundings. He saw Vincent and Teddy kneeling twenty meters away, staring up the pipe.

71

Emmis and Rat were checking a set of bodies they found already inside, dragged there and feasted on by the mountain lion. Their uniforms showed them to be Imperial troops, most likely a patrol that was ambushed by the lion. Johnny looked toward the entrance of the pipe and saw Owl and Malik checking piles of debris. Bull was setting down the lion's carcass, Johnny could still see his blade in its chest. A sharp pain alerted him to what Doran was currently doing. He looked down as Doran was threading a needle and its attached thread into and out of Johnny's skin on each side of the wound. He worked quickly and quietly as he alternated between sewing the stitches and using an alcohol swab to clean the area around each wound.

Shuffling feet alerted Johnny to someone's approach. He turned his head and saw Emmis coming to kneel beside him.

"How is he Doc?" Emmis asked.

"He'll be fine once I stop the bleeding and finish sewing him up. He's going to have a headache for a while, and some impressive scarring, but he'll live," Doran answered. "Damned stupid of him if you ask me."

"Yea, but it was some badassary on a whole new scale," Teddy intoned without turning around. "Oh, by the way, I have your hatchet."

"Thanks," Johnny answered, his voice a little thick.

"One question: why did you not just let us shoot the damn lion?" Emmis asked.

"Felt like the right thing to do?" Johnny asked sarcastically. Emmis tilted his head, signaling he wasn't buying it. "We are too close to the camp. Your weapons don't have silencers on them, any shots would have been like sending up a flare. Even if we weren't around when they came to investigate, they would find our trail and either send out an alarm or follow us. Too bad too." Johnny finished, looking back at the lion.

"Too bad?" Doran asked, looking up at him.

"Yea. I could make a new coat out of it," Johnny responded. He looked back down at his arm. Doran had almost all of the blood wiped away and his wounds stitched. He was right about the scars, the claws had dug in deep. Doran finished his sutures and then began to wrap a bandage around his upper arm. Once it was covered, he tied it off. Johnny felt the chill of the wind on his skin where his sleeve had been torn. Johnny pulled his bag around, unzipped it and pulled and old t-shirt from the bag. He reached for his knife, then remembered where it currently was, so he pulled one of his throwing knives.

He cut the sleeves off the t-shirt and then tugged them over his torn sleeve. Once they were in place, he put the remains of the t-shirt back in his bag and slung it back on his shoulder.

He moved his arm around, feeling the tightness and tug of his wound and new stitches. He made sure that the sleeves covering the tear and bandage would not move. Once he was certain, he picked his balaclava up and slid it over his head. He adjusted it, then picked up the goggles.

He put them on, but not over his eyes yet. He stood with help from Doran, swaying slightly as he regained his balance. He nodded to Doran, who let go of his arm, then slowly walked over to the dead animal. He crouched by its head, laying a hand on it.

"Sorry," He said softly, closing his eyes. He moved his hand and gripped the handle of his knife. With a quick, strong yank, Johnny pulled the knife free. He looked down at the blood, still fresh, dripping off the blade. He leaned over and picked up a scrap of a dead imperial soldier's uniform and wiped the blade clean. He made sure no blood remained before sliding it back into the sheathe on his shoulder. He looked at the lion one last time before standing. He cast his gaze around the makeshift den the lion had made. The bodies were old, more than a month. The marks on the bone showed prolonged feeding. He moved back up the piped to where Emmis was standing.

"The grate is half way up the pipe," Jonny said. Emmis nodded. "You ok?"

"I will be. Headache mostly," Johnny replied.

"Very well. Vincent, Teddy, move forward. Keep your eyes peeled," Emmis ordered. Vincent and Teddy stood, Teddy turning and holding out the handle to Johnny's hatchet. Johnny took it with a nod of thanks, then placed it in the sheathe on his back. He went to pull his rifle, but figured it would be more of a hindrance in the confines of the tunnel. He pulled his backpack around and opened it. He withdrew the battle rifle he had packed, then zipped the bag back up. He pushed it back onto his back and pulled the sling out of his pocket. He clipped the sling to the end of the buttstock and then to a swivel piece on his left shoulder. He pulled a fresh magazine out of his cargo pocket and seated it into the magazine well with a click. He pulled the charging handle back to seat the first round. He pulled the bolt back slightly to ensure the round went in. He extended the buttstock to his personal choice. He looked up to see the amused surprise in Emmis's eyes.

"Had a feeling it might come in handy," Johnny explained. Emmis nodded, accepting the explanation. They set out behind Vincent and Teddy as they walked down the pipe. As they got deeper into the pipe, the ambient light died, causing Johnny to lower the goggles over his eyes. The pipe washed out in a green hue. Johnny counted off the distance in his head, trying to keep it accurate to his memory. It took them nearly twenty minutes to cover the distance. In fact, they almost walked past it. Johnny looked up and spotted it just as he was moving under it.

"Here," Johnny said. The group came to a stop as Johnny inspected the grate. It was just as he had remembered. The pin was new, but the hinge was old and covered in rust. "Any of you got any oil or lubricant?"

He heard a couple of chuckles in the darkness. He looked back down to see Bull walking up, holding a bottle of some kind out. Johnny took it from him and inspected it. Once he opened the cap, he knew exactly what it was. It was an oil based lubricant for the bolt of Bull's weapon. Johnny smeared some over the hinge, letting it soak in for a few moments, before adding more. He looked at Emmis.

"Help me with this," Johnny said. He pulled the pin with a slight rasp of metal on metal.

He pocketed the pin and gripped the grate. A slight layer of rust had built up on both the grate and the surrounding metal. Emmis reached up and grasped the grate as well, and with a short tug, pulled it loose. Once it was free of the rust, they began to open the grate slowly, pausing to add oil to the hinge every time it squeaked. Finally, they worked it all the way open, swinging it back and forth to work the oil deeper in the metal. Johnny handed the oil bottle back to Bull, and nodded to Emmis. The marines set up a perimeter, Teddy and Vincent facing forward up the pipe, Rat and Malik facing back down the pipe, and Bull, Doran, and Owl holding the grate. Emmis and Johnson shouldered their rifles and waited. Johnny used the grate to climb up into the access shaft, using a hand to keep his battle rifle banging against the walls and floor. The access shaft was not as tall as the pipe, causing Johnny to stoop. He turned and held out a hand, pulling Emmis up as soon as the marine grabbed hold. Johnny shuffled back to allow room.

"The shaft is sixty yards long at an upward angel. At the end is a vertical section, four feet tall," Johnny explained. "The sounds of the pump house should cover any noise we make."

"Any way to know if there are people in there before we enter?" Emmis asked.

"Yes. The pump house has automatic lights that flip on when someone is inside. So unless they broke the lights, we should be able to tell before we pop that next hatch," Johnny answered.

"So they are going to pop on if we enter?" Emmis asked, slightly alarmed.

"No. The sensor is by the door. I can show you how to disable it once we are inside."

He turned and headed up the shaft. It was slow going since they couldn't stand up straight. Johnny kept his ears open as the sounds of the pump house became louder. Johnny felt a slight change in the temperature as the heat of the pump house radiated through the pipe. He reached the vertical section of the shaft as the heat caused sweat to begin to form. He paused in the vertical shaft and waited for Emmis. Once Emmis was in position, Johnny unclipped his rifle and set it aside. He reached up and felt through the grate until his fingers brushed against the pin holding it shut. He felt around the pin until he felt the head. He used his fingers to slide the pin out, managing to catch it before it fell into the shaft. He pocketed it as well. He nodded to Emmis. Both men gripped the grate and pushed, popping it open, the sounds of the pump house drowning out the snap of the rusted metal. Johnny pushed it open enough to allow him to crawl up and into the pump house. Holding it with one hand, he pulled his knife and wedged it into the space between the grate and the floor, keeping it open. He gripped the floor with both hands and then pushed off with his legs, pulling, and then pushing himself up and out of the hole.

Once he was in the building, Johnny took a knee, keeping his right hand near his throwing knives, prepared to launch one or more at anyone in the pump house. Convinced that they were alone, Johnny turned and gripped the grate, pulling it completely open. He grabbed his knife and put it away before reaching into the hole. He grabbed Emmis's hand and pulled him up into the pump house. Once Emmis was on his feet, Johnny pointed at the door to his left, ten feet away. His finger was pointing to a small box just above the door, indicating the sensor that would turn on the lights. Emmis nodded his understanding. Johnny motioned for Emmis to move along the wall to the back of the house. Once they were in the back corner, Johnny finally spoke.

"The pump house is twenty-five by thirty. As you can see, the machinery takes up most of the center space. The whole thing is powered by solar panels on the roof and the water that rushes through the pipes. The sensor for the lights has a breaker on the wall over there," Johnny said, pointing toward a jumble of electrical cables and panels. "I'll show you which one to cut."

Johnny led the way past the running machines to the electrical systems and popped open a breaker box. He first pointed to and then flipped a breaker switch wrapped in orange tape.

Once it clicked, he nodded to Emmis.

"That will kill both the internal and external lights attached to sensors," Johnny said. He led Emmis over to the door and waved a hand in front of the sensor. He chuckled when he saw Emmis tense up slightly at his movement. He sent Johnny a withering look. Johnny shrugged an apology, then motioned him to the door. Emmis stood behind him as Johnny gripped the handle. He turned it enough to release the catch. He pulled it open enough to peer outside. He spotted a tent directly in front of the door, less than ten feet away. It was as tall as the pump house, casting the intervening area in shadow. Johnny opened the door further and stuck his head out. He looked around, trying to spot trouble. After a few moments, he eased himself out of the door and into the snow. He moved forward a bit to allow Emmis to follow. Johnny stopped and turned to Emmis. He pointed to the dozens of tracks went across the back of the tent to either side. Troops frequented the path. Johnny moved forward to where the tracks all commingled.

He could hear the snores and deep breathing of people sleeping through the wall of the tent. Further away, he heard voices talking and laughing. He cast his view into the snow for the reason why. He spotted the butt of a cigarette sticking out of a print. He picked it up and held it out for Emmis to see. The troops went back there to smoke. Johnny did not see a large collection of discarded butts, so either most of them took the butts with them or they only went back there sparingly. He dropped the butt back into the snow and waived Emmis back toward the pump house. They quickly slipped back inside and Johnny silently shut the door. He led Emmis back to the access shaft and then turned to speak with him.

"Gonna have to watch out for that," Emmis said, referring to the smokers who stood back there.

"They don't use it often, guessing only when storms crop up. That side of the tent is on the lee side of incoming storms," Johnny replied. Something was bothering his thoughts, but he could not put a finger on it. "Let's get back to the others. After you."

Emmis lowered himself into the shaft silently and moved far enough down to allow Johnny to join him. Johnny gripped the grate and lowered it enough that Emmis could hold the grate by himself. Johnny squeezed underneath it and dropped into the shaft. He took a moment to grab the rifle he left there and clip it back on his shoulder. He then helped Emmis lower the grate the rest of the way. Johnny pulled one of the pins from his pocket and replaced it enough to make it seem as though the grate was still secured, but out enough it would only take a finger to pull it back out. Once that was finished, he nodded to Emmis, signaling that he was ready to go. Emmis led the way back down the shaft, moving slightly faster than they had when they had when they moved up. Emmis made it to the pipe's grated quickly. He dropped down into the pipe and moved to the side to allow Johnny to drop down. Johnny stood in the pipe and looked around. The Marines had not moved from when they had left.

"How'd it go?" Owl asked.

"The shaft will put us inside the camp unseen. Looks like we found our new insertion point," Emmis replied. He looked at the mission clock on his wrist band. "We need to move. Sunrise is coming."

Johnny nodded and moved past Vincent and Teddy, taking point once again. The dull throb in his head suddenly vanish as he set his mind to the next objective. He moved at a jog, trying to make up the lost time from his skirmish with the mountain lion. Ten minutes after they set off, Johnny's goggles began to register the lighter hue of the open sky over the snow. He slowed as he reached the exit, looking down to check for fresh tracks. The unit, taking his cue, slowed and waited until Johnny was satisfied. Johnny was certain he and the unit were not going to run into another surprise attack, he left the pipe and turned to the northwest. They came out of the pipe at a higher elevation than the valley. There was a vast, open field with few trees to stop the snow fall. Here their pace slowed. Without roads or tree cover, the snow was deeper. Johnny turned to the unit and signaled that they fall in a straight line. He was hoping that their overlapping tracks would fool anyone who came across them into thinking it was a herd of deer or pack of wolves that made them. He spotted the rocky cliffs across the field. There were a handful of caves they could use as shelter until the flyby. He kept the pace steady as they neared their destination, the features of the terrain becoming more prevalent.

Johnny slowed as his feet went from ground under the packed snow, to ice. He looked up at the cliff, seeing the river pouring over the top of the cliff, cascading down to the pool it had dug out in the earth millennia ago. All of it was frozen in a single instant of time. He carefully led the marines across the pool and then behind the waterfall. He spotted the cave in the darkness, hidden behind massive boulders that had fallen from the cliffs long ago. It would allow the Marines to set up camp and even start up a fire to keep warm, the glow would be shielded by the stones as long as they were far enough back. He stopped the group outside the cave, peering inside.

"Stay here," Johnny said. "I'm gonna go check it out." He unclipped the sling of his rifle and handed it to Vincent, the closest marine. "Hold that."

He stepped up to the entrance of the cave and pulled his shotgun. He held it out in front of him one handed as he drew a hatchet as well. He stepped cautiously, trying to discern any breathing or growls. The cave would be perfect for any creature trying to get out of the cold and into shelter. He was also looking for signs of predation, carcasses and bones. He was nearly a hundred feet into the cave and still saw no signs of anything taking shelter. He went as far as he could, the cave dropped a dozen feet into an underground pool that fed an underground river. He swept the cave once more as he made it back to the entrance. He lowered the shotgun and stowed the hatchet as he walked back out under the frozen falls. He turned to the Marines and stowed his shotgun.

"It's all clear in there," Johnny said reaching for his rifle. Vincent handed it over, Johnny reattaching the sling. He turned and led the Marines into the cave. He took them all the way back to the drop off and dropped his bag. "We can rest here."

The Marines looked around a bit confused.

"Weren't we supposed to be going to the rally point?" Teddy asked, looking between Johnny and Emmis.

"We are at the rally point." Johnny answered. "What?" Johnson asked, confused.

"It's above us." Johnny answered. "About sixty feet up." He pointed toward the ceiling. Emmis checked his wrist band, switching from the radio settings to the map feature. It showed that they were, indeed, in the correct spot.

"He's right. We are right where we are supposed to be," Emmis said. He checked his timer and map once more, before launching into a string of orders. "Bull, Vincent, get the gear unpacked, this is home for the day. Doran, Teddy, get the uplink set up outside, try to keep it out of sight. Owl, see if you can find a trail up to the top of the cliff, I want you on overwatch. Johnson, you are his back up. Malik, Rat, let's get some lights set up in here." The Marines waited a single moment before jumping into action. "Johnny?" He turned toward Johnny.

"I'm going to show Owl and Johnson the easiest trail to use. Then I'm going to go find some firewood. Lights won't keep you warm in here." Johnny answered. Emmis nodded his approval. Johnny motioned to Owl and Johnson to follow and the trio moved out toward the cave's entrance. Once they were outside, Johnny led them further to the north, along the base of the cliffs, looking for a specific feature. He found it fifty yards down. A partial landslide had caused the cliff to lose most of its vertical face, allowing one to easily scale most of the way up the cliff. An unfortunate tree near the edge had fallen, creating a natural ladder to scale the rest of the distance.

"Be careful. The tree probably has ice built up on it," Johnny warned them as he pointed up the slide to the tree. Owl and Johnson nodded their thanks and began the climb. Johnny turned from them toward a stand of trees a hundred yards further down. He moved through the snow, keeping an eye on his surroundings. Not only could there be predators stalking about, but he couldn't risk being spotted by an Imperial patrol. He looked to the east, seeing the horizon becoming lighter as dawn approached. He reflected on how insane his life had become in the last twenty four hours. He entered the stand of trees and pulled one of his hatchets. He searched for a suitable tree, not too large, yet big enough to stand losing a few branches. He saw a few good candidates on his first sweep, finally choosing a fallen oak, leaning against a still standing tree. He looked around to ensure no one was near and then began to hack at the tree. He started with some medium sized branches, gathering them into a pile as he cut them off.

He started to build up sweat as he worked, his breath beginning to come in ragged gasps from exertion. Once he had a dozen or so large branches, he stowed his hatchet and gathered them into his arms. He turned back toward the cave and set off along his original tracks. It took him a little longer to make the trip back due to the load in his arms. He passed by Teddy and Doran as they were finishing up their task of setting up the satellite uplink. The uplink was a small satellite dish, set up on a collapsible tripod. They were adjusting the angle so it pointed up into the open sky. As Johnny stepped by them, his foot bumped something. Doran looked back at him.

"Careful. We laid out a pair of cables stretching back into the cave," Doran said. "Stay to the right and you'll be fine."

"Thanks," Johnny replied, stepping to the right a couple of feet to ensure he wouldn't trip over the cables. He moved to the back of the cave, where Bull, Emmis, and Vincent were setting up the camp. Vincent was setting up a pair of laptops, the end points for the cables attached to the dish outside. Emmis was pulling water and MRE packs from a couple of the bags and Bull was moving medium sized rocks to the center, arranging them into a circle. Johnny stepped to the side of them and set the armload of branches on the ground. He pulled his hatchet once more and set to cutting a few branches into three or four pieces. He took one of the larger pieces and used his hatchet to shave off thin strips to use as kindling. He took several pieces and arranged them into a pyramid in the stone circle. Once the pyramid was set, Johnny pulled an old butane lighter from his pocket. He walked back to the wood pile and grabbed a handful of the shavings, taking them over to the stone circle. He pushed the shaving in open spaces in the pyramid, trying to keep them from getting too packed, allowing air to move through. Once he was satisfied, Johnny flipped the lighter and sparked the flint, causing a flame to ignite. His goggles took a moment to adjust to the sudden, bright light. He held the lighter to the shavings until the flame caught and began to burn. He shifted his position and held the lighter to more shavings until the flame caught there as well. He stepped back, flipping the top of the lighter back down to snuff its flame. He watched as the two sections of shavings he lit began to burn in earnest, catching the edges of the larger pieces. In a few moments, the fire would fully catch.

Johnny looked over at the remaining branches and did the math in his head. It would last them half the day, hopefully. He cast a glance at the pile of MRE packs and narrowed his eyes. The marines had only brought enough food for themselves, not counting on an extra mouth to feed. Johnny gave himself a little nod. He has had to fend for himself so far, he can still do so now. He pocketed his lighter and turned away from the fire and headed back toward the entrance of the cave. He was near the entrance when a hand was laid on his shoulder. He turned to see who it was and saw Emmis staring at him.

"Where you going?" Emmis asked.

"Think I can do better than MREs," Johnny answered. "We can spare some food for you," Emmis countered.

Johnny nodded, "I know. But it's ok. Fresh meat will do us some good."

"Dawn is in a couple of hours."

"I'll be back before then," Johnny replied. Emmis looked like he was going to try and stop Johnny, but, in the end, released his grip on Johnny's shoulder and nodded. Johnny turned back to the entrance and walked out. He stopped next to Doran and Teddy, still fiddling with the satellite dish. He cast his gaze around the field and decided to head southwest. He couldn't explain how he knew or why, but he just knew. He turned to the right and began his walk, deciding to follow the cliffs for as long as possible. He picked up his pace to a light jog and headed into the snow.

Emmis watched Johnny until he disappeared around the face of the cliff to the southwest. He looked at his wristband and calculated the time. Dawn was in two hours and forty five minutes. He hoped it was the right call to let Johnny go. He switched the display to the radio settings and pressed a finger against Owl's name.

"Owl."

"Yea, boss?" came Owl's response a split second later.

"Johnny left the camp, moving southwest. You have a visual?" A few seconds of silence ticked by.

"Yea, I've got him, he's entering what looks like a small, wooded grove not too far from here. There a problem?"

"No. Just keep an eye out for him." Emmis requested. "Not a problem boss. Owl out."

Emmis stood there for a few more seconds and then turned back into the cave. The fire Johnny had started had finally caught the wood and was burning with a nice intensity. Emmis reached up and removed his goggles as he approached. Bull and Vincent were huddled over the laptops, their backs to the fire. He noticed that they, too had shed their goggles and facemasks, enjoying the warmth of the fire on their backs. Emmis walked by them and took as seat, pulling his facemask over his head, running. He unclipped his battle rifle and set it to the side. Bull looked up from the laptop he was staring at.

"The kid?"

"Breakfast run." Emmis answered. Bull looked up in thought before shrugging and going back to the laptop. Emmis looked across the fire as Doran and Teddy walked up to it. They both unclipped their battle rifles, setting them down on their packs before sitting. They pulled their goggles and facemasks off and settled down comfortably.

"Johnny's out on a breakfast run," Emmis said before they could ask. Teddy and Doran looked at each other for a moment before looking back at Emmis.

"Was he taking special orders for this run? Cuz I could kill for an espresso and bacon egg sandwich," Teddy responded, drawing laughs from the group. He leaned over to pull his pack closer. He opened it and pulled a collapsible decanter and a sealed bag of coffee grounds. "Coffee anyone?"

"You need to ask?" Vincent asked sarcastically, without turning around. Teddy nodded as he stood and headed to the cave's entrance once more.

"Where ya going?" Bull asked, looking over Vincent.

"To pack this thing with snow. Keeps me from having to use our own water," Teddy answered. He was gone for a few moments as the rest of the team in the cave settled into the warmth of the fire. Emmis stared at it for a few moments before broaching a subject that had been on his mind. He pressed Owl's and Johnson's names on his wrist band, making sure they were included in the discussion.

"Gents," He began. "I want your honest opinions: What do you think about Johnny?" He asked. The three marines around the fire looked at each other and then at Emmis before answering.

"He's got skills. Scary skills, but useful," Vincent was the first to answer.

"I don't know how he is holding it together," Johnson replied over the comm. "He's literally lost everything he has ever known in the last day: his home, his family, maybe even himself."

"I hear that. You get a good look at his eyes when he's focused on the hunt or when he was staring down that first lion?" Owl asked. "There's not much I fear, but he made the short list. I'd hate to be on the receiving end of his rage."

"No one would have survived that fight with the second lion, and he came away from it with what is tantamount to a flesh wound and a head ache, all the while killing a full grown lion with a knife," Doran added. "I've never seen anyone with those kinds of reflexes."

"Let's be fair," Teddy chimed in, walking back up to the fire, Malik and Rat on his tail. "The kid ain't human. He's more primal than that. He was reading the terrain more than anything, he spotted signs most of us would have dismissed, and it was like he knew which one of those wolves would attack before it did. Living out here like he and his family have been has turned him into a new kind of beast. Then the Imperials killing his family and destroying his home caused something to snap in his brain. Instead of reacting like a 'civilized' person," Teddy said, using his fingers to denote quotes, "He did what any predator would do to someone encroaching or disturbing their territory and or home: He went on the offensive and sent a message. And let me tell you," He added, placing the decanter in the flames, "that message was a brutal fuck you and your army. Those imperials never stood a chance."

"The way he looks at you sometimes," Malik intoned. "It's not so much that he is looking at you, but into you. Gauging your soul."

"He'd make one hell of an operator though," Rat chimed in.

"I think that would only work if they just let him loose and told him to hunt anything that he came across," Doran added. Emmis nodded as he let their words sink in. Then he began to think of how he would write the recommendation he was thinking about.

"Why you asking sir?" Vincent asked.

"I'm thinking of recommending Johnny to be selected for a position as an operator with us or one of the clandestines," Emmis answered. The marines around him nodded as they thought about the repercussions of such a recommendation.

"I think that would be a good idea," Teddy said. They all turned their attentions back to the fire and the laptops.

It took nearly an hour for the snow in the decanter to melt and then boil, then for the coffee to heat up. Emmis had, several times, gone to the mouth of the cave to look and see if Johnny was on his way back. Each time he had asked Owl, he had gotten a negative response. He wasn't worried, yet, but the horizon to the east was getting lighter and lighter, to the point that they no longer needed their goggles to see clearly. He decided to wait another half hour, then he would send three of the guys to follow Johnny's path. He had just walked back to the fire, accepting a fresh cup of coffee from Teddy, when one of the laptops made a chiming sound. He walked over and stood behind Vincent to check it out.

"Satellite is coming into orbit, be another hour or so," Vincent said. "Once it is over us, we should be able to get a direct link to command, sir."

"Good, keep me apprised," Emmis responded. He walked over to where Malik and Rat were playing chess, checking his watch for the umpteenth time. He watched the game for a while, when he started to feel uneasy. The half hour was almost up when he decided to cut it short and send out a party. He walked to the entrance of the cave, stood there for a few moments before marching back to the fire.

"Teddy, Rat, Malik, get your gear. You're heading out to find him," Emmis ordered. A sudden voice behind him nearly made him drop his coffee.

"Find who?"

Emmis and the Marines spun toward the entrance of the cave. Their surprised looks were greeted by the appearance of Johnny standing at the entrance, the large body of an animal slung over his shoulders, the glare of the fire casting just enough of a conflicting shadow to keep what it was hidden. Johnny stepped further into the cave, the light of the fire and chemical sticks Rat and Malik had set up revealed the animal to be a large deer. Johnny walked around the back of the fire and flipped the deer's carcass off his shoulders to the ground.

It hit with a thud and laid still. He stood up straight and rolled his shoulders, working out the kinks that had formed during his hike back. He walked over to where his pack was and pulled his rifle from the sling on his back, setting it down, barrel pointing up and toward the wall behind it. His battle rifle and shotgun followed suit. After that was done, he moved back to the deer and pulled his knife from its sheathe on his shoulder. He began to cut into the deer, starting the process to skin it. The Marines around the fire looked on in silence as he worked, the only sounds filling the cave were the fans of the laptops, the crackle of the fire, and the tearing of ligaments as the knife loosened the skin.

"Sooooo…you weren't kidding when you said he went on a breakfast run?" Teddy ask, tearing his eyes away to look at Emmis, who shrugged in response.

"I figured he would get a rabbit or squirrel or something else small, not a full sized deer," Emmis responded, shifting his gaze from Johnny to Teddy and then back to Johnny, who had finished with the opening cuts and had begun to actually pull the skin off, using his knife to aid the process.

"If one of you could get a large, flat stone and put it on top of the fire, we can start cooking this meat," Johnny requested, not turning around. The Marines looked at each other before realization of what Johnny wanted dawned on Teddy's face.

"AH! How about a grill stand instead?" He asked, diving back into his bag. He pulled his hand out holding a folding camp grill. He unfolded it and placed it over the fire, the flames just licking over the top of the bars.

"You just happened to have one of those in your pack?" Rat asked incredulously. Teddy shrugged.

"Never know when you'll go camping."

The sound of sizzling fat and meat filled the cave as Johnny turned around and laid a large cut of the deer's side on the grill. Soon the cave was filled with the smell of cooking meat, causing every mouth in there to water. Johnny set his knife on the deer's pelt as he moved to his bag and removed the t-shirt he had cut the sleeves off of. He also took the opportunity to pull his goggles and balaclava off, stowing them in a cargo pocket. He carried the shirt back over to the deer. He picked up his knife and cut down the side seam of the shirt, laying it open on the ground. He turned back to the deer and began to cut more steaks from it. Teddy decided to be the impromptu grill master while Johnny was busy and used his knife to turn the grilling steak over. The flames jumped and dances as juices, blood, and fat fell into the fire.

Johnny worked in silence for twenty minutes as he cleaned every usable piece off the carcass, setting each cut of meat on the shirt. As he finished, so did the meat on the fire. While he had been working, Bull had found a large, flat river stone in the cave and set it down next to Teddy. Doran used a couple of alcohol swabs to 'clean' the stone's surface before Teddy transferred the fully cooked slab of meat to it. Once it was there, he set about cutting the meat into even strips for everyone. He doled them out evenly, taking one for himself last.

Johnny finished cutting the meat from the deer and stood, stretching out his legs. He stabbed a second large chunk of meat and set it on the grill before stooping to pick up the pelt. He stepped around the crackling fire and carried it to the entrance of the cave. He set it down, fur to the ground and spread it out, using his throwing knives to secure it. He proceeded to use his hunting knife to scrape any remaining tissue from the skin. Once he was satisfied with his work, he walked back to the fire and sat down, using a piece of the destroyed shirt to clean his blade. He scooted to the side to make room as Emmis walked over to him, handing him a cup of fresh coffee. Johnny replaced the knife in his shoulder sheathe and accepted the cup. Emmis took a seat next to him as Johnny took a long, grateful sip.

"Thanks," Johnny said.

"No problem. You provided the food, we could certainly provide the drink," Emmis responded. Johnny nodded and grinned.

"You were right, by the way," Johnny said in a low voice. "About?"

"I had planned on getting something small, but figured what the hell once I saw this guy walk into my sights. There's enough of us here to eat most of him throughout the day," Johnny said. "And what we don't take, something else will. Saw signs of a bear and her cub out there."

"Are we in danger?"

"No," Johnny replied simply. "I left the entrails and such back at the kill spot. They'll eventually follow the smell back here, then they'll wait until we leave before moving in."

"Planning on keeping the skin?"

"Yep. I need a new coat, Doran and that mountain lion tore the sleeve on this one."

Emmis chuckled and looked around. His Marines seemed happier since they were eating fresh food. He nodded a couple of times, realizing how much Johnny had done for them.

"Rest up, link up is in a few hours." Johnny nodded and stared into the fire, taking another sip of coffee. He had been up since yesterday morning, not counting the hour or so he was unconscious, and yet he didn't feel tire. Just the opposite in fact, he never felt more alive or energized. He could get used to the new feeling.

Johnny watched the Marines laugh and joke in silence as the time wore on into dawn. He envied them, in a way. He wished he could laugh like that again, but he knew deep down he no longer could. He felt that something was broken, he no longer felt the urge to laugh for a laugh's sake. He peered across the fire at Emmis as the captain spoke to Rat and Malik, who had taken over the watch on the laptops. He turned his gaze to the entrance of the cave as Owl and Johnson walked in. They had been up on top of the cliff since Johnny had led the team to the cave on over watch duty. He had showed the others the way up when Emmis had told Vincent and Doran to relieve them. They were removing their facemasks as they approached the fire. Johnny nodded to them and then pointed to the pile of cooked strips of deer meat sitting on a stone next to the fire.

They nodded their thanks and walked to Teddy, who was pouring two cups of coffee for them. Johnny rolled his neck to loosen his muscles. He stood and turned to the entrance, feeling the need to get some fresh air. He stepped outside, then around the frozen fall. He gazed off to the range to the east, watching the sky turn a lighter blue as the sun was beginning its climb. The sky above the range appeared to be getting darker. He knew it was a trick of the sunlight on the atmosphere, but he also felt that it was a lot like himself. The dark being beaten back to allow for something new to take its place. He hoped whatever he was becoming was worth the loss of feeling he endured thus far. He turned his gaze from the range to the field in front of him. It was still and silent, almost too peaceful to Johnny's senses. He reflected on how ridiculous that would have sounded to him two days ago. It struck him on how much he had been through and lost. He heard the sounds of foot falls echoing against the walls of the cave. He stepped to the side to allow the new arrival room to stand next to him. He didn't turn to the man next to him, instead continuing his survey of the snow covered field.

"See anything interesting?" the voice of Bull broke the silence.

"Nothing worth noting. A small herd of deer are about to leave the safety of that grove trees to the north there," Johnny responded, nodding in the direction of the trees. He felt Bull turn his head to look. After a few moments, he saw the first of the herd step cautiously out of the tree line, pausing once for a minute, its ears twitching back and forth, alert for any danger. Sensing none, it began to move further into the field, shortly followed by two, then three, then several other deer. Johnny watched the deer out of the corner of his eyes as they began their trek across the field. Bull chuckled and shook his head.

"Now how did you know that?" Bull asked.

"The early light caught the shine of their eyes as couple of times. The trees have lighter colored bark than their fur, so it's a little easier to discern their movements from the other shadows cast by the trees themselves," Johnny explained. "Once you silence everything else, it's easier to see and hear the things that are out of place." He looked at Bull. "For instance: the bear and her cub I clocked a few hours ago have left their little stand of trees and moved into the field. They are moving slowly this direction, cautious, but determined. They'll probably pass us during the day, heading for the stand the deer just left. The elder one will watch this area until we leave before bringing her cub in. Once inside, they will settle here for a while. I'm gonna make sure they stay here and not follow us."

"How?"

"The deer scraps and anything we don't eat. It will keep them occupied for a bit." Johnny explained.

"No, how do you know they left the stand?" Bull asked. Johnny nodded his understanding. "If you listen to the wind coming around the cliff, you can hear her huffing and snarling at the cub when it wanders too far," Johnny explained. They stood there silent, listening to the wind for a few seconds. Then Bull heard it, a light, but steady huffing sound behind the wind's normal howl.

"Well I'll be damned," Bull said softly. "Where did you learn all of this?"

"Can't explain it," Johnny answered truthfully. He couldn't really explain it, but when he surrendered to his rage and primal feelings, he began to understand the world around him in a whole new way. He looked once more toward the range to the east, the light of the approaching dawn was now well and truly up them. Johnny estimated that they had maybe twenty minutes before the sun crested the ridge. "C'mon, we should get inside." He pressed

Vincent's name on his wristband, opening a private comm channel. "Vincent. Sunrise over the range is in twenty minutes. You guys might want to find a way to make yourselves unnoticeable."

"Thanks for the heads up. We've been digging out a little nook up here, should allow us to stay small." Vincent responded. Johnny turned around and headed back into the cave, followed closely by Bull. The two made their way to the fire as both laptops made chiming sounds.

"Boss! Sat linkup is starting," Rat shouted. "Time to completion is six minutes." The marines in the cave moved to surround the laptops as rat set up a small projector looking device. He plugged it into both laptops. The projector warmed up as it activated, drawing power from the laptops themselves. Emmis knelt down next to Rat as the status bar finished loading. Johnny, standing behind the group, watched as an image of the earth materialized on the screen, then on the wall of the cave as the projector caught up. It was a topographical map, zooming in to North America, then closer to the Rocky mountain range, then closer onto Colorado. The image scanned back and forth until it locked onto the satellite dish the Marines had set up outside. The image tightened onto the signal, then focused the resolution so the detail was nearly perfect. Johnny could even see Vincent and Doran on the cliff. He was pretty impressed with the image. A steady set of beeps began to sound from the second laptop.

"Sir, command is ready for link up," Malik said, turning to Emmis. Emmis nodded and motioned for Malik to connect the call. "Raptor nest, Raptor nest, this is Raider Eight. How copy?"

"Raider Eight, this is Raptor Nest, we read you Lima Charlie," a female voice responded. The image on the screen of the laptop resolved to show the face of a young, red haired woman, her freckles accentuating her face. "You boys in position? Sat images are only showing two at the rally point."

"Affirmative Raptor, those are our over watch team. We are actually sixty feet below the point. Our guide was able to show us a cave more suitable to conceal our presence for the day," Emmis explained. He tapped Malik on the shoulder. Malik moved away from the laptop, making room for Emmis to sit down in his place. Once he was settled Emmis looked directly into the laptop. The woman on the screen looked off to the left as someone spoke to her. She turned back toward the camera, a slight confused look on her face.

"Copy that Raider eight, we received word from Stallion twelve that the civilian you encountered volunteered to lead you..." She trailed off as someone once again spoke to her. "Standby Raider Eight…General Quincy wants a word."

"Standing by Raptor Nest," Emmis replied. He looked at the Marines assembled around him. They all looked back with confusion and worry. The screen on the laptop shifted from the young woman to the face of a weather beaten one of a man who had a very rough life. His steel gray eyes stared into the screen a few moments before he spoke. His voice was just as worn and gravely as his face. Too many years of hard drinking and smoking Johnny assumed.

"Raider Eight, this is General Quincy," The General said.

"Yes, sir, we're reading you loud and clear," Emmis responded. The general's image nodded. "We have an update to your current objectives, Raider. Lieutenant, bring up the camp on the monitor," The general said to someone off screen. The laptop with the projection of the surrounding landscape shifted to the east until the valley with the many tents and buildings the imperial forces put up took up the entire screen. The image zoomed in and focused on a large building just north of the center of the camp. It was a brick and stone building, two stories tall. There were several satellite dishes and antennae attached to it at various points. Johnny spotted three imperials on the roof, one on a first story outcropping, the other two at the very top. Judging from the amount of haze coming from the two at the top, they were smoking. Their AKN98 suppression rifles were hanging at their waists, the one below them was pacing around the roof, his rifle in his hands and at the ready. Johnny could even see the man's footprints in the snow behind him. "Two days ago, one of our high altitude UAVs was shot down near your area of operation. An Imperial patrol got to the crash site before our recovery team."

"What did they get, sir?" Emmis asked.

"The internal CPU. This unit has a backup system that stores all of the images it took until techs are able to erase it. The footage includes our own lines as well as footage of the main imperial base in Colorado. The passive GPS signal indicated it was on the move, now it is sitting inside that building." The general explained. The second laptop switched its graphics from standard image to thermal signatures. There was a pulsing light inside the building, signaling the CPU's location. "The CPU went into active location mode as soon as their techs plugged it into their computer systems. Our techs are monitoring what they are doing remotely."

"And that is?" Vincent asked.

"They are trying to access the information on the CPU, but are having issues getting through the encryption and security programs. They have been ordered to initiate the thermal core if the imperial techs get through the security," The general explained. "But we are hoping that you can get to it before we need to."

"What else is on that CPU?" Emmis asked.

"A set of viruses and Trojan worms our techs programed into every drone CPU. When plugged into an unauthorized system, it automatically downloads everything it can on that system and any system attached to it. It also uploads a serious virus to the system that allows us to not only access their systems remotely, but crash them as well when we want to," The general answered. "Normally the CPU would send a burst transmission containing the information it gathered, then we would trigger the self-destruct initiative."

"But it's not working, is it?" Vincent asked.

The general looked a little uncomfortable as he answered. "No, something inside that building is keeping the CPU from sending the information. That's why we need you collect the unit while you execute your mission."

Emmis nodded as he assimilated the information and thought it over. "We'll have to adjust our assault plan, but we can get it done," Emmis said.

"Very good, captain. Now let's get your plan laid out," The general responded. "Lieutenant, you're up."

The screen changed again back to the young woman. She shuffled a few pieces of paper before launching into her briefing. "Satellite images from the last flyby shows at least one hundred and thirty eight imperial troops in residence." She nodded to someone off screen.

The projection changed to a set of stills taken at night using thermal or infrared images. The stills showed different parts of the camp up close, then the whole camp at a wide angle. Johnny spotted no outlying troops outside the fences. Neither were there any on the ridges around the camp to give them an elevated view.

Stupid, Johnny thought. He had instantly spotted nearly a dozen places where he could set up and cover almost the entire camp. The images stopped on a set of tents, similar to the one he and Emmis saw outside the pump house. Emmis must have had a similar thought.

"Stop the images," Emmis said. "Is there a concrete structure next to these tents? Off to the side, near the western perimeter."

The lieutenant looked through a few images before finding one. She displayed it through the projector. There were four tents, surrounding what appeared to be a set of barrels. Their bright centers showed burning fires inside them. Behind the back of the west tent, the group could see the front of the pump house. Johnny could also see several pairs of imperial troops marching around the outside of the tents, but never moving near the pump house.

"Who or what are in those tents?" Teddy asked.

"Those tents hold most of the prisoners you are going after," the lieutenant replied. The image shifted to infrared, showing dozens of figures in each tent. Another image was put up showing a group of the prisoners standing in the snow. They were wearing thin jackets and no gloves. Some had used socks to cover their hands. Doing a quick calculation in his head, Johnny counted fifty three prisoners in the tents. That means there were three missing.

"Fantastic," Emmis said. "Our guide showed us a back way into the camp. It sits in that pump house behind the tents. We can sneak the prisoners out quickly and quietly."

"What do you mean?" The lieutenant asked, confused.

"There is a pipe that runs down the mountain to help keep flooding from overwhelming the town during the thaw. There is an access shaft that runs from the pipe to the pump house. The shaft ends at the floor of the house. It will allow us to move into the camp and move the prisoners out without raising an alarm." Emmis explained. "Teddy that will be yours, Johnson's, Vincent's, and Owl's job. Set it up how you want. Johnny will show you the quickest path to the exfil. The rest of us will snag the CPU and make our way out. Plan to take out the lights still holds, Bull and Rat will handle that. Malik and I will provide over watch. Doran, I want you to stick with Teddy's team. Some of the prisoners might need aid. Johnny, after you show Teddy's team the trail, I need you to stand by to lead my team out of the area as quickly and quietly as you can." Emmis said, looking back at Johnny. Johnny nodded.

"I can show Teddy and Owl the trail while it's still daylight, it's easy to follow and once you hit the halfway way point, you won't leave any tracks." Johnny replied. "As for your team, captain, I'm going to need an overview of the camp."

"Bring it up," Emmis said, turning back to the laptop. The Lieutenant on the screen nodded and the projection widened to show the entire valley. Johnny studied it for a few minutes, committing every detail to memory, judging the best course they could take. He saw several possibilities before settling on the best course. He pointed to the small drainage ditch running southeast out of the camp.

"Here. Here would be your best exit point. The ditch should be clear of deep snow." He stepped up to the projection and traced his finger along the ditch as it ran out of the valley to a dry creek bed sixty meters from the valley. "Follow the ditch to this creek bed. From there it's a sprint to the forest here." He followed the creek bed to the beginning of the forest, where the trees became incredibly thick. "Once you reach the tree line, you'll be able to follow my signs, I'll teach you them, to the meet point here." He brought his finger back around to the north side of the hills ringing the valley. "I'll meet you here." He pointed to a small group of rocks on the map.

"Why there?" Bull asked.

"Once you make your way out of the camp, it's all about getting clear as fast as possible."

"Once you hit the forest, you should be able to shake most of your pursuers because of how dense the trees are. It's my job to make sure we disappear once you clear the forest. So that's what I will be doing. I'm going to be keeping an eye on our actual escape route as well as anyone that is still chasing you. It'll be quicker for me to get the trail ready and for you to move without me tagging along." Johnny explained. Bull mulled his words over in his mind before nodding his understanding.

"Kickoff time is 00:30. I want Teddy's team in place by 00:00. My team will be in place on the north side of the valley by 00:10. Johnny, I want you to be in position by 01:00 at the latest. Does that give you enough time to prep the trail?" Emmis asked. Johnny worked the time table through his head.

"That'll be enough time," Johnny answered.

"Perfect. For now, let's get you, Teddy, and Owl out there. Owl and Teddy should be able to run that trail blindfolded and backward." Emmis ordered. Johnny nodded and moved to his gear. He picked up his weapons and placed them in their holsters. He heard Emmis giving last minute orders to his men. Johnny clipped the sling of his battle rifle to his shoulder and turned back around. Teddy and Owl were picking their gear up and adjusting the straps and slings to make themselves comfortable. Johnny nodded to the two of them and headed over to the entrance of the cave. He stopped long enough to check the deer hide he had laid out. It was coming along fine. He pulled out his balaclava and slipped it on before exiting the cave. The sun was just over the horizon, its rays reflecting off the frozen waterfall in front of the cave. He turned to the two marines behind him.

"We can hug the cliff most of the way around the field. After that, there is a short ridge that will keep us hidden as we approach the pipe." Johnny said. The two marines nodded as they donned their own facemasks. Johnny turned to the south and set off. It took them nearly an hour to make their way around the cliff to the ridge. He didn't want to risk moving across the open field during the day. The light wind throughout the night would have covered their original tracks they made before. Once they were at the ridge, Johnny picked up the pace and cut down the time it took to reach the pipe. He slowed as they approached the pipe, the memory of his hand to claw fight the last time they had approached the pipe still fresh in his memory.

He shouldered his rifle and stepped lightly as he approached. The sounds of the boots crunching in the snow behind him sounded like cannon fire to his ears. He moved to the side of the pipe and then peered in. He saw no signs of anything in the pipe, but gave it a few moments before proceeding. He stepped in the pipe and took a knee, listening. He was listening for anything out of the ordinary, but just heard the wind rushing through the pipe. He stood back up, waved the marines forward and headed down the pipe. Johnny kept his senses peeled as they approached the access shaft. Once there, he pulled the pin back out, handing it to Teddy. Together, they lowered the grate silently, they assisted each other into the shaft. Johnny led them to the exit inside the pump house, pausing at the end to listen for anything out of the ordinary. Once they were satisfied there was nothing in the pump house, Johnny pulled the pin holding that grate closed. Owl and Teddy held it open as Johnny climbed up and out of the shaft. He gripped the grate and opened it all the way, then moved back to assist the others through the opening.

He showed them where the power and breaker boxes were and what to cut when the time came. He also explained what the area around house and tents was like before waving them back into the pipe. They lowered the grate back into the place and headed back down the shaft. They exited the shaft into the pipe and moved back up toward the exit. Once they were there, they paused to rest. Johnny looked toward Teddy.

"Where's the exfil point?" Johnny asked. Teddy turned to his wrist band and pressed a few icons and buttons. The wrist band on Johnny's wrist chirped twice, drawing his attention to it. He looked at the screen and watched as it showed a map of the surrounding area. Johnny recognized it as the same map as the one projected on the wall of the cave. Three markers were glowing on the map, indicating their position, the cave, and the exfil point. Johnny looked closer at the third point's location. It was north by north east of the valley, nearly ten miles out. He worked out the best path for them to take. He was staring at the map when a revelation hit him.

"Let's head back down the pipe," Johnny said. He led them back down to the wash and then paused at the entrance. He brought the map back up and showed Teddy.

"Whatcha got?" Teddy asked.

"This creek bed," Johnny replied, pointing to the map. The creek bed was down the road they came up before. It connected to another road that led into Silverton itself. The creek he was pointing at went under that road, just outside the city. He then traced it, it circled around the town at the base of the mountains. As Teddy watched, he saw that the creek came within a mile of the exfil point. He began calculating the time it would take as Johnny spoke once again. "Depending on the condition of the prisoners, it will take nearly three hours to get to the exfil."

"This path will keep you all out of sight, and keep your tracks to a minimum. I'll take you to the start of the creek bed, all you have to do is follow it. I will also leave a marking to show you where to leave the creek bed."

"What kind of marking?" Owl asked. Johnny looked at Owl, then back to Teddy.

"The same one I left over the dead recon soldiers." Johnny answered. Owl's eyes showed confusion, but Teddy simply nodded. "Come on, let's go." He stood and set off down the wash to the road. He stayed off the road in the scrub bushes and trees, to keep their trail signs to a minimum. He kept the pace quick and steady, covering the distance to the bridge he had pointed out on the map in just over a half an hour. He stopped at the bridge to allow Owl and Teddy to rest. Johnny searched for an easy way down before seeing the signs of a deer trail ten feet to the side of the road. He moved over to it and looked down the slope. It was steep, but not dangerously so. Still, he decided they should make a safety for those that were going to go down.

"Teddy, you guys have any rope?" Johnny asked, turning to the two marines. They looked at each other before Owl unslung his bag and opened it. He pulled out a bundle of climbing rope and tossed it to Johnny. Johnny caught the rope and began to unravel it. He pulled a D-ring from his bag and tied the end of the rope to it. He searched for and found a thick conifer behind him, walking over, he slung the D-ring around the tree, catching it as it curled around the trunk. He clipped the ring to the rope and pulled hard, causing the D-ring to tighten to the tree. He tugged it a couple of times to ensure it wouldn't slip free. He walked back to the bank, picked up the rest of the bundle and hurled it as hard as he could out over the creek bed. The rope straightened out as the end tied around the tree stopped the forward momentum of the rope, gravity then took hold, causing the rope to fall against the bank, its free end laying at the bottom.

Johnny inspected his handiwork and nodded. He turned back to Teddy and Owl and made his way over. He accepted a bottle of water from Owl. He lowered the balaclava and took a deep swig of water before handing it back.

"Thanks." Johnny said, handing the bottle back to Owl. "That should help get your people into the creek bed. I'll make sure they have a safe area to climb out of it."

Teddy and Owl nodded. Johnny replaced his balaclava and took a look around. He could see the darkened buildings of Silverton and his mind flashed back to a time when it was a thriving town full of amazing people. He should feel sad about its current state, but all he felt was loss. He stared for a few moments longer before turning back to the road.

"Let's get moving." Johnny said. Teddy and Owl nodded, standing back up and hefting their weapons. Johnny set the pace once again, slightly faster this time, confident in the trail.

They made it to the pipe in less than half the time it took to get to the creek. They paused a few moments to rest, before heading up the pipe. Johnny led the way once again, keeping it steady. He wanted to get them back to the cave as soon as possible. The day was going to go faster than they thought. It took nearly an hour and a half to get back to the cave. Johnny paused as he got to the entrance and turned around. He felt the wind pick up and blow loose snow and ice across the ground. He sniffed the air and smelled the sharp, crispness that comes hand in hand with snow. He narrowed his eyes at the horizon, before turning back and heading into the cave. He checked the deer pelt once more, hoping it would be finished by the time they had to leave for the mission.

He walked to the back of the cave, passing a fresh pile of cut timber. Someone must have been worried they would run out, Johnny mused. He stopped by the fire to accept a steaming cup of coffee from Doran before moving over to his bag. He set the coffee down before removing the sling from his shoulder. He set his rifle on his bag and then pulled his balaclava over his head. He stuffed it into his pocket, picked up the cup of coffee, and moved over to where the remainder of the cooked deer was stacked on a rock. Johnny picked up a small piece and took a bite from it. As he savored the flavor, he walked over to the laptops and observed as Emmis worked with the other Marines to finalize their plans. He looked up as Johnny approached. "Got them squared away?" Emmis asked. Johnny nodded.

"Yep. The trail is easy enough to find if you know what to look for. It will keep the prisoners out of sight and danger. The trail is longer the way I pointed out, but only by a half hour or so. Should keep them safe." Johnny replied. Emmis nodded.

"And our trail?"

"I'm going to head out here in a few to walk it. I should be back before night fall," Johnny replied. "I'm also going to make sure I leave a false trail, hopefully draw some of them off."

"Good plan. Need any help?" Bull asked. Johnny turned to him and shook his head.

"No. Thanks, but I'll move faster on my own," Johnny replied. He popped the rest of the deer meat into his mouth and washed it down with the coffee. He turned back to his gear and picked up his rifle, setting it to the side, leaning against the wall of the cave. He picked up his bag and moved back to the pile of cooked meat. He chose several large pieces and put them in his bag. He closed the bag and slung it over his shoulder, turning back to grab his rifle. He secured the sling and pulled his balaclava from his pocket, sliding it over his head as he turned toward the exit.

"Be safe out there," Emmis shouted to Johnny's retreating form. Johnny paused and looked back at the Marines, a look of amusement in his eyes.

"Where's the fun in that?" Johnny asked, sarcastically before turning back to the exit, hefting his rifle, and venturing out into the snow once again.

Emmis watched Johnny leave the cave, an uneasy feeling forming in the pit of his stomach. A fear in the back of his mind wondered if that was the last time he and his men would see the primal young man again. A lot was riding on his shoulders, so much so that Emmis was sure it would break lesser men. He shook his head slightly to clear his thoughts and turned back to the monitors and projection behind him. They had a lot to prepare for and precious little time left. He was playing out scenarios in his head, then the options they had to overcome them. The curve ball headquarters threw them forced them to deviate from their current objectives, but not by much. There were still three prisoners missing from the camp, and he knew without evidence that one of them was the intelligence asset they were after. That would also fall on the shoulders of himself, Bull, Rat, and Malik. He was certain that the three prisoners were in the same building as the CPU, but the satellite's scans could not penetrate the walls.

"Think we'll see him again?" Bull asked, sitting down next to Emmis. Emmis sighed, betraying the uneasy feeling he had.

"I think so. Kid's a survivor and fighter." Emmis responded.

"Never met anyone like him," Bull said, trying to keep the conversation going. "Me neither, but he reminds me of those explorers from the history books."

"How's that?"

"Those men we used to read about in school, you know, taming the wilds of America with nothing more than their wits and nerve," Emmis responded. "And you know, after watching the kid, I'm beginning to think that they didn't conquer or tame the wilds, but understood them on a primal level."

"Could be right, sir, could very well be right." Bull said, nodding.

"Enough of that, let's get a rotation started. I want eyes on these screens from here on out. Let's make sure we know the patrols down to the smallest details. Two hour shifts here, two up top, four resting. Set up a watch schedule,

I'll take Malik up top with me to start off. We leave here by 23:00." Emmis ordered.

"Got it sir," Bull responded, pulling out a pen and small notebook from his cargo pocket. Emmis stood and called for Malik to join him. They left the cave and moved to the top of the cliff to start their watch. Emmis couldn't help but marvel at the beauty of the area around them. The sun reflecting off the snow and ice, causing it all to sparkle like a billion diamond chips. He then thought about how such beauty also hid the worst dangers he and his men could ever go up against. They all may die and lose the war, or survive and win, but the land would always remain to outlive them all. It was a sobering thought for Emmis.

They day seemed to drag on into sunset as the Marines prepared for their mission. As night was falling, Emmis was in his rest period, just having fallen asleep next to the fire. His unconscious mind slipping in and out of dreams as he slept. He knew he wouldn't be completely rested, they were too close to kickoff and his body was beginning to pump endorphins and adrenaline into his veins. He could feel the tension emanating from his marines as well. It always happened when they got close to mission start time. It was all they could do to keep a calm exterior, whilst on the inside, a storm raged and threatened to break that calm.

Emmis woke with a small start as the bolt on Bull's squad suppression weapon slammed forward with a snap. Emmis's hands went straight to his battle rifle as the adrenaline surge brought him to a fully awake state. It took a few heartbeats for his brain to acknowledge that he was not in any danger before he relaxed his grip on his weapon. He looked around as he brought a hand up to wipe the rest of the sleep from his eyes. His gaze stopped on Bull and his eyes narrowed slightly in annoyance. Bull looked contrite as he realized his fault.

"Sorry, sir," Bull said sheepishly. "The bolt catch slipped." He finished closing the top of his weapon and set it down.

"No problem," Emmis replied, his voice still thick with sleep. He sat up all the way, rolling his shoulders and neck to relieve the tension that had built up while he dozed. He looked around to see the others working diligently. He checked his watch and saw that they only had a few hours left before they needed to set out. He looked to the entrance of the cave to see the encroaching darkness creeping up on them. His eyes narrowed as his brain told him something was missing. It took a few moments before it hit him. The deer pelt Johnny had stretched out was gone. "The kid back?" He asked looking back toward Bull.

"Back and gone," Bull replied. "Ghosted in about an hour ago, took the pelt, left a map, and then headed out again before anyone knew he was here."

"Map?" Emmis asked. Bull handed him a scrap of paper Johnny had left. It was a rough outline of the valley and the surrounding area. He left small drawings on the spots where Emmis and his team were to escape the camp and then into the forest. Emmis stood, stretching out his back, still looking at the map. He accepted a cup of coffee from Vincent as he stepped up to the projection on the cave wall. He held the map up as he studied them both. His eyes suddenly widened as he realized what he was looking at. "I'll be damned." He said softly.

"Sir?" Teddy asked from his seated position in front of a laptop. Emmis turned to the marine.

"Since you all have been sitting here, have any patrols gone near this section of the fence?" Emmis asked, pointing to the indicated section at the southeastern side of the camp. Teddy narrowed his eyes, squinting at the section, before turning to the notes they had been taking throughout the day. His eyes widened in surprise.

"No, sir. Each patrol has cut across in front of these tents here, instead of continuing behind them to follow the fence line. What's up?" Teddy responded. Emmis held up Johnny's map.

"Johnny drew this map for us. He's circled this section of the fence, indicating that this is our exit point." Emmis said. He ran the scenario through his mind. A blind spot in their patrols was priceless information to him. He smiled as he estimated their chances now. Time to get to work. "Alright, wake everyone up, bring in the team up top. Time to finalize our plans." Emmis ordered, turning from the projector and walking over to his gear. His Marines jumped into action, rousing those that were asleep and using the comm to bring in the two up on over watch. Emmis quickly got his gear in order and then move to the laptops to assist Teddy in getting the two teams' plans set. He looked briefly at the cave entrance and saw that night had truly fallen. His mind wandered briefly to their trump card out there, waiting to strike at the imperials like the wolves they had seen in the forest the night before.

100

The next couple of hours went quickly for the unit and, before they knew it, they were leaving the cave to begin their mission. Each Marine pulled their facemask down, once again becoming anonymous ghosts in the night, then placing their night vision goggles on their heads. Teddy and his team split off as soon as they left the cave and headed along the cliff to the trail Johnny showed them. Emmis led Bull, Malik, and Rat in the opposite direction to their insertion point. The moon was out and bright in all its splendid glory, casting its light upon the land, allowing both teams to move without the aid of their night vision goggles. Emmis was confident that the imperials were not monitoring the field they were crossing, but he still moved with caution, taking his team along the outskirts of the trees. He kept his ears and eyes peeled for any hint of danger, as they moved through the snow. His instincts kept telling him to put some distance between themselves and the total abyss the trees caused. He was able to just barely swallow the fear in his gut and keep moving. They kept their pace steady, periodically looking at the maps on their wrist bands to ensure they were still on track.

Emmis led the team to the base of a small hill separating their target valley from the field they were in. He allowed his team a few moments to rest before leading them up the hill. He waved a hand out to his side, signaling that his men should spread out. Emmis shouldered his rifle, but kept the barrel pointed down. It was ready to swing into place in a microsecond, but kept his vision clear. He cast a glance to either side of himself, to get an idea of where his three men were. Bull was to his left, his weapon held at his hip, the linked belt of rounds running up over his arm and back to his pack. Emmis knew there were ten thousand rounds in the bag, all linked together to give Bull the ability to lay down a truly impressive amount of fire on his own. Rat was to his right, the barrel of his shorter battle rifle dancing in the moonlight as he made his way up the hill. Malik was further out to Rat's right. Emmis could see Malik cast his gave to the right every now and then, keeping an eye out for trouble.

The team made it to the top of the hill ten minutes after they started, slowing as they reached the crest. Emmis moved to be slightly ahead of them to ensure he was the first to the top. He began to crouch as he crested the hill, trying to keep his profile as low as possible. He reached the top and spread out prone, laying in the snow, feeling the chill of the packed snow under his body seep into his clothes. He heard the others follow suit with a handful of gasps as their senses registered the cold underneath them. Emmis could see the glow of the camp's lights just over the ridge as he crawled forward, using his feet and elbows to propel him along in the snow. His head finally cleared the top of the hill, and for the first time since they had accepted their mission, was able to see the camp in real life. He cast a wide gaze over the many tents and quickly constructed concrete buildings in the valley. He spotted the tents being used for the imperial motor pool near the one makeshift entrance they had set up into the valley. He saw a handful of two man patrols walking lazily around tents and buildings, a four man post at the gate, and the three imperial troops standing on their target building. He quickly checked the timer on his wrist and then looked back toward the camp.

"Generator tent at our two o'clock," Malik whispered over their team channel. Emmis slowly turned his head to look in Malik's indicated direction. He spotted dozens of cables and wires leading to a particularly large tent eighty feet from the fence at the bottom of the hill. If he listened carefully, Emmis could hear the hum of the large pieces of equipment from their position. He was about to turn his gaze to the fence, when something caught his eye. He brought his rifle to his eye, peering through the combat scope. He saw a familiar shape on the backside of the tent just out of his line of sight.

"Malik, Rat, move along the ridge to the right there. I want to know what's on the backside of that tent," Emmis whispered into his comm. He received acknowledgements from both Marines as they shuffled backward until they were lower than the crest. Emmis turned to the fence and cast his gaze along it, looking for a weak point. He saw that instead of setting up their own perimeter on the side facing Emmis and his team, the imperials just augmented the standing fence by weaving concertina wire through and above the chain link fence that had been there before. "Bull, see anything?"

"I do." Bull responded. "Twenty meters to our right."

Emmis looked straight ahead, then counted the distance to his right. He immediately saw what Bull had seen. The fence bowed outward where two of the fence posts had begun to fall into the ditch that ran below it. Adding to its desirability as an entrance point was a large tent near it casting a shadow upon that entire area. It would be simple for Emmis and his team to use the ditch to cut through the fence and move into the camp. From there, two of his men could easily get to the generator tent to set their explosives and back. Using the point in the fence, Emmis began to trace the route he would lead his men to get to their objective. He noticed that most of the tents were placed haphazardly instead of straight lines. They could use the imperial's arrogance and overconfidence to their advantage to get to their objective. Getting out would be the trick after that. He could see a large open space on the other side of their target building. They would have to time their explosive distraction perfectly to give them time to cross that open ground. Until then, they would have to do things quietly. He reached into a pouch on his belt and pull two barrel attachments.

"Psst, Bull, catch," Emmis whispered, tossing one of the attachments to Bull. Bull was able to catch it without moving too much. He looked at it and then back at his commanding officer quizzically. "We're going to try and keep this quiet for as long as possible."

"Ah, got it," Bull responded. He shifted the position of his weapon so he could pull his service pistol out of its holster. Emmis followed suit, setting his battle rifle down, pulling his pistol out. He quickly and quietly threaded the suppressor to the barrel. Its metal upon metal whispering into the night. Approaching footsteps to his right signaled the return of Rat and Malik.

Emmis turned slightly, his pistol out and ready just in case, ensuring the approaching steps were indeed that of the two marines. Rat led the way, dropping back into the prone and shuffling back into his original position.

"Whatcha see?" Emmis asked.

"They have a couple dozen barrels stacked back there," Rat responded, taking a quick draw from his water bag in his pack. "Can't say for sure, but it's most likely fuel for the generators." Emmis shook his head.

"Little too confident aren't they?" Malik asked sarcastically.

"Yeah, just a bit." Emmis replied. "Attach suppressors, we are going to stay as quiet as possible. Once we are inside, Rat and Malik will set up the generators. Bull and I will cover. After that, we'll move to our objective."

"When are we moving?" Bull asked, anticipation in his voice.

"As soon as Teddy's team is in place." Emmis answered. No sooner had the words left his mouth, then Teddy's voice broke through.

"Team two in position."

"Copy team two. Give us ten to get target one set." Emmis ordered.

"Copy team one, standing by for ten." Teddy responded. Emmis looked at the three marines to his left and right.

"Let's get moving." Emmis ordered. He held both his rifle and his pistol out as he pushed with his knees, forcing his body over the crest and onto the opposite slope. He paused long enough to turn his body around, keeping his feet in front of him. He used his feet and elbows to guide the direction and speed of his slide. He heard the marines behind him follow suit and started to pray that one of the imperials didn't decide to look at the hill at that moment. Emmis made it to the bottom of the hill and into the ditch without an issue. He slung his rifle onto his back, tightening the straps to keep it from bouncing around while he moved. He paused to lower his goggles, the light from the moon and stars cutting out almost completely once in the ditch. He moved forward to allow room for the others, giving them time to place their goggles over their eyes and for Bull to sling his weapon on his back. Malik helped him tighten the straps around it to keep it in place.

Leading with his silenced pistol out front, Emmis led the group single file down the ditch to the low point in the fence Bull had pointed out earlier. Emmis stepped a few feet further to set up a forward guard while Malik stopped a few feet before to set up a rear guard. Bull paused to hand his pistol to Rat before reaching up to grip the bottom of the fence. He realized as soon as he grabbed it, that they wouldn't have to cut through it. The fence was loose enough at the bottom that he could simply pull it out enough to allow the others to crawl underneath it. Once he had the fence out enough, pulling slowly to ensure that the fence made no sound, he planted his feet.

"Go," Bull whispered to Rat. Rat nodded and ducked under the section bull had pulled out.

He scrambled up the side of the ditch, making sure he was careful where he placed his feet. Once he was up out of the ditch, he moved forward a couple of feet to make room. "Malik, go."

Malik lowered his rifle as he turned around. He, too, ducked under the bottom of the fence before climbing out of the ditch. He stepped to the right once he was out, his weapon pointed toward the generator tent. Before he had stopped moving, Emmis turned to duck under the fence, making sure to duck lower than necessary to keep the stock of his rifle from hitting the bottom of the fence. He quickly climbed out of the ditch and turned around. He sat flat on the ground and used his feet to push the bottom of the fence out.

"Rat, give me a hand," Emmis whispered. Rat turned to see what Emmis was currently doing, then followed suit, making sure to leave enough space for Bull to climb up. Once they had their feet set, Bull slowly release his grip on the fence, allowing Emmis and Rat to take the full weight of it. Once he was confident they were not going to slip, Bull dropped to the prone to crawl under the fence. He slowly stood, trying to discern if he was going to get hung up on it. He saw Emmis nod, signaling he was not hung up. Bull climbed up out of the ditch, accepting his pistol from Rat. He took a few steps forward and pointed his weapon to the left side of the tent.

He heard Emmis and Rat shuffle backward slowly, allowing the fence to return to its natural position. The two Marines stood and moved away from the ditch. Emmis moved to the corner of the tent and peered around it.

He spotted two Imperial troops standing at the top of their target building, their backs to him. He waved Bull to cross the area between the two tents in front of them and take up position at that corner. Once Bull was in position, Emmis waved Rat and Malik toward the generator tent. His two marines were completely silent as they set off. Briefly, Emmis had the feeling of being watched and his mind wondered where Johnny was at that moment. He shook the thought from his mind and brought it back to the task at hand.

Teddy knelt next to the door in the pump house, patiently watching the timer on his wrist count down. They had managed to get to their positions in the pipe faster than expected, so he and Johnson set up a few surprises for anyone who followed them both inside the pump house and the access shaft. He positioned Doran slightly down the pipe from the access shaft to act as a first aid station. Vincent was inside the access shaft to act as a guide for the prisoners.

Owl was at the pipe's entrance to the wash as their look out. Teddy was certain that no one would follow them from the field at the top of the pipe. He had Johnson rig up an early warning system to give them a heads up. Teddy cast his gaze around the pump house, his goggles washing the entire room in a green glow. He was going to leave Johnson at the door to keep an eye out for trouble and to keep the prisoners calm and orderly.

He looked once more at the timer on his wrist and watched as it ticked down to zero. His comm unit activated at nearly the same instant, causing Teddy to jump a little.

"Party poppers set," Rat's voice whispered over the comm, indicating that they had set the charges on the generators. Teddy nodded to himself. Time to get to work. He waved Johnson over, then pressed a button on his comm to switch to the team's channel.

"Time to move. Doran get prepped for wounded. Vincent, you're their guide through the shaft. Johnson, you've got my back?" Teddy asked. Johnson nodded. Teddy turned to the door and gripped the handle. He took a few deep breaths to calm himself and then slowly turned the handle, releasing the catch. He quietly eased the door open, the moon casting its light into the opened door. He eased his head out, expecting to hear a shout of alarm. Hearing no such shout, Teddy released the door and stepped out into the snow. He looked around, making sure that the area was clear. Once he was certain their infiltration had gone unnoticed, he moved to the back of the tent in front of him, pulling his combat knife from the sheathe on his side. Once at the back of the tent, he slowly cut into the material from the bottom. He could barely hear the fabric tear as the sharpened blade made its way up, pausing when there was a break in the snores on the other side of the tent wall. The snoring continued after a few seconds, letting Teddy know that he had yet to be discovered. Once he had a good twelve inch cut into the bottom of the tent, he replaced the knife back onto his belt. He looked around once more before dropping prone to crawl through the tear into the tent.

Once he was through the tear, he got up into a kneeling position, shouldering his rifle and sweeping his gaze through the rest of the tent. There were a dozen cots set up around the tent, a prone, sleeping form on each. A few shivered as the wind leaked through the tear in the tent, the cold seeping into their skin. The clothes they had been provided was enough to keep most of the cold out, but not enough to allow their survival for extended periods of time. He spotted very few blankets among them all. Their conditions both saddened and enraged Teddy. He took a deep breath to swallow his rage before moving to the nearest cot. He pulled a chemical light stick from his pocket and prepared to crack the tiny glass tube inside it to mix the light giving chemicals. The nearest cot held a small frame, shivering under its blanket against the cold. Teddy could see that it was a man as he approached. The man's beard and hair was long and shaggy, showing a long period of captivity. Teddy approached silently, lowering his rifle as he settled next to the man. Teddy released his rifle and reached out, his hand hovering above the man's mouth. He lowered his hand over the man's mouth, causing the man to jerk awake in fear.

Teddy used his other hand to snap the chemical stick and shook it to mix the chemicals together.

"Easy, pal. I'm a friend," Teddy said softly, holding the stick up to his face, its light casting its shine upon him. It took a couple of seconds for Teddy's words to register in the man's head. Teddy saw a tear form in the man's eye as he realized what Teddy's presence meant. "I'm gonna take my hand away. You gotta keep quiet, ok?"

The man nodded. Teddy took his hand away and stepped back as the man sat up, his tattered jacket showing he was a sergeant in the army. The tear in his eye threatened to turn into a raging torrent as his eyes adjusted to the semi-darkness, allowing him to get a good look at Teddy.

"Who are you?" The man asked, his voice breaking with emotion.

"Sergeant Theodore Roosevelt, United States Marine Corps. Teddy for short. And we be the cavalry," Teddy said, smiling under his face mask.

"Sergeant Anthony Lashe, alpha company, third armored," the sergeant said to Teddy's unasked question. Teddy nodded.

"Okay Sarge. We're here to get you out. Wanna help?"

"We?" Lashe asked. He looked around expecting to see more heavily armed Marines in the tent. His eyes showed his disappointment at seeing no one else.

"My team has a way out through the building behind this tent." Teddy answered. He moved over to the tear he had cut and opened it enough for Lashe to look out of. Lashe could see nothing other than an open door. He was beginning to think was just another way for the imperials to mess with them all, when Teddy waved his chemical stick up and down slowly. A second chemical stick responded inside the building. Lashe could just make out another body inside the door. Willing to give them the benefit of doubt, Lashe turned toward Teddy.

"What do you need?" Lashe asked, his voice strengthening. Teddy nodded.

"Help me wake the others in here first," Teddy answered, handing a few chemical sticks to Lashe. Lashe snapped the first and shook it as Teddy turned to the next cot to wake up its occupant. It took less than five minutes to wake the fourteen men in the tent and let them know who Teddy was. The three marines in the group smiled broadly as they recognized the uniform. Teddy quickly found the highest ranking person in the tent, an Air Force Master Sergeant, and brought him over to the tear in the tent. He pointed out where Johnson was before he spoke.

"We are getting everyone out, but we can't just let you all head in in a large group. Master Sergeant, I need you to stagger the groups while I get the other tents over here," Teddy explained. The Master Sergeant nodded, before turning to the prisoners in the tent and arranging them into smaller groups of four. Teddy turned to Lashe. "Give me another hand?"

"Sure thing," Lashe answered, stepping away from his group. Teddy pulled him to the side.

He handed Lashe his extra knife and another handful of chemical sticks.

"Head to the tent to the left, wake everyone up, and get them ready to move when I get there." Teddy ordered. Lashe nodded.

"Shouldn't be a problem. The imperials stop patrolling the tents at night, too damn cold for them." Lashe said, a flash of anger pierced his eyes for a moment. Teddy nodded.

"Fantastic. Let's move," Teddy said. He used his knife to open the tear wider, before exiting. Lashe followed, his blanket wrapped around his shoulders. Lashe headed to the left, while Teddy headed to the right. He neared the corner when he thought he heard the zip of a round flying through the air. He paused and peered around the corner, expecting to hear more rounds.

When no more were heard after a few moments, he moved around the corner and to the side of the next tent. He stopped next to the wall and listened for anything out of the ordinary. He then cut the wall open and slipped inside. A cot was immediately to his right, the occupant stirring from the sudden chill. Teddy quickly stowed his knife and used his free hand to cover the mouth of the cot's occupant, this one a woman. She fought him slightly, forcing him to use more pressure. He leaned down to bring his face next to hers, pulling another of his dwindling supply of chemical sticks from his pocket. He quickly snapped the capsule and shook it to mix the chemicals together. He brought it up to allow her to see him. Her sleeve had ridden up her arm slightly, showing the bottom half of an eagle, globe, and anchor tattoo on her forearm.

"Easy devil dog," Teddy said softly. His words pierced her brain and she instantly stopped fighting him, her eyes growing wide. "Sergeant Teddy, at your service. I'm going to remove my hand now." She nodded as Teddy removed his hand and stepped back.

"First Lieutenant Amelia Mott," she said.

"Well, ma'am, y'all ready to get out of here?" Teddy asked, throwing all the charm he had at her, lifting his goggles from his eyes. She flashed an amazing smile at him and nodded.

"Yes…yes we are sergeant."

"Good, let's wake everyone up," Teddy said. Stepping to the next cot. He and the lieutenant woke up the other twelve women in the tent and let them know what was going on. He was pleased to see that not only did they all have blankets, but they all had thick coats as well. A dark thought crossed his mind as he thought about how they may have gotten the coats, but he quickly dismissed it seeing more than a few of the women sported bruises on their arms and faces. It was getting harder for him to bury his rage and not go after the nearest imperial he could find. He led the women to the cut in the tent and pointed to the corner of the first tent.

"Lieutenant, there's an air force Master Sergeant directing traffic, so link up with him."

"Take those blankets and any extra warming gear you all have. Most of the guys in the other tents don't have anything to keep them warm. I'm going to the next tent," Teddy said. The lieutenant nodded set about getting the other women to gather their blankets. Teddy moved to the cut and turned the corner around to the back of it. He stopped cold when he spotted the body of an imperial soldier laying in the snow behind the tent. He reached for his rifle, stopping only when he realized no one was around. He quickly picked up and armload of snow to cover the body. He noticed the wound in the side of the man's head and knew without knowing that Johnny had dropped him. Once he dropped the snow onto the body, further obscuring it from sight, Teddy picked up his pace. It took another five minutes to wake and arrange the eleven men in the tent furthest from the pump house. These men were mostly officers, many had been beaten severely according to a major in the tent. Teddy quickly filled them in on their plan before leading them to the fourth tent. The fourteen men inside the tent had already been woken up by Lashe and were more than ready to leave. Teddy led them back to the first tent as the last group of women made their quick dash to the pump house. The Lieutenant and Master Sergeant were there waiting. Teddy stopped and watched as the Master Sergeant sent the next group on.

Lashe approached Teddy and handed him the knife Teddy had lent him. Teddy accepted it with a nod, before replacing it back into his pack. He pulled his rifle back around and checked it to endure nothing had happened to it. As he was lowering it, the Major approached him.

"What's the plan Sergeant?" He asked Teddy. Teddy turned to him and wince slightly at all the wounds on the Major's face.

"Maybe you should head out with the others wounded now, sir," Teddy recommended. The Major shook his head.

"I'll be one of the last. Now tell me what is going on," The major answered. Teddy sighed and nodded.

"My men are leading you guys through an access shaft to a drainage pipe. Once there, we will lead you to an exfil point where there should be a flight of helicopters waiting to take us to the nearest bar." Teddy explained. The major nodded, looking toward the opening in the tent as the next group left. Teddy did a quick count. They could easily get the last of the prisoners into the pump house. "We're all going now."

Teddy waived to the remaining prisoners and followed them out of the tent. They entered the pump house, following the directions of Johnson as he pointed to the grate in the floor. Teddy paused long enough to pull his goggles back down over his eyes. He saw that Johnson and Vincent had rigged up chemical lights to lead the prisoners. Teddy was the last to enter the pump house, closing the door behind him. He watched as the prisoners filed into the shaft. Johnson stepped up next to him, sensing the unease in his fellow Marine.

"What's up?" Johnson asked. Teddy looked to the prisoners, then to Johnson. "Johnny's out there somewhere," he said softly, continuing before Johnson could ask.

"Dropped one of the imperial guards without a sound."

"The captain told him not to engage," Johnson replied.

"I know, but there's nothing we can do about it now." Teddy said. He watched as the Major was the last to drop into the access shaft. "Besides, I feel better knowing he is watching out for the others. Don't you?" Johnson nodded.

"Yea, I do," he replied. Teddy turned to the door, a thought crossing his mind.

"Got another claymore in there?" He asked. Johnson nodded, catching Teddy's drift. He pulled a thin block from his bag and turn to the door. He stopped four feet from the door itself and set the claymore down, angled up slightly. He used the adhesive strips attached to it to keep it in place. Once he was sure it was set, he flipped the laser trip wire switch on top of the device and stepped away. Both Teddy and Johnson could see the lasers emitting from the top of the claymore in their night vision goggles. They moved back to the shaft. Johnson dropped down into the shaft and waited. Teddy took one last look at the door before pressing the all channel button on his wrist band.

"Shepherds are on the move. Fifty four accounted and present. Moving to pick up," Teddy said into his microphone as he dropped into the shaft.

Johnny had been laying at the top of the southern ridge for most of the day. After setting up the trails for both teams, ensuring they could see and read the signs he left, Johnny had the idea of doing some reconnaissance of his own. He scouted the best way up the ridge and, once getting to the top, sat and observed the camp below him. He spotted dozens of blind and vulnerable spots throughout the camp. He thought it strange that such a camp would have so many weak points, but then reminded himself that they were in enemy territory. They were far enough from anything important that the imperials in the camp felt they were safe enough without the extra security. He knew that the marines were still trying to find a good escape route out of the camp when he spotted the fence. He watched as a patrol moved along the fence, then turned and walked in front of a pair of tents instead of continuing along the fence line. He watched that area as the next patrol did the same thing, and then a third. After the fourth patrol, he was convinced none of them would go behind the tents. There was the exit for the Marines. Johnny left his position on the ridge and made his way to the point in the fence he had observed. He noticed that the old chain link fence was still in place, its ties rusted and corroded. He managed to work one of the ties loose near the bottom of the fence, allowing enough space for him to crawl under.

He slipped through the fence silently and made his way to the tents in front of him. He peeked around the corner and spotted imperial troops moving about, oblivious to his presence. He thought about venturing further into the camp, but figured he had tempted fate enough for now as he backed away from the tent and back to the fence. He slipped under it and made his way around the hills back toward the cave. He paused at one of the old ranger boards long enough to pull a scrap of paper from it. He sat on a nearby rock, pulling a pen from his pocket.

He closed his eyes and brought up the over view of the area to the forefront of his mind. Once he was sure he had the details straight, he opened his eyes and began to draw. He sketched out the outline of the camp, circling the point in the fence he observed and writing exit next to it. He then drew the paths of the trails for both teams, circling where they needed to exit. He checked his sketch for a few moments and then stood, stuffing the pen back in his pocket. He folded his makeshift map and slid it into a magazine pouch.

He picked up his rifle and set off back to the cave, making sure to stay in the trees and hug the base of the cliff. The entire way back he was thinking of how to broach the subject of his involvement to Emmis. He knew Emmis wanted him to stay out of the fight and wait for them by the trail to lead them out. Johnny, however, knew that he could do more by posting up on the ridge he found earlier and provide cover. In his head, the argument went in circles with every point he made having a counter point. In the end, he resolved to just bring the subject up and see how well it went. He neared the cave just as the sun was beginning its descent to the west, already the shadows began to lengthen. He entered the cave and noticed that most of the Marines were resting by the fire. He stopped next to the deer pelt he had laid out and checked it. It was ready for the next step of processing. Unfortunately, Johnny had neither the time nor the supplies to finish it, so he rolled it up instead. He unslung his bag and used the unused straps to attach the rolled up pelt to the bag like a blanket. He slung his backpack back on and looked to the back of the cave. He spotted Emmis asleep on his back, his breathing steady and deep.

He had a sudden thought that won over any and all arguments. The best way to win this particular argument was to avoid it all together. He pulled the map he drew from his pouch and unfolded it. He set it on the ground just at the entrance, using two rocks to hold it in place.

He took one last look at the Marines. He sighed and left the cave. He was halfway back to his spot on the ridge before he looked back, expecting to see two of the marines following him. When he couldn't see them, he shrugged his shoulders and continued on. It was nearly sunset when he reached the bottom of the ridge once again. He looked up at the ridge, then to the west at the setting sun. He may make it to the top before total night fall he told himself. He shifted his battle rifle to his back and began his climb. It took him nearly a half hour to climb the first half of the vertical face. He stopped on a ledge to catch his breath, but stood straight when a gust of wind whipped across him. He could smell it in the air. That crisp tang of an approaching snow storm. He looked to the east and narrowed his eyes, trying to see the encroaching clouds. They were still on the other side of the range, but he estimated it would hit them while they were on the mission. Could add a new level of difficulty he mused. He turned back to the cliff face and continued his climb. It took another half hour to finish his climb. He stopped and rested once he was at the top, feeling a thin layer of sweat beneath his clothes.

He stood up straight and brought his rifle back around. The lights in camp were snapping on as the darkness began to settle around them. He moved back to his position and knelt in the snow. He set his battle rifle down and pulled his main rifle from the holster on his back. He brought the rifle up, resting his eye on the scope and swept his sight from the concrete building to the tents containing the prisoners and back. He moved a few feet to the right and slightly forward, giving him an unobstructed view of the entire camp. Satisfied with his position, he dropped the bipod of his rifle and set it in the snow. He checked the time on his wrist band as the sun fully set behind the western mountain, allowing the night to fully drop upon the land. He moved back and retrieved his battle rifle, setting it next to his other rifle. He unslung his back pack and set it down, moving his battle rifle to sit atop it. He lay prone in the snow and scooted forward to his rifle. He adjusted his position to allow the rifle to sit comfortably in his shoulder and his eye to reach the scope. He pulled a fresh magazine for it and set it next to the rifle within easy reach of his right hand. He then settled in, allowing his muscles to relax. He had a few hours before the mission was set to start. Once he was relaxed, his mind began to wander.

He realized that he was never as calm as when he was behind the scope of his rifle or hunting. He swept his gaze across the camp again, marking targets in his mind. He was committing their paths and habits to memory. He counted nearly fifty of the imperial troops moving about in the open, with less than half of them patrolling the camp itself. He brought his sight to the four tents housing the prisoners. A few were standing outside around the burning barrels, trying to stay warm. He watched them for a half hour before they decided it was too cold and headed into their assigned tents. Johnny shifted his gaze to the concrete building and watched the three imperial troops standing on its roof. He noticed one was chain smoking cigarettes like a chimney. The fact that he felt secure enough to signal his position with a lit cigarette annoyed Johnny. He was tempted to shoot the burning carcinogenic from the man's lips, but restrained himself. It would do no good to give away his position just yet. Instead he studied the imperial soldiers, noting where their body armor stopped, where the common place of their grenades were, and how most had discarded their helmets for thick, wooly hats to keep warm.

He checked his wrist band for the time. The marines should be on the move by now. He looked to the pump house first, keeping an eye on the door for any movement. He waited a few minutes before sweeping his gaze along the crest of the hills surrounding the camp. The moon was bright, illuminating the hills enough to allow Johnny to see without the aid of his night vision goggles. He saw no movement on his first sweep and was considering returning his aim to the pump house, when a quick flash of shadow on shadow caught his eye. He brought the reticle of the scope to rest on where he saw the movement and waited. Another flash of movement at the top of the hill came and went. Then another and finally a fourth. Johnny was certain it was Emmis and his team. He watched them for a moment before switching his aim to the pump house.

Seeing no movement at the door after a couple of minutes, Johnny shifted back to where he spotted Emmis. He saw the team come over the top of the hill and begin their slide to the bottom. He followed their slide for a moment, before sweeping his sight across the camp, searching for any sign that they had been spotted. Seeing none, he shifted his aim back to the team, losing them once they reached the ditch.

He swung his aim back to the pump house in time to see the door swing inward a couple of inches. He was squinting to see any movement. He kicked himself internally as he remembered his night vision goggles in his cargo pocket. He quickly pulled them out and donned them, before returning his eye to his scope. He manage to see one of the Marines dash from the pump house to the back of the first tent. Johnny swept his sight around the tents, searching for trouble.

He was returning his sight to the first tent when he spotted movement past the far left tent. He swung his gaze over and settled it on the form of an imperial soldier walking steadily toward the tent. Johnny estimated the distance and wind speed and direction. He shifted his aim up and slightly to the right, so the reticle was leading the soldier's movement. He took a deep breath and let it out slowly, his finger resting lightly on the trigger. He thumbed off the safety and added pressure to the trigger, gently squeezing it backward. He paused between breaths and squeezed the trigger back fully. The rifle bucked against his shoulder as the pin and hammer ignited the powder in the shell. The round left the barrel with a barely audible pop. Johnny brought the rifle back to its original position as the round sped toward its intended target.

Johnny watched as the soldier's head pitched to the side, a light spray of blood and brain tissue ejecting out into the snow. The soldier dropped, his forward momentum causing him to fall on his face. Johnny kept his sights on the prone form for a few more seconds, ensuring it was indeed dead, before swinging his sight up. He spotted small groups of prisoners rushing across the open expanse into the pump house. Johnny smiled as he saw a marine rush to the next tent. He kept his attention on the escape as the marine left the second tent minutes later. He moved around the back of the tent and spotted the body, coming to a halt and looking for any signs of trouble. Johnny watched as the marine picked up an armload of snow and spread it over the body, concealing it. He moved on to the forward most tent and cut open the side, quickly disappearing inside. Johnny took an opportunity to swing his sights over toward what he had identified as the generator tent. He spotted two heads peeking out between a pair of tents near it. Emmis and his team were waiting for Teddy's team to finish Johnny figured.

He swung back to the prisoners' tents as the marine led the last of the prisoners into the pump house. Johnny waited until the door was closed before swinging back to where he had spotted Emmis's team. It took a little more than twenty minutes start to finish for Teddy's team to clear all of the prisoners out of the camp.

"Shepherds are on the move. Fifty four accounted and present. Moving to pick up," Teddy's voice said over the comm. Johnny nodded to himself. Fifty four saved thus far, turning into a good night. He watched as Emmis's team left their positions behind the tents and began to snake their way to the concrete building. They made it as far as the nearest set of tents to the building when one of the roof guards approached them. Bull's hulking form had barely managed to duck out of sight before the guard got within sight. Johnny set his aim on the guard and waited. The guard stood there for a few minutes before turning to head to the other side of the roof. Johnny led his path in the scope until he was at the center of the roof. He squeezed the trigger once more, feeling the familiar buck of the rifle. He steadied his aim in time to see the round tear through the man's neck, nearly severing his head completely. Johnny quickly shift his aim to the other two on the higher roof. Other than taking a look behind them, they appeared to have heard nothing at all. Johnny shifted his sight back to the spot Emmis and team were hiding in time to see them run to the building. He tracked their movement until they entered the building through a side door. Johnny kept his gaze on the building, waiting for the team to exit. He was starting to get slightly worried, which nearly turned into a full blown panic attack when a multitude of sirens began to blare. Johnny calmed himself as a door on the side of the building burst open, Rat and Malik leading. The two marines exited the building at a run, followed by four more people in prisoner garb, three men and a woman. Emmis followed them, then Bull, who turned and let out a sustained burst from his rifle back into the building at their pursuers. The group was nearly half way to the tent lines on their way to the fence line Johnny had pointed out to them, when a group of imperial troops surrounded them. Johnny counted twelve in all so far, with more scrambling out of tents. Johnny took a deep breath to calm himself as he prepared to try something desperate. The Imperial troops were standing close enough together that he wouldn't have to move too much. He ran his next action through his mind to ensure he could work the action smoothly. He took a deep breath, gripped the bolt with his right hand, put his finger on the trigger, and began to pull it backward.

Emmis slid to a stop in the snow beside the four prisoners they had released. Rat and Malik stood in front of the group, their rifles leveled at the dozen imperial troops standing in their way. Emmis turned to his left as more troops were exiting their tents in various states of dress. Everything had been going so well too, until Emmis pulled the CPU from the terminal it was attached to. Then it was all alarms and running. They burst out into the camp hoping to reach their exit before they could be caught. Now he looked on as their exit was cut off. Emmis held his rifle in one hand, the detonator to the explosives rigged to the generators in the other. His thumb was on the button as he looked back at Bull, who had his weapon leveled to their rear. He simply nodded at Emmis once.

"Fuck it," Emmis said resolutely. He triggered the detonator. Time seemed to slow to a crawl as several things happened at once. There was a terrific flash behind them as the generator tent exploded in a magnificent fireball, lighting up the night sky. The resulting concussion flattened the tents surrounding it, the flames engulfing a few. The sudden loss of power sent most of the camp into darkness as the lights failed nearly simultaneously. But most shocking of all was the sight of the twelve imperial troops falling to the ground in quick succession as if they were marionettes whose strings had been severed. Flashes of blood and bone sprayed across the snow as they fell. The team and rescued prisoners sat there stunned for a split second before Emmis's senses came crashing back to reality.

"Move!" He shouted, breaking everyone out of their fugue. Rat and Malik burst forth in a sprint, each giving their rifles a quick burst, cutting down panicked and confused imperial troops as the left their tents. Emmis was just behind the prisoners, taking aim at a half dressed imperial sergeant who was bringing his own weapon, a combat shotgun, to bear, when the imperial's head whipped to the side, a piece of his skull exploding outward while the body fell to the ground. Emmis sent a silent thanks to Johnny, who was up there somewhere. He refocused his attention back to the front where Rat was sliding through a hole in the perimeter fence. Rat stood and pulled the hole wider as the others reached it. Emmis was surprised to sense no return fire nor pursuers yet, just panicked cries and secondary explosions as the barrels of fuel that had been stacked behind the generator tent caught fire and detonated. Emmis paused at the fence to allow Bull to go first and took a look back at the camp. He saw dozens of forms outlined by the flames running back and forth, a few stopping to survey the line of dead. No one was rushing to organize a pursuit just yet. Maybe they could put some distance from the camp before anyone did take charge. He ducked under the fence and nodded to Rat.

"Johnny?" Rat asked. Emmis nodded.

"Probably," Emmis responded. The two marines turned to catch up to the group. "Neat trick," Rat chuckled. Emmis smiled. Indeed it was.

Johnny meanwhile had a smile of his own on his face. His plan had gone off without a hitch. He cycled the bolt as quickly as he pulled the trigger, moving his aim smoothly along the line of imperial troops. He watched the line begin their fall as he ejected the empty magazine and quickly inserted the fresh magazine. He shifted his aim to follow the team as they resumed their escape, pausing to squeeze off a round at a half dressed imperial soldier holding a shotgun. He watched as the team reached the fence, then turned his sights back to the camp. He started to search for targets of opportunity, hopefully officers. He looked for anyone trying to restore order to the camp. His first target was gather a group of soldiers around the prisoners' tents. Johnny rested his sight on the man's head and squeezed the trigger, feeling the rifle buck. Seconds later, the man's chest seemed to explode outward as the large caliber round tore through him. The troops around him scattered. Johnny followed one, got his sights ahead of him, and squeezed the trigger once again. The body did a cartwheel as the legs gave out and it hit the snow face first.

He swept his gaze across the camp, cycling the bolt. He stopped when he spotted a group of five around the line of bodies he created. He steadied his aim and his breath as he squeezed the trigger and cycled the bolt, squeezing it a second time as he shifted his aim to the right.

He cycled the bolt once again as the first round slammed into the forehead of his first target. The man to the target's left turned his head in time to catch the second round through the throat. Again, the survivors scattered for safety. Johnny was sweeping the courtyard, firing at anyone he spotted, dropping five more. He paused to take a good look at their handiwork. Dozens of bodies laid unmoving in the snow, the burning tents casting an eerie glow over the prone forms. Shadows and figures darted from cover to cover, fearing to stay out in the open too long lest they be the next to fall. Johnny grinned once more, removing his eye from the scope of his rifle. He gathered the empty magazine, stuffing it into his cargo pocket before getting up into a kneeling position. He thumbed the safety on his rifle back to the on position as he lifted it from the snow. He reached up and collapsed the bipod, feeling the heat off the barrel. He replaced the rifle back into the holster on his back. He picked up his battle rifle and clipped the sling back onto his shoulder, then reached for his pack. He slung it around his shoulders, checking the straps before standing.

He gripped his battle rifle, keeping his finger off the trigger, as he turned away from the camp. He made his way to the cliff and looked down. The area at the bottom looked clear, but something was telling him to be careful. He slung the battle rifle over his back and began his climb down, ensuring he had three points of contact before moving. It took less time for him to climb down than he thought it would. Once he was at the bottom, Johnny took a moment to catch his breath. It was coming out deep and ragged, his lungs burning in the cold. His muscles felt as though they were on fire as he stretched them out. He pulled a bottle of water from a side pouch on his back and unscrewed the cap. He lowered the front of his balaclava and was lifting the bottle to his lips, when all the warning bells in his head told him to drop to the ground. Listening to the bells without hesitation, Johnny dropped as though his legs had vanished, hitting the snow hard. A dozen shots rang out into the night, the rounds impacting the cliff behind where he had been standing a split second before, gouging out chunks of rock.

Johnny rolled to his right, pulling his rifle around as he did. More shots rang out as the snow and ground he had been laying on was chewed up. Johnny rolled into a kneeling position, bringing his battle rifle to bear and flipped the safety to burst fire with his thumb. Without actually aiming, he let loose three five round bursts into the darkness of the forest. Several of the rounds tore into the bark of a few trees, their splinters exploding outward. As soon as the last round was fired, he dove forward into a roll, trying to get to cover behind a fallen tree.

More shots split the air above him as he slid into the tree. He lifted his rifle and let loose another burst, dropping it below the tree just before the return fire chewed into the bark. Johnny knew he should have been feeling fear, having never been on the receiving end of such accurate fire, but all he felt was anger. He used his elbows to push himself down the log while the enemy's fire continued to chew into the tree above where he had been. He was six feet down and risked a peek above the tree. He spotted four imperial troops leaning out from behind the safety of large trees. From this angle he had a line on two of them. He lifted his rifle and took careful aim. He squeezed the trigger, feeling the rifle buck against his shoulder five times, the spent shells ejecting into the night, the moon glinting off them. He shifted his aim and fired again, the bolt slamming back indicating it was empty. He stayed up long enough to see his aim had been true as the first burst caught the first trooper center mass, the rounds punching through his inadequate vest. Blood sprayed onto the bark of the tree next to him and into the snow behind him as an invisible hand yanked him back onto the ground.

As he fell, the trooper next to him caught three of the five rounds of his second burst.

The rounds climbed up the man's body. One into his chest, one to the neck, and his head snapped to the side as the third round caught him the temple. The last two rounds impacted the tree above the trooper's head, tearing the bark away. The trooper was punched into the tree, where he slid to the ground in a heap. Johnny dropped below the tree he was behind just before the other two troopers let off a barrage of return fire. Johnny thumbed the magazine release as he pulled a fresh one from his pocket. He pressed the bolt catch release and heard the bolt slam home. He stayed down as the barrage of rounds continued to tear into the bark and zip over his head. Johnny was starting to worry that he was pinned, when his ears caught a familiar sound under the din of the shots. He heard the mechanical release of the magazines catches on the imperial rifles. Stunned to realize they were both reloading at the same time, Johnny launched himself over the tree. He launched into a sprint as soon as his feet were back on the ground, letting loose two bursts from his rifle at the remaining troopers. He sprinted to the nearest tree as the troopers finished their reloads and fired into the darkness where they had last seen him.

Johnny waited for the break in their fire, then spun around the tree, aiming his rifle. He saw one of the troopers lean out and fired off a burst, the trooper ducking behind his cover just in time to avoid Johnny's fire. Johnny was thinking about rushing forward, when he was hit from behind. The second trooper had used his comrade as a decoy to flank Johnny. He tackled Johnny into the snow, Johnny's rifle breaking free of its sling to slide into snow out of reach. Johnny managed to roll onto his back as the imperial trooper tried to stand and bring his weapon to bear. Johnny grabbed hold of the weapon with both hands, twisting the barrel away from his face, causing the trooper to fall to his knees, straddling Johnny's torso. The two of them wrestled for control of the weapon, their strengths nearly matched.

"Hěn kuài, tā kāi qiāng ba!" Johnny heard the trooper above him yell. Not understanding the words, Johnny caught movement out of the corner of his eye as the second trooper stepped from around his cover. The second trooper began to lower his rifle when the context hit Johnny. Taking his left hand from the rifle, Johnny threw most of his strength into a straight punch into the trooper's face, stunning him. Johnny reached down, taking advantage of the situation, and jammed his thumb onto the trigger of the imperial rifle. The weapon's bolt began to slam back and forth as the weapon fired on a cyclic rate, the spent shells raining down into the snow. His hand began to burn as the barrel became red hot from the amount of fire it was pouring out. Johnny gritted his teeth and used his strength to lift the barrel up, the line of rounds chewing up the ground as it led straight to the second trooper. The trooped began to jerk as the rounds climbed his legs and up his body. Dozens of rounds chewed him up before the bolt slammed back in the open position. It seemed to take a while for the body to crumple to the ground as Johnny turned his attention back to the trooper above him. He looked up just in time to take a fist to the face, snapping his head to the right.

Stunned, Johnny's grip eased on the rifle, allowing the trooper to pull it from his hands. Though his jaw ached, Johnny quickly recovered as the trooper pressed the magazine release.

As the trooper reached for a fresh magazine, Johnny launched a kick to the inside of the man's thigh. The trooper grunted in surprise and pain as his leg shot out behind him. Johnny rolled to his knees, gripped the rifle from the trooper's grip and sent it flying away into the trees. Johnny turned back to the trooper, reaching for his pistol on his right leg, when the trooper came back up slashing at Johnny with a wicked looking combat knife. The blade cut into Johnny's jacket and skin, causing Johnny to turn away. He could already feel the blood begin to flow down his arm.

He flexed his hand, testing its mobility as he reached up to his shoulder with his left hand.

He pulled his own combat knife from its sheathe on his shoulder. Johnny straightened up and looked at the trooper before him. The trooper had dropped into a ready combat stance, his knife blade out. Johnny slid his right foot back slightly, crouching slightly, his left hand out, blade up. The trooper yelled in anger and launched himself forward in a stabbing lunge. Johnny parried with his own blade, the sound of metal sliding against metal as he turned his body, pushing the trooper away. The trooper stumbled as his forward moment was not impeded. He managed to recover and bring his blade up as Johnny followed the parry with an over hand stab. The two locked blades, using the forearms of their free hands to brace themselves. Johnny could see through the green haze of his goggles his sleeve had turned dark from blood soaking into the fibers. He could feel the raw nerves around the wound scream in agony, causing him to grit his teeth.

The two pushed against each other in a battle of strength and will, knowing that the first person to falter would be the first to die. The trooper's eyes showed a hint of fear through the rage. In an act of desperation, he lunged forward, using all of his strength to knock Johnny off balance. It was only through supremely bad luck that, at that same instant, Johnny went to plant his foot better and stepped upon a hidden patch of ice under the churned up snow. Johnny's foot slipped out from under him as the trooper pushed, causing Johnny to fall backward. The wind was knocked from his lungs in an explosion of air as his body hit the ground hard, followed up by the weight of the trooper, who dropped on his chest. The trooper had reversed the grip on his knife and stabbed down, barely giving Johnny enough time to block the strike. He locked his arms together as his eyes focused on the dancing tip of the blade above him. He felt his strength waning as the trooper above him put his full weight behind the blade. Johnny watched the blade inch closer and closer, trying to think of a way to get free.

The trooper's eyes showed his utter joy as the blade finally began to pierce Johnny's skin, drawing blood. Johnny felt the skin above his right eye tear incrementally as the blade bit into him, the pain just beginning to register. Panicking, Johnny lunged his torso up in an attempt to unseat the trooper, who push down at the same time. Johnny felt a flash of pain as the trooper was unseated. Johnny rolled to his left, feeling the knife tug his goggles down and bite into his cheek. He rolled free, coming to his feet, feeling blood run freely down his face, obscuring the vision in his right eye. The trooper rolled up to his own feet, holding his blade up, Johnny's blood dripping from its tip. He laughed wickedly as he reached into the snow at his feet. Johnny's blood ran cold as the trooped pulled Johnny's knife from the snow. He held both blades and laughed even harder at his imminent victory. Johnny tried to wipe the blood from his face with his right hand and reached to his back with his left. His fingers closed around the handle of one of his hatchets when the trooper lunged at him with a roar. Pulling the hatchet free from its quick release sheathe, Johnny whipped it up underhand, wide blade up. He first felt the blade bite into the trooper's chest, quickly followed by a dull, wet slap as the hatchet bit through the trooper's clothes and chest. He grunted in surprise, eyes going wide in shock and fear. The blades fell from his suddenly lifeless fingers as he sank to his knees. Johnny released the handle of his hatchet, leaving it embedded in the trooper's chest. He stepped back and reached behind him with his right hand. The trooper looked up at him in fear, the blood running freely down his chest, pooling in the snow. Johnny pulled his other hatchet free of its sheathe and raised it. The moonlight glinted off the razor sharp blade as Johnny brought it down with all his strength, burying it in trooper's neck, severing his spinal cord.

The trooper fell to his side in the snow, the light in his eyes going dim. Johnny watched for a moment before the downside of his adrenaline rush and the loss of blood caused him to become unsteady on his feet. He swayed slightly as his legs became weak. He stepped back to catch himself and ran into a tree. He leaned against the tree, trying to restore his energy and strength, but failing. His legs finally gave out, causing him to slide against the rough bark to the ground. Distantly, he could hear approaching footsteps. He pulled his pistol with his left hand and took deep breaths. He was having trouble focusing with his left eye. He couldn't see from his right but contributed that to the amount of blood on his face. The footsteps were closer now, but still sounded distant for some reason. He raised his pistol to shoulder level, ready to confront this new threat. His hand shook violently as his strength failed him. How annoying, he thought. He tried to squeeze the trigger when he spotted something moving, but it was just too hard. A hand appearing from nowhere startled him as it grabbed the top of his pistol.

"Easy Johnny!" Emmis said, gently but firmly pulling the pistol from Johnny's failing grip.

Lights began to pop on as the others joined them. Johnny smiled. He could rest now. His eyes began to close, allowing him to the rest he felt he deserved, when they shot open once more as Emmis slapped his face. "Hey! Stay awake buddy, don't fall asleep on me."

Emmis shook Johnny to wake him back up as he saw Johnny's eyes start to close again. He was in bad shape. Emmis and the others had followed Johnny's trail from the camp. They picked up their pace once they reached the turn off point, the snow not as thick on the ground due to the dense tree cover. They were halfway to the meet up point when the sounds of a gun battle echoed through the forest. Emmis and the group paused for a moment to discern whether or not they were being fired upon. Once they realized they were safe, Emmis had his team hand the prisoners they saved the teams' side arms and sent off at a run to get to the battle. They could see the shots flashing between the trees as they approached. The firing suddenly stopped as someone burned dozens of rounds off at a cyclic rate. They then heard cries of anger and pain. Then it all stopped. The echoes died, leaving an eerie silence in the forest. He led the team to a few meters from where they heard and saw the battle before they slowed, unwilling to rush into a potential ambush situation. He waved to his men to spread out as they approached.

Emmis saw a body fall to the side and another back into a tree and slide to the ground. He picked up his pace as the body against the tree pulled a pistol from a hip holster. He recognized Johnny as he lifted the pistol. Johnny's hand shook violently as he appeared to have lost the strength to hold the weapon. Emmis quickly closed the distance to the young man and grabbed the top of his pistol.

Emmis looked over Johnny with severe concern as the rest of his team and the prisoners searched the battle site. Johnny had a cut in his face three inches long, bisecting his right eye. His balaclava had soaked up quite a bit of blood, but a lot of it was still free flowing. Another gash had been opened along the inside of his right forearm. It, too, was also bleeding freely.

Emmis set Johnny's pistol to the side and reached for his first aid kit.

"Rat! Get over here!" Emmis yelled, a little more loudly and harshly than he had meant. Rat came running over and slid to a stop beside them.

"Dear god," Rat said, moving to Johnny's side and pulling his own first aid kit out. He paused to rip open the sleeve of Johnny's jacket and then pulled a bottle of water from his pack. He opened it and let it run down Johnny's arm to clear the blood from the wound. The action elicited a sharp gasp of pain from Johnny. "Good, he felt that." Emmis nodded and began to remove the remains of the night vision goggles from Johnny's head.

"Bull, police the bodies and weapons. Malik, take one of the others and scout the trail," Emmis ordered as he stuffed the goggles into a cargo pocket. He gently pulled Johnny's balaclava down and over the top of his head to get a clear look at his wounds. He accepted the bottle of water from Rat, who proceeded to pull a wrap bandage from his kit. He placed a line of gauze along the wound before wrapping the bandage tightly around Johnny's forearm. Emmis used splashes of water to try and clear most of the blood, again eliciting a groan of pain from Johnny's lips. He then placed gauze over the wound, trying to stay away from Johnny's eye. He paused to press a button on his wrist band. "Teddy, what's your status?"

A few seconds of silence followed, then Teddy's voice broke through.

"We just left the trail at Johnny's marking," Teddy responded. "Eta 20 minutes to rendezvous."

"Copy Teddy. Have Doran set up a first aid station when you get there," Emmis ordered. "Not a problem, sir," Teddy said. There was a length of silence before he spoke again.

"What's going on sir?" Emmis hesitated, unsure of whether or not he should tell them what had happened. In the end, the more they knew, the better prepared they would be to help him.

"Johnny's been injured pretty good. He's gonna need a lot of help," Emmis said, looking up at Rat. Rat caught his gaze and shook his head solemnly. He finished wrapping Johnny's arm, staunching the flow of blood and shifted to help Emmis with the wound on Johnny's face. He used a small amount of water to soak a stack of gauze and then placed it over Johnny's eye.

They then used three wrap bandages to secure the gauze to Johnny's face. Emmis, satisfied with Rat's work, stood and turned to the battle site. Bull and three of the prisoners were using red lens flashlights to search the ground. Bull saw Emmis looking around and joined him, holding Johnny's battle rifle. "What happened here?"

"One hell of a fight from the looks of it," Bull responded. He turned and walked a few feet toward the cliff, shining his light at its base. "Johnny came down the cliff there. The troopers came from the forest there," he said, turning and pointing his light into the forest. "They let loose a sustained burst at Johnny, which got buried into the cliff." He pointed his light at a set of holes that had been chewed out of the cliff face. "Johnny must have hit the ground before they fired. He rolled to the left there, avoiding another burst of fire. He got to either his knees or feet there, most likely his knees, and let loose a burst of his own in their direction." Bull shined his light at the disturbed snow and scattering of empty shells. He then pointed at the trees and highlighted the impacts in the bark. "He moved to this tree here and fired at least five shots, before sliding on his stomach to this position here and firing ten rounds from this point." He led Emmis along the tree, showing the impacts from the trooper rounds and the piles of shells from Johnny's rifle and the empty magazine. "His shots from here were on point, perfect angle to get these two here," Bull said, shining his light on two of the dead troopers. "He left his cover and made it to this point. He fired at least one burst from here before he lost his rifle." Bull showed the tracks Johnny left moving from cover to cover. There was one last group of shells to mark Johnny's position.

"Lost his rifle?" Emmis asked. Bull held up Johnny's rifle.

"Yea, looks like one of the remaining troopers acted as a decoy, while the other one, that one that lost the hand to hand, flanked Johnny. They wrestled on the ground for a minute." Bull said.

"How did the decoy die?" Emmis asked. Bull pointed to the sixty or so shells grouped together on the ground.

"My guess is someone jammed the trigger on that rifle over there down and burned through its clip at the decoy," Bull responded. He walked over to the last trooper and rolled the body over to show the two hatchets embedded in it. "At some point Johnny lost his knife as well, I'm guessing after he got the wound on his face, judging by the blood in the snow. He ended it though with those freaking hatchets." Emmis nodded, taking in the information. Ambushed and yet still managed to kill all of them, Johnny was even more impressive than Emmis had originally thought. He looked back as Rat helped Johnny take a drink of water.

"Gonna be able to arm our guests?" Emmis asked.

"Yea, there's enough to go around, three mags each." Bull answered.

128

"Good, get them squared. Then hand your weapon and pack off to Rat, I'm gonna need you to help Johnny down the trail." Emmis said. Bull looked at him for a moment and nodded. "We are gonna head out as soon as Malik gets back and we get Johnny's gear passed around." He turned and led Bull back to Johnny, who was slipping in and out of consciousness. He knelt next to the young man and looked at Rat. "How is he?"

Johnny turned his head and looked at Emmis, his left eye seemed to have trouble focusing.

"Eh, I've been better, could use a drink," Johnny said thickly, a smile touching his lips.

"Ready to move when you are."

Emmis smiled under his facemask. "I bet you are, but do me a favor and let Bull help you walk." Emmis responded. Johnny nodded.

"Might be a good idea."

"Let's get some of this gear off you," Emmis said. Johnny leaned forward off the tree to allow Emmis and Rat access to his gear. Emmis removed Johnny's pack and set it aside as Rat pulled his hunting rifle from its holster. Rat set it against the tree and then pulled the shotgun at his lower back from its holster. He pulled his own pack around and opened it. He placed the shotgun inside and closed the pack back up before putting it back on his back. He picked up Johnny's hunting rifle and was in the process of attaching a makeshift sling to it, when Emmis stopped him. "Not that, Rat. I want you to carry Bull's weapon."

"On it, sir," Rat responded. He stood and moved to Bull, slinging his battle rifle on his back. Bull handed his squad weapon to Rat, then unslung his pack of ammo and helped Rat adjust it on his own back. Malik and the prisoners walked over as Bull was adjusting a few straps on Rat.

Emmis picked up Johnny's pack and handed it to the female prisoner. "We're going to distribute Johnny's gear to help Bull carry him to the rendezvous point. Malik, don't forget his bladed weapons. The rest of you will carry the rest. I've got his hunting rifle," Emmis said. The people around him nodded and voiced their acceptance of his orders. The female prisoner slung Johnny's pack onto her back and picked up one of the fallen imperial battle rifles. She popped the magazine, checked the number of rounds in it, and then reinserted it into the magazine well. She cycled the bolt and made sure the safety was on. She accepted two more magazines from another of the prisoner and slipped them into her pockets. Malik walked over to the trooper's corpse and pulled the first hatchet from its chest with a wet snap. He used the jacket on the corpse to clean the blade of all the blood. He set it aside and gripped the handle of the second hatchet. He tugged twice and couldn't dislodge the weapon. He put his foot against the corpse's shoulder and tugged once more, finally freeing the blade and nearly severing the head completely. He clean the blade just like the first and picked up both hatchets. He pulled his pack around and opened the top of it. He placed the hatchets in the bag and looked around for Johnny's knife. He spotted it and the trooper's knives in the snow. He picked both up and placed them in the bag as well. He closed his bag and slung it back onto his back.

He picked up his rifle and turned to Emmis. He walked over and held both Emmis's weapon and Johnny's hunting rifle as Emmis and Bull picked Johnny up off the ground. Bull threw one of Johnny's arms around his neck and lifted him onto his shoulders with barely a grunt. Emmis helped Bull adjust Johnny so both were comfortable. Emmis stepped back and accepted his rifle. He slung the rifle onto his back and then accepted Johnny's hunting rifle. He looked at Bull once more.

"All good?" He asked.

"Yep, He's not that heavy," Bull responded. "Besides, it's only five miles to the rendezvous."

Emmis nodded and turned to Malik. Malik nodded, understanding the unspoken order. He set off down the trail, taking point as the others fell in step behind him. Bull, carrying Johnny was in the center, while Emmis and Rat brought up the rear. Emmis made sure to tell everyone to shut their flashlights off, bathing them in nearly complete darkness once more. Malik set the pace as a steady quick march, but not fast enough to wear Bull out. He kept his eye peeled for any trouble as they moved through the dense forest. He checked his wrist band every so often to ensure he was on the right path. After nearly forty minutes and three miles of trail, he waved the formation to a halt. He had spotted movement up the trail, a wisp of a shadow against the pale snow. The formation came to a halt, with two of the prisoners taking up a guard position in front of Bull. Malik waited for there to be any more movement. He brought his rifle to his shoulder, thumbing off the safety. He put his finger against the trigger, ready to fire.

A quick series of red flashes up the trail signaled the approach of friendlies. Malik relaxed his grip on his rifle and stood. He looked back at the group behind him.

"Friendlies," he said softly. He heard the group release a collective breath and stand.

They moved forward slowly until Malik could make out the two forms of crouching marines off the main trail. As they stood, Malik walked up to them.

"Teddy, Johnson, good to see you guys," Malik said.

"Same. How's Johnny?" Teddy asked. Malik stepped to the side, allowing the arrivals to get a view of the group.

"He passed out completely once we started down the trail. My guess is shock and maybe loss of blood," Malik responded. As the group caught up to them, Malik could see the concern in Teddy's and Johnson's eyes as Bull carried Johnny by them. Malik nodded to Johnson and then stepped back to the head of the group, Johnson falling in step beside him. Teddy waited until Emmis and Rat caught up to his position and fell in step beside them.

"Doran's got an aid station set up at the LZ," Teddy informed Emmis. Emmis nodded, trying to keep his mind off the young man slung over his weapon specialist's shoulders.

"How are the other prisoners?" Emmis asked.

"Some had busted bones from some enthusiastic beatings, mostly the officers. The women haven't said much, but they have some serious bruises from restraints and periodic beatings," Teddy responded. "They are in high spirits now that they are away from the camp, but I, and Doran, suggest some serious help for them when we get back to base."

Emmis nodded and looked up the trail in time to see Johnny slip from Bull's shoulders and crumple to the ground. Panicked, the three marines ran up the trail to check on him.

Johnny began to regain consciousness slowly at first, pain exploding behind his right eye as he was bounced along. Confused, he tried to look up, only to have pain explode once more in his head. The pain was a mixed blessing as it caused him to waken fully. He was just beginning to identify his surroundings when his mind clicked into overdrive, causing him to remember the fire fight and subsequent hand to hand combat he had engaged in. Fearing that he had been captured by another unit of imperial soldiers, he pushed off whatever he was being carried by. With a groan, Johnny felt the sensation of falling for a moment before he hit the ground with a crunch. He heard several footsteps running toward him as he reached for his pistol. His blood ran cold when his hand gripped nothing at his hip.

"Easy Johnny," Emmis's voice called out. Flashlights flipped on around him as his vision slowly returned to his left eye. He worried about his right, unable to see anything out of it. He reached up and felt the bandages around his face, remembering the sensation of the blade of a knife cutting into his skin. He looked around as the marines looked down at him, concern evident in their eyes. Emmis knelt and place a hand on Johnny's shoulder, keeping him from standing. "Easy, Son, you're safe. Take it slow, you've taken quite a beating."

"Should have seen the other guy," Johnny said thickly. He grinned slightly as he heard chuckles from the other marines. He rolled on to his backside and brought his knees up. A large hand reached down to assist him. Johnny took the hand and was more or less pulled up to his feet. Still a bit unsteady, he felt Bull place both hands on his shoulders until he stopped swaying. Johnny, nodded, once he was sure of his own legs. His head throbbed behind his eyes once more, though not as sharp as it was before. Bull stepped back and Johnny looked around the trail. He spotted one of his markings on a tree nearby, signaling that they were within a mile and a half of the landing zone. He swung his gaze to Emmis, spotting the barrel of his rifle on Emmis's back. "See that you grabbed my gear."

"Yea, we dispersed it amongst the group to make you a lighter load for Bull to carry," Emmis nodded. "We'll hold on to them until Doran can get a look at you."

Johnny nodded, then wished he hadn't as a wave of nausea and lightheadedness wash over him. He caught himself as Emmis held out an arm to brace him. Johnny nodded to him and then straightened himself up. He looked up the trail.

"Let's get moving," Johnny said. The marines nodded and turned back to the trail, getting back into their original positions with Bull keeping step beside Johnny just in case. Johnny kept pace with the group, though he felt weak and drained. He kept his ears open for any signs of trouble, still kicking himself for not spotting the imperial team before they had fired at him. He thanked his instincts, though. They were the only things that saved his life. He promised himself that he would not allow that to happen again. He walked in silence, periodically looking up at the sky to see the stars peeking through the branches of the trees. A sharp gust of wind blew across them, bringing a familiar scent to his nose. "When is the pick up?"

"In three hours," Bull responded, looking at the time on his wristband. "Why?"

"Storm's rolling in," Johnny answered. "Two hours at the most."

"Great," Bull said, a hint of sarcasm in his voice. Johnny grinned, once more falling silent and turning his attention back to the trail. It took nearly a half hour to get to the clearing.

Johnny first heard the sounds of voices echoing softly through the tree. He then spotted the group of prisoners huddling together, trying to stay warm. He saw Doran off to the side, using a large rock to spread his medical gear out. They stepped into the clearing, when Johnny's instincts drew his attention to a tree across the clearing. He swung his gaze to a large conifer just inside the tree line. He spotted the glint of moonlight off the lens of Owl's scope.

"What d'you see?" Bull asked. Johnny nodded his head toward the tree.

"Owl," Johnny replied. Bull looked at the tree and narrowed his eyes. He finally saw a shape in the tree and chuckled.

"How do you do that?"

"I dunno, to be honest. I just know," Johnny said. Malik and Johnson led to group over to Doran first, who began to look over everyone. He grabbed Johnny's arm and pulled him over to the rock.

"Sit," he ordered. Johnny sat on a rock next to the larger one.

"Emmis, you might want to get some fires started. Storm's going to roll through in an hour or so," Johnny said as Doran pulled his right arm out straight. Doran unwrapped Johnny's arm and began to pull the gauze away. Johnny looked down at his arm as the cold air met the raw nerves. It stung sharply at first, but faded quickly. He watched as Doran probed the wound, then reached for his set of needles and sewing thread. He looked up at Johnny as he threaded the needle.

"This is going to hurt," Doran said. Johnny nodded his understanding as Doran ripped open an alcohol swab. He quickly rubbed it around the edge of the wound and tossed it aside, ignoring the quick draw of breath from Johnny at the sting of the alcohol. Doran looked up at Johnny once more, getting a nod to continue from the young man. Doran pinched the two sides of the wound together near Johnny's wrist and pushed the needle through the skin, drawing it and the thread through. He worked quickly and quietly as he repeated the process, closing the wound on Johnny's arm. Doran deftly tied the end of the thread to finish the process. He used a small pair of scissors to cut the thread and set the needle aside. He picked up Johnny's arm and twisted it to the side to inspect his handiwork. Seemingly satisfied, he unwrapped a new bandage and wrapped it around Johnny's arm, covering the wound.

Once that was done, he had Johnny face him. Johnny turned slightly so that he was face to face with the corpsman. Johnny winced slightly as Doran began to unwrap the bandages around Johnny's head. He proceeded carefully as he unwrapped the last of the bandages. His face showed concern as he tossed the bandages to the side and started to pull the gauze away from Johnny's face. Johnny spotted some of the gauze as Doran tossed them away, many soaked through with Johnny's blood. Once his cheek was clear of gauze, Doran used a fresh alcohol swab to clean the wound on Johnny's cheek, again ignoring the sharp intake of breath from Johnny.

"Hold still," Doran ordered quietly. He picked up the needle once more, using the swab to clean it, before threading a new line through it. He used one hand to pinch the sides of the wound together and began to stitch Johnny's face back together. He was working quickly until he got near Johnny's eye, slowing down his movements so as not to accidently damage Johnny's eye more than it had been. He finished sewing Johnny's cheek, tying the end to keep it from coming loose. He repeated the process with Johnny's forehead, stopping once again just above his eye.

Doran set his needle aside and took a couple of deep breaths, his concentration causing him to hold his breath at times. He rubbed his hands together to warm them before continuing. He reached up and began to lightly peel the gauze from Johnny's eye. Johnny could feel a slight tugging as parts of the gauze had dried to both blood and skin. Johnny tried to keep his breathing calm and normal as the pain began to return. His sight from his right eye was blurred and distorted as the gauzed was pulled away completely. Doran's eyes narrowed as he surveyed the damage.

"Try not to blink at all," Doran ordered softly. "I'm going to clean your eye as much as possible and then put fresh gauze on it." He reached for a new alcohol swab.

"That bad, huh?" Johnny asked as Doran opened the swab and began to dab around Johnny's eye. Doran sighed.

"The sooner we get you to a full facility, the better. They may be able to save your eye and your sight," Doran responded truthfully. Johnny nodded slightly as Doran pulled his hands away. Doran pulled open a new package of gauze and a tube of some kind. He popped the cap, squeezed some clear gel like substance onto the gauze, and set the tube to the side. He rubbed the gel over the gauze and turned back to Johnny. "This is going to be cold."

Doran slowly pressed the gauze to Johnny's face. Johnny felt the cold gel against his face. He mused how he felt the cold gel, but not the pain he should be feeling from the raw and open nerves. The sound of tape tearing drew his attention to Doran, who had released the gauze and picked up a roll of medical tape. He pulled a five inch strip off and then tore that in half. He used the two pieces to secure the gauze to Johnny's face. He pulled a new wrap bandage from his bag and unrolled it. He quickly wrapped the right side of Johnny's face. He made sure the bandage was tight, but not oppressively so. He sat back once he was finished and surveyed his handy work.

"That should do for the time being," Doran said. Johnny nodded, feeling a dull pain behind his eye. He swung his gaze around the clearing, spotting Bull, Malik, and Johnson carrying armloads of cut timber from the surrounding forest. He looked away from them as footsteps in the snow grabbed his attention. Emmis approached both Doran and Johnny, carrying Johnny's pack and battle rifle, Johnny's hunting rifle still on his back. He set Johnny's pack down next to Johnny and pulled his hunting rifle from the makeshift sling on his back. He opened the bolt and handed the rifle to Johnny, who accepted it gratefully, checking the opened chamber like his father had trained him to do, before closing the bolt and locking it down. He put it in the holster on his back and picked up his pack. He opened it and reached inside. He pulled both pistols from the pack and checked their chambers. He ensured they were on safe before slipping them into the holsters on his hips. A gust of wind caught his attention. He looked up at the sky as the first of the clouds cleared the tree line.

"I'd have the guys dig pits into the snow before building the fires. The pits will keep the fires from being easily seen and protect the flames from the wind," Johnny said, reaching back into his pack and pulling out his shot gun. Emmis nodded and turned to the group.

"Dig out pits first guys, down to the dirt, five foot diameters," Emmis ordered. A chorus of 'aye sirs' responded as the marines and many of the prisoners began to dig out the snow.

Johnny opened the breach of his shotgun, checked the shells, and closed the breach. He slipped it into its holster and reached back into the pack. He pulled out his hunting knife, slipping it into the sheathe on his shoulder. He dug around in his pack and then looked up confused. Emmis saw the confusion and then realized its cause. "The guys still have your hatchets. They used them to cut some of the fire wood."

"Ah, no worries then," Johnny replied. Emmis held out Johnny's battle rifle. Johnny accepted it, pulled the charging handle back, locked it, and hit the magazine release. He counted ten rounds still in the magazine, but pocketed it any way. He pulled a fresh magazine from his pouch and inserted it into the well. It clicked into place with a satisfying snap. He pressed the bolt release and listened to the bolt slam forward. He flipped the safety back on and closed the ejection port. He set the rifle down and stood, slinging his pack onto his back. He adjusted the straps back to their original positions. He picked up his battle riffle and clipped tried to clip the sling back onto his shoulder. When he couldn't locate the clip, he took a closer look at the end of the sling. It had been ripped off during the wrestling match. Johnny shrugged and held his rifle with both hands.

"Thanks Doran," Johnny said, turning to the corpsman. Doran looked up at him for a moment, before turning back to pack his medical supplies.

"Only wish I could do more," Doran responded. Johnny nodded and stepped away toward where Bull and Rat were setting up the first fire. Johnny stopped at the edge of the pit and watched for a moment. He smiled slightly as Rat cursed when their pyramid of wood collapsed. Johnny shook his head and went to the next pit where one of the prisoners had finished setting up. The prisoners began to search for a way to start the fire, when Johnny hopped into the pit, pulling his lighter from his pocket. He flipped the flint, catching the flame on the wick. He held the lighter to a smaller piece of wood until it caught. He shielded the brand new flame with one hand, using the other to hold it against a larger piece of wood until the flame caught its bark. Once he was sure the flames would keep burning, Johnny snuffed the flame on his lighter and replaced it into his pocket. He climbed out of the pit as prisoners began to huddle around the growing flames. He returned to the pit where Bull and Rat were still trying to build their fire. Johnny decided they had failed long enough. He jumped into the pit and took over building the fire.

"Thanks," Rat said sheepishly. Johnny nodded and set the lengths of wood up. He pulled his knife from his shoulder and used it to shave some thin strips from one of the larger pieces. Once he had enough, he pulled his lighter out once more and ignited the shavings. He made sure the flames wouldn't gutter out before climbing out of the pit to join Bull and Rat. Bull pulled one of Johnny's hatchet out of his pack and held it out to Johnny, handle first. Johnny accepted the weapon and slipped it into the sheathe on his back.

"Thanks," Johnny said.

"No problem. Has a thousand uses," Bull replied. Johnny grinned. "Don't I know it."

"Teddy has your other one. He's in the third pit over there," Bull said, pointing toward the tree line. Johnny looked over and could see bobbing heads as Teddy's team of diggers cleared out more snow. Johnny looked to the sky as the first of many fat, heavy flakes began to fall. The prisoners huddled closer to the fires, trying to stay warm. He once again mused upon the fact that he didn't really feel the cold like he should. He knew he should be shivering and huddling close to the fire like many of the others, but it just didn't register the same in his brain. He looked back toward the pit Teddy's team was working in just as a flash of light signaled the start of their fire. He saw Teddy climb from the pit and move toward them. Johnny looked at the time on his wristband and then toward the sky once more.

"How long?" He asked.

"Forty minutes if they are on time," Bull responded, understanding the Johnny's question. "Why?"

"Snow's going to get thicker by then," Johnny replied.

"How do you know?" Teddy asked, joining them. He held out Johnny's other hatchet.

Johnny took it and placed it in the remaining empty holster on his back. It was strange, but once the hatchet slipped into place, he felt whole once more. He turned his attention back to Teddy's question. He ran the question through his mind a bit before answering, trying to find the right words.

"Instinct, I guess is the best way I can describe it," Johnny answered. "Instinct and experience."

The marines nodded, accepting his explanation. They no longer had any doubts Johnny was right. Teddy turned to Bull.

"Let's get a rotation started. Two man teams?" Teddy asked.

"Yea, grab Malik and take the west, I'll take Johnson and post at the east. Rat, you grab Doran and watch the south trail we came up," Bull replied.

"I'm on it," Rat said, moving to go inform Doran of their orders.

"Where do you want me?" Johnny asked. The two marines looked at him with concern and slight confusion in their eyes.

"Wouldn't you want to rest?" Teddy asked. A dangerous look entered Johnny's eye, one that sparked a primal fear in both marines.

"Why don't you post up with Owl to the North?" Bull asked. Johnny nodded and lifted his rifle. He set off to the tree he had spotted Owl in earlier. He walked to the base of the tree and leaned against the bark.

"Anything moving out there?" He asked. To anyone looking upon the situation, it would have appeared that Johnny was speaking to either himself or the thin air.

"Not much. Had a rabbit go by a bit ago," Owl answered softly. "How's the eye?"

"Hurts a bit, but not as bad as it had earlier. Arm itches," Johnny replied. Johnny looked at the time on his wristband. They still had a half hour before the helicopters were due to arrive. The snow had started to fall more rapidly as they observed the forest ahead of them. Johnny felt the wind pick up through the trees as the clouds built up above them. He focused his ears to pick up any sounds rushing through the trees. His mind began to wander to what was ahead

138

of him once they reached the base. Emmis had mentioned something about a recommendations once they returned. Johnny began to fear what would happen now that his right eye was essentially shot. He hoped that they would believe that his injury would not hinder his performance nor his talents in the field.

He was so wrapped up in his thoughts that he nearly missed the new sounds approaching on the wind. He tried to identify the sounds when Owl dropped from the tree into the snow next to Johnny. Johnny turned to him.

"Choppers are four minutes out," Owl said. Johnny's ears continued to pick up the noise in the wind. He filed the noise as approaching helicopters in his memory. He looked to Owl, about to ask how things were going to go, when he spotted movement further in the forest. It first appeared to be a trick of flying snow in the wind, but his left eye processed the information it saw in an instant. He focused on the battle rifle, the helmet, and then the other shadows darting between the trees. Quickly gripping Owl with his right hand, Johnny spun the two of them behind the large conifer tree, just as dozens of rounds split the air where they had been. Johnny kept his momentum up as he moved from the safety of the conifer to the cover of a large maple three feet away. He slid into a kneeling position behind the tree and brought his battle rifle to his shoulder. He spot sighted the first imperial soldier he could clearly see, flipped the safety off, and pulled the trigger. The battle rifle bucked against his shoulder five times, each time a spent shell went spinning into the darkness around him, each shot a mere whisper thanks to the suppressor on the end. He saw the soldier he was aiming at drop backward as the rounds impacting his body overcame his forward momentum. The muffled sounds of several more shots erupted from his left as Owl spun around the base of the tree, spotted a target, and fired a set of rounds. The staccato of battle rifle rounds began to permeate the silence of the forest as the group of Imperial soldiers realized they had lost the element of surprise.

"Enemy contact, North by Northwest. Multiple units," Owl's voice said over the comm. Johnny sighted down his rifle at a second target, this one carried a belt fed weapon. Johnny squeezed the trigger again. He felt the rifle bounce against his shoulder. He watched as one of the rounds sparked off the top of the weapon. The soldier dropped in the snow with a splash of blood and snow. He shifted his aim at a third and fired just as the soldier let loose a barrage of his own. Johnny had barely enough time to duck behind his cover before the rounds ripped into the bark of the tree and split the air. He heard the crack of the Marines' weapons from the other side of the clearing.

"Set up a fall back line in the fire pits. Bull I want that weapon of yours set and firing in two. Teddy, Owl, Johnny, Malik, you four hold as long as you can until we have the line set. Bull and Rat to one pit, Johnson and I will take the second. Doran get the flares set and ready. Move Marines!" Emmis ordered, his voice cutting through the clamoring of the weapons. Johnny swung around the other side of the tree and peered down the sight, targeting the closest soldier he saw. He pulled the trigger once, letting the rounds fly, before shifting his aim to the right and firing again, catching a second soldier as he made for the cover of a nearby tree. He looked up from his sight as the two soldiers fell into the snow. The group of enemy soldiers was larger than he had thought. He could see at least fifty moving amongst the trees. And they were getting closer. They were within sixty yards, darting between trees, slowing their pace as they came within range. One soldier armed with a belt fed weapon took cover behind a fallen tree.

He quickly set his bipod on the tree and began to fire sustained bursts, the booms of his weapon resounding through the trees. Johnny ducked behind his cover as one round bit a softball sized chunk from the bark.

He spun to the other side and quick sighted the gunner. He pulled the trigger of his rifle, feeling the bolt lock back. He cursed as he saw three rounds impact the tree the gunner used as cover and the other two were lost in the darkness. Johnny spun back behind cover as he reached for a fresh magazine. He pressed the magazine release, sliding the spent magazine out, sliding the fresh magazine in with a solid click. He realized, as he slid the empty magazine into his cargo pocket, that he had one full magazine left. He hit the bolt release and felt and heard the bolt fly forward. He waited for a lull in the fire as the rounds pounded the tree behind him. He heard the last round impact the tree and spun around the base. He felt and heard errant rounds flying around him as he took a better aim at the gunner who was busy hammering Owl's position. Johnny steadied his breath and his aim, before gently squeezing the trigger. His rifle bucked against his shoulder as the first round left the barrel. He knew instantly that the shot was good. He was unable to witness the initial hit as several soldiers jumped the gunners cover and let loose a hellish barrage. Johnny spun to the opposite side in time to see the second and third rounds hit the gunner, causing him to jerk to his left, along with the barrel of his weapon, cutting down several of the soldiers that had left cover in front of him. Most took rounds to their legs and knees.

Johnny brought his rifle up and sighted the three remaining soldiers and quickly pulled the trigger of his rifle twice, sweeping his barrel across the three. They dropped in the snow as more rushed forward. Johnny brought his sights on an officer, preparing to fire when Emmis's voice broke through the sounds of the battle.

"Teddy, Malik, fall back. We have you covered. Johnny, Owl, give it a sixty count, then fall back. Owl drop markers at your position," Emmis ordered. Johnny squeezed the trigger of his weapon and watched the officer fall in a splash of blood. He shifted his aim and dropped a radio man as he went to jump a fallen tree. The man fell in a tangle of limbs and flying snow. Johnny counted the sixty seconds in his head, looking over at Owl as the last few seconds ran out. Owl nodded his head, signaling Johnny to move. Owl spun around the base of his tree and let loose a dozen rounds, covering Johnny who sprinted from his cover to Owl's cover. Johnny moved past Owl to another tree just at the tree line and stopped. He swung around and let loose two bursts at the approaching imperial troops as Owl left his own cover to sprint past Johnny. Johnny watched as Owl dropped three cube like objects at the base of the conifer he had been using as cover before he sprinted past Johnny, tapping him on the shoulder as he moved past. Johnny spun around and sprinted across the open snow of the clearing, Owl just a few feet in front of him. Enemy rounds zipped by him and bit into the snow around their feet. He could see the heads of the other Marines poking just above the edge of the pit. He and Owl were closing in on the third pit, which was currently empty.

"DROP! NOW!" Teddy yelled over the comm. Johnny and Owl dove into the empty pit, narrowly avoiding the freely burning fire, as a rocket thundered over them, exploding somewhere further into the clearing. The roar of the Marines' weapons specifically that of Bull's belt fed weapon almost drowned out the fire of the imperial troops. Johnny rolled to his knees and moved to the lip of the pit and peered above the edge. The imperial troops were at the tree line, taking cover behind individual trees. Johnny spotted a dozen or so bodies in the snow just outside the tree line. Johnny brought his rifle up and fired a burst into a group of imperial troops gathered around a particularly large tree. His bolt locked back as his rounds bit into the group, dropping three of them.

"Damn!" Johnny cursed, hitting the magazine release. He yanked the spent magazine out and stuffed into his cargo pocket. He was reaching for the last magazine when a yell above him drew his attention. One of the imperial soldiers had made it through the fire to the pit Owl and Johnny had taken cover. The soldier was swinging his weapon around, Johnny could see his finger going for the trigger as Johnny reached behind his back. His hand gripped the stock of his shotgun and tugged it free. He swung it back around and shoved the barrel at the soldier, pulling the trigger all the way back. Both barrels fired with a tremendous boom as the buckshot tore through the air and then the soldier, throwing the body back several feet. Johnny popped the breach and let the empty shells eject into the snow. He cradled the open shotgun with his right arm as he drew two fresh shells from his vest. He inserted the shells and flipped the barrels up, closing the breach. He returned the shotgun to its holster and pulled the last full magazine from its pouch. He inserted it with a snap and hit the bolt release. He paused as the sounds of rotors punctuated the sounds of the battle.

"Highball three, this is Raider Eight. We have engaged the enemy danger close. Requesting a gun run, over," Emmis said over the comm. Johnny and Owl popped up and opened fire into a group of imperial soldiers trying to skirt the tree line. They dropped as the combined fire peppered their bodies.

"Raider Eight, this is Highball two seven. We read you Lima Charlie. Gun run in thirty, mark targets," a terse female voice said over the comm.

"Roger Highball two seven, markers set, enemy in the trees," Emmis responded. Johnny sighted another officer and pulled the trigger. The man dropped as four of the five rounds cut through him.

"Copy Raider Eight. Wild Dogs on approach from the east, gun run danger close," the voice responded. Johnny went to pop up again when Owl pulled him down.

"DOWN! DOWN! DANGER CLOSE!" Emmis shouted. The roar of high powered engines drowned out all sounds as Johnny looked up in time to see six sleek and deadly looking attack helicopters blaze over them, the multi-barreled cannons on their bellies spitting fire at an insane rate. Three fired rockets from the pods on their sides, the following explosions rippling through the ground. Johnny covered his head as spent shell casings dropped upon him and Owl. He heard the whine of the helicopters' engines as the pilots executed tight turns to come back around for another run.

"Highball two seven, two six, two two, and two four on approach. Prep for landing," the voice said.

"Alright boys and girls," Emmis shouted. "We are going to make this quick! We'll cover, all prisoners will run to the choppers. Split into three groups. Don't look back and don't slow down until you are on board. Johnny, Owl, you still with us?"

"We're still here," Owl said as enemy fire chipped the snow above their heads. Johnny popped up and let loose a burst into the forest, watching at least one soldier drop. The attack choppers finished their turn and came back over the marines and prisoners, again unleashing certain death and destruction upon the imperial troops as the massive rounds tore through thick trees and bodies like fire through paper. Rockets splintered trunks and blew craters into the snow, throwing enemy soldiers around like dolls. Johnny looked back as four massive helicopters flared in and landed quickly, their ramps dropped revealing several armored troops bearing belt fed weapons.

"GO! GO!" Emmis yelled. Johnny turned back to the tree line and let loose three aimed bursts at darting soldiers as the prisoners left the two pits in three lines. Johnny spotted a pair of heavy gunners setting up to fire upon the prisoners near a tree that had been hit by one of the attack helicopter's rockets. He brought his rifle up and squeezed the trigger, feeling his rifle buck against him as the last rounds of the magazine left the barrel, the bolt locking back. Johnny watched the rounds hit the first gunner as the second finished setting up. Johnny reached for his pistol, unsure of whether or not he could hit the second gunner, when a sustained burst of fire ripped through the gunner. Johnny followed the tracer's line back to Bull's position. Johnny pulled his pistol and took carefully aimed shots at soldiers that poked their heads from cover.

He watched the attack helicopters begin a second turn to make a third run when his comm activated.

"Highballs two six, two two, and two four are full and away," the voice said. Johnny heard the massive engines spin up to full power as the massive machines begin to lift off. "Highball two seven is ready for you. Let's move marines, meter's running."

Johnny and Owl moved to the back of the pit as the attack helicopters finished their turn and made a third run. The attack helicopters had just passed over their heads when Emmis came over the comm.

"Move! Move!" Emmis ordered. Owl and Johnny burst from their cover, moving as fast as their legs would take them. The rest of the marines had left their cover at the same time, sprinting ahead of the duo, all making their way to the last helicopter. Johnny could see the two armored marines laying down sustained streams of fire into the forest. Johnny saw the first of the marines enter the helicopter when his instincts told him to look to his left. He turned his head and saw two soldiers clear the trees at an angle to the helicopter. His blood turned cold as he recognized a shoulder mounted launcher in the hands of one of the soldiers. Johnny slid to a stop, taking a knee. He brought his pistol up one handed and squeezed off several rounds, hoping the distance was short enough. He felt immense joy and relief at the sight of the rocket soldier jerking around as the pistol rounds punched into him. His joy was short lived as the second soldier turned his sights on Johnny and let loose as burst of fire. The first round felt like a hammer to his thigh, punching his leg out to the side. The second round punched into his body at his left shoulder, causing him to pinwheel backward as the last round slammed into his back, throwing him into the snow. His sight immediately began to go black as his body began to go into shock. His last vision before losing consciousness was the soldier that shot him being turned into red and pink mush as seven weapons turned their fire onto them.

Rat was the first to make it to the ramp, running up into the belly of the helicopter past the heavily armored and armed crew members. He winced slightly as the roar of their weapons bit sharply into his ears. He spun around in time to see Johnny come to a sliding stop on his knee. Johnny lifted his pistol and fired off several rounds. Rat followed Johnny's aim and spotted a rocket soldier drop from Johnny's perfect aim. He then watched in horror as the soldier beside the dead rocket trooper turn his weapon toward Johnny and begin to fire. He watched Johnny's body spin to the side as rounds tore into him.

"Johnny's hit!" Rat yelled, bringing his weapon up at the imperial soldier. Bull, Teddy, Malik, one of the armored crew members, Emmis, and Johnson all turned as well and let loose sustained bursts at the soldier, who proceeded to vanish in an explosion of mist. Doran and Owl turned around and ran back to Johnny's prone form. They slid to a stop and reached down, each taking an arm. The two lifted Johnny up and began to drag him toward the chopper. The rest of the marines took up position around the ramp and kept a sustained rate of fire, covering Owl and Doran. Rat stepped to the side as they dragged Johnny up into the helicopter. The rest of the marines followed as the attack helicopters came around for a fourth run. Rat turned to Doran and Owl as they set Johnny on the floor of the helicopter, Doran whipped his bag off his back and opened it. Rat and Owl pulled their combat knives from their belts and cut open Johnny's clothes to assist Doran. They heard the ramp close as small arms rounds pinged off the hull as the engines roared. The helicopter shook as it started its climb back into the sky. Emmis and the other marines stood around and watched as Doran, Rat, and Owl tried to stop the bleeding.

"Doc?" Emmis asked Doran. Doran looked up at Emmis, cold resolve in his eyes. He slowly shook his head side to side, then returned to his duty. The helicopter flew the rest of the way in complete silence.

Colonel Huang Xu Lin looked upon the clearing with a mixture of rage and disappointment on his weathered face. He watched recovery teams sweep the forest for both survivors and the dead. Bodies were carried from where they had fallen to be laid in neat lines near the group of vehicles Lin and his men had arrived in. The clearing was a massive graveyard for the imperial troops sent. Nearly one hundred soldiers had died here, scores more at the fallen prison camp miles to the south. His men had arrived shortly after first light to the camp, the fires from the destroyed generators and fuel barrels still burning with an intense fury. Half of the tents in the camp had succumb to the fire, dozens of soldiers burning inside. He could hear the sizzle as freshly fallen snow was devoured by the immense heat. He sent many of his men to quell the fires, sending the rest to police the bodies. He sent four of his recon platoons to scout the immediate area. Two came back with troubling news.

First platoon had found the disappearing tracks left by Emmis's team when they had infiltrated the camp. They followed the tracks up the hill to its crest, finding their observation point. They began to follow the tracks down the opposite side to the field in the next valley.

They quickly lost the tracks as the whipping wind and heavy snowfall had obscured the rest of the tracks. They cast their sights in a hundred yard zone and could not pick up the tracks once more. The turned and headed back toward the base to report. The passed the opening to the drainage pipe, completely ignoring it.

Third platoon had climbed the northern slope, following the directions of the battle reconstruction specialists. According to survivors, the camp had succumb to extremely accurate sniper fire that covered the escape of the Americans. They finally reached the top and began their search. They expected to see several firing positions, given the amount of dead men in the camp. Finding nothing initially, they were about to give up, when one of the soldiers kicked up three spent shell casings in the snow. Dropping to a knee, he brushed the snow away and found more than a dozen casings. Calling the others to him, they searched the immediate area, but could find no more evidence of firing positions. They collected several casings and continued their search, heading to the edge of the cliff. They looked down the cliff and spotted the four dead men at its base.

They radioed the camp and directed second platoon around the hill to the spot they found. Second platoon searched through the dead men until they came upon the body of the man Johnny engaged in hand to hand combat. Upon turning the body over, nearly every member of the platoon lost control of the breakfasts they had earlier that morning. Their medic was able to discern the different wounds and find the killing blows. The rest of the platoon was able to remap the battle and judged that the four men had engaged a single individual. They found the tracks of others joining the site, but estimated they had arrived after the fight. They were ordered to wait until first and third could join them, then follow the path they had discovered.

Lin had watched as the dead were lined up in front of the command center, each one covered in a tarp, their identification tags taped to their chests. The fires had been reduced to smolders, still steaming in the snow, the count had been made. Forty nine soldiers had died in the raid. No prisoners nor American commandos had been found amongst the dead. The raid was nearly perfect. It pissed Lin off to no end. These…barbarians, these godless cretins had killed dozens of his imperial majesty's soldiers and suffered no casualties of their own. His rage built to a boiling point. First his favorite reconnaissance unit goes missing after what should have been a simple extermination of three civilians. Now a secret prison camp had been assaulted with many dead. To top it off, the company sent to reinforce the camp had gone silent during the march. Things could not get much worse he thought. He was wrong.

His radio came to life as the commanding officer of third platoon requested medical support. Lin ordered most of his men to the trucks and had third platoon map out the route they should take. It took nearly an hour to traverse the thick snow and crap trail. Lin spotted smoke rising from the tops of the trees as they got closer. He swore violently when they cleared the trees and entered the clearing. The far side of the clearing was smoking and showed signs of what appeared to be artillery strikes. Many of the trees had been blown in half, some still burned from the strikes. Bodies laid strewn out all around the tree line, the snow stained a deep red from the amount of blood spilled. His men rushed from their vehicles without an order from him and began to search for survivors. Of which, there were very few that would survive their wounds. As the survivors were debriefed, the medics making sounds of annoyance as the officers questioned their charges.

The stories were all very similar. Their company officer had decided to cut through the forest from the main road to cut down on their travel time, when they had happened upon the clearing and the Americans. They had slowed to try and keep the element of surprise, hoping to ambush the Americans and recapture both the prisoners and the American commandoes. That element was lost when someone not dressed as a commando opened fire, killing their company officer. Their second ordered an immediate attack. The commandoes quickly formed a defensive line and held it for several long minutes, their fire accurate and sustained. The company had continued to press their advantage, appearing to gain the upper hand. Until the helicopters had arrived.

Several helicopters made a half dozen runs over the company, loosing hundreds of thousands of rounds into the forest, cutting down a great number of the company. Rockets followed the heavy rounds, blasting trees and soldiers apart. A few of the survivors spoke of four massive American helicopters landing near where Lin had parked his convoy. The survivors saw the prisoners load into three of the machines and escape. The fourth waited until the commandos had boarded before taking off. One of the survivors did state that he saw one of the commandos, the one dressed more like a woodsman, fall from accurate fire from a single soldier, who died when several weapons were turned on him. Lin had a couple troops check the area the survivor had indicated. They found a significant pool of blood, with a trail leading toward the trees. The trail disappeared suddenly. Lin's rage was tempered slightly as the news that at least one of those hated barbarians had been cut down.

Lin peered into the sky as one of his captains ran up to him. The captain saluted and stood still until Lin turned to the man. He threw a half salute in the general direction of his head. The captain snapped his salute and reported. One hundred thirty six dead, eighteen wounded. Fourteen would most likely not survive the trip back to base. Lin stared at the man as his rage flared up once more. Nearly one hundred and fifty of empires best to kill one beast. He wished his calls for permission to use the Dragon's Wrath initiative would be heeded and approved. Deployment of Dragon's Wrath would sweep away the American defenses like dead leaves in the wind. He may have to think about defying the orders of his superiors and use the system, no matter the cost in so called innocent lives and international condemnation. The world would bow to the emperor sooner or later, might as well show the world their teeth and prove their might.

He looked around the clearing and sneered at his men. He would not achieve the glory nor respect he deserved if incidents like the one here continued. He saw himself in royal gold with the title of a lord of the land, second to only the emperor himself. It would be his and his alone. He would put the fear of the gods in his men and whip them back into the perfect unit he wanted. He began to shout orders to have his men start the process of packing the dead into the bed of the trucks. His officers snapped into action, berating and whipping the men into action.

Lin smiled. Soon enough indeed, he thought to himself. Visions of glory danced in his eyes.

Johnny's mind drifted between the realms of reality and the quasi realm of the unconscious. He stood in the field once more, the fog hanging heavy around him. He looked down at his hands, noticing the rifle in his left and the hatchet in his right. He paled when he saw the blood drip from the blade of the hatchet. It dripped into an already deep pool around his ankles. The sight of ripples in the blood drew his attention. He looked up to see a figure stepping through the fog, approaching him. Johnny lifted the rifle, cradling it in his elbow. He put his finger against the trigger and held the rifle steady. He lifted the hatchet slightly, ready to swing it if need be.

He narrowed his eyes as the figure began to resolve into a solid object. Johnny gasped as he stared at himself standing at the edge of the fog. His doppelganger stood their silent, his hunting rifle cradled in both hands. He tilted his head to the side and gave the real Johnny a curious look. Johnny lowered his rifle, sensing no danger from his double. He took a closer look at the double as the stared each other down. His double was slightly larger than Johnny was currently. His arm muscles were more defined as they gripped the rifle. But it was the full beard his double was sporting that caught him the most off guard. He didn't have the full growth yet. It was the look in the double's eyes that was the most telling however. They showed age in them, yet they still held that same primal feature that others had seen in Johnny's eyes. The scar down the right side of his face was faded from time. A second figure appeared in the fog, this one lower to the ground. Johnny recognized the shape of the shadow as a dog. He was half right as the wolf from his first dream appeared beside his double. The wolf looked at Johnny first, before looking up at his double. It took a few steps forward, turning its eyes back on Johnny.

This is what could be, the wolf said, Johnny hearing the words in his head. He narrowed his eyes at the wolf.

"Could be?" he asked. The wolf nodded.

Yes. This could be you. If you adjust your course, the wolf replied. "What?" Johnny asked confused.

Your anger has served you well. It has given you the drive needed to survive, but you must not let it overcome what and who you are. You must temper your anger. Use it to fuel your actions, but not your motives, the wolf said. It narrowed its eyes as Johnny's eyes softened, realizing that he had indeed been letting his anger drive both his actions and his motives. It relished the kills he made during his time with the marine unit and his massacre of the imperial recon unit that attacked his home. It may have, if he was being honest with himself, been the factor that drove him to reckless actions that caused his injuries.

How much blood must be spilled to satisfy your anger's hunger for revenge? Would this do? The wolf asked. It lifted its muzzle and let out a terrific howl. The fog dispersed outward as if a great wind pushed it. Johnny's eyes widened in fear and revulsion as the scene before him was revealed. He, the wolf, and his double stood in a clearing, much like the one he and the marines defended. The ground was covered in a lake of blood. He spotted hundreds of bodies lying half submerged all around. While most wore the uniforms of the imperial army, more than a few sported the camouflage of the United States military forces. Johnny felt sick as he spotted the wounds in the nearest corpse. They were perfect matches to the hatchet he held in his hand.

This enough for your rage? Should we add more to your count? The wolf said as several imperial soldiers rose from the blood and dropped to their knees, their heads bowed. Johnny's hand shook violently, the blade of the hatchet danced back and forth. An internal battle began as his rage howled for the blood of the soldiers, whilst his intelligence, compassion, and instincts called for a stay of his hand. Johnny's double and the wolf watched stoically as Johnny battled for control of his blood lust. Finally, his rage was overcome as his hand opened, dropping the hatchet with a splash into the blood. His rifle followed suit as Johnny dropped to his knees, a wave of emotion overcoming him. He felt the first tear in the corner of his eye. The rush of loss hit him like a bullet, causing him to cry. The wolf approached him, the blood beginning to recede as it approached. Johnny felt the wolf's fur as it rubbed its muzzle on Johnny's cheek. Johnny looked up into the wolf's eyes, a sincere look of understanding in the brown eyes.

Good. Now your path comes to a divide. Its destination now one of your choosing, the wolf said. Johnny took a few deep breaths, trying to calm his emotions. He was confused by the wolf's statement.

"My choice? What do you mean 'my choice'?" Johnny asked. What could have passed as a smile crossed the wolf's features.

You'll see, the wolf said. The fog rolled back in quickly, obscuring Johnny's sight to the point where he blacked out completely.

The steady beeping of medical machinery resonated through Johnny's skull, the steady tone drawing Johnny's consciousness back to reality. He tried to take a breath and began gagging and choking on the tube in his throat. His left eye flew open, panic setting in as he continued to choke. He lifted his arms and felt something tear out of his skin as he reached for the tube. Several pairs of hands gripped his arms, forcefully pushing them back down as voices filled the room and Johnny's ears.

"Doctor! He's waking up!" a high pitched female voice yelled. Johnny's eye focused on the bright light above him as he continued to panic. He felt the tube begin its way out of his throat, causing him to gag as another voice spoke.

"Easy son. We're pulling the tube out, just relax," A powerful male voice said. Johnny felt the tube pull fully out of his throat and suddenly felt the urge to throw up. He manage to swallow the urge as he looked around. He was in a large room with high ceilings. The lights above him were harsh and brilliant, nearly blinding him. Several people stood around him, their faces covered with white facemasks, their heads with some kind of blue sock cap. Each wore blue scrubs and gloves stained with blood as they continued to hold Johnny down.

Blood's probably mine, Johnny mused as he spotted one of the nurses approach holding a syringe. The clear liquid inside distorted the light as she gripped a small tube leading from Johnny's arm.

"This will help you relax," She said softly as she pushed the needle into an opening on the tube and pressed the plunger down. Johnny felt a quick sensation of cold running through his arm before he started feeling drowsy.

His left eye was getting harder and harder to keep open as the anesthesia began to take effect.

"Kid's frickin strong," Someone said as Johnny began to drift off.

"He's gotta be with as much blood he's lost and the trauma he's sustain," another responded. Johnny was unable to hear any more as he drifted fully off.

He regained consciousness slowly this time. He knew he was lying down, the pressure of the bed on his back told him so. He slowly moved his fingers as he opened his left eye. He was slightly concerned that he was still unable to see out of the right, but figured they had bandaged it more to let it heal. His eye took a moment to focus, but he soon knew that he had been moved. The ceiling in this room was not as high and the lights were softer on his eye. He felt the weight of a blanket on his legs and looked down his body. He moved his toes and saw the blanket shift in response. He tried to move his arms, but felt a slight tugging sensation. He looked over at each and spotted the IV tubes sticking out of his skin, two of them sticking out of the bandages on his right arm. He turned his head to get a better view of the room, taking notice of the single dresser and the TV on the wall. To his right was a large window, the shade drawn down at the moment. He could see the sun's rays poking out from the bottom of it.

"Ah, you're awake," a deep male voice said from his left. Johnny turned his head quickly, wishing he hadn't as a wave of nausea washed over him. He spotted a middle aged man standing in the doorway to the room, the door shutting slowly. He was average height and a little on the large side. His face was friendly looking, the age and laugh lines visible from the distance between them. He wore small rectangular glasses on the end of his nose, a white lab coat over a tan uniform, and a stethoscope around his neck. Johnny could see gold emblems glinting in the light on the man's collars. He chuckled slightly as he saw Johnny's eye swim around slightly, indicating the nausea. "I wouldn't move too quickly, you're still pumped full of some pretty intense meds."

Johnny place his accent to the Midwest, Ohio or Indiana. The man approached Johnny's bedside and held out an open hand.

"I'm Doctor Benjamin O'Malley, US Navy," the doctor said. Johnny took his hand and shook it. He noted the eagle emblem on one side of the doctor's collar and a medical symbol on the other.

"Johnny," Johnny replied thickly. "Where am I captain?"

"Ah, recognize the insignia?" Benjamin asked. Johnny nodded. "Dad was military, grandpa before him."

"That would explain it. To answer your question: Welcome to Camp Liberty," Benjamin said.

"Liberty?" Johnny asked, trying to figure out where Camp Liberty was. Unable to figure it

out he looked to the doctor for the answer.

"We're right outside Colorado Springs," Benjamin said. He leaned over and checked a few of the screens next to Johnny's bed. He looked away from the screens and pulled a penlight from his breast pocket. He clicked it on and quickly flipped the light onto Johnny's left eye and then away, judging the response of his pupil. He repeated the process a couple more times, before shutting off the light and replacing it into his pocket. He nodded as he stepped around the bed.

"What about the marines and prisoners?" Johnny asked as his mind flashed back to the battle. The doctor looked up at him for a moment, before turning his attention to Johnny's arm.

"Everyone else made it back with little to no injuries. Thanks in large part to your efforts I hear," Benjamin said as he lifted Johnny's arm to check the bandages. Satisfied, he gently placed Johnny's arm back at his side and looked up at Johnny's face. "You, on the other hand, suffered some pretty severe injuries we need to discuss."

"Go ahead," Johnny replied. The doctor moved to the edge of Johnny's bed and picked up his chart. Benjamin flipped through a couple of pages and read quietly for a moment before speaking.

"Let's start with your arm," Benjamin said. "You sustained some pretty severe trauma to your muscle tissue from the knife cutting into you. There was also some tendon damage that we can try to fix. The biggest problem is going to be the nerve damage. You'll be able to move the arm perfectly fine, but the surface nerves are more or less dead."

"Meaning I won't be able to feel," Johnny said calmly. Benjamin nodded.

"It may not be permanent, we will have to monitor it," Benjamin said. "Moving on to the ballistic trauma. You suffered three gunshot wounds to your right thigh, left pectoral region, and right shoulder. The wound to your thigh was a through and through, mostly muscle damage and a slight crack to your femur from the bone ricocheting off it. No permanent damage, though the round missed your femoral by a couple of millimeters. The round you took to your shoulder embedded itself in the bone. While nearly breaking your scapula, we were able to pull the round out and repair the bone with a polymer solution. Your shoulder is going to be stiff for a bit, but you'll make a full recovery. The chest wound was the most severe. It nicked your aorta, causing massive blood loss. The corpsman on scene was able to slow the bleeding, but it was a close thing."

"Remind me to thank Doran the next time I see him," Johnny replied. Benjamin nodded his agreement.

"Your eye, however, is an entirely different scenario," Benjamin began. "Though there was a slight penetrating trauma to your eye, repeated blows, and extended use had damaged it permanently. We may be able to try a new experimental procedure, but I'm still waiting on the ok from on high."

"What kind of experimental procedure?" Johnny asked. Benjamin looked at him for a long moment before answering.

"There are a few people who want to speak with you first. I think I'd better let them explain," Benjamin said. He set Johnny's chart back on the edge of his bed and moved toward the door. "Get some rest, I have a feeling you're going to need it."

Johnny watched Benjamin open the door and leave. The door closed slowly as the questions began to crowd Johnny's thoughts. He turned to the blank television before him, contemplating on turning it on, when a massive yawn hit him. He tried to stay awake, but was still so weak. He laid his head back, unsure if he was not asleep before his head hit the pillow or not.

He was unsure of how long he had slept, but he was awakened by the warning bells sounding in his head. His instincts told him he was not alone in the room. His eye snapped open wide, instantly focusing to the soft light above him. He raised his head and look toward the TV. Leaning against the dresser, his legs crossed at the ankles and both hands resting on the dresser, was a middle aged man in a very expensive looking suit. His gray hair gleamed in the light as he looked at Johnny. Johnny didn't sense anything dangerous about the man, so he began to wonder why his instincts were still telling him that he was in danger. Johnny looked toward the door to the room and spotted two large shouldered men in suits, their hands crossed in front of their chests. Johnny noticed that their arms were not crossed tightly and that their right hands were close enough to the edge of their suit jackets that it would take microseconds for them to pull the pistols hidden under there. Johnny could see the slight bulge and distortion the pistols caused in the lining of the jackets.

He could not see much of their upper features because of the tinted glasses they were wearing. He looked away from the two guards and looked toward the window. Two more guards of similar build and dress stood by the window looking stoically across the room. Johnny returned his gaze to the man in front of him. The man had a slight smile on his weathered face, watching Johnny assess the room. He waited until Johnny's focus was back on him before speaking.

"You know who I am son?" The man asked, a slight New England accent in his voice. Johnny cocked his head slightly taking in details of the man's clothes. He spotted the small United States flag pin on the man's collar. He had seen many politicians where something similar in public. His gaze was drawn to the man's right hand where a class ring shined in the light, a large golden H in the center of the stone. His left hand had a golden ring on his wedding finger and a large, silver watch further up on his wrist.

"You are a politician of some kind. Pretty high up the chain judging from the four man security team in the room. Went to an Ivy League school, most likely Harvard from the ring on your right hand. Your wedding band is old, you've been married for a while. You have money judging by that large watch on your wrist and the fancy suit," Johnny said, his eye narrowed slightly as the grin on the man's face widened. The man chuckled lightly.

"Very good. All correct, and yes, I did attend Harvard," The man said. He pushed off the dresser as he uncrossed his legs and stood straight. He clasped his hands behind his back. "My name is Gerald Winters. I'm the current president of the United States." Johnny's eye widened at the introduction.

"A pleasure," Johnny replied. The president grinned again.

"I don't take offense to you being unaware of who I am," the president said, walking around to the side of the bed. Johnny followed his movements. "From what I understand, you had been out of touch with the outside world for quite some time because of the invasion. I...I am sorry for your loss." Johnny nodded his thanks. "I was briefed on your actions out there. You took on a seasoned imperial recon unit, killing every member, by yourself. Then you led a marine Special Forces team through enemy held territory, showed them the best way to infiltrate an enemy encampment, slip over fifty prisoners out without alerting their guards, and then covered the second team's escape with constant and accurate rifle fire from an elevated position when they had been spotted. And after all that, you stood side by side with those same marines as enemy reinforcements from another nearby camp came up you all. Did I miss anything?"

"Not that I know of. I really didn't do much," Johnny said. A genuine smile crossed the president's face at Johnny's words.

"On the contrary. The Marines were equipped with combat camera modules and the surveillance satellite stayed on station. We saw the whole thing from a bird's eye view. You are well and truly impressive," The president said. Johnny's eye narrowed in suspicion. He had the feeling the president was buttering him up and dancing around his true motive.

"So what do you want from me?" Johnny asked. The president grinned as he pulled a chair close to Johnny's bed and sat down. He crossed his hands over his lap and stared Johnny in the eye, his expression becoming serious.

"I have an offer for you, young man. One that only comes around at the rarest of times and only to extraordinary individuals," The president began. "There is an opening to join a team of unique specialists. These specialists operate outside the normal chain, tackling the most difficult jobs that come up. Their purpose is to assist the United States from behind the scenes, whether that be espionage, sabotage, assassinations, or general reconnaissance or misdirection. There are many perks to being a part of this unit, but there's also a pretty significant price."

He paused to let Johnny absorb the information, watching his expression as he mulled the idea in his head.

"What's the price?" Johnny asked.

"Death," the president said simply. "Each member of the unit officially dies upon their joining. All records of them cease, fingerprints and DNA are wiped from official systems. The only record you will have once you join will be a false name that leads to an empty grave with a simple marker. There's more, but until I get your agreement to join, I can't say much more."

Johnny stared at the president for a few moments, trying to judge whether he was being honest or not. He had fully intended on volunteering for the service while working with Emmis and his marines, but with the injury to his eye, he was unsure if they would take him. Now here was an offer to not only fix his eye, but give him the opportunity to do more than he thought he could accomplish. He gave the thought another heart beat to consider the offer before looking up at the president once more.

"I'm in," Johnny said. A massive smile broke upon the president's face as he stood up. "Fantastic," he replied. He waved a hand toward the guards at the door. The one on the left lifted his wrist to his face and appeared to speak into his watch. Johnny figured that there was a comm set in the watch. The two guards stepped aside as the door opened. Doctor Benjamin entered, carrying a clipboard. He smiled as he looked up from the board in his hand to Johnny and the president.

"Sir?" Benjamin asked simply.

"He's agreed," the president answered. Benjamin's smile widened as he stepped toward the bed.

"Good. Now Johnny, it is Johnny correct?" Benjamin asked. He continued when Johnny nodded. "Ah, great. Now Johnny, we are going to perform an experimental procedure to try and fix your right eye. The procedure involves implanting cybernetics to replace the damaged sections of your eye. This could include any nerve, ocular, or muscle damage. I've been looking through your chart here and, in my opinion, we will be replacing most of your eyeball itself. Any questions?"

"Basically, you're replacing my eye with a high tech camera," Johnny replied. Benjamin nodded.

"That's the most simplified way of explaining it, yes. If the procedure succeeds, your eyesight will be better than perfect. It should take no longer than ten hours to complete the procedure once we begin. You will be out for the entire thing," Benjamin explained. He set the clipboard down and pulled a syringe out of his pocket. He held it up in front of Johnny. "Once we start this, there's no going back. You'll officially be deceased and your old life will be eradicated." Johnny grinned slightly at Benjamin's statement. He had already given up his old life once his family was killed. He looked at the president, then back to Benjamin. He took a deep breath, then made his decision.

"Let's do this," Johnny said. Benjamin gave him a small smile and pushed the needle into the IV tube. He depressed the plunger and watched the liquid enter the tube. Johnny felt a cold sensation, then immediately felt drowsy. He was having a hard time keeping his head up as he looked over at the president.

"I'll see you when you wake up, Johnny. Then I'll explain everything," The president said. To Johnny, his voice sounded like it was coming down a long tunnel. His eye finally closed as the injection knocked him out.

Benjamin watched as the anesthesia finally took hold and worked its magic on Johnny. His left eye closed and he began to breathe deeply, signaling he was truly asleep. He looked up at the president and nodded. The president's face showed concern.

"Sir?" Benjamin asked. The president looked at the doctor for a long moment before answering.

"I was just wondering if he truly understands the decision he just made," The president replied. He looked over Benjamin's shoulder as the door to the room opened and five nurses walked in. Benjamin and the president stepped back as the nurses surrounded the bed and began to move it toward the door. Benjamin looked at Johnny once more before turning to the president, a look of tired determination in his eyes.

"Did any of us?" Benjamin replied, before turning on his heel and following the nurses to the operating room. The president stood there, staring at the floor for a long while after.

Johnny woke slowly to the sound of talking, his head still thick and groggy from the anesthesia. He slowly opened his eyes, seeing nothing but blurred colors and blobby shapes. He blinked a couple of times, having to force his eye lids open each time. They wanted to stay closed. His sight began to clear, the shapes and colors sharpening to reveal the room he had been in before. He saw that someone had turned on the TV, a local news station was playing a story. He went to turn his head when something new appeared in his eyes. A green box surrounded the TV, followed by a list of numbers and letters. He recognized the first line as the TV's brand name and size. The next set of numbers listed the height off the ground and distance away from him. The third set of numbers and letters were the power and energy requirements for the TV. He looked closer, trying to read the smaller numbers, when the TV became larger all of a sudden. He jerked back in response before realizing his eyes had zoomed in on the screen. A new box appeared around the anchor as her face appeared. The line of texts next to the woman listed her name, age, and location. He was getting so wrapped up in what he was seeing, that he didn't hear the door open.

"I see you're awake, good," the President said as he walked in, followed by Doctor Benjamin, and the security detail. Johnny looked over at the president, his eyes automatically refocusing. A box appeared around the politician, followed by a list of descriptive texts.

NAME: Gerald Thomas Winters
OCCUPATION: President of the United States
AGE: 52 YEARS, 8 MONTHS, 15 DAYS
HEIGHT: 64 INCHES
WEIGHT (ESTIMATED): 184 LBS
ARMAMENTS: NONE DETECTED
HOME ADDRESS: WHITE HOUSE
SPOUSE: Nichole Jennifer Winters (MAIDEN NAME: MILLER)
CHILDREN: 3 (ANNA ELIZABETH (AGE 22), FRANKLIN ROGER (AGE 28), MARTIN EUGENE (AGE 19))
POLITICAL AFFILIATION: DEMOCRAT
NATIONALITY: AMERICAN
MILITARY RECORD: N/A
HOME STATE: MAINE
CRIMINAL RECORD: N/A
...CONTINUE?...

Johnny blinked at the information and turned his eyes on the security detail. The information from them was generally the same. Though each one had the green boxes around them turn yellow as the armament descriptor listed large caliber pistols on their persons. Johnny watched as they walked, a smaller, red box appeared on their chests in the general area of the listed firearms. He began to smile as he turned his sight on Benjamin. His smile quickly turned to a frown as he read what was displayed.

NAME: Benjamin O'Malley
OCCUPATION: None found
AGE: None Found

HEIGHT: None Found
Weight: None Found
ARMAMENTS: Three syringes (5 GAUGE NEEDLES (Minimal Threat)), 1 Scalpel (Medium Threat), .44 Caliber Pistol (Smith & Wesson Model 682) (6 Rounds) (Solid Nose) (EXTREME THREAT)
HOME ADDRESS: None Found
SPOUSE: None Found
CHILDREN: None Found
POLITICAL AFFILIATION: None Found
NATIONALITY: None Found
MILITARY RECORD: United States Navy
RANK: Captain, O-6
SPECIALTY: Medical Doctor
CRIMINAL RECORD: None Found
...CONTINUE?...

Johnny watched as several yellow boxes appeared on Benjamin's body, followed by a brilliant red box over his hip. Johnny guessed the red box was the pistol. He titled his head as the box around Benjamin changed from red to green to yellow and back. It flashed so fast, Johnny was afraid his eyes were broken already. Benjamin took a look at Johnny's face and chuckled.

"Having issues identifying me?" Benjamin asked. Johnny's eyes narrowed as Benjamin chuckled again. The president looked between Benjamin and Johnny before understanding what was going on, adding his chuckle to Benjamin's.

"Maybe I should explain. Doctor O'Malley here is a part of the unit you just joined. He is the chief medical officer in fact. Maybe I should start from the beginning," The president said. Johnny nodded and turned his gaze onto the president. "August nineteenth, seventeen seventy two, a special meeting between members of the continental congress was held in Boston. Thomas Jefferson, Benjamin Franklin, George Washington, Paul Revere, Thomas Adams, and Samuel Adams were all in attendance. They all knew war was on the horizon. They also knew that their chances of victory was slim. At the recommendation of both Washington and Samuel Adams, the group invited a little known, but successful pirate named Alexander Patrick Wolfe." Johnny's eyes showed the surprise at the name, wondering if it was the same Alexander

Wolfe in his family tree. "Wolfe, at the time, was notorious for two things: Capturing ships much, much larger than his own, and his undeniable loyalty to the colonies. He was wanted by the British for attack, boarding, and looting thirty nine vessels bound for both England and the New World."

"The members attending the meeting originally wanted to hire Captain Wolfe as a Corsair. They would pay him and his crew for every ship they sank and for every piece of valuable cargo they brought back to the patriots. Once the meeting began, however, Wolfe knew his future would end quickly. Once the British knew of him, they would send an armada to hunt him down. Win or lose, he would never survive the revolution. He came up with a new plan. Over the course of his lifetime, he met and befriended many exceptional people. Most of them had no love for the British for one reason or another, a few he knew would love the adventure, the rest would do what he asked for the pay. He proposed the formation of a special unit of the continental forces. One that would operate outside all normal chains of command and laws of the land, policing themselves and dealing with perpetrators on their own. Only a handful of people would know who the members of this unit were: The current commander of the nation, the leader of Congress, a member of the judicial branch, and a member of the ranking members of the military. These four men would hold the secret, passing it on to those that replace them. Two of the four would hold the knowledge of the unit's current home base." The president paused to allow the information to take hold in Johnny's mind. The door to the room opened and a nurse came in pushing a cart of drinks and snacks. He waited until the nurse left the room before continuing.

"The question arose on how the members of the unit were chosen and what their mission would be. It was Benjamin Franklin who came up with the size of the unit and how they were chosen. He proposed that the unit be made up using one person for each state in the union plus the unit commander. Each new member would be sponsored by a senior ranking member of the unit. The final decision would come down to the Commander of the nation. Though the unit would attempt to keep full numbers, there have been times where the unit's numbers have dropped to alarming numbers as members died," The president explained. "The mission of the unit came down to Captain Wolfe. He knew standard warfare would only get the burgeoning United States so far in a war against the British Empire. To win they would need to employ guerilla and secret warfare. Not just in the New World, but also in Britain itself. The unit

162

had to be made of operatives who could engage the enemy in battle, trick them in public, or confuse them from within their own ranks. The men and women Captain Wolfe had in mind were perfect for said mission. They were, after all, thieves, pirates, mercenaries, and former soldiers. It took two days of back and forth before the members unanimously agreed to the formation of the unit. They took an oath to keep the secret. Over the next several months, Captain Wolfe contacted and arranged for Franklin, Samuel Adams, Washington, and Jefferson to meet and agree to each person's joining the unit. The term Minutemen was first used to describe the patriots who took up arms at a moment's notice. Certain groups have claimed the name for one purpose or another, all for their own personal edification and glory. We use it as the call sign for the unit. To date, there are fifty three spots in the unit, one for each state. On active duty, there are fifty two Minutemen right now, including Benjamin."

Johnny looked over at Benjamin, who gave him a quick smile. Benjamin held out a carton of juice. Johnny took the drink and took a long pull from the straw, the juice tasted amazing to him.

"Each member of the Minutemen has a specific function or trait that sets them apart from everyone else. Whether that be martial skills, or infiltration, each one contributes to the mission at large. After the revolution, Washington, realizing just how vulnerable the brand new nation was, shifted the mission of the Minutemen. Instead of focusing on just the threat from Great Britain, the Minutemen would focus on all threats to the nation. Captain Wolfe new that to be effective, the Minutemen had to remain a secret. He decided to keep their engagements to the shadows as much as they could. Upon the outbreak of the civil war, one of the men sworn to hold the secret of the Minutemen gave the identities of the Minutemen at that time to a member of the British Parliament and a high ranking confederate officer. They began to hunt the Minutemen down. Several of the operatives and their families were killed before the rest of the Minutemen and the other secret keepers found out about the betrayal. The surviving Minutemen hunted down the member of parliament, the confederate officer, and then the secret keeper."

"You're not talking about Lincoln, are you?" Johnny asked incredulously. The president shook his head.

"No, the chief justice of the supreme court at the time. One of the Minutemen poisoned his bourbon one night. Made it look like natural causes,"

The president replied. "After that incident, one of Lincoln's last actions was to enact the cover for all Minutemen. Upon their joining, all Minutemen are declared officially deceased. Minutemen have saved this country countless numbers of times from the worst things possible. All without letting the world at large know of their existence. During World War II, Roosevelt began the practice of adding military titles and ranks to Minutemen, allowing them to blend with normal military units and keep questions from being asked. At times, members of the OSS and later the CIA would cross paths with the Minutemen, but luckily, their cover has yet to be compromised. Those agents that gleaned the truth usually ended up as members themselves." The president took a sip from the drink he picked up. "Today, the minutemen are spread thin and are hard pressed. They are engaged in operations all throughout the western United States. They are operating as saboteurs, assassins, intelligence gatherers, and pathfinders. The operative you are replacing was one of the Minutemen's top hunters."

"Hunters?" Johnny asked, lifting an eyebrow. The president nodded and waved for Benjamin to continue. Benjamin took a deep breath before speaking.

"The Minutemen Hunters are specialized solo operatives. They are given a list of targets and objectives, then allowed to execute those objectives their way. Out of all the operatives, Hunters have the widest ranging and cross over skills. Assassination, sabotage, intel gathering, they do it all. We used to keep balanced numbers when it came to each 'job' the Minutemen have. Unfortunately, over the past few decades, our number of Hunters has dwindled to one."

"High Shot was our last hunter. He died a couple of years ago. His position has been vacant since. We are hoping you will fill that position. Your actions and skills during the mission were exceptional and, quite frankly, brilliant," Benjamin explained.

"What happened to High Shot?" Johnny asked.

"We can get into that later, if time permits," Benjamin replied.

"Enough history, for the moment. Let's move on to his new software," The president said. "Yes, sir," Benjamin replied. "Johnny, there was a slight problem when we were installing the new cybernetic hardware and software. Your brain couldn't handle the difference between the two. We had to compromise and ended up installing the cybernetics in both of your eyes."

"The base setting of your eyes is set to identification and intelligence briefing, as well as identifying any weapons or threats in your immediate vicinity. We can customize it all later, after you get a chance to get use to them. Your eyes can also shift between the different spectra of visual and a few non-visual spectra of colors. They can also shield themselves from normally debilitating flashes of light almost instantaneously. The programing in the software will allow you to sync with electronic scopes and video equipment. We can even communicate to you through text through your eyes."

Johnny frowned. He was not comfortable knowing that they would have the ability to see through his eyes at all times without his knowledge or permission. Benjamin caught the frown and understood its meaning.

"No, we won't be able to see through your eyes, unless you allow it and activate that function," Benjamin said, heading off Johnny's question. "First thing we are going to do is get you used to your eyes, showing you how to switch between the different modes and functions. That should take up the next week or so. After that, we are going to test your skills in a live exercise using sim and shock rounds...In three weeks, we should be heading back home. You'll be meeting a few of the others in the coming days, the rest as time goes on. I...I should tell you that a few of them aren't going to like you starting out. High Shot was family. His loss hit us all pretty hard."

Johnny nodded. He had grown up on stories of how close military units became, especially units with unique specialties. He was fine with any animosity, he didn't join to be popular or make friends.

"Good, now that we have you all briefed and set, I will leave you in the very capable hands of Benjamin here," The president said. He stood up and held out his hand. Johnny grasped it and gave it a small shake. "Welcome to the Minutemen hunter. I expect great things from you."

Johnny nodded, releasing the president's hand. The president nodded to Benjamin, then headed for the door. One of the guards opened the door as the president reached it, standing aside to let the commander and chief exit first. The four guards followed the president out, leaving Johnny and Benjamin alone. Benjamin waited until the door fully closed before turning back to Johnny.

"First thing's first," Benjamin started. "We need to move you from this room. Captain Emmis and his men have been by each day to check in on you. We've been careful to keep them away from this room and from speaking with anyone other than our personnel, who keep the pretense that you are still critical and unable to receive visitors. We can't very well tell them you are dead and then see you as you walk around. So let's get you out of here. There's a set of cammies, boots, and a cover in the dresser. Get dressed as quickly as you can." Benjamin began to remove the IV's from Johnny's arms as he spoke. Once Johnny's right arm was free, he stretched it out and flexed his fingers. He could feel the pull of the tendons in his arm, trying to work the stiffness out of his arm. The last IV came out of his left arm and he stretched it as well. He rotated his arm at his shoulder, feeling the tightness caused by the wound and stitches in his chest. He pulled the covers off his body and looked at his thigh. A set of stitches could be seen just below the leg of his boxers. He swung his legs out of the bed and set his feet on the floor, feeling the cold in his soles.

He put his full weight on his feet and stood, grimacing slightly at the dull throb in his thigh. He hobbled over to the dresser, Benjamin watching Johnny closely. Johnny reached the dresser and paused to catch his breath. He still felt a bit weak. He pulled the dresser open and found the set of green cammies neatly folded at the bottom of the drawer. He pulled out the blouse to find a green undershirt and black socks. He set the blouse down and pulled the t-shirt out. He set the shirt down and grabbed the bottom of the hospital gown. He quickly stripped the hospital gown off and picked up the shirt and cammies. He hobbled toward the restroom, stumbling only once as his leg threatened to give out on him. Benjamin started toward Johnny, but stopped when Johnny waved him off. Johnny made it to the restroom, closing the door behind him. He set the cammies on top of the sink and then put his hands on the side. He put his weight on his hands, taking deep breaths. He looked up at his reflection in the mirror. The software in his eyes began to identify him. He already knew everything, and did not want to see what came up. He willed it to stop and, to his surprise, the program halted. He took a long look at himself. His face seemed to have aged, his four day growth of facial hair giving him a rugged look. His eyes looked as they always had, though if he focused hard enough, he swore he could see the aperture of the camera in his right eye. The stitches on his face crisscrossed the angry red line where the imperial soldier had cut him open. He raised a finger and traced the line down his face.

He turned his sight away from his face to his chest. The line of stitches the doctors had placed in his skin to close the wound were packed tightly together, giving the impression it was just one large piece of string. He turned slightly to get a look at his back. A second line of stitches marked where the third gunshot wound was. He turned back straight and gave his entire form a look. He was beaten up and slightly broken, but he was still standing. He mused how his condition matched that of the United States at that time. He also knew he would become stronger in spite of the wounds he had suffered. He looked at his reflection a few more moments before pulling on the t-shirt. He felt the fabric tug slightly on his stitches, but he did not feel any of them pull out. He adjusted the collar a bit, then picked up the blouse. It was the standard MARPAT green, its digital pattern seemed to shift slightly in the light. He unbuttoned the garment and slipped his arms through the sleeves, once again wincing at the tightness of his shoulder and chest. He buttoned up the blouse and took a long look in the mirror. The word MARINES was stitched above the left breast pocket, while HUNTER was above the right. He wanted to chuckle at the name, so much for a false name.

He pulled the pants up his legs, easing his right leg in first, the muscles protesting slightly. He put his left leg through, pulled the pants up and secured the belt around his waist. He stepped back and looked at his reflection. He remembered seeing pictures of his father and grandfather in their uniforms. Without the beard and the wound on his face, he looked a lot like them. He turned away from the mirror, opened the door, and left the restroom. Benjamin was sitting beside the bed, his feet up on the blankets, his hands on his stomach, watching the TV. Johnny shook his head as he hobbled back to the dresser. He pulled out the socks and closed the drawer. He pulled the lower drawer out and found a pair of combat boots. He retrieved those as well and moved to the empty chair on the other side of his bed. He sat down slowly, trying not to stretch his thigh muscles too much. Once he was settled, he pulled the socks and boots on.

"You kinda look like you belong in that uniform," Benjamin said as Johnny laced the boots tightly. Benjamin swung his legs off the bed and stood as Johnny pushed himself off the chair. Benjamin dug into his pants pocket and pulled a pair of what appeared to be strings with hooks out. "Here, these are to blouse your boots."

Johnny accepted the items and bent down, wrapping them around the tops of the boots and securing the hooks together. He quickly tucked the ends of his pant legs under the bands and stood back up. He felt the tightness in his thigh begin to work itself loose. He stood and looked at Benjamin. Benjamin regarded Johnny for a few moments before speaking.

"Something's missing…AH! I know what it is," Benjamin said. He reached back into his pocket and pulled two pairs of silver bars from his pocket. He walked over to Johnny, pulling the caps off the pins on the backs of the bars. He gripped the end of Johnny's collar and pushed the pointed pins through the fabric, recapping them once they were set. He repeated the process on the other collar and stepped back to inspect his work. "There we are. Congratulations, Captain Hunter."

Johnny looked down at the bars on his collar and then up at Benjamin. "Just like that?" He asked incredulously. Benjamin nodded.

"Just like that," Benjamin replied. "Keep the facial hair for now, you'll pass for one of the many hundreds of special operatives around this base. We are not going far. Follow me."

Benjamin turned toward the door and Johnny followed, picking up the cover as he moved. Benjamin opened the door and stepped out into the hallway. He turned to the right and continued on. Johnny stepped out of the room and took a look around. Dozens of doctors and nurses milled about, going about their duties. A few guards stood every few meters, their hands tucked behind their backs, but Johnny knew it would take them mere seconds to pull the pistols attached to their hips. Each time he stopped his gaze on a person, the identification program started its run. He shifted his gaze each time it started, not giving it time to complete. He heard announcements and the beeping of machinery coming from different rooms. He turned to his right and spotted Benjamin standing in front of the elevators. Johnny moved quickly to join him.

"Keep the cover off until we get outside," Benjamin said softly. Johnny nodded his head almost imperceptibly. "We are going to make a quick stop by my office to gather somethings."

The elevator bell sounded and the doors opened a second later. Johnny and Benjamin stood to the side to allow a doctor and her gaggle of nurses to exit before they stepped on. Benjamin pressed the button for the first floor and stepped back. The doors closed slowly and Johnny felt a pull in the bottom of his stomach as the elevator descended. The two stood in silence as time seemed to drag on. The pull in their stomachs settled as the elevator stopped.

The doors opened and they stepped off. Benjamin turned to the right and swore, quickly turning around.

"We gotta move!" He said insistently. Johnny nodded and followed Benjamin to the left down the corridor. He looked over his shoulder as they reached a corner and spotted what caused Benjamin's outburst. Captain Emmis, Teddy, and Bull were standing at the front desk, speaking to the receptionist. He ducked around the corner as Teddy looked up down the hall. Benjamin and Johnny quickened their pace as Benjamin led him down a maze of hallways and corridors, finally stopping in front of a solid door labeled 'SPECIAL CLEARANCE AUTHORIZED PERSONNEL ONLY.' Benjamin paused just long enough to press his hand to the middle of the door. Johnny heard the locks buzz and click as they unlatched in sequence. Benjamin pushed the door open and stepped inside. He held it open long enough for Johnny to enter and closed it quickly. The locks latched close once more, securing the door, bathing the two of them in darkness. His eyes automatically kicked into night vision mode, allowing him to see everything in sharp detail. The room was twenty by twenty with no windows to the outside. He did see another door directly across the room. Five large desks sat in the center facing each other. A large computer tower stood tall at their center. Though he saw no actual computer screen, he did see keyboards set into the wood of each desk. Ten large TVs were attached to the wall to Johnny's left, off currently. Benjamin took a deep breath and let it out slowly. He reached over and pressed his hand to the wall beside the door. The lights in the room snapped on, along with the TVs and computers. Johnny's eyes switched back to normal vision a micro second later. The computer tower projected four holographic screens onto each desk. Each screen projected a different set of data and images. The TVs were each showing a different news broadcast.

"Welcome to satellite station Echo," Benjamin said, stepping further into the room. He stopped next to the closest desk and pressed a few keys on the keyboard. Johnny heard the locks on the far door disengage and start to swing open. Benjamin stepped toward the door, waving for Johnny to follow. Johnny stepped further into the room, looking around in wonder, when an image on the TV caught his eye. It showed four massive helicopters landing at an airfield, dozens of ground personnel rushing out to them. Three dropped their ramps and out came the prisoners he and the marines rescued. Benjamin looked back at Johnny, then to the TV. He stopped and pressed a key on the nearest keyboard. The sound on the TV was turned up as the sounds of cheering overcame the sounds of the helicopters' engines. The camera followed the prisoners as dozens of corpsmen and medics rushed to help them. The camera zoomed out and a reporter came into focus. The reporter was wearing a light blue winter coat, her hair blowing around in the wind.

"Not since the Great Raid of 1945 in the city of Cabanuan in the Philippines, rescuing more than five hundred Allied service members, has the United States staged a rescue against all odds. We're being told by officials familiar with the operation that a single Marine special forces unit launched a raid against a fortified Imperial camp deep into enemy held territory, rescuing more than Fifty American service members that were being held there. Our sources state that the mission was completed with no loss of life to the unit nor to the prisoners. Details are still fuzzy, but we are being told that hundreds of Imperial soldiers lost their lives during the raid. Many families can indeed breathe easy knowing their loved ones are once again safe here at Camp Liberty. We'll keep you informed as the story progresses. Frank, back to you," The reporter said. The image switched back to a middle aged man who was wiping a tear from the corner of his eye. The sound cut out as Benjamin pressed a button on the keyboard.

"This is what we can accomplish, tenfold," Benjamin said. Johnny nodded, turning toward the older man, a crooked grin on his face.

"Then what are we waiting for?" Johnny asked. Benjamin smiled and waved a hand, signaling Johnny to follow. The door led to a smaller room with a single desk. It was a pretty ostentatious office with many decorations and pictures upon the walls and bookshelves. A number of books crowded the shelves as well. Benjamin walked behind the desk and pulled open a small drawer. He pulled out a Navy cover. He closed the drawer and reached under the center of the desk. He pressed a recessed button. Johnny's eyes widened as a hidden door to his right slid into the wall, revealing a short corridor. Johnny could see a small window allowing sunlight in. Benjamin donned the cover and headed down the corridor, Johnny following closely. Benjamin pressed a button as he reached the end of the corridor. Johnny looked back in time to see the hidden door close. Benjamin pushed open the outer door, a blast of cold air hit them both. He and Johnny stepped out into the cold winter air, the sunlight shining down on them. Johnny looked around and noticed they were in a tight alley between the hospital and another building.

"This way," Benjamin said. He led the way down the corridor to the street. They paused as they left the alley. Johnny saw hundreds of people moving up and down the sidewalks, dozens of vehicles ranging from small carts to large military trucks on the road. Johnny felt a little uncomfortable being in the center of so many. He found that odd. He used to be surrounded by hundreds when he played for Purdue University. He should be used to it. Johnny turned and followed Benjamin, who led the young man down the block to the corner. They returned salutes as they passed by lower ranking service members. When they reached the corner, Benjamin pointed to a small, older four story building across the road.

"That's where we will be staying while we are here," Benjamin said. He and Johnny waited until the cross walk turned and moved with the crowd. They walked around the back of the building. The snow had been cleared from the sidewalk, but was still two feet deep around it. Benjamin climbed the stairs on the porch and stopped at the door. He knocked three times and waited. Johnny looked around, the feeling of being watched becoming an overwhelming sensation. He looked behind himself and then up the side of the next building. He focused his gaze on a window on the fifth story. His eyes zoomed in and the program scanned the window. The program located and identified a small security camera in the window's shadow. His vision flipped between several modes until it stopped on an ultraviolet mode. He could see the infrared laser emitting from the camera and trailing down to the area Johnny and Benjamin were standing. His vision switched again to a stranger mode. He could see different cables and wires crises crossing through the walls of the building he was looking at. Or more accurately, he realized, he could see the energy field given off by the different cables.

He discerned that the cables with more power running through them had a brighter field than the others. He found the cable running into the camera and began to follow its path. It ran down the outside of the building to the ground, then across the short space between the two buildings. He was slightly confused when the energy field disappeared as soon as it hit the building Benjamin and Johnny were waiting to enter. He turned back to Benjamin, his vision returning to normal, as a slight buzzing sound emitted from the door and the lock released. Benjamin pulled the door handle and the door opened. He held it open and waited for Johnny to enter. It was like night and day when he walked across the threshold into the building. The outside was old and looked like it needed maintenance and work done on it. The inside was sleek and shining. The walls were metallic with lights running along the floor and ceiling on both sides. The floor was stone, marble Johnny guessed. The ceiling was solid metal just like the walls. It was warmer inside, the difference in air pressure causing the warm air to rush toward the outside. Johnny stepped further in to allow room for Benjamin to enter. He walked in and closed the door. Benjamin stepped around Johnny and led the way down the hall.

"This is Liberty Barracks. This is where the Minutemen hold up when we are in this area."

"We refitted this old tenement building when Camp Liberty was established a few years ago," Benjamin explained. They continued down the hall until it exited into a large room. Johnny saw several offices along the sides, their doors closed and their lights off. "First floor is dedicated to Admin details, intelligence analysts, and emergency funds." Benjamin led Johnny to an elevator on the far side of the room. He pressed a button and waited. The elevator opened silently and the two men entered it. There were no buttons Johnny saw. "Four." Benjamin said. The elevator closed and Johnny felt the elevator start up, but never felt the pull usually caused by moving elevators. It took only seconds until the doors opened again to a similar room as the first floor. The major differences came from the pool table, couch and chairs around a massive TV, a small kitchen occupied the far end, and a table with four chairs around it. There were six closed doors along the side. Benjamin led Johnny out of the elevator and to the third door on the right. "Fourth Floor holds all the living spaces and rooms. This will be yours while we are here."

Benjamin pressed his hand to the wall next to the door. It opened silently, revealing a medium sized room. A full sized bed was against the far wall, its sheets made up neat and tight. A small nightstand was beside it with a single lamp. A dresser stood opposite, its dull gray finish matched the walls.

"It's not much to look at, but it'll do," Johnny said. Benjamin grinned and stepped toward the dresser. He pulled out the top drawer.

"All of your gear is in here."

Johnny walked over and looked into the dresser. His original clothes were neatly folded in the bottom of the drawer. His hunting knife and hatchets were resting upon the garments.

Johnny reached down and pulled his hunting knife out. He rolled it over in his hands and let out a weary sigh.

"Do me a favor? Give this to Emmis. Tell him I said thanks," Johnny asked. Benjamin looked into the young man's eyes for a moment and then nodded. He took the weapon from Johnny's hand and turned to leave.

"Get some rest, Tomorrow we start your training," Benjamin said. He stepped out of the room and the door closed. Johnny looked at the door, then back at his gear. Things were changing for him. He hoped it was for the better.

Benjamin walked back to the hospital, his mind deep in thought. Johnny had agreed to the terms of the Minutemen so readily. It bothered Benjamin on one level. Minutemen were ghosts, shades of the past that reap a terrible vengeance on the present. He saw the same surveillance footage the president had, sat in on the same debriefing of the Marines who worked alongside the young man. He had other members of the Minutemen intelligence section working to get the full background on Johnny. Benjamin had gone through the man's personal effects after the surgery and while they were waiting for Johnny to wake up. He found a small pendant on a silver chain in the effects. The pendant had an insignia that Benjamin had only seen in one other place. He endured that the president had not seen it, uncomfortable questions would have been raised. He would speak to Johnny further about it later, for now, he had to inform a group of Marines that their friend had not survived.

He reentered the hospital through the same door they had left earlier. He walked into his office and sat down, tossing his cover onto a shelf behind him. He pulled the knife Johnny had entrusted him with from his pocket and set it down on the desk in front of him. He pulled the blade from its sheath and took a look at it as the light reflected from the blade. It seemed a simple enough weapon, he could discern no special qualities from it. There was a small stain of dried blood upon the blade near the hilt, but other than that, it was a clean and well maintained weapon. Benjamin stared at his reflection in the blade for a moment longer before reaching for a drawer to his right. He pulled it open and reached inside, pulling a small cordless phone out. He pressed it against his ear and waited for the phone to connect.

"Yes?" a quiet, female voice spoke through the earpiece. "This is Doctor O'Malley," Benjamin said.

"What can I do for you Doctor?"

"A group of Marines will be stopping by, led by a Captain Jacob Emmis. They'll be inquiring about a patient named Johnny. J-O-H-N-N-Y. When they return, please give me a page," Benjamin requested. There was silence on the other end as the woman took down the notes.

"Aye, doctor. I'll have the front desks keep an eye out," the woman said. The call disconnected. Benjamin went to set it back into its receiver, when it buzzed three times and stopped. Benjamin reached under the lip of the desk where the drawer closed and pressed a small recessed button residing there. He placed the phone back against his ear and waited.

"ID?" a metallic voice asked.

"Stitch. Oh one seven seven two five," Benjamin responded. He waited as the computer recognized both his voice and access code. It took mere moments, then another female voice spoke.

"Stitch, Wildkat," The voice was quiet, yet higher pitched. "What's up Kat?" Benjamin asked.

"Did he agree?"

"Yes, we have a new hunter," Benjamin responded. He could hear the disappointed sigh on the other end of the line. He closed his eyes and shook his head slightly. It was an old and tired argument that had been circulating through the unit since High Shot had died. He had been a mentor to most of the Minutemen. Benjamin, like the others, still felt his loss, but they had to move on. It was their duty and responsibility. "Kat, I'm not going to rehash this out with you over the phone. Shot's gone, we needed a new hunter. This young man may not be a former Delta operator, but his skills certainly warrant his place amongst us."

"I still think it's a god damned mistake," Kat said vehemently. The call cut out suddenly. Benjamin let out a weary sigh and set the phone back into the receiver. He closed the drawer softly, when what he really wanted to do was slam it with all his might. He knew it would be a mistake and a waste of both his energy and the potential damage he would do to the desk. He looked down at the knife still in his hand, his thoughts drifting back to Johnny. It was true that Johnny did not have the experience nor the training that High Shot had when he joined the Minutemen, what he had though, was more potential and skills than any other Hunter the Minutemen had since Benjamin had first joined all those years ago.

He heard a slight beep sound from his belt as he sat there thinking. He reached down and pulled the small cell phone he had clipped to his belt. He looked at the tiny screen and read the short text.

Your requested party has arrived. Reception Desk Four. The screen read. Benjamin nodded and took a couple of deep breaths. It was time. He replaced the phone back onto his belt and then picked up the sheathe. He slipped the blade back into it and stood from his desk. He slipped the weapon into his pocket and left his office. He made his way to the south entrance to the hospital. He slowed as he reached the double doors leading to the reception area. It was crowded with civilians, nurses, and service members, all waiting on words from loved ones or the doctors working to save their loved ones. He spotted Emmis and three other Marines standing near the back corner, waiting patiently. He took another deep breath and pushed the door open. He affected a look of remorse mixed with professionalism as he walked calmly toward the group. The massive marine named Bull spoke softly to the others around him as Benjamin approached. They all turned toward the doctor and waited calmly, though he could feel the tension radiating from them. Benjamin did notice that he had been wrong about one of the marines. The insignia of a chief petty officer and corpsman decorated the collar of one of the men's cammies.

Instinct took over as they all recognized the insignia on Benjamin's collar as the four troops popped to attention. Benjamin waved them to at ease and took a deep breath.

"Captain Emmis?" Benjamin asked. He saw the tall, dark skinned man nod slightly. "If you gentlemen will follow me?"

Benjamin turned and led the group through the reception area, accepting a carefully prepared chart from a special nurse of his as he passed the desk. He led the group to an empty screening room just outside the reception area. He turned as he entered and waited for the group to enter before closing the door.

"Please, if you would all make yourselves comfortable," Benjamin requested as he quickly flipped through a few pages on the chart. He had had one of his operatives make up a fake chart showing the damage to Johnny's body was too severe for them to repair. Benjamin took a deep breath before beginning. "You are all here to inquire about a one Johnny No Last Name?"

"Yes, sir. He was brought in three days ago with severe gunshot wounds to his chest, shoulder, and thigh, as well as severe lacerations to his face, right forearm, and left shoulder," the Corpsman responded. Benjamin saw the name Doran on his chest. Benjamin nodded.

"Of course," Benjamin said, he consulted the chart. "I am sorry to tell you that Mister Johnny has passed." He saw a gamut of emotions play across the faces of the men around him.

"What happened?" Emmis asked, his voice cracking as he tried to keep his emotions in check.

"We worked on him for twelve hours, but the trauma to his chest was the worst of his injuries. His aorta was lacerated by the round bisecting his body. We induced a medical coma while we tried to stop the bleeding and repair the damage. We had thought we had stopped the bleeding and transferred him to a recovery room. We missed a small tear in the lining of his lung as well as a tiny nick in his femoral, most likely caused by a bone splinter from the bullet hitting the bone," Benjamin read off the chart. "He went into arrest as his lung collapsed causing a tension pneumothorax. As nurses attempted to resuscitate, the slight tear in his femoral ripped open completely, causing internal bleeding. He woke for a moment before we realized how bad the internal bleeding was. He slipped back into a coma and before we could fully stop the bleeding, he went back into arrest. We were unable to revive him a second time."

Benjamin paused to let the men to absorb the information. He hated that he had to lie to them, but history had proven the need for anonymity. The men were silent for a moment, when Bull's emotions overcame his composure. He let out a howl of grief filled anger and flipped the empty bed he had been leaning on like it was nothing. The bed crashed to the floor with a bang. The smallest of the marines moved over to comfort him. The corpsman stepped up to Benjamin.

"Sir?" He asked, holding out his hand. Benjamin nodded and handed over the chart. Doran looked at it for a while as Emmis stepped forward.

"Did...did he say anything when he woke up?" Emmis asked, his eyes were fighting back the tears. Benjamin nodded. He pulled Johnny's hunting knife from his pocket. He held it out to Emmis.

"He wanted you to have this. He said 'thanks' right before he passed," Benjamin said. Emmis took the knife from him, holding it almost reverently in his hands.

"Do you know who he was Doc?" Emmis asked. Benjamin shook his head.

"Just that he as a civilian that assisted you on your mission, and that his actions were enough to warrant his burial in Arlington," Benjamin responded.

He watched Emmis pull the blade from its sheathe and turned it over in his hand.

"What about the remains?" The small marine asked. He had been trying to calm Bull down.

The name Roosevelt was on his cammies. Benjamin had foreseen the question.

"I have been told that a special detail will be taking the remains from the airfield tonight. Congress will be conveying the Gold Medal and the Presidential Medal of Freedom upon the remains in a special ceremony tomorrow, with a full service graveside tomorrow evening," Benjamin responded. He felt a tad better. Everything he told them about the ceremony and the awards had been true. It was a standard cover for those Minutemen not previously part of the military. The casket would have a false body made up to look like Johnny. The replica would look indistinguishable from the real man. Emmis nodded.

"He deserved it…and more. If you'll excuse us, sir, we need to go speak with our command," Emmis said. He held out his hand to Benjamin. "Thank you, sir."

Benjamin shook Emmis's hand and looked at the other men in the room. Emmis waved them out of the room, then followed. He slipped the blade back into the sheathe, then placed it into his cargo pocket. Benjamin felt a twinge of guilt at the looks of pain and anguish on their faces. He knew it was for the best, but it didn't mean he had to like it. He would pull strings to ensure that the marines would be able to attend the service, and get some leave time after. They deserved that much. He stepped out into the hallway and watched the men leave. He let out a weary sigh, suddenly feeling drained. He slowly made his way back to his office, mentally preparing himself for the next stage. The training program they planned on putting Johnny through may end up breaking the young man both physically and mentally.

He entered the outer office and paused as the door closed. The door to his inner office was ajar. He stopped at the nearest desk and opened the bottom drawer. He pulled out a Colt M545 semi-automatic pistol. The weapon was an advanced version of the ones the military carried. It fired the standard .45 caliber round that had been a favorite of the US military for nearly two hundred years. The major differences came with the velocity of the rounds, the firing mechanism, and the caseless rounds in the magazine. The weapon held three times the number of rounds the standard weapon held. Each round had a small charge on the end that would propel it from the chamber. From there, built in concentric magnetic rings would increase the velocity exponentially until the round left the barrel itself. It was next generation technology, only available to the Minutemen for the time being. Benjamin thumbed the activation switch, turning on the battery powering the magnets. He pointed the gun at the door and stepped slowly toward it. He slowly pushed the door open, preparing to open fire.

"We need to update the security on these doors," a deep gravelly voice said as the door opened. Benjamin blew out a sigh of relief and lowered the pistol. He grinned at the man sitting behind his desk. The man was the oldest living member of the Minuteman and the unofficial leader of the unit. At nearly fifty years old, his silver hair was still full. The beard hanging off his face gave him a slight Viking look. He looked up at Benjamin as the doctor walked up to the chair in front of the desk and sat down. "Ben, how's things?"

"So far so good Din," Benjamin answered. "Just left the Marines Johnny had helped." The man sitting across from Ben leaned back in the chair, lacing his fingers behind his head.

"And?"

"They bought the story. As far as they are concerned, Johnny died on the table. They're on their way to speak with their CO, presumably to request leave to attend the burial," Benjamin responded. Din nodded, his face showing him deep in thought.

"We'll make sure they get the leave." Din said. Benjamin had met the man known to the Minutemen as Odin, Din for short, nearly thirty years ago. He had been brought to Benjamin's operating table in extremely bad condition. Benjamin had spent nearly two days saving the older man's life. After the surgery, Din had disappeared. Benjamin had forgotten about him until one night he came home and there Din was, sitting in his living room, wearing a strange uniform, drinking a scotch. Din had explained who he was and what the Minutemen were, then offered Benjamin a spot with the unit. Benjamin had agreed after a few days of thought. He had become one of Benjamin's closest friends over the years. Din sat back forward, placing his elbows on the desk in front of him. "Tell me about the new kid."

"Johnny's got everything we've been looking for in a hunter," Benjamin said. "Did you get a chance to watch the sat vid?" Din nodded. "Apparently, it was just half of the story. The marines we debriefed said that Johnny had tracked down and then ambushed an imperial recon platoon that had attacked his home. The marines stated that every imperial soldier had been killed. He then voluntarily led the marines through enemy territory unnoticed to a safe location. He showed the marines a way to enter the camp unseen from two different locations, get the prisoners out, again unseen, and then provided extremely accurate sniper fire to cover the team's escape. He won a hand to hand fight with a larger, more skilled enemy combatant."

"Though not without injury to himself," Din interrupted.

"True, but it seemed to hardly slow the kid down," Benjamin responded. Din nodded and waved for Benjamin to continue. "The only thing that brought the kid down was the three rounds he took, and even then, he woke up half way through the surgery."

"What about his past? I know you took something from his personal effects," Din said.

Benjamin nodded.

"It's in the center drawer," Benjamin replied. Din leaned back and opened the drawer. "When the president was filling Johnny in on our history, he got this funny look on his face when the name Alexander Wolfe was mentioned. I checked his gear after the surgery on his eyes."

"That's when I found that."

Benjamin pointed at the pendant as Din pulled it from the drawer. Din held the chain near the pendant and looked at the symbol on it. His eyebrows lifted in surprise as he recognized the symbol as well. His eyes shifted from the symbol to Benjamin.

"Does he know?"

"Uncertain," Benjamin replied. "I want him fully committed and his initial training complete before I broach the subject."

Din nodded, mulling over what he had been shown. The revelation behind the pendant could send Johnny into a tail spin. It could also cause him to harbor a feeling of superiority and the need to command. Though from what he had been told about the young man made him doubt that would happen, he wanted to be absolutely sure. They could not afford a struggle for control at this critical stage. The Minutemen were spread out to each front of this war and places beyond. A power struggle could rip the unit apart. Din set the pendant back into the drawer and stared at Benjamin.

"What's the schedule?"

"Next several days are going to be him getting accustomed to his new hardware and software. I want him completely comfortable with his ability before putting him through the maze," Benjamin explained.

"Martial training?"

"Glitch and Haywire are arriving tonight. They'll be running the Maze as well as handling his hand to hand and advanced weapons training. Bandit and Kat are supposed to be coming in to handle his infiltration and surveillance training, but…"

"Kat still having issues with replacing Shot?" Benjamin nodded.

"Yea. She's feeling that we are betraying his memory by replacing him."

"We can't mourn forever, and we need a hunter. Maybe now more than ever," Din said, an ominous tone infecting his voice.

"Din?" Benjamin asked. Din looked into Benjamin's eyes and for the first time, Benjamin saw Din's true age show through.

"We've gotten word that the Emperor may be creating a new special unit of his own. He is banking on the success of his military advisors and leaders here in the states to spur his new initiative on. We need Johnny to pick up where Shot left off. The list is only getting longer," Din replied. He pulled a piece of paper from his pocket and handed it to Benjamin. Benjamin took it and opened it up. His eyebrows rose in surprise as he saw the sheer number of names on the list. Only the first twelve had been crossed out. "Our young hunter is going to be busy."

Benjamin nodded and folded up the paper. He placed it in his pocket and looked at his leader.

"Means I should get to work then." Benjamin moved to rise. Din waved him back down into his chair. He spun around and pulled a bottle of amber liquid and two glasses from the shelf behind him. He set the glasses down on the desk and pulled the stopper out of the top of the bottle. He poured a couple inches into each glass. He put the stopper back and set the bottle down in front of him. He slid one of the glasses over to Benjamin. He raised his glass in a silent toast.

"It'll wait until tomorrow. Let him rest for the night." Benjamin lifted his glass and then took a long sip, feeling the alcohol burn slightly as it ran down his throat.

Johnny woke early the next morning with a groan. He had slipped in and out of sleep as his eyes kept flashing scrolling lines of code every couple of hours. He pushed himself out of bed and set his feet on the floor. He braced himself as he pushed off the bed to a standing position. His thigh muscles were tight as they stretched fully out. He stretched his arms above his head, feeling the tightness in his shoulder and chest. He lowered his arms slowly, feeling his tendons pop slightly. He moved over to the dresser, still limping slightly. He pulled the top drawer open and looked inside. He spotted his original gear again. He closed the drawer and opened the second drawer. He found pants and shirts neatly folded and stacked. The quick count in his head told him there were enough clothes for ten days, all of the clothes were black. He pulled out a single pair of pants and a shirt, setting it on the top of the dresser. He closed the drawer and pulled the third one open. He found boxers and socks in it. Again he pulled a single pair of each and set them on top of the dresser.

He moved over to the bed once again, pulling the old shirt off and setting it down. He stripped off the clothes from yesterday, moving carefully so as not to pull any of the stitches in his leg or chest and back. He turned to the dresser and started to get dressed in the fresh clothes. He felt rejuvenated once he had them on. He turned back to the bed and folded the old clothes and stacked them next to the dresser on the floor. He moved to the night stand where he had dropped the cammies when he went to bed. He folded the cammies and set them on top of the dresser. He picked up the socks and sat down on the edge of the bed to put them on. He winced slightly as he bent his right leg to pull the sock on. He searched for and found his boots, pulling them on and lacing them up tight. He lowered the pant legs down over the boots and stood. He limped lightly to the door and pressed his hand against the wall next to it. The lock released and the door popped open an inch. Johnny gripped the edge of the door and opened it all the way, stepping into the main room.

The lights snapped on overhead as he stepped out of his room. He looked around and found it just as empty as the day before. He looked to the small kitchen area and his stomach emitted a grumble. He realized that he hadn't eaten in days and limped his way over to the counter. He paused to lean against it, taking his weight from his leg momentarily. He took a couple of deep breaths, trying to calm the slight shake in his muscles. He kept most of his weight on the counter and moved around it to the cabinets and fridge. He opened them and surveyed his options. He pulled a box of cereal out of the cabinet and the gallon jug of milk from the refrigerator. He set them both on the counter top and searched for a bowl and spoon. He finally found a bowl, slightly larger than the cereal bowl he had originally wanted. He shrugged and set it next to the bowl of cereal and continued to look for a spoon. He opened the last drawer on the counter and smiled as the many pieces of silverware reflected the lights above them.

Johnny pulled a spoon out and moved back to the bowl. He poured a large amount of cereal into the bowl, following it up with enough milk to make the flakes float. He replaced the milk in the refrigerator and moved back to the bowl. He gently lifted the bowl and limped over to the table. He set the bowl down and pulled the chair out. He sat down, wincing slightly, and pulled the bowl toward him.

He ate slowly, relishing the taste of the cereal, thinking he had never tasted anything as good as that simple food. The room was so quiet he thought he could hear the crunch of the cereal between his teeth echo off the walls. He stared at one such wall, devoid of all color and decoration, and let his mind wander. He tried to see his future, or more specifically, the future he wanted. He was slightly annoyed that he could envision nothing more than what the next few days held once his training began. He thought about the last few days and the decisions he had made. He could still feel the rage burning deep inside of him, but knew that to let it run wild and burn everything in its path would be a mistake and lead to nothing more than ruin. His mind thought about the dreams he had had and couldn't decide if they were truly visions or if they were the delusions of a broken mind trying to make sense of its suffering and loss.

His ears picked up the hiss of the elevator doors opening. A few seconds later, the doors hissed close. The muffled shuffle of boots on the carpet approached from behind. He closed his eyes and pictured the movement. The steps were light, but spread, meaning whoever it was stood taller than Johnny. He opened his eyes and focused on the door handle to the refrigerator. The software zoomed in on the handle and the image resolved, he could clearly see the person's distorted image reflected in the metal. The software filled in the resolution and color gaps and became a hard image in his vision. The person approaching was indeed taller than Johnny, but not as heavy. The man had blonde hair and fair skin. He was wearing a business suit, dark gray, with a navy blue tie. Johnny blinked and his vision returned to normal as the man came within a couple steps of him.

"Johnny?" The voice was soft, with a southwestern twang at the edges. The man stepped to the side of the table and looked down at Johnny. Johnny looked up at the man and the software in his eyes started their process of identification.

NAME: Franklin West
OCCUPATION: None Found
AGE: None Found
HEIGHT: None Found
WEIGHT: None Found
ARMAMENTS: (1) 9 mm pistol (GLOCK M773 (15 Rounds) (Hollow Point) (Intermediate Threat))
HOME ADDRESS: None Found
SPOUSE: None Found
CHILDREN: None Found
POLITICAL AFFILIATION: None Found
NATIONALITY: None Found
MILITARY RECORD: United States Army
RANK: O-4, Major
SPECIALTY: Technician (Cybernetic, Holographic, Fiber Optic, Electrical, ETC.)
CRIMINAL RECORD: None Found.
...CONTINUE?...

"Can I help you?" Johnny asked, looking up into the man's face. It was reassuring, trusting even. Franklin held out his hand. Johnny took it and gave it a small shake.

"Flipswitch," Franklin said.

"Flipswitch?" Johnny asked, raising his eyebrows. Franklin smiled as he released Johnny's hand and pulled the chair next to him out. He sat down and unbuttoned his suit jacket.

"Call sign. We all have them, even you," Franklin explained. "Please, keep eating. I'm here to fill you in on what's going to happen in the next few days and get your training started." Johnny nodded and continued to eat as Franklin reached over to the center of the table and pressed a hidden button. The table top slid back a few inches and a set of small posts rose. The tips of the posts began to glow and hum slightly. An image of a human eye appeared a foot above the table, rotating slowly. Johnny paused halfway into a spoonful of food to stare amazed at the hologram. Franklin smiled again and coughed lightly. "This is your eye before the surgery." Sections of optical nerves and bundles of neurons became highlighted. "These are the sections of the neurons and nerves we attached the cybernetics to. We spliced the nerves and circuitry together flawlessly to allow your normal electrical impulses to power the equipment. Here," a single strand of nerve endings was highlighted in a different color, "is where we attached the broadcast terminus, which will allow you to broadcast what you are seeing either live or to a special cloud database we are setting up."

"Broadcast? How?" Johnny asked. Franklin made a waving motion against the hologram.

The hologram of the eye shifted into an outline of a human body. A set of armor pieces slid over the body until they fell into position. Franklin pointed toward the helmet piece and waited for the image to enlarge. The helmet became a wire frame showing the internal circuitry and individual linking armor pieces. Near the left ear of the helmet, a thin rod began to pulse blue.

"This is the transmitter inside what is going to be your helmet. It will link up wirelessly to the transmitter in your eye. This one will link up to our satellite networks and give you access to the Minutemen systems," Franklin replied. He waved his hand and the image of the eye reappeared. He moved his hand over it again and the hologram showed pieces of a camera system were replacing parts of the eye. "Simply installing the camera in your pupil and iris proved too complex and problematic. Stitches decided to fully replace the eye itself."

"Stitches?" Johnny asked.

"Doc Benjamin." Franklin replied. "While both of your eyes look real, they are, in fact, both fake. You will still feel periods of dryness and strain as your muscles and nerves become accustomed to the new technology. We designed the software along similar lines to the Neuro-cyber prosthetics that have been used for the last ten years. The software in your eyes is actually ten years ahead of what the outside world has access to. Your brain controls the different functions of your eyes. You think it, and if it is programmed, it will happen. The transmitter also functions as a connection point between your eyes and any weapons equipped with electronic sights." He paused to let the information sink into Johnny's brain as he used both hands to turn the image and readjust the iris. "We've added an adaptive color program to the irises and lenses to give you some control over how your eyes appear. It will also allow you to fool most iris scanners."

"Most?" Johnny asked between mouthfuls.

"The most advanced iris scanners will be able to detect the difference in your eyes and may lock you out, but those types of scanners are in the White House and Pentagon. The ones you run into won't pose a problem." Franklin explained. Johnny nodded as he heard the elevator doors open again. This time the footsteps were heavier, closer together. He recognized the footfalls.

"Hello Doc," Johnny said. He set down his spoon and picked up the bowl. He drank the last of the milk in the bottom of the bowl. He set it down and leaned back. He looked at Franklin's face as he looked between Johnny and the new arrival, confusion and amazement pasted to his face. Johnny heard Benjamin chuckle as he stepped to the other side of Johnny. He pulled out an empty chair and sat down.

"Good morning," Benjamin replied. He looked at Johnny. "How are you feeling this morning?"

"A bit unsteady, but alright considering." Johnny answered truthfully. Benjamin nodded. "Good. We are going to keep your physical exertion to a minimum for the next week. We will be putting you through some physical therapy for the next two weeks to work you back up to full health. The third week is when we will see what you can really do," Benjamin said. Johnny nodded and pushed his chair out. He stood slowly and picked up his empty bowl. He limped over to the sink and washed the bowl out, setting it on the counter to dry. He turned back to Benjamin and Franklin as they stood from the table. Johnny limped back over to them and leaned against the table.

"When do we start?" Johnny asked. A big smile broke upon Benjamin's face. "Right now."

The next four days went by like a blur for Johnny as every morning Benjamin or Franklin would meet Johnny for breakfast. They then led him down a floor to one of their labs where they walked him through each and every setting in the program of his eyes. They drilled how to switch between the different settings and features with nothing more than a thought. Johnny was amazed at what his eyes could now do as they ran different tests and set up scenarios for him. Each day he found he could switch the different sights and modes faster and faster, with much less lag time and much more ease. He learned he had modes that would allow him to see through different materials or trace the path of electronic signals. He could spot hidden weapons under clothes or body armor and could follow the path of laser sights to their source.

He was getting stronger, too. Benjamin had started him off slowly on the first day, working the muscle mostly to loosen it back up. Johnny still limped slightly, but it was not as pronounced as it had been that first day. He was starting to get a little stir crazy too. Benjamin had told him that, for the time being, he was confined to what he now knew to be called Liberty House One. He had almost the full run of the place, though a couple doors still did not open to his palm and his eyes could not penetrate the material the walls were made out of. He shrugged it off and figured he would figure it out sooner or later. He watched the news late into the evenings and read a few of the books provided by the Minutemen on a tablet he found in the drawer of the nightstand. He read up on the history of the war, trying to figure out where things went wrong and how the US had been pushed so far back.

After the massive storm chains that ravaged large sections of the United States, as well as hurricane Louis that nearly wiped out Puerto Rico, the New Asiatic Empire sent what was supposed to be massive shipments of humanitarian aid and supplies. Ten thousand cargo ships holding hundreds of thousands of containers docked in the major ports of Honolulu, San Diego, Los Angeles Santa Monica, San Francisco, Portland, and Seattle in the span of two days. Just as the sun set on the second day, the Empire struck. Each container held either troops or armored vehicles, allowing nearly one million of the Empire's finest to invade. Hundreds of submarines launched multiple missile strikes, having used the cargo ships as cover. The missile strikes had been aimed at civil and military defense structures, nearby bases, docked ships, and more than a few hospitals. The strikes nearly crippled the cities as officials and leaders reeled from the surprise assault. As a response to the assault began, thousands of fighters, bombers, and interceptors came from seemingly nowhere to capitalize on the initial surprise and wiped out most of the US air power on the west coast. The Marines of Camp Pendleton, the Navy at Coronado Island, and many army units were among the first to recover and began their counter attack, slowing the Empire's initial push out of most of the cities.

The overwhelming force of the Empire's attack on Honolulu caused the island state to fall in less than one day. According to the intelligence provided by the Minutemen, the Empire had turned the islands that made up Hawaii into a massive prison complex housing more than three million prisoners to date. The US, realizing the Empire had won the opening moves, ordered a full retreat to what was now being called the Washington Line. In a preemptive move, the pentagon had ordered all air defense units to set up along the Line, from the northern most point in Montana to the southern point in Texas, following the contours of the Rocky Mountains. Still needing to cover the retreat of the west coast forces, hundreds of pilots volunteered to provide what air support they could. Most did not return. The Empire moved to capitalize on their victories by destroying the US defenses on the eastern side of the Rockies. Instead, they ran into an impenetrable wall of anti-aircraft fire.

After that, it turned into a ground war that has all but halted the Empire's advance. Johnny read report upon report of US units slowing the enemy's advance but not stopping it. The extreme winter that has set in has been their only saving grace. The Empire was unprepared for the snow. The US used their knowledge of the land to strike a thousand different times along the Line using guerrilla tactics. It was a smart move, but one that only scratched the enemy. While annoying, they didn't provide the breach the US needed to turn the war around.

Johnny was reading about the last major offensive the US took that nearly resulted in disaster as the Army's 227th armored was decimated by four Imperial divisions as they tried to secure the only remaining superhighway through the mountains, when his door opened. Benjamin poked his head in.

"Got a minute?" Benjamin asked. Johnny set the tablet down and swung his legs out of bed. The physical therapy was working, he didn't feel much if any pain at all any more.

"Of course. Come on in," Johnny said. He went to stand but Benjamin waved him back down.

"Sit, sit. This will only take a minute," Benjamin said as he walked into the room and closed the door. "I just wanted to try and explain a few things before we start the next stage of your training. You've been doing far better than we would have thought. The ease of which you took to your new eyes and their amazing abilities is astounding. Tomorrow you will begin your hand to hand and advanced weapons training. Your instructors have been here for a few days, observing your progress. I can postpone it if you feel you are not yet capable to engage in physical activities." Johnny thought about it for a few moments before looking at Benjamin.

"No. I'll be fine," Johnny replied. "Who are these instructors?"

"You'll meet them tomorrow," Benjamin said. "I'll let you get back to your reading." Benjamin nodded to Johnny, turned and left the room. Johnny waited a few moments, imagining what kind of advanced weaponry he would be trained on.

He woke the next morning at the same time as always. He made his way to the showers and waited for the water to warm. He stripped down, tossing the clothes from yesterday into a pile under where his towel hung. He stood under the spray for several long minutes, letting the warm water cascade over him. He felt his muscles relax after days of tension and physical therapy. He closed his eyes, relishing the warmth spreading over him. A quick flash of images caused his eyes to jerk open. His breathing increased slightly as he tried to make sense of the images he saw. He could have sworn he saw his family. He shook his head to clear his thoughts. His family was gone, he had to come to terms with their deaths. He finished his shower, shutting off the water, and reached for his towel. He dried his face as he stepped to a mirror over a nearby sink. He used the edge of the towel to wipe the steam from its surface and took a look at his image. His face was healing quickly, the angry red line now thin and starting to dull. He had begun to let his beard grow out, but could still see where the scar dipped under the hair.

He shook his head at how strung out he looked. He turned away from the mirror as he dried the rest of his body off. He tied the towel around his waist and picked up his discarded clothes. He stepped out of the shower room and was halfway across the main room, heading for his temporary bedroom, when he had the feeling he wasn't alone. He stopped and turned his head toward the kitchen area.

Three people stood around the counter, staring at him. The first was Doc Benjamin. Though the good doctor was wearing some kind of body armor, his face was uncovered. He stood, leaning against the counter, a steaming cup of coffee in his hand. The next figure was slightly shorter than Benjamin, and slimmer. Johnny would have to guess they were most likely just over one hundred pounds without the armor. They were wearing the same type of body armor as Benjamin, with a few changes. The solid armor pieces on their forearms and biceps were thicker. Johnny could see the thick knuckle pieces on the gloves holding the coffee cup. Johnny looked over the rest of the armor and spotted thicker pieces over the figure's chest and abs. He couldn't see the figures legs, but would guess that the armor pieces were thicker there as well. Johnny couldn't see a face. The figure had yet to remove their face shield and helmet.

The helmet had a picture on it that seemed to fade in and out in the light, a skull wrapped in what looked like twisted blue lightning. The third figure stood by the stove, the sounds of bacon sizzling against the heat. The smell was beginning to permeate the room. This figure stood as tall as Johnny and slightly wider. His armor was very different from the others. Slots in the armor designed for ammunition magazines dotted the armor. Slots on the forearms were sized for pistol magazines, the ones on his chest were for larger weapons. The armor was also smooth where it was thicker, and more encompassing. Johnny could tell where joints were, but couldn't see between the pieces of the armor. The man's face was soft, almost joyful as he looked at Johnny. His tanned skin shown with a thin sheen of sweat from the heat of the stove. Johnny spotted a helmet on the counter behind the man. Its armor was as smooth as the other pieces the man wore. The face mask had a laughing skull barely visible on its face. The man smiled as Johnny looked at the three of them.

"Mornin'," The man said. His thick Texan accent caught Johnny by surprise. "Breakfast'll be ready in five. Go on and get dressed. You'll need to eat before we get started."

Johnny looked at Benjamin, who nodded, before continuing to his room. Two things stood out as Johnny entered. The pile of old clothes that had been accumulating next to his dresser was gone. He shrugged that away, figuring someone had taken them to get washed. The second was a set of new clothes

189

sitting on his bed. He dropped the old clothes he was carrying next to his dresser and moved to his bed. He reached down and picked up the first item. It was thicker than a normal shirt, but not heavier. He looked closely and his eyes zoomed in to the individual strands of fabric. Not fabric, he saw, not exactly. It was indeed woven, but it was some kind of metal material. His eyes identified the strands as a titanium tungsten alloy. He blinked and his eyes zoomed back out. He looked over the rest of the shirt and spotted tiny hooks on the biceps, forearms, shoulders, neck, back, wrists, and chest. He set the shirt down and picked up the pants. They, too were made of the same material, with identical hooks along the legs and waistband.

He figured they were meant to be worn over the normal gear he had been wearing. He set the pants back down and moved over to the dresser. He tossed the towel off to the side as he open the drawers of the dresser and pulled out fresh clothes. He quickly donned them and moved back to the bed. He pulled on the pants first. He let out a small noise of surprise as the waist band suddenly tightened around him. It loosened slightly, then tightened once more before finally fitting perfectly. He ran his hands along the waist. The pants fit perfectly against the ones underneath. He shrugged as he pulled the shirt up and over his head. He held his arms out as the shirt tightened against his body. The sleeves tightened around his wrists and then loosened enough for him to move, but he couldn't fit a finger between his skin and the sleeve.

The same occurred around his neck, at first becoming so tight he thought he would suffocate, then loosening slightly enough to allow him to breathe easily. He looked down to check out the new outfit, then moved around his room, testing his mobility. Unable to sense any hindrances in his mobility, he left his room. The smell of cooked bacon was overwhelming to his senses, causing his mouth to water instantly. Benjamin and the two newcomers were still standing around the counter as Johnny approached. The man cooking turned and set a full plate of eggs and bacon on the counter beside him.

"Sit, eat." He told Johnny as he turned back to the stove. Johnny nodded and stepped up to the counter. He picked up the plate and a fork, then moved to the table. Benjamin and the other Minuteman followed. Benjamin set a fresh cup of coffee down in front of Johnny and took a seat beside him. taste.

"Thanks," Johnny said, picking up the cup and taking a long drink, savoring the bitter.

"You're going to need it," Benjamin responded. He looked at the Minuteman across the table. Johnny followed his gaze and saw the person nod. They reached up and slid three latches at the bottom of their helmet. Johnny's eyes widened as a mass of blonde hair fell from the helmet as it was removed. The Minuteman fully removed the helmet and set it aside on the table. She shook her head slightly to unbundle her hair. She looked from Benjamin to Johnny. Her face was round, showing slight Asiatic features, but tight, a slight scar across her left cheek.

Her nose had a small bend to it, signaling it had been broken and reset more than once. Her bright blue eyes stared with intensity into Johnny's. Her small lips were compressed in a tight smile.

"Johnny, this is Haywire, your hand to hand combat instructor," Benjamin said, motioning to the woman. "And the master chef over there is Glitch, your advanced weapons instructor." Glitch turned and threw a slight wave. Johnny nodded in response. He focused on each for a second and sent the command to have the identification program run. Her name was listed as Katherine Brown, currently a Captain in the United States Army. His name was listed as Diego Vance, a Lieutenant Commander in the United States Navy. The program found no weapons on Haywire's body, but dozens of red boxes appeared on Glitch's. The program detected seven small caliber pistols, three large caliber pistols, and a dozen small bricks listed as HWX-098 breaching charges. Johnny's eyes showed his surprise at Glitch's armaments as he shut the program down.

"Ben, want anything?" Glitch asked from across the room. "Yes, please, scrambled," Benjamin replied.

"Order coming up. Haywire?"

"Same," she answered simply. Her voice was soft. Johnny had a hard time placing the accent from just the one word. He turned back to his own plate, shoveling a forkful of eggs into his mouth. He ate in silence for a few moments, before his instincts told him that she was still staring at him. He looked up and raised an eyebrow in a silent question. She cocked her head to the side and appeared to be trying to choose the words to her question carefully.

"Do you have any experience or training in hand to hand combat?" She asked. Northwestern United States, Johnny thought, placing her accent finally. He had a friend in college from a small island town in Washington. The accents were nearly identical.

"I won this fight," Johnny said, pointing toward the healing wound on his face. "Also won a fight with a cougar. Other than that, just a handful of kickboxing lessons in high school. Tended to try and avoid conflicts as much as possible." He heard Ben chuckle lightly at his words.

"You **barely** won that fight," he said.

"Still won. I'm standing, he's not," Johnny replied, his eyes taking on hard edge for a split second as he remembered the fight.

"True enough." Ben agreed. Haywire nodded a few times.

"It's going to be my job to teach you how to truly master hand to hand combat. It's going to take years to teach you everything. For the next week, I'll be teaching you the basics. I wish we had more time, but..." She said.

"That's enough Haywire," Ben interrupted. Johnny looked from Ben to Haywire, confused. "But?" Johnny asked. Ben looked at him for a moment before answering.

"A situation may be forming that we will need to address. But until we get solid details, it's better if you just focus on your training," Ben explained. Johnny narrowed his eyes at the doctor.

"C'mon Stitches, gotta give the kid more than that," Glitch called out. "Can't. Word from on high."

"Hmph, whatever," Glitch responded. He shrugged and turned back to the stove. Johnny

stared at the doctor for a few more moments before understanding the matter was closed. He shrugged his shoulders and went back to his food. Ben found it to be the best time to change the subject.

"Haywire is indeed here to show you the basics on how to survive a hand to hand encounter. While Glitch is here to train you up on your basic armaments," Ben said.

"Oh yea, we gonna get you outfitted with gear you've only seen in sci-fi movie and video games," Glitch said as he walked over to the table and set down two plates in front of Ben and Haywire. "Eat up now."

The group ate the rest of the meal in silence. Johnny removed the dirty dishes and placed them in the deep sink to clean later. Ben finished off his coffee and stood.

"Time to get started." He waited as Glitch and Haywire retrieved their helmets. He led the three Minutemen to the elevator and waited for it to open. They all stepped inside and waited for the doors to close. "Range."

The elevator started down. Johnny estimated that they had gone further down than the first floor. His suspicions were confirmed when the elevator doors opened, showing a large, wide room that ran at least one hundred meters back. Brilliant overhead lights snapped on in sequence, illuminating the entire room. Pillars, set six feet from each other, marked the individual lanes of fire. A collapsible table was stretched between each pillar. Ben led the group off the elevator and turned to the right. The room, Johnny saw, hooked around the back of the elevator and into a fully stocked gym. A set of mats had been set up in the center for people to spar. The group stopped to appreciate the set up. Haywire stepped away from the group and over to a small bench beside the ring. She set her helmet down and stepped into the ring. She stopped just short of center, her hands clasped behind her back, her feet set shoulder width apart.

"Step into the ring," She commanded. Johnny nodded and stepped forward. He stopped equidistant from the center as she did and waited. She took a deep breath. "Hit me." She said simply. Johnny looked at her slightly confused. "I said: hit me." Johnny shrugged and dropped into a combat stance, his hands in front of his face, his right foot slightly back and his left slightly forward. He pulled his right arm back and threw his full weight into a straight punch at Haywire's face. He began to worry as she stood still. He started to pull back on his punch when she finally made her move. Johnny let out a yelp of surprise as he was pulled forward and then suddenly found himself on his back, the wind knocked from his lungs. He coughed a couple of times to clear his airways and breathe in again. "Stand."

Johnny groaned as he pulled himself to a sitting position and looked around. Haywire was standing in her original position, her hands still clasped behind her back. Johnny, however had ended up behind her original position near the edge of the mat. Ben and Glitch were off to the side, leaning against the wall. Smiles were pasted to their faces as they shook their heads in amazement and knowing. Johnny pushed himself back to his feet and moved back to his original position. His muscles and joints popped slightly as he moved. He rolled his shoulders and swung his arms slightly to work the tension out of them. He stopped at his original start point and retook a combat stance. He again launched a right handed punch, throwing his entire body into the punch. He didn't try to pull the punch this time, but paid sole attention to Haywire. She stood completely still again, until his punch was an inch from her face. Time seemed to slow as she moved and Johnny watched. Her hands whipped from her back and up. Her left hand gripped Johnny's right wrist, her right hand gripping the front of his shirt. She twisted slightly, bringing her right foot forward up against the insole of his left foot. Then she added her own strength, pulling down on his right arm, forward using her right hand, and ensuring his foot didn't move using her own foot. The result was a sort of somersault for Johnny. His forward momentum, increased by Haywire pulling him forward, was altered by her pulling down on his right arm, causing his center of gravity to shift. And it was finished off with Johnny being thrown over her thigh, causing his feet to leave the ground. Again, Johnny landed with a thud on his back, staring up at the ceiling, the air exploding from his lungs. He laid there for a moment, running the entire sequence of events through his head, trying to figure out a way to counter it.

"Stand." Johnny nodded as he pulled himself to his feet. He was working a counter to hers in his head as he stepped back into his start position. He looked at her as he dropped back into a combat stance. She stood still as a statue, waiting. She nodded once. Johnny again launched a right handed punch, just as fast as the first. This time, as it neared her face and she began to move, Johnny pulled the punch back and swung his left hand in a cross. He saw the look of surprise in her eyes, as Haywire was forced to adjust her own actions. She leaned back just in time to avoid the devastating blow Johnny's punch was intending to inflict. She brought her left hand up in front of her face as Johnny's left passed in front. She gripped his wrist and yanked, forcing Johnny to continue along that trajectory. Johnny felt the tug and allowed his body to continue to twist. As his back turned toward Haywire, he threw his right elbow back in a strike. Anticipating the move, Haywire used her right forearm to block the strike. Johnny felt the solid appendage stop his strike, feeling it all the way up his arm. Haywire reversed her arm and hooked in around Johnny's elbow. She pulled his arm backward quickly. He felt the stitches in his shoulder strain and pop slightly. As soon as his arm was far enough back, Haywire locked her own arm in place, keeping Johnny from being able to move. She repeated the motion with her left arm, pulling it backward to lock both of his arms behind his back. She became slightly concerned with how easily Johnny had allowed her to immobilize both of his arms.

Johnny had anticipated her counters as well, allowing her to focus on his arms. While they had been moving, Johnny had moved his left leg between hers and behind her left foot. As soon as she locked his arms back, he twisted his right shoulder forward, using his size and strength to pull her off balance. He pulled his right arm as hard as he could and felt her left foot leave the ground as it pulled over his leg. He continued to twist and felt her weight upon his back as he pulled forward. Her grip on his arms loosened as her momentum launched her forward. He pulled his arm around and threw her to the ground. Recovering almost immediately, she spun on her back, gripping his right arm with both hands and scissoring her legs between his. She rolled, pulling on his arm as her legs swept his out from under him. Johnny fell to his side as Haywire took advantage of his fall and rolled on top of him. She straddled his waist, using her legs to pin his. She held on to his right wrist as he held her left. They pushed back and forth, each trying to outmuscle the other and gain an advantage. After a few moments of this stalemate, Johnny looked up into her face and saw a broad smile form.

"Very good," she said, sitting up, letting go of his wrist. He let go of hers as she swung her leg over his body and moved off him. She pushed herself to her feet and held out her hand. Johnny pulled his feet to his backside as he gripped her hand. With a mighty heave, she pulled him up to his feet. She held onto his hand for a few seconds before releasing it. Johnny let out a breath and realized just how much energy they had used in their short bout. "You sure you've never had any training?"

"None," Johnny said, giving his head a slight shake.

"Then how?" Haywire asked as she led Johnny off the mat to a set of lockers. She opened the first and pulled out a bottle of water. She handed it to him and then pulled a second out. He opened his and took a drink before answering.

"I read your body movements," Johnny said, blushing slightly at how it sounded in his head. Haywire gave him a slight grin at his embarrassment. She understood what he meant.

"Is that how you survived out there?" Ben asked from across the room. Johnny looked at him and then screwed up his face in thought. He nodded after a few moments.

"Yea. I read the way the wind blew through the trees, the way the snow shifted along the ground, even how the animals adapted to their surroundings," Johnny explained. "As for the men I killed, I studied them as they ran or took cover or moved into firing positions. I used the same skills to take them down

195

that I used on any other creature I have hunted before. These just happened to be better armed and more numerous."

"Hehehe, nice," Glitch said. Johnny took another drink of water and recapped the bottle.

He set it to the side and stepped back onto the mats.

"Ready for more," Johnny said. Haywire nodded and set her own water aside and joined him on the mat. She began to walk him through various counters and counters to those counters. Johnny kept quiet as he absorbed the information given by Haywire. She ran him through hand to hand drills for hours, learning basic moves and repeating them. Benjamin stepped forward after five hours of drills. Johnny and Haywire separated from their last round of drills, each showing a thick sheen of sweat on their faces, their breaths deep, signaling their exertion. Benjamin handed each a fresh bottle of water.

"Well done. I think that's enough for today," Benjamin said. Haywire nodded her agreement.

"I think so too. Tomorrow we will kick it up a notch," she replied. Glitch stepped forward on to the mat, a broad grin on his face.

"My turn now?" He asked. His grin broke into a smile when Ben nodded. "Fantastic. This way young man, time to show you your new toys." He gripped Johnny by his shoulders and led him back out to the range area. He directed Johnny to lane six and had him stand still. Glitch moved to the pillar between lanes six and seven. He pressed his palm against the pillar and stepped back. A split appeared in the pillar and extended upward five feet from the floor. Once the split completed its path, the two sides of the pillar pulled apart from each other, disappearing into the curves of the rest of the pillar. A rack of pistols extended from the pillar with a hiss.

Johnny did a quick count and stopped at sixty. The rack finally stopped extending and Glitch moved beside Johnny, a massive smile plastered to his face.

"Amazing isn't it?" Glitch said. "A rainbow should shoot out every it opens." He smacked Johnny on the back and stepped up to the weapons rack. He pulled a pair of large caliber pistols from the center. He turned and held them out, grips toward Johnny. "Recognize these?"

Johnny took the pistols from Glitch and looked at them. They were the ones he had been wearing when he had left home. He was slightly concerned that they felt heavier than he remembered. He turned them over in his hands, examining them carefully. He noticed the barrels had been extended a half inch, but he could not see any other changes. He looked back up at Glitch.

"They're mine," Johnny replied. "They're heavier than I remember." Glitch nodded. "Very good," Glitch said, smiling. "They are yours, with some adjustments. First there is the electronic sights that link up with your cybernetic eyes. Go ahead, take aim down range."

Johnny nodded and turned down range. He gripped his pistols tightly as he lifted his right arm to shoulder level, his pistol pointing straight. His hand was unwavering as he stood there, wrist locked. A small crosshair appeared in his vision. A set of numbers beneath the crosshair showed distance, elevation, and wind speed. He moved the pistol side to side and up and down, watching the crosshair follow his movement. He lifted his left hand and watched another crosshair appear beside the first. He moved the pistols independently and watched the crosshairs respond. A small grin appeared on his face as he imagined what an advantage this would give him in combat. He lowered the pistols and watched the crosshairs fade away. He turned back to Glitch.

"The electronic sighting in the grips connect to your eyes as soon as your hands touch them. Once we get your gloves fitted, there won't be such a lag in the movements. Remember that there will be a certain amount of lag, especially if you are swinging your weapons quickly. You'll have to judge and estimate your aim in those cases," Glitch explained. "Second adjustment are the barrels. We've equipped them with electromagnetic rings along the barrels."

"Effectively turning them into rail guns?" Johnny asked. He lifted his right hand so the barrel was pointed toward the ceiling in front of his eyes. He couldn't see the rings with his normal vision, but when he sent the command for a deep scan, he could see the thin rings circling the barrel every quarter inch. Four tiny wires connected each ring together and then to a tiny power source near the firing spring. He blinked and his vision returned to normal as he looked at Glitch. Glitch nodded and turned toward the rack again, this time pulling a handful of magazines from it. He set the magazines on the firing table and turned back to Johnny.

"Yep. It increases the velocity of each shot by a factor of five, and the range by a factor of three. Go ahead and put a few down range," Glitch said. Johnny turned down range and set the pistol in his right hand down on the table. He picked up a fully loaded magazine and inserted it into the magazine well in the pistol of his left hand. He pulled the slide back and let it slam forward. He ensured the safety was on and set it down. He picked up the remaining pistol and another fresh magazine. He inserted the magazine and pulled the slide back. He let it slam forward and checked the safety. He picked up the second pistol and held them both with the barrels pointed up. He nodded that he was ready. Glitch stepped to his right side and pressed a recessed button on the pillar twice. The floor twenty meters down range slid to the side and two manikins rose up from the floor. Johnny's eyes immediately scanned them and identified them as synth flesh over ballistic gel and synthetic bone composites. They were as close to real bodies as one could get without using actual people.

"Range is hot. Shooter on the line, you may fire when ready," Glitch said. Johnny nodded and lowered his right arm out straight. He saw the crosshair appear and moved his arm so it settled on the chest of the right target. He flipped the safety off with his thumb and took a deep breath. He let it out slowly and squeezed the trigger. The pistol barked loudly and bucked in his hand, the slide launching back far enough to eject the spent shell. The spring reached its maximum stretch before pulling the slide back forward to insert the next round into the chamber. His attention, however, was on the manikin. Less than half a heartbeat after Johnny squeezed the trigger, the round completed its flight, impacting the manikin. With the added velocity the electromagnetic put into it, the results were devastating. The solid nosed round hit the manikin with the same force as a standard fifty caliber round. Thousands of pounds of force and pressure ripped through the synth flesh. The round continued through the ballistics gel and bone, its velocity barely slowed by the resistance. The wake of the round caused more damage as it rippled through the body. Johnny stared in amazement as the body was ripped apart by a single forty five caliber round. He saw a blast of concrete dust and chunks as the round impacted the far end of the range. The remains of the body finally splattered against the floor along the path of the round. Johnny thumbed the safety back on and set both pistols back down on the table. He turned to Glitch, who was laughing hysterically.

"What the hell was that?" Johnny asked, still amazed by what he saw. Glitch continued to laugh as he stepped up and picked up the pistol Johnny had just fired. He ejected the magazine and pulled the slide back to eject the live round. He then pressed a small button under the barrel. A small compartment slid open, a tiny tab jutting out slightly. Glitch pull the tab and the small power source attached to it out.

"This is the power source for the electromagnets. I preset it to maximum earlier. At that setting, the battery will dump every scrap of power into the rings, and then, in turn, to the round as it travels along the barrel. The result is what you saw: The power of an anti-tank weapon in the size of a standard round," Glitch explained, getting control of his laughter. Johnny nodded as he processed the information.

"Will the weapons still fire if the battery dies?"

"Of course. The rounds won't be enhanced by the electromagnetic rings, but yes, they will still fire normally," Glitch said as he set the spent battery down and pulled a fresh one from his pocket. He inserted it and closed the compartment. He then turned the pistol upside down and showed Johnny a small, round switch on the underside. "This is how you adjust how much energy each shot will use, if any. Now we have it set up that you can switch the amount of power remotely using your head gear, but we haven't tested it. The markings here are in increments of ten, starting at the zero mark here." He turned the switch to "0" and turned the pistol back over. He inserted the magazine and pulled the slide back. He flipped the safety off and pointed the pistol downrange. He squeezed the trigger five times, the pistol barely bucking in his grip, the shells ejecting to the ground. Johnny watched the rounds impact the target on the left with splashes of ballistics gel. He flipped the safety back on and set the pistol down. "I would recommend using the power supply only when necessary. The rounds as they are will punch through most types of light armor. The power source will let you shoot through walls and heavy armor."

"Reload and get ready. I'm gonna start throwing up random targets and see how you do."

Johnny nodded and picked up his pistol. He ejected the half spent magazine and picked up a fresh one. He slid it into the well with a snap. He picked up both pistols and pointed them down range. He took a deep breath and nodded. Glitch reached over and pressed three buttons. The first button dropped the destroyed targets back into the pit. The second told the computer to begin picking targets at random distances, heights, and amount of cover. The third began the program. A siren blared throughout the range as more doors opened in the floor. The first target to appear was ten feet out. It popped up quickly. Johnny pointed his right hand at the target and squeezed the trigger twice. The pistol bucked in his hand as two empty shells went spinning off. The first round took the target in the head, tearing the top off, the second buried itself in the target's chest where the heart would have been. The target was immediately pulled back into the pit as the computer registered the kill. More targets popped up. Johnny worked quickly, but methodically. He dropped target after target. Most of them took a single round to the head or chest, though a few took as many as three. The slide on the pistol in his right hand locked back as he fired the last round. A new target appeared thirty feet out. He brought his left arm around, bringing the crosshair to rest on the target. He squeezed the trigger and then swore internally as a solid piece of metal slid up in front of the target. He saw the round spark as it ricocheted off the armor and into the ceiling. He began to set the pistol in his right hand down, thinking he should switch the power on the battery up, when a new set of numbers and letters appeared under the crosshairs.

PWR: 60%

Johnny didn't give it a second thought, but instead pulled the trigger. The pistol barked loudly, bucking back into his hand. He watched as a hole appeared in the armor with a small spark. The target seemed to jump up slightly as the enhanced round tore it clean in half. A second target appeared behind the same cover, the top of its head barely visible. Johnny shifted his aim and fired. Again, a hole appeared in the armor and the target disappeared. Johnny shifted his aim as more targets appeared behind varying pieces of cover. He worked his way through the targets, adjusting the power behind each shot silently. Finally, he pulled the trigger and felt the pistol buck. The round impacted the wood cover he was aiming at, but didn't penetrate enough to hit the target. The counter for the power level in his eye read "0," signaling the battery was spent. Johnny narrowed his eyes in frustration as he adjusted his aim up slightly and squeezed the trigger. The slide locked back as the last round left the barrel. A heartbeat later, he saw a splash of gel as the round tore through the top of the target's head. Another siren sounded as the destroyed targets and their cover dropped into the floor. The doors slid shut over them as Johnny set both pistols on the table. He surveyed the range, noting the splashes and piles of gel that marked where targets had been.

He turned to Glitch, who had taken a step back to join Haywire and Ben. The looks of astonishment and amazement covered their faces as they looked between Johnny and a screen that had descended from the ceiling above him.

Johnny took a step toward them and looked the screen. It showed every target that had popped up. Each target showed where the rounds hit by placing a red "X" on each strike. A string of numbers under the targets showed his accuracy and time between shots. The time between shots had gotten progressively shorter as he went down the line. His final accuracy rating was ninety seven percent. The entire exercise was timed as ten minutes forty six seconds. Another screen popped up and Johnny saw his time at the top of a list of other times. Odin and High Shot were listed as second and third with times of ten minutes fifty two seconds and ten minutes fifty five seconds respectively. Johnny looked back at the trio in front of him.

"So…how did I do?" He asked. Silence dragged on for a few seconds before Glitch broke out into a hysterical laughing fit. Ben joined in after a second. Even Haywire giggled softly.

"That was something else," Glitch said. "Normally newbies don't even make it to the board."

"And you not only made it, you destroyed the boss's time."

"He also beat High Shot's," Haywire said, pointing to the screen. "And that's surprising why?" Johnny asked.

"Because High Shot was a former Delta operator who had been listed as one of the best shooters in the world," Ben explained.

"Ah," Johnny responded.

"Who trained you?" Glitch asked, stepping up to the line. He pressed a button on the pillar and watched as a gang of robotic cleaners swarmed from the walls and began to clear away the mess Johnny had made.

"My father and grandfather taught me the basics. Learned most of the rest by trial and error. Grandad used to say I took to fire arms like a fish to water. Anything placed in my hands became an extension of my own body," Johnny said, remembering the times his father and grandfather had taken him out to their homemade range. A look of sadness reached his eyes before he could stifle it. He quickly squashed the feeling, hoping no one had seen it. He was slightly unsuccessful, judging by the look in Haywire's eyes.

"I'd say they were right, going from the evidence," Glitch said, motioning to the range. "Take a few moments to relax while the bots clean up the mess. Then we'll run through another simulation. We'll change up calibers and types of pistols."

Johnny gave him a crooked grin. He was never more relaxed then when he had weapons in his hands. Glitch had him try out dozens of types of pistols, ranging from amazing wheel chambered revolvers to an experimental machine pistol that fired caseless rounds using nothing but electricity and magnets. Johnny felt exhilarated after several hours of firing hundreds of rounds. He made sure he felt comfortable with both the weapon and the connection in his eyes before he was ready to call it a day. Glitch stood by with an impressed look on his face as Johnny picked up weapons he had never touched before and quickly became not just accustomed to them and their mechanics, but was able to show advanced proficiency with them. He finally called it a day when he looked at the watch in his forearm armor piece and saw that it was nearly eight o'clock. He and Johnny pulled two sets of the weapons he had fired and carried them into the elevator. The others would be cleaned by the computer's automated systems. Johnny had been persistent that he clean a few of them.

They walked to the table once they were back in the residential wing and set the weapons down. Ben moved to the kitchen area and began to pull dishes and materials out to make dinner. He figured a nice large meal would be fitting for the end of a long, hard day. Johnny and Glitch set about disassembling the weapons, setting them out in a close pattern to keep the pieces from intermingling. Haywire sat on the couch, half watching TV, half watching Johnny as he focused on his task. She had been wary of his skills and even more so of his presence in the unit.

She still mourned the loss of High Shot, like the others, but after watching and sparring with him throughout the day, she was willing to say she may have misjudged him. High Shot had been an amazing operative and invaluable part of the Minutemen, and his loss was felt by all, but even he had said that the group needed a better hunter. Haywire was almost certain they may have gotten just that. While they had sparred, she had seen the flickers of a primal force show in his eyes. It scared and, if she was being completely honest, excited her. She hoped he would survive what Odin and Stitches had planned for him.

Johnny spent the next week learning more and more from Haywire as she expanded his training in hand to hand combat. He was getting faster and stronger as his wounds healed more and more. He no longer felt any pain or tightness in his muscles as he moved. On the seventh day, Haywire decided to pick up the pace and see how well he had absorbed her lessons. They faced each other on the mat, silently waiting for one of them to make the first move.

Johnny's facial expression was neutral as his eyes flared in anticipation. Haywire showed nothing but a calm exterior. Johnny was almost surprised when she made the first move, throwing out a straight kick with her right leg. Johnny blocked the kick and subsequent left cross she threw. He launched a right punch at her chest and followed with his own left cross when she countered. She spun out of the way of the left, only getting grazed by his outer knuckles. They went back and forth for minutes, each attacking while the other countered. Glitch and Ben watched on, whispering to each other about who had the upper hand.

The bout lasted for twenty minutes, neither showing any signs of slowing or faltering. In fact, it appeared that they were increasing the speed and ferocity of their strikes. The sweat on their faces shone brightly in the light as they moved back and forth. Finally, Haywire smiled demonically, as Johnny appeared to take a misstep and get slightly off balance. She took a step forward and launched a devastating round house kick, aimed for his chin. Her sense of victory was short lived, however, as a crooked grin broke upon Johnny's face and that same primal look appeared in his eyes. Instead of stepping or leaning back to avoid the kick, Johnny regained his balance seemingly effortlessly and stepped forward. He braced his left arm, tightening the muscles and took the kick into his bicep with a short grunt. As soon as her leg made contact, he wrapped his left arm around her leg, pinning it against his body. He reach over and gripped the outside of her leg with his right hand. He loosened his hold with his left hand slightly as he pulled hard with his right, spinning her around. He retightened his grip and pulled backward, causing her to lose her balance on her remaining leg. She caught herself as she hit the mat with her hands and tried to push herself up before Johnny could follow up her fall. Unfortunately, she was not fast enough. Johnny had released her leg and dropped atop her, straddling her waist.

Haywire managed to spin herself to her back, facing Johnny. She arched her back, trying to dislodge Johnny. Instead, she opened the opportunity for Johnny to wrap his legs around hers and pin them down. She threw an awkward punch up at him, getting desperate. Johnny caught her hand and pulled it down across her chest, pinning it to the floor on the opposite side of her body. Johnny pressed the forearm of his free arm against her neck, adding enough pressure to start cutting off her oxygen and blood supply to her brain. Her mind reeled for a half second before realizing that she had no way of escaping. She started to feel lightheaded as the effects of lack of oxygen began to set in. She quickly smacked her hand against the mat three times, signaling her surrender. There was a joyous whoop from Glitch. Johnny, hearing the smacks against the mat, immediately sat up, relieving the pressure on her neck. He let her hand go as he unwrapped his legs from hers. He rose to his feet as she coughed to clear her airway and take a deep breath. He stepped back and held out his hand as she turned her flushed face toward him. She gripped his hand and allowed him to pull her up to her feet. Her face was still flushed and she couldn't tell if it was from embarrassment, lack of oxygen, or something more...primal. She held his hand for a moment longer than necessary before letting it go. She turned to regain her composure as Johnny turned to Glitch and Ben.

"Well done!" Ben said, holding out his hand. Johnny shook it as a grin broke upon his face.

Glitch stepped up and smacked Johnny's back playfully.

"Nice job kid, Stitches here owes me twenty bucks," Glitch said. He looked over to Haywire as she picked up as towel and bottle of water. She began to wipe the sweat off her face when Glitch spoke again. "When was the last time an untrained newbie forced you to tap out?"

"Never," Haywire responded. She unscrewed the cap on the bottle of water and took a long drink. She set the towel down and picked up a second bottle of water. She walked over and handed it to Johnny. He accepted it with his customary crooked grin. She blushed slightly as she turned away from him. She started walking toward the door of the gym. "Well done. We'll continue your training when you get back. Stitches, I'm hitting the showers."

"Ok. We'll see you in a bit," Ben replied. Johnny walked over and picked up an unused towel and wiped the sweat from his face. He set the towel down and opened the water. He took a deep drink as Ben and Glitch spoke quietly to each other. He recapped the bottle and turned the duo. "Time for your last weapons session?" Ben asked. Johnny nodded and followed them out of the gym to the range.

Haywire stepped from the elevator with a sigh. She dragged her feet as she made her way to her quarters. She stopped to take a look at the door to Johnny's quarters. A tangle of emotions welled up in her as she thought about the young man who just pinned her minutes ago. She pushed those emotions back, trying to discern if they were just because he was an amazing specimen of the opposite sex that proved himself in the ring against her, or if she was actually attracted to him. She shook her head and turned back to her door. She pressed her hand to the side of the door and waited for it to unlock. Once it unlatched, she pushed it open and moved into the room, the lights popping on automatically. She reached under the armor on her forearms and unhooked the tabs holding her gloves in place. She pulled them off and tossed them on to her bed. She bent down and pressed the release tab on her boots, feeling them loosen from her feet and ankles enough to kick off. She repeated the process on her pants and pushed them down her legs. She lifted her feet one at a time as she pulled the armor off. She stood slowly, feeling her muscles pop and pull at the movement. She stood fully and tossed her pants onto her bed alongside her gloves. She reached under her arms and was pressing the release tabs when a voice startled her. She spun in place and took a fighting stance.

"What's gotten you all sweaty Wire?" a female voice said softly. Haywire relaxed as her eyes adjusted to the dark corner and the form of her comrade appeared. She was quietly leaning against the corner of the walls, her arms crossed over her chest. She pushed off the wall and stepped into the light, the black shading of her armor seemed to absorb the light. Her helmet had the depiction of a snarling panther fading in and out in the light. She moved with ease as she stepped over to Haywire's bed and sat down. Haywire ignored her question as she thumbed the release tabs on her armor. She grabbed the edge of the sleeve on her right arm and pulled as she withdrew her arm from the sleeve. She ducked her arm under her armor and slipped it up her body and over her head. She pulled her left arm from the sleeve and tossed the armor onto the bed beside the others. "Could it be that the newest societal reject has our own martial master all hot and bothered?"

"What do you want Kat?" Haywire asked as she turned to her friend. She set her hands on her hips and glared at the mask staring at her.

"I want to know why he is here," the woman said, cocking her head to the side. "Because he needs some basic training before Odin sends him out," Haywire answered.

"We don't need him," The woman said, venom dripping in her voice. "We don't need anyone to replace…"

"We do. And he is not replacing anyone," Haywire said, cutting her friend off, knowing where the conversation was heading. "High Shot can never be replaced, but we need a Hunter, and Johnny's the best we've found."

"Oh? On a first name basis with this one, are we?" the woman said, sarcasm and revulsion in her tone. "You go ahead then. I'll prefer to keep him nameless. Why get to know someone who will be dead in a couple of weeks anyway."

Haywire's anger flared at the disdain in her friend's voice. Again, she wondered why she jumped to the defense of a man she met a few days ago. She took a couple of deep breaths and turned to her dresser. She pulled a clean towel from the top drawer and turned to the door.

"You might want to give him a chance, Kat. He might surprise you," Haywire said as she moved to the door. "I'm going to take a shower, lock the door when you leave." Haywire stepped out of her room and made her way to the showers. She turned on the spray in the first stall and waited for the water to warm up. She stripped off her undergarments and stepped into the spray, letting the water rinse away the sweat that had built up on her skin. Her mind flashed an image of Johnny straddling her waist during their sparring match. She sucked in a breath sharply as her eyes snapped open. She lowered her head and let the water roll over her, trying to figure out her own emotions toward Johnny.

"Damn," She said softly.

Johnny stepped up to Range six and waited as Glitch pressed the button to open the weapons racks. Over the week, he had worked with pistols, battle rifles, large caliber machine rifles, shotguns, grenades and explosives, and sniper rifles from all over the world. Each time he showed rapid familiarity and mastery on each and every one. He was impressed with how the Minutemen had upgraded his own weaponry as well as other standard weapons. This time, when Glitch opened the racks, a set of what appeared to be launchers dominated the selection. Glitch pulled the first one out and held it like it was his own child. The launcher was three feet long with five barrels on one end, each about three inches in diameter, and a single five inch diameter opening on the other. It had a single pistol grip on the bottom with a twin finger trigger. A pad half way down the tube marked where one would put their shoulder. An eye piece was against the side, but looked like it flipped out perpendicular to the launcher. Glitch ran a hand along its length and looked up at Johnny.

"This is my baby," Glitch said. "Mark twenty two Cyclone Shoulder Mounted Launcher. I customized this one with five tubes, each containing a hellfire laser guided missile. Same as the ones on the smaller UAV's. Each missile has also been upgraded with a HX-12 charge surrounded by a tungsten casing and a thermite tip. Will ruin just about anyone's day. We'll be working with these today. We are going to start with something different first."

Glitch placed the Cyclone launcher back onto the rack and picked up a longer, squarer weapon instead. This weapon was four and a half feet long with twin barrels that ran nearly three feet of its length. It had a pistol grip and trigger assembly. A rounded shoulder stock showed it would fit neatly around the entire arm. A squared box was attached to the bottom that looked as though it could detach from the weapon itself. A short, squat charging handle ran from the end of the barrels to above the trigger assembly. Glitch turned and set the weapon down on the table and stepped back to allow Johnny a close look. Johnny took a closer look at the barrels and saw a set of half rings lining the insides of each barrel and the barrel themselves were about two inches in diameter.

"Say hello to the Snare launcher," Glitch said. He stepped up and pulled the box from the magazine well. Inside, the rounds were separated into two sections, six rounds to a section.

Unlike normal rounds, these were nearly perfectly round, like ball bearing. His eyes identified the casings as ferrite magnetic composites surrounding small fission charges. "This weapon fires what is basically an electromagnetic bolo. The power source charges the casings of each round. That keeps them close together until the field meets something metal. Once that happens, the rounds come together, their casings crack and they explode. If one of the casings cracks prematurely, they explode."

"So…basically it's a grenade launcher that fires magnetic grenades?" Johnny asked. Glitch nodded.

"Yep, with a range of just under a mile. The range is determinate on how long you charge the magnets along the barrels. The half rings on the insides of the barrels create the 'string' of electromagnetism that keeps them close together," Glitch said. "We'll start with this one. First, let's ensure our safety." He reached into the opened pillar and pulled a handle down. Johnny felt a sudden jolt of static electricity and looked down range. He could see motes of dust impact something with a small zap. He looked over at Glitch. "Electro static shield. It'll keep shrapnel from coming back at us." Johnny nodded and stepped up to the table. He reinserted the magazine and pulled the charging handle back. The weapon began to hum as Johnny picked it up and put it around his shoulder. Glitch pressed a button against the pillar to his right. At the end of the range, a tank facsimile rose from the floor. Johnny adjusted the sync between his eyes and the sights and waited. "Fire when ready." Johnny nodded and held the trigger down. The humming increased as the power built. Sparks of electricity danced along the inside of the barrels as the power reached maximum. Johnny released the trigger and felt the weapon bounce hard against his shoulder. He also felt a static jolt as the weapon launched the two rounds. Johnny zoomed in on the rounds and followed their trajectory. He could barely see the arcs of electricity dance between the two rounds. They impacted a corner of the target, they whipped inward against the armor. Johnny blinked as the rounds exploded upon contact. His vision returned to its default setting as the concussive blast hit them like a wave. The flames and shrapnel weren't far behind. Johnny instinctually ducked as the flames raced at them, only to stop at the barrier. He saw arcs of electricity where the flames touched the invisible mesh. He saw more solid shrapnel pieces hit and fall to the ground, still smoking from the explosion. Johnny looked at Glitch and grinned.

"Very nice," He said. Glitch nodded and took the weapon from Johnny, replacing it onto the rack. He pulled another large bore weapon and handed it to Johnny as the sprinklers kicked on to suppress the flames at the end of the range.

"Moving on to the next," Glitch said. Johnny's grin became larger as he realized his entire afternoon would be spent firing high explosive rounds.

Johnny and Glitch stepped off the elevator hours later, smiles of utter joy plastered to their faces and their ears still ringing. They were patting themselves down, trying to shake the dust and ash loose from their clothes and armor. They looked up as the elevator closed and found the main room of the residential floor a tad full. Johnny recognized Flipswitch, Haywire, and Ben sitting around the table. Their conversation had been interrupted as the two newcomers stepped off the elevator. They had decided to remove their armor and all three were in normal clothes. Johnny could see the beginning of a tattoo on Haywire's left arm. A fourth person was sitting on the couch watching the news. They were in their armor and helmet, making identification impossible. Ben stood as Johnny and Glitch made their way to the table.

"Looks like you two had fun," Ben said bemusedly. Johnny grinned and nodded.

"Who doesn't have fun blowing stuff up?" Glitch asked. Ben smiled and turned to Johnny. He waved over the fourth person, who stood. Johnny began to take in the details of the person's armor. It was covered with intermingling patches of dark and light grays, giving them a not quite solid shape as they moved. Their helmet, like the others, had an almost indistinguishable picture on it. This one was a skull with a bandana around its nose and mouth. The armor pieces over their under armor was sleek, almost metallic. The pieces were not as thick as Glitch's nor Haywire's, but also didn't have the circuitry nor scanners that Ben's or Flipswitch's did. Johnny ran a scan of the armor and his eyes widened as the results came back with dozens of error messages. His armor was reflecting the scans, sending false information back.

"Johnny, let me introduce you to Bandit," Ben said. Johnny held out his hand. Bandit took it and gave it a small, but firm shake. "He and Wildkat are going to be training you on an introductory course in infiltration and information gathering."

"Cool," Johnny replied. "And Wildkat is?"

"She's here somewhere. I'm sure she'll introduce herself, either today or tomorrow morning. Now, about this course, it's not going to be as fun and action packed as shooting weapons all day or sparring with Haywire, but I will expect you to pay attention," Ben said, looking straight into Johnny's eyes.

"No worries," Johnny answered. He looked from Bandit to Ben. "If you guys will excuse me, I need to go get out of this gear and get a shower."

"Of course," Ben said, stepping aside. Johnny nodded to them and made his way to the door to his room. He pressed his hand against the side and waited. The door popped open and he stepped inside, reaching under his arms to flip the release tabs on his under armor shirt. He was pulling it and the shirt underneath over his head, when his instincts warned him he was not alone in his room. The door shut with a click as he pulled the garments off and tossed them onto the bed. He slowed his breathing and let his ears pick up any noise in his room. He heard a second breath a half second behind his. He took a step toward his dresser, purposely keeping his back to the far corner of the room, where the light didn't quite reach. He pulled open the fourth drawer and pulled a fresh towel from it.

"You must be Wildkat," Johnny said, seemingly to thin air. He tossed the towel over his shoulder and turned to the corner. His eyes automatically adjusted to the half-light and the form of a person could barely be seen. "A pleasure."

Wildkat stepped from the corner, her exterior showing a calm demeanor, while internally she was both pissed and impressed. Normally, no one would have known she was there until she decided to make herself known. Yet, this…man not only knew she was in the room, but where she was. He had sensed her presence and dismissed her as being nonthreatening. It pissed her off that he would make such assumptions. She calmed the fires of rage in her heart and strode over to his bed. She turned and sat down on the covers, still staring at him. She could see what Haywire saw in him, physically speaking. He was handsome in a roguish, rough way. The scars on his chest, back, and face only accentuated those looks.

"You must be Stitches' newest find. Hmph! I still don't see what he does," Wildkat said.

Her Georgia accent was thick in places. "Don't get comfortable. I'll teach you what I can while you are here, but I doubt you'll be able to use any of it."

Johnny frowned at how much disdain and malice she laced in her words. He narrowed his eyes as she stood and made her way to the door. She started to open it when Johnny spoke.

"And why's that?"

She stopped and turned her head to look directly at him.

"Because you'll be dead in a couple of weeks," She said calmly. She opened the door fully and stepped out. Johnny watched her in silence as the door closed once more. A small grin formed at the corner of his mouth as he thought about how much he wanted to prove her wrong.

Johnny awoke the next morning much earlier than usual. His instincts told him something was wrong and roused his brain from its normal REM sleep to its almost fully awaken state. His room was still dark, and it took a split second for the night vision mode to kick in. His heart and brain kicked into overdrive as he saw an arm begin its downswing at him, a stick of some kind gripped in its hand. Johnny threw his arms up in a cross and caught the arm on its down strike. He felt the hit travel up his arms. He grit his teeth as he pushed the arm up and away, using his feet to kick off his blankets. He rolled to the floor as the arm came back down, striking the bed with a sharp thud. Johnny hit his chest on the floor and pushed up. He swung his legs around, catching and sweeping his assailant's legs out from under them. He pushed himself to his feet and looked down at the figure on the floor. He started to move forward when his instincts yelled at him again. He dropped into a crouch as a second assailant moved out of the shadows and launched a swing at Johnny's head. The strike sailed harmlessly over him. Johnny pushed back with all his strength, twisting his body around. He tackled the second assailant around their waist. He launched the both of them to the floor, dropping all of his weight on the person's chest, forcing the air to explode from their lungs.

Johnny used his forward momentum to roll off the downed assailant and back to his feet. He spun, swinging his leg out in a round house kick. Catching the first assailant in the side as they moved to rejoin the fight. Johnny heard a grunt of pain and surprise as his kick sent the assailant into the wall next to them. Johnny brought his foot down and rushed the stunned figure, using his left forearm to jam the figure's head back into the wall. He kept his arm there, adding pressure, trying to choke the figure out. He threw a hard uppercut into the figure's side four times, trying to do as much damage as possible as quickly as possible. He was so focused on damaging the figure in front of him, he didn't notice the second figure get back onto their feet, swaying slightly. They recovered enough to rush at Johnny, swinging their weapon at his back. Johnny took the first to his back, just over his kidney, causing him to snarl in pain. He let go of the first assailant and spun out of the way as the second strike came flying in. Johnny avoided it, allowing the strike to his the first assailant's arm. Johnny stopped his spin and launched a straight kick into the second assailant's chest, putting all of his strength into the kick. The second assailant landed on the bed in a tangle of limbs and sheets. Johnny dropped his left leg and immediately pivoted on it, bringing his right leg up. He swung it into the first assailant's abdomen, causing them to double over. Johnny brought his leg down, stepping forward and swinging his knee up into the assailant's head. The figure dropped like a puppet with its strings cut. Johnny turned his attention back to the second figure as it managed to swing itself off the bed. They each took a step forward, each preparing for their own individual strike. When the door slammed open and the lights snapped on. Johnny grimaced as he turned away, the sudden brilliance overwhelming his night vision.1

"Enough!" Ben yelled, stepping forward in between Johnny and his assailant. Johnny blinked several times as his eyes switched back to normal vision. He stood back up quickly, the adrenaline still pounding through his veins. Ben stood in front of him in full armor, the visor of his helmet reflecting the light. Johnny could see deep red slashes running from top to bottom and left to right. The slashes intersected, mimicking stitches, forming a red cross. The image faded in and out in the light. His hands were up, palms facing both Johnny and his remaining assailant. Johnny could hear the faint crackle and hum of running electricity coming from his palms. Johnny shifted his gaze from Ben to his assailant, his eyebrows lifting slightly in surprise as he stared into the helmet of Wildkat. He lowered his arms and relaxed slightly, his pulse banging in his neck. Wildkat lowered her arms, a baton of some kind in her left hand. She turned to Ben.

"What the hell do you think you are doing Stitches?" She asked angrily.

"Stopping the two of you before things get out of hand," Ben answered calmly. He lowered his hands and stepped away toward the other assailant. Johnny looked in that direction and narrowed his eyes. Bandit was lying against the wall, his head lolling back and forth lazily. Ben took a knee and held Bandit's head in his hands. He flipped the quick releases on the bottom of the helmet and pulled it gently off Bandit. Johnny watched silently as Ben set the helmet aside. He ran the ID program as soon as he got a good look at Bandit's face. It was rough, angular. A pencil thin mustache decorated his upper lip. His pale blue eyes were having a hard time adjusting. The program in his eyes finished their run, identifying Bandit as William Kidd of the United States Navy. Ben held Bandit's head with one hand while he held his hand three inches above. Johnny's eyes detected an infrared beam as it scanned Bandit's head.

"Wha hit me?" Bandit asked, a little delirious. Ben shushed him as he finished his scan. He looked at the top of his forearm for a moment before looking back up at Bandit. He pointed his right index finger and a bright light popped on, emanating from its tip. He moved the light between Bandit's eyes, judging their response. He repeated the process for a few moments before the light shut off. Johnny turned to the door as it opened again. Haywire and Flipswitch stepped inside, both in full armor. They looked from Johnny to Wildkat to Ben and Bandit on the floor.

Johnny turned his attention back to Bandit when the latter spoke again. His southwestern accent slurred slightly. "Wha's goin on? Wha the hell hit me?"

"Easy, you have a minor concussion and two broken ribs," Ben said, reaching to his side and pulling a short syringe out. He stabbed it into the side of Bandit's chest and depressed the plunger. "And it was Johnny that took you down. Nice moves, by the way." Ben said, turning to Johnny. He then looked toward Haywire and Flipswitch. "Get him out of here and onto the couch." Haywire and Flipswitch nodded and stepped by Johnny, who moved out of the way. Ben stood and stepped to the side as Haywire and Flipswitch each gripped one of Bandit's arms and pulled him slowly to his feet. They threw his arms around their shoulders and more or less dragged him from the room. Ben watched them leave and then turned his attention to Wildkat and Johnny.

"Again, I ask: What the hell do you think you are doing?" Wildkat asked, nastily. Ben was radiating a cold fury as he stepped up and looked down into Wildkat's visor.

"What was **I** doing? What the **HELL** do you think you were doing?" Ben asked, furious. "I was doing what I was ordered to do," Wildkat answered.

"Your orders were to assess his reaction to a sudden and unprovoked assault, not to try and kill him," Ben nearly yelled. "You were out of control."

"I had everything under control, and he's not dead nor even seriously injured," Wildkat retorted, waving her hand toward Johnny. Johnny had crossed his arms and leaned against the wall, watching the back and forth.

"And what would have happened if I had not intervened?" Ben asked. Wildkat raised her hand as if to say something, but Ben cut her off. "Get out of here and prepare his training cycle." When Wildkat didn't move, Ben took another menacing step toward her. "Move."

She hesitated for a moment, before lowering her hand and leaving. She gripped the edge of the door and slammed it shut behind her with a loud bang. Ben and Johnny stared at it silently for a few moments, before Ben turned to the younger man.

"Let me check your back," Ben said. Johnny stood and turned around, allowing Ben to check the strike Johnny had taken. Ben poked and prodded around the forming bruise. After a few moments, Ben pulled his hands away. "You'll be fine. Mostly surface and muscle bruising. I will want to check again in a couple of days to ensure that your kidney isn't damaged." Johnny heard the tearing of wrapping paper and then a cold and hot sensation as Ben pressed some sort of compress against his skin. He felt Ben's hands pull away, leaving the compress.

"Bandit going to be okay?" Johnny asked. He turned around and looked into Ben's facemask. Ben nodded.

"He'll be fine." Ben responded. He moved toward the door. "Get dressed and come out for breakfast."

With that, Ben left the room, leaving Johnny standing all by himself. He waited a few moments before moving toward his dresser. He peeled off the pants he had been sleeping in and pulled open the drawers. He quickly dressed in the under armor and stretched. He felt the muscles in his back protest as the bruise continued to form. He put his boots on and bent over to lace them up, a grimace forming on his face as the bruise sent twinges of pain through his back. He stood back up and left the room. The main room was a buzz with activity as everyone moved about. Haywire was assisting Ben, who was checking over Bandit, still woozy from the concussion. Flipswitch and Glitch were preparing a large breakfast for everyone. Wildkat was the only one who wasn't to be found. Johnny moved past the couch as Ben scanned Bandit's head once more.

Haywire had removed her helmet and was holding Bandit up. Johnny stopped at the end of the couch and looked down, concerned.

"He alright?" Johnny asked.

"Yes, yes, he'll be on his feet in a couple hours," Ben said, not looking up from staring at his forearm. Bandit looked over toward Johnny, his eyes swimming slightly from nausea. He finally focused on Johnny.

"Yeah, I'll be fine once I get some of that godly go juice in me," Bandit replied. "What?" Johnny asked.

"He means coffee," Haywire said. Johnny nodded his understanding and moved over to the kitchen area. The grill began to sizzle as Glitch dropped several pieces of bacon onto the top of it. Flipswitch was setting a handful glasses and mugs on the counter. Johnny grabbed one and moved to the coffee maker. He poured a full mug and took it back over to the couch. He held it out to Bandit, who took it with a grateful nod. For the first time in a long time, he felt comfortable in surroundings that didn't involve the forest or constant danger.

After breakfast, Ben and Bandit, who was now moving and talking without a concussed slur, took Johnny down to the second floor. They entered a room with dozens of free standing doors and monitors on desks and attached to walls. Wildkat was leaning against one of the doors, her helmet still on. Johnny nodded to her as he entered. He felt her eyes on him as he moved to stand near a set of computers set into the side wall. Bandit walked over and whispered something to her before turning around to address Johnny.

"Welcome to the infiltration course of your initial training session," Bandit said. He waved his arms around the room. "Here we will teach you the finer skills of lock picking, hacking, bypassing and fooling security systems. The electronics portion of your training will be slightly easier due to your upgraded peepers. The last few days, we are going to throw curveballs at you." Bandit walked around, motioning to the different locks and computers throughout the room. "The last day of your training will take place in what we call the Maze. The Maze will force you to use everything you have learned and every instinct and skill you brought to the Minutemen. Are you ready?"

"Let's get started," Johnny responded with a grin. Bandit nodded and turned to the closest door. He pulled it open and then removed a small bag from it. He walked over and handed it to Johnny.

"These are yours." Bandit said. "Take care of them."

Johnny turned to the nearest table and set the bag down. He untied the strings and unrolled the bag. The bag had dozens of small pockets sewn into the lining. Each pocket contained two pairs of lock picks. Johnny pulled one from a pocket and held it up in front of his eyes. The ID program ran a quick scan and came back with a titanium alloy. He replaced the lock pick and looked up at Bandit and nodded.

"Time for your first lesson," Wildkat said, motioning to the door she was leaning on. Johnny nodded and stepped forward. He pulled a lock pick set out and knelt in front of the lock. "Insert the picks carefully. Normally we would tell you to fell for the crenellations, the different bumps caused by the tumblers, but with your new eyes, you should be able to 'see' the interior of the lock."

Johnny nodded and began to blink rapidly, each blink shifted between the different modes programmed into his eyes. He stopped when the door became clear, almost like a mesh outline. He focused on the lock and watched as it resolved into a more solid shape.

"Focus and it'll be like an X-ray or deep radar scan. You should also be able to see the ends of your picks," Wildkat explained. "Move the picks until you find different tumblers that will move. Move the picks to push the tumblers in their 'open' positions and the lock disengages."

Johnny focused both on what he was seeing and the words he was hearing. He saw two tumblers that could move. He adjusted the picks and felt and saw the tumblers shift. He felt a sense of accomplishment and pride as the tumblers locked into their open position. He gently pulled the picks from the lock and then gripped the door handle. He twisted it and pushed it open. He stood back up and looked to his two instructors. Bandit had a small grin on his face, Wildkat merely nodded once.

"Well done. Moving on to the next."

Johnny spent the next several days going through the different types of locks and security systems, learning to bypass or pick the systems. Each day, the locks became more and more difficult, the systems more intricate. Bandit and Wildkat taught Johnny how to splice into systems and fool the cameras attached to them to see nothing. He was taught by Ben and Flipswitch on adjusting the color spectra of his eyes to fool retina scanners. He was becoming more and more comfortable with the skills he was learning and speed at which he learned them.

On the fifth day, Bandit and Wildkat switched things up on Johnny and threw in shifting light intensities, from complete darkness to strobing to blinding lights. They added laser trip sensors and even patrols consisting of his five instructors.

On the sixth day, Johnny awoke to an empty residential floor. He dressed in his usual under armor and went out to the kitchen to make himself breakfast. He sat down with a cup of coffee and a bowl of cereal. He ate slowly, contemplating the last few weeks. He noticed the way his muscles were outlined under his skin, musing on how much more fit he was becoming since joining the Minutemen. He remembered his time in high school and college, seeing the gym rats that were pumping iron every day to become massive muscle men. While he had no attention of becoming as large as they had, he did like the feeling he got when he looked in the mirror and saw the new him. His face had almost completely healed, the angry red giving way to a paler hue. He looked down at his forearm, seeing the scar on it as well. He shoveled a spoonful of cereal into his mouth as his gaze shifted from his arm to a piece of paper in the center of the table.

He frowned at his lack of attention. He should have seen the paper when he sat down. He picked up the paper and read the small note written on it.

Johnny-

Come down to floor two, room five. Press your palm against the left side of the frame. A number pad will appear against the door. Press 08-19-1772.

Ben

Johnny set the paper down and hurried to finish his breakfast. He washed it down with his coffee, regretting it slightly as the scalding drink burned his mouth. He quickly cleaned up and washed the dishes he had used. He made his way to the elevator, wondering what was in store for him today. He pressed his palm against the wall to the right of the door. He waited for the doors to open, quickly stepping inside once they did. As soon as they closed he spoke.

"Two." Johnny felt the elevator descend for a few moments before stopping once again. The doors opened silently, allowing Johnny to step off the lift. He walked down the right side of the corridor until he found room five, using his ultraviolet sensors in his eye. He stopped and looked at the door. He took a deep breath and pressed his hand against the wall where he had been directed. He waited a few moments. A keypad suddenly popped into his vision. He quickly entered the code, his mind reflecting on the conversation he had had with the president during his stay in the hospital. August nineteenth, seventeen seventy two, the date the members of the continental congress met to form the Minutemen in the first place. He stepped back as the computer inside the door read the code and unlatched the locks. The door popped open an inch, allowing him to pull it all the way open. He stepped inside and the lights popped on. The room was completely empty, save for a manikin in the center, pieces of armor attached to it, a helmet over its face. This helmet had a blank facemask. The armor pieces were not as thick as Haywire's or Glitch's, but not as thin as the others' either. They also did not have smooth edges. The edges were jagged along the forearms, as if they were bladed. The upper arms covered the biceps from nearly the shoulder to the elbow. The chest piece covered the entire chest, with a small gap around the diaphragm area. Another piece covered the abdomen. The thigh pieces ran from the tops of the hips to the top of the knee. The shin guards ran from the bottom of the knee to the ankles. Johnny walked around behind the manikin and checked out the back pieces. Several small pieces extended from the back, each standing a half inch tall. Johnny ran a finger between two of them, wondering what they were for.

"Like the armor?" Ben's voice asked. Johnny looked around the manikin and saw Ben standing near the door. He was in full armor again. He stepped forward and put a hand on the chest piece. "This is the Mark VIII Stalker gear. High Shot designed it a few years back. We had just begun to actually build it, when he died. We have refitted it to your specs, should fit you like a glove." He ran a hand over the chest piece. "This is just the base model, mind you. There are several ways we can customize it for you. Now, let's get you suited up." He turned from the manikin to the door as it opened once more. Bandit and Glitch stepped in. "We're going to show you how to fit each piece to your under armor and activate the circuitry inside."

"Circuitry?" Johnny asked as Bandit pulled the forearm piece from the left arm and moved next to Johnny. He pulled Johnny's left arm up and had him hold it there as he fitted the forearm piece onto Johnny's arm. The piece tightened as soon as Bandit stopped moving it. It adjusted a few more times before becoming snug on his arm. Glitch followed suit with the right arm while Bandit pulled the upper arm piece off the manikin and attached it to Johnny's arm.

"The armor has Nano circuitry running through both the solid pieces and under armor. It reacts not just to your body, but also to the environment around you. Once the gloves are in place, the circuit will be complete and give you total access to the armor's special features,"

Ben explained. "In this case, the skin of both the solid pieces and the under armor have Nano receivers and shifting color optics, allowing you to change the color scheme, making it easier to blend with your environment."

"What? Like an invisibility mode?" Johnny asked incredulously as Bandit and Glitch attached the leg pieces to his legs. Ben shook his head.

"No, not at all. Think ghillie suit without the actual suit part or hanging pieces," Ben replied. "Should give you the advantage of staying unnoticed going from one type of terrain to the next without having to change your exterior clothing. One of the features High Shot designed. The other is a shifting energy and thermal signature. The exterior of the armor keeps you from almost all versions of thermal and energy detecting equipment, as long as you don't overheat the armor or allow too much energy to build up inside the internal circuitry."

Johnny contemplated his words as Glitch and Bandit snapped the clamps of the body armor into place. The armor adjusted again, first tightening against his chest before loosening enough to allow him to breathe. He looked down as he moved his arms around. The armor did have a sort of shifting color feature to it, almost like his eyes could quite decide what the true color was. He looked back up as Ben pulled the helmet from the manikin. It, too, was different from the others. Bandit's helmet was angular, with a sloping forehead that swept back into an almost pointed ridge. Ben's and Glitch's was more egg shaped, smoothly curved. The helmet Ben held in his hands had a smooth facemask with no distinction between the visor and the lower facial portion, except the shapes of two eyes. It had a short ridge above eye area which led to a smooth rounded head. It, too, showed the same color shifting that the other armor pieces displayed.

"The solid pieces of the armor have a solid, lightweight titanium alloy covered bay thousands of layers of woven spider silk Kevlar. You could take a fifty caliber standard round to the chest without it penetrating. The shock and force will still kill you, however, so I would avoid it if possible," Ben explained. Johnny looked up at him with a cocked eyebrow.

"Thanks, I'll remember that," Johnny replied. He shook his head in mock amazement. "Come on, a short walk will allow you to get used to the weight and way it shifts as you move," Ben said. He held the helmet under his arm and waved Johnny to the door. Johnny followed Ben out into the corridor, amazed at how so much armor could feel so light. If he had to guess, he would have said he was wearing no more than ten extra pounds of clothing. Ben led the group further down the corridor to a door at the end. He pressed he free hand against the side and waited for the door to open. Once it opened, he motioned Johnny in first. Johnny entered and a single bright light popped on over a small table at the center of the room, a pair of gloves with armored knuckles and fingers sat in the center. As he approached the table, he spotted a small envelope under the gloves. He stopped by the table and waited for Ben. Ben stepped up beside Johnny and set the helmet down. "Go ahead and put the gloves on."

Johnny looked at Ben for a moment, then picked up the gloves and slipped them over his hands. As soon as they were on, they began to mesh with the sleeves of the under armor until there was no way to tell where the gloves stopped and the sleeves started. The under armor adjusted again and became skin tight. The process continued throughout the rest of the under armor, causing it all to become skin tight around him. He flexed his fingers a few times, amazed that he could not tell that there was material over his skin. He looked up at Ben and nodded. Ben picked up the helmet and held it out to Johnny.

"Now this," Ben said reverently. Johnny took the helmet and moved it around in his hands, getting to know every millimeter of it. He turned it upside down and looked into the interior.

Unable to see much, he did see a thin screen between the armor and where his eyes would sit in the visors. "It's a tradition in the Minutemen, the offering of their first facemask, or in this case, their first helmet. By putting on the helmet, you swear to abandon your previous life, the identity you used to know. Minutemen swear to fight in the shadows, unknown, unacknowledged by the greater world. From this point forward, the only ones who will mourn your passing will be the men and women who stand beside you. We fight the evils no one wants to know about, the dangers hidden in outlandish conspiracy theories. We try to stop a threat before it becomes known. Now you must decide: will you accept the cost?"

Johnny stared into the helmet, letting the words sink in. An eternal battle began as his emotions fought back and forth, coming up with reasons not to accept. In the end, he squashed them all and lifted the helmet. He slid it over his head and let it settle into position, bathing Johnny in near darkness. Only the light filtering through the eye slits allowed him to still see Ben who stood in front of him. The padding around the base of the helmet extended and touched the neckline of the under armor, causing it to shift and merge together, truly sealing Johnny into his armor completely. He felt a surge of static electricity run from his chest over his skin and down his extremities. He felt the serge up his neck and then everything happened at once. Internal lights in the helmet snapped on, as well as the screen in front of his face. An internal diagnostics began to run, the display running on the screen.

MARK VIII STALKER V1.0
INTERNAL DIAGNOSTICS RUNNING…NO FAULT
EXTERNAL DIAGNOSTICS RUNNING…NO FAULT
USER INTERFACE DIAGNOSTICS RUNNING…NO FAULT
INTERNAL SYSTEMS STARTING…DONE
USER INTERFACE STARTING…DONE
EXTERNAL OPTIC SYSTEMS…SCANNING…CONNECTEDSYNCING
OPTICS SYSTEMS…WORKING…COMPLETEDISPLAY…ACTIVE
CALLSIGN: HUNTER
ACTIVE OBJECTIVE…UNKNOWN
INTEL…UNAVAILABLE

Johnny watched as the screen between his face and the exterior of the helmet dimmed and a set of displays appeared. The screen displayed temperature, current weapon interface, and optics from his eyes.

"The screen will work with your eyes. You'll get to the point where you won't be able to tell the difference between the two after a while. And let me be the first to welcome you to the Minutemen," Ben said, holding out his hand. Johnny took it and gave it a slight shake. "Now, to the exercise at hand. This is your last test before the Maze. I'm going to leave the room."

"Read the objectives on the note in the envelope. As soon as you have read the note, you'll have ten minutes to complete the course. Fail and you'll run it again later. It changes each time, so I suggest you complete it the first time around. Good luck."

Ben released Johnny's hand and moved to the door. He opened it and left, leaving Johnny alone. Johnny waited a few moments before turning to the envelope. He picked it up and tore the top off, amazed at the amount of fine motor control he had with the gloves. He pulled out the note and dropped the envelope back onto the table. He unfolded the sheet of paper and quickly read the instructions.

Welcome to the last exercise. You will have Ten Minutes to navigate the course of locked doors and computers. Your objective lies on an unmarked computer somewhere along the course. Find it, download it into your armor's internal databanks. Once you have the objective, make your way to the end of the course. Good Luck.

Johnny read the note once more to make sure he read his objectives correctly. As soon as he was done, he set the note down. A timer appeared in the top right corner of his display, starting at ten. It began to count down just as the lights snapped off. He blinked and his eyes automatically shifted to night vision. He saw a door across the table from him and moved to it. He grinned as he opened the door. He suddenly felt like he was truly having fun.

Ben watched the door close, before turning and walking to the next room. He opened the door, causing Glitch and Bandit to turn toward him. They both nodded their heads in greeting and stepped aside to let Ben move to the bank of monitors at the other end of the room. A familiar figure sat in the center seat, with Wildkat to his right. The chair to the left was empty, waiting for Ben. He nodded a greeting to Haywire and Flipswitch before taking his seat.

"Well said," Odin commented as Ben sat down. "He's just about ready to begin."

"I don't see why you gave him High Shot's prototype," Wildkat said dejectedly.

"Because it needed to be tested and it was designed to be worn by a Hunter," Ben replied, exasperated by the old argument.

"He could have been given a set of the old—" Wildkat began.

"Enough! He's starting his run," Odin said. All eyes turned to the monitor as Johnny opened the first door. They watched in silence as Johnny moved through the course with a seeming familiarity. He popped locks with ease and bypassed scanners in seconds as he made his way toward his objective. He was ahead of the estimated time by nearly a minute when he ran into his first obstacle. A mark twenty iris scanner. He first tried to fool the scanner with a simple shift in the color of his irises. When that didn't work, he tried to hack it remotely, causing the terminal to partially lock down. He ended up following the many wires until he found the two he needed. He spliced the power cable with the main terminal cable, causing the internal functions to short circuit and default to the open position. This burned up his lead, however, and costing him precious seconds. He picked up the pace as much as he could, working his way through the lasers in the next room, bending and twisting like a cat. He reached the other side and quickly picked the lock. He reached the room with the objective computer. The group watched as he pushed the tip of his pinky into a USB slot and waited ten seconds. He pulled his finger from the computer and move to the far door. He had recovered his lead, only twenty seconds this time as he made it through the door. He had two rooms left until the exit. He hacked the second to last door and stepped inside. Immediately, hundreds of laser trip wires snapped on. Johnny hesitated a second and then began to move forward. He made it a few feet, when the lasers began to move. Johnny slid to a stop just as one of the lasers cut a path in front of him.

The group watched as precious seconds ticked away and Johnny stood still, as if unsure what to do.

"He's not going to make it," Wildkat said, a slight tone of victory in her voice. She looked back at the screens, and was suddenly thankful she had her helmet on. Else the others would have seen her cheeks burn with embarrassment. Johnny had chosen that moment to rush forward, dodging and swaying around the lasers. He moved with such speed and intensity that it appeared that he had done the course before. He dropped into a slide as he neared the end and a pair of lasers cut in front of him at waist height. His slide was stopped short by the door at the end. He quickly stood and began to pick the lock. The timer ticked down to forty seconds when he popped the door open. The timer stopped as Johnny stepped into the following hallway, with thirty six seconds left.

"That's that," Odin said, standing from his chair. "How's he ranked?"

"First at the range, fourth on the course," Ben replied. "We won't know where his final rank is until he runs the maze tomorrow."

"Fine. Get him back to the residential floor and resting," Odin ordered. He turned and nodded to the others before walking to the door. He opened the door and stopped, he turned to the room. "I don't want any of you discussing how High Shot died with him until he completes his first mission, understood." A chorus of acknowledgements sounded from around the room.

Odin left the room and made his way to the elevator.

Johnny walked the remainder of the corridor, trying to bring his breathing back under control. He felt the adrenaline slamming through his veins like a drum. His eyes and the computer in his armor had calculated the speed and movement of the lasers, allowing him to make his way through without issue. He felt a twinge of pain from his knees with every step. He had misjudged the speed of his slide and ended up slamming into the wall harder than he wanted.

He made it to the end of the hall and opened the door. The next room contained a spiral staircase leading up. He began to climb the stairs, absentmindedly running through the different programs contained within the armor. He finally came to the landing at the top and saw another door. He stepped up to it and pushed. The door opened into the common room of the residential floor. He looked around. He was standing in the kitchen area. He stepped up to the counter and set his hands down on it. The door closed silently behind him, becoming flawless with the rest of the wall around it. He let out a couple of deep breaths, calming down. He reached up and found the three clasps holding his helmet on. He flipped them and waited for the under armor to separate. He felt the fibers pull away from themselves. He pulled the helmet up and over his head, setting it lightly down on the counter. He turned the face toward him, looking deep into the eyes for a moment. He turned from the helmet, stepping the few feet over to the refrigerator. He opened it, pulling a fresh cold bottle of water from it. He was closing the door, when the elevator doors opened. Ben led Haywire, Glitch, and Bandit off. Johnny pulled out four more bottles of water and set them on the counter. Ben and the others approached, reaching up and unlatching their own helmets. Ben pulled his off and set it on the counter in front of him. The others followed suit, accepting bottles of water from Johnny.

"Well done kid," Glitch said, opening the water and taking a long pull from it. Johnny nodded his thanks. He took a drink from his own bottle, savoring the taste, when the elevator opened once again. Flipswitch stepped off, carrying a small laptop. He walked with a purpose as he stepped around the edge of the counter and next to Johnny. He set the laptop down and opened it. It booted right up to a desktop menu. Flipswitch pulled out a USB cable and plugged one end into the laptop.

"First off, well done. You ranked fourth amongst the Minutemen currently serving," Flipswitch said. "Second, let's get that intel out of your armor. Turn around please."

Johnny picked up his bottle of water and turned his back to Flipswitch. He heard a slight scraping sound as the man behind him opened a section of

Johnny's armor. He heard the wire get plugged in, followed by a short electrical jolt in his back. His eyes flashed a bunch of lines of computer code, causing him to blink several times. A few seconds later, he felt a tug as the wire was pulled from his armor and then the click of the section closing again.

"There we go, all done," Flipswitch said. He turned back to the laptop and began typing.

Johnny turned back to the group in front of the counter.

"What now?" Johnny asked, looking at the clock on the wall. It was just after noon.

"Now we relax, or more specifically, you relax. You're running the Maze tomorrow, best to be relaxed until you run it," Bandit answered.

"And what is the Maze?" Johnny asked, suddenly feeling anxious as he saw all the knowing, mischief smiles around him.

"Can't tell you that, sorry," Glitch said. "But for now, get out of that armor and relax. I'll cook us up a big lunch and we'll just sit back and chill." Johnny nodded and walked around the counter, picking up his helmet. He moved toward his door, feeling, for the first time since joining, a bit apprehensive.

Johnny was woken by Ben early the next morning. He was told to get a shower and dressed, get breakfast, and then head to the ground floor. Johnny nodded, suddenly wide awake. He grabbed a fresh towel from his dresser and headed for the shower. His dreams the night before and thoughts while standing under the hot spray was convoluted with memories of the past and imagining what the future held. He rinsed the soap from his body and shut the shower off, using the towel to quickly dry his body. He wrapped the towel around his waist and pulled the screen back to step out. He looked down to ensure the towel wouldn't slip off. When he looked up, he became so startled he nearly slipped and fell. Wildkat was leaning against the wall across from the shower, her arms crossed in front of her. She wasn't wearing her helmet, allowing Johnny to see her face for the first time. Her brunette hair was cut in a pixie style, her hazel colored eyes shone brightly as she stared at him. Her lips were compressed in a tight line as her delicate nose twitched from her breath. Her fair skin shone slightly in the light.

"How long have you been standing there?" Johnny asked, taking hold of the knotted end of the towel to ensure it would stay in place. He saw her eyes flit up and down his body.

"Not long. Just wanted to wish you good luck in the Maze today. And…just rely on your instincts. They've served you well so far," She replied. She pushed herself off the wall and stared at Johnny for a few moments. She turned and headed for the exit. She stopped at the door and turned, a small, sly grin on her face. "Now I know what all the fuss was about for Haywire."

With that, she pushed the door open and left. Johnny stood there, stunned for a few moments, just staring at the door. He couldn't be sure, but felt that Wildkat was warming up to him. He shook himself out of his thoughts and moved to the exit of the shower room, pushing the door open. He was slightly surprised to find the main room empty. He quickly made his way back to his room. He tossed the towel into the corner and started pulling the drawers open.

He paused when he saw a small note on the top of the dresser. He quickly read it and set it back down.

Johnny-

Cammies and combat boots. The rest of your gear will be waiting for you at the Maze.

-Ben

Johnny pulled a set of black cammies from the bottom drawer, along with the normal tan boots the Marines wore. He closed the bottom drawer and pulled the second one open. He pulled a pair of his boxers, a pair of black socks, and an undershirt out. He quickly dressed, leaving only the blouse of the camouflaged utilities off. He quickly put the boots on and laced them up, using the elastic bands around the tops of the boots to blouse the bottom of the trousers. He closed the second drawer and pulled the top open. He dug around inside until he found the Captain's bars he had worn before out. He carefully attached them to the collar of the blouse and stepped back to inspect his work. Satisfied he got it right, he picked up the blouse and left the room. He set the blouse on the back of the couch and went to the kitchen area. He made himself a light breakfast and sat down at the table. Though he didn't particularly feel like eating, he knew he had to. He quickly finished his bowl of cereal and washed it down with coffee. He washed out the dishes and set them off to the side.

He walked back to the couch and picked up the blouse, quickly donning it and securing the buttons. He walked over to the elevator and pressed his hand to the side and waited. The doors opened silently and he stepped inside. He told the computer he needed to go to the ground floor and waited. The doors closed and he felt the elevator descend quickly. A few minutes later, he felt the elevator come to a stop. The doors opened and he stepped out. He didn't see anyone standing around the elevator, so he decided to check the door Ben had first showed him. He set off down the hall, nearly reaching the door, when a voice stopped him in his tracks.

"You the hunter?" a male voice called out, a Cajun tang in it. Johnny stopped and turned around. A stocky, bearded man stood at the end of the hall where Johnny had first come from.

Johnny walked back to the man. He stopped a couple of feet from him. The man wore the same type of utilities Johnny wore, the only difference was a set of golden oak leaves on the collar. The name on the blouse read Le Phantome. His eyes identified him as Charles Le Phantome, Major, United States Marine Corps.

"Yes," Johnny answered. Le Phantome smiled broadly, his perfectly white teeth in contrast with his dark skin. Johnny saw shades of gray permeate his chest long beard and the temples of his crew cut hair. He held out his hand. Johnny took it and gave it a short shake, feeling the calluses on the other man's hand.

"Junker," Le Phantome replied. He released Johnny's hand and motioned for Johnny to follow. Johnny fell in step behind the man as he led Johnny to a second door.

"Junker?" Johnny asked. Junker turned his head and looked over his shoulder at Johnny. "Yep. I handle all the vehicles for the Minutemen," Junker answered. "If it drive, flies, swims, or dives, I build them, maintain them, and repair them."

The two men left the building and stepped out onto the sidewalk. Johnny reached into his cargo pocket and pulled the cover for his utilities out. He flipped it to open it back up and placed it on his head. Junker led them across the sidewalk to a HMMV sitting idle alongside the sidewalk. Junker walked around the back of the HMMV and opened the driver's side door.

"Get in," he ordered. Johnny nodded and opened the passenger door with a heave. He got in and pulled the door closed with a bang. Junker settled in the driver's seat and pulled his door closed as well. He adjusted his position and then pressed a button. The HMMV lurched forward into gear and Junker pressed the accelerator. Johnny looked out the window and saw hundreds of soldiers and marines walking along the sidewalk, going about their lives. He saw a few laughing, joking with each other, while others looked sullen. "Survivors." Junker said, bringing Johnny's attention back to the present.

"Survivors?" Johnny asked. Junker nodded.

"Most of those men and women out there just got here. They mostly come from the Army's 223rd and 387th armored. They were protecting the Denver line. Massive artillery barrage by the Imperials nailed them pretty good. They were evacuated from their positions, most went to the Denver fall back, but more than a few ended up here," Junker explained. Johnny nodded and looked back out the window. Junker took a quick look at Johnny as he turned a corner. "Itching to get back out there, yea?"

"Just a bit," Johnny said softly. They drove the rest of the way in silence. Junker pulled up in front of a large set of warehouses and came to a stop. He put the HMMV in park and looked at Johnny.

"Go inside that door there," Junker said, pointing toward the nearest door to the warehouse. "There will be instructions inside, as well as the gear you'll need. Good luck, son, you're going to need it."

Johnny nodded his thanks and opened the door. He stepped out into the cold and closed the door with a bang. He walked calmly to the door of the warehouse and gripped the handle. He paused for a moment, a thought of self-doubt began to form in his mind. He quickly stifled it and twisted the handle. He pulled the door open and stepped inside. There was nothing but darkness as the door shut behind him. He blinked quickly and switched his vision to night mode. The room was about the size of the bedroom he had been using. A door at the far side of the room had a set of lockers next to it. Johnny took a step toward the lockers, when a set of words scrolled in front of his eyes.

WELCOME TO THE MAZE, HUNTER OPERATIVE YOUR ARMOR IS IN THE FIRST LOCKER
THE SECOND WILL BE FOR STORING YOUR CURRENT ATTIRE
THE THIRD CONTAINS ALL EQUIPMENT NECESSARY FOR THE COMPLETION OF THE MAZE
YOUR OBJECTIVE IS AT THE END OF THE MAZE UTILIZE ALL THE SKILLS YOU HAVE LEARNED THUS FAR YOU HAVE TWENTY MINUTES TO COMPLETE THE MAZE GOOD LUCK

Johnny read the lines quickly and moved to the lockers. He opened the first and second lockers. He felt a thrill of excitement as he saw his armor hanging in the locker. He pulled the utilities off quickly and stored them in the locker neatly folded. He put the boots in the bottom of the locker and closed it. He pulled out the armor and just as quickly as he undressed, he donned his armor. He slipped the boots and gloves on, feeling complete as the armor tightened back to skin tight levels. He pulled the helmet out and placed it on his head, feeling the under armor completely seal. He waited as the armor powered on. His visor powered up, switching to night vision as well. He stretched his fingers back and forth and rolled his shoulders. He felt a level of confidence he never noticed before. He turned and stepped up to the third locker. He opened it and looked inside. A rifle hung from the hook in the back of the locker. He looked at the shelf above and found a pistol. He pulled the pistol out of the locker and watched as both his eyes and the armor synched up with the pistol's software. His program identified the pistol as a MP456 semi-automatic pistol. The magazine was loaded with mark seven training rounds.

Each round delivered a debilitating shock to whomever it hit. Johnny checked the chamber, ensured the safety was on, and then placed the pistol against his right thigh. He heard a set of clicks as the armor extended a series of clips to keep the pistol in place. He checked to top of the locker and found five magazines for the pistol. He placed them along his right forearm, watching as a set of clips locked them into place. He shook his arm to ensure they stayed, then pulled the rifle from the locker. His program identified it as a Colt Arms M816 battle rifle with a thirty round magazine. He found a pouch of seven magazines in the back of the locker and used his left hand to attach them to his chest. He hefted the rifle and stepped toward the door.

He stepped up to the door and ran a quick scan on it. No security devices, nor visible traps. He gripped the handle with his right hand, using his left to keep his rifle shouldered. He twisted the knob and pushed the door open. His instincts screamed at him to drop as soon as the door opened. He listened and dove forward, landing behind a stack of barrels as several rounds split the air where he had been a second before. He brought his feet around and rose into a sitting position, his pulse slamming in his veins from the burst of adrenaline his body gave him. He blinked twice, switching from night vision to infrared. He looked around his position, hoping to locate the laser sight he thought he got a glimpse of. He grinned as he spotted the thin line of light. He followed it back over the barrel until he got to a position where he was going to risk exposing his position. He gripped his rifle tightly as he ran the connection program between his eyes and the tiny camera at the tip of the forward sight. His eyes snapped to a new view, the barrel of the rifle extending from the bottom of his vision. He inched it around the side of the barrel to his left. His vision was slightly distorted for him as he tried to adjust minutely from the buttstock, causing more wild movements at the barrel. He steadied it and finished the turn. He spotted the laser sight once more and followed its path back to the shooter. He could see the shooter's shoulders and head sticking up over a stack of what appeared to be lumber. Johnny steadied his hands and, in turn, the sight of his rifle. He rested the crosshair on the figure's head and let out a breath. He squeezed the trigger twice, muscling the rifle to keep it from jumping out of his hands. The rifle barked twice, close enough to sound like one long shot, two shell casings flew from the ejector to clatter along the ground. He brought the rifle back under control in time to see the figure jerk twice as the electrically charged rounds impacted them. Johnny grinned as he spun to his feet and rushed forward, blinking to return his vision from the front of his rifle to his normal eyes, he blinked again to switch his vision back to night vision.

He took a look at his surroundings as he moved deeper into the room. The warehouse was open, with hundreds of pieces of equipment and debris lying about to provide cover and hiding spots. He made it forty meters toward the center, when rounds sparked off the floor to his immediate left. Johnny dove to the right behind a forklift as more rounds ricocheted off the metal. Johnny popped up over the top of the forklift's hood and swung his gaze toward the location where the shots came from. He spotted three figures dodge between places of cover, moving toward him. A fourth was kneeling on a gantry twenty feet off the ground. Johnny ducked again as the sniper swung his rifle in Johnny's direction and let loose a small burst. Johnny heard the rounds hit the hood and a few flew off over his head. Johnny popped back up and quick spotted the sniper, firing off three rounds in quick succession. He ducked down to avoid the next burst of incoming fire. He looked around, knowing he had to move, or risk getting cornered. He spotted an open hatch in the floor. Hoping it was a trench used by mechanics, Johnny sprinted from his cover as another burst rattled against the lift. He dropped to a slide as he reached the hatch. He felt a tug in his gut as he dropped into the hatch. He dropped to his knees with a thud. He looked up and smiled. It was indeed a mechanic's trench. It ran most of the length of the warehouse, and in this case, ran toward his objective. He moved in a crouch as fast and silently as he could, looking back occasionally to ensure he wasn't being followed.

"Where the hell did he go?" Glitch called over the team's comm. He had rushed the final dozen yards to flank the newest operative. He spun around the back of the forklift, leveling his battle rifle, relishing the moment when he would let a burst fly into the unfortunate young man's back. Instead, he found nothing but a few spent shell casings. He pressed his hand against the side of his helmet and spoke again. "Anyone see where he went? Flipswitch? Haywire?"

"Flipswitch has been neutralized. Johnny put all three rounds into his chest. Stitches is down as well," Haywire answered. "I didn't see him move. Looks like he got by us." Glitch turned and looked at Haywire and Junker, both walking calmly toward Glitch's position, both looking behind every scrap of cover, hoping they saw Johnny before Johnny saw them.

"Odin, be advised, Hunter slipped the snare," Glitch said, looking at his two companions. "He's headed your way."

"Copy," came the gruff reply. Glitch was about to ask where he and the other two should redeploy, when Junker jerked to his left, two stun rounds taking him in the chest. Glitch spun toward the shots, just as Haywire dropped, taking three to her back. Glitch dropped to his knee and swept his gaze along the warehouse in front of him. He squinted as he thought he saw a shadow move against another shadow. There were three quiet flashes, illuminating the oil drums the barrel was sticking out from. Glitch felt as though he had been hit with a set of hammers as the rounds impacted his chest plate. The sensation was immediately followed by an intense burning sensation as the electricity was discharged through his torso. He gritted his teeth as the stun rounds immobilized him. The last thought to run through his head before he passed out was how?

"Glitch, Haywire, and Junker are down," Wildkat's voice came over the comm. Odin nodded silently as he looked over the warehouse.

"Hunter?" He asked.

"Unknown," she responded. "He flanked them somehow and dropped all three. He's ghosted again. You think he can get by you?"

"Maybe," Odin answered, a smile forming on his face. He hadn't seen such a talented new operative in decades. He squinted toward Wildkat's position, unsure if he saw the movement he thought he saw. "Kat?"

"I got him," Wildkat answered. He watched as she dropped from her elevated position behind where they had seen the movement. He watched the area for a couple seconds, before he saw two flashes. The open comm channel between himself and Wildkat deteriorated into static for a few moments. "Wildkat is down," Odin said flatly. He rolled his shoulders, preparing to face his newest charge. He felt exhilarated at the opportunity.

Johnny moved slowly down the corridor made by the giant containers on either side of him. He had stowed the rifle onto his back when he moved into the confined area. He held his pistol in both hands, its barrel sweeping the area in front of him. He was feeling extremely pumped after flanking the last three figures. He thought about leaving them alone, but figured it would be better to ensure they couldn't follow rather than hoping they wouldn't. He was nearing the end of the corridor, when he suddenly felt that he was walking into a trap. He paused and looked around his immediate area. He spotted a darker corner than the surrounding area and moved into it. He turned his back to the corner and took a knee. He slowed his breathing and quieted it to a whisper. He strained his ears, trying to detect any kind of sounds around him. He tilted his head slightly as he heard the shuffle of fabric against metal, just as whisper, followed by the slight creak of a stressed, taught strap. He stilled his breathing all together as the sound approached. He placed his index finger against the trigger and steadied himself. He narrowed his eyes as a shadow passed above him. A figure dropped from above at the end of the corridor. They made no noise upon landing. Johnny gave them a heartbeat of a pause, allowing them to stand slightly, giving him a larger target. He pointed the barrel of his pistol at the figure and squeezed the trigger twice, the pistol barked and bucked in his twice, illuminating the corner he was crouching in, slightly washing out his vision. The figure jerked twice and dropped to the ground. Johnny nodded and turned away.

He stood and walked to the end of the corridor. He navigated the twists and turns of the warehouse, making his way toward his objective. He stopped as he spotted a small dome in the center with a single door. He crouched next to a stack of tires and shifted his gaze around the open space between his position and the door. He started to stand again when he saw three flashes out of the corner of his eye. He dove behind the tires just as the three rounds hit them with dull thuds. He used his arms to move him further into cover. He got to his knees and peered over the stack of tires. He ducked again when two more flashes from the muzzle of a weapon lit up the opposite side of the clearing. Johnny moved in a crouch, turning around and moving from the tires to a stack of metal crates. Three more rounds split the air behind him. He moved quietly, listening for any other movement besides his own. He held out his pistol as he reached the corner of the stack. His barrel had just cleared the edge, when a hand reached around and pulled him off balance. He jerked forward, nearly losing his balance completely and falling on his face. His pistol was pulled from his grip and tossed away. He heard it clatter against the floor meters away. Johnny regained his balance in time to see another pistol being brought up to fire. Johnny, reacting quickly, struck out and grabbed the top of the pistol. He pushed the slide back, ejecting the chambered round. He used his index finger to flip the release catch. He pulled the slide toward his body, pulling it from the rest of the pistol completely. He tossed the slide away as he threw a punch with his other hand. The figure he was fighting blocked the strike with the now useless weapon.

Johnny brought his free hand back around to block his opponent's follow up strike. They sparred back and forth for long minutes, each striking and countering, trying to force a mistake. Johnny thought he had gained the upper hand when he felt his latest strike hit his opponent's chest with a solid thud. His victory was short lived, however, as his opponent grabbed his arm and twisted his torso, pulling Johnny off his feet. As Johnny lost his balance, his opponent swept their foot forward, kicking Johnny's legs out from under him. Johnny's eyes widened as he fell forward. He used his free hand to catch his fall, turning it into a roll as he ducked his shoulder. His opponent was forced to let go of Johnny's arm, lest he get pulled down as well. Johnny hit his shoulder against the floor, swinging his legs up to bring himself all the way around. His hand now free, Johnny swung it behind his back and gripped the pistol grip of his rifle. He gave it a small tug, disengaging the clips. He completed the roll and came up to a kneeling position. He spun toward his opponent, bringing his rifle to his shoulder. He knew he had no time to actually aim, so he just pointed the barrel in the general direction of his opponent and squeezed the trigger twice. His opponent had started to launch himself forward, trying to take advantage of the situation he created. He stopped short as Johnny spun to face him, rifle leveled. He tried to dodge, but he was not quick enough. The rifle barked twice, bouncing against Johnny's shoulder. The force of the rounds impacting his opponent's chest threw him backward to the ground. His unconscious body slid into the darkness. Johnny took a couple of deep breaths, trying to calm his nerves and slow his pulse. He slowly stood and thumbed the safety back on. He slowly turned, his instincts on high alert, searching the shadows for any more movement.

He approached the door to the dome slowly, his rifle sweeping back and forth, following his gaze. He stopped by the door and ran a scan on it. He found it contained a simple tumbler lock and an electronic seal in the frame. Johnny set the rifle to the side of the door. He pulled the side of the frame off with a heave. He quickly pulled a bundle of wires out and searched for the two he needed. Upon finding them, he scraped the covering from the wires and pressed them together, shorting out the electronic seal. He released the wires and took a step to the side. He dropped to a knee and reached under the forearm piece of his right arm and pulled his lock picks from a built in sleeve. He quickly worked the picks in the lock, setting the tumblers to their open positions. He grinned as the last tumbler clicked open. He pulled the picks from lock and replaced them in their sleeve. He retrieved his rifle and stood. He placed his finger on the trigger and tucked buttstock under his arm, keeping it tight and level. He gripped the door handle and readied himself for anything. He twisted the handle and shoved the door open, preparing to fire. He relaxed when he found an empty room with a central pillar standing a few feet up from the floor. He lowered the barrel as he approached the pillar. A small red button was placed at its center. Johnny stepped up next to the pillar and looked at the button. His eyes widened as a new set of orders crossed his eyes.

Press the button

Johnny arced an eyebrow as he read the words. He shrugged and reached out and pressed the button. The lights above him snapped on, washing out his vision. Johnny turned away and blinked several times, returning his vision to normal. A buzzer sounded throughout the warehouse, echoing off the empty spaces. The sound of mechanical locks unlatching echoed around the dome, followed by the walls lowering. Johnny brought his rifle to his shoulder and spun it around as a new sound arose. He quickly relaxed as he recognized the sound as clapping hands. He lowered his rifle as the wall in front of him lowered, revealing the Minutemen he had been training with standing in a line, clapping loudly. All except for the center operator. Johnny didn't recognized him. His armor was thick, almost as thick as Glitches. It was scratched and dented in areas, showing a lot of use and experience. Johnny looked closer at the operator's helmet. It showed a skull with its right eye covered by an eyepatch. He stood as tall as Johnny, but was wider at the shoulders.

"Well done, Son. Been a long while since someone bested me in a one on one," the operator said. "Nice move with the rifle." He stepped forward, lowering his hands. "My name is Odin. I lead the Minutemen. I want to officially welcome you to the unit. Ready to put the kid's toys away and get down to the real thing?"

Johnny grinned behind his facemask and lifted his rifle and set it on his shoulder. "Let's do this," Johnny replied.

Johnny followed Odin and Ben out of the elevator back in the Liberty Barracks. They were driven straight back by Junker after they changed into their military utilities. Johnny noticed the three stars on Odin's collar. They stepped off on to the second floor, heading toward a door halfway down the corridor. Johnny waited silently as Ben pressed his hand against the wall next to the door and waited until it unlocked. He pushed the door open and waited for Odin to enter first. Johnny followed Odin, with Ben bringing up the rear. The room was filled with computers, monitors, and data banks. A large, solid metal table sat in the center. The computers and monitors displays hundreds of different screens with thousands of different pieces of data. Odin walked around the far side of the table and placed his hands on the top of it. A hum of electricity sounded from the center of the table as the top began to glow.

"Johnny, I wish we had time to celebrate your joining, but unfortunately we don't have time," Odin said. His face showed his age as he stared into Johnny's eyes. "We'll arrange for a small celebration when you get back. Has Ben explained what a Hunter does for the Minutemen?"

"A bit, yes. Hunters take on a multitude of missions involving many different skill sets."

"They can be sent out into the field for extended periods of time," Johnny answered. Odin nodded and waved his hand over the table. A hologram program began to run. A dozen screens popped up over the table. He reached out and pressed a hand against one particular screen. The others dissolved, leaving the one Odin chose. The image expanded showing a list of names. Johnny estimated that there were nearly a hundred names on the list. The first ten were red, while the rest were blue.

"Hunters are some of our best operators. The current mission we had assigned High Shot hasn't been issued in over one hundred years, not since world war two," Odin said. He waved at the list. "This list contains all the names of Imperial officers, diplomats, known agents, and so called heroes of this war. Almost every one of these men and women have committed atrocities in the name of their emperor and their own base desires. Removing them from the field would damage their war effort and allow the United States forces to make their push back toward the coast. While your mission objectives will vary, you will have one constant objective from here on out: Kill the people on this list. Do you understand?" Johnny peered at the names for a moment, seeing the possibilities and the path his future was about to take. He looked from the list to Odin's eyes. He stared at the older man for a moment before answering.

"Yes."

Odin nodded. "Good. Now down to business." He pressed three names on the list. The rest of the list dissolved, leaving the three names hanging in midair: Tajiko Myn, Shen Myn, and Ken Myn. The names dropped down near the top of the table and spread out, leaving a few inches in between. A picture appeared above each name. The pictures showed Asian men around the same age. The man on the left sported a large burn on his left cheek, the center man sported a full beard, and the one on the right was clean shaven with an arrogant smirk on his face. "These three men lead the Imperial's famous Tiger Companies."

"Tiger Companies?" Johnny asked. Odin nodded.

"Officially the Alpha, Bravo, and Charlie companies of the infamous 344th armored division, first battalion. They led the assault through the streets of San Francisco and the complete destruction of two small towns outside the city," Odin said, waving his hand over the table. The pictures shrank in size and more images scrolled across, showing battle scenes of tanks firing upon entrenched positions and American troops. "Five weeks ago, one of our infiltration specialists managed to recover a set of orders. The orders were for these three to lead their companies to Denver and begin the Imperial siege of the city, breaching the Line and making way for the rest of the Imperial forces to move through the mountains and into the Midwest."

"We've been monitoring their movements and have concluded that they are indeed on their way. The Imperial army has already begun their artillery barrage against the city. Damage has been minimal, but that could change quickly. The pentagon is worried that the barrage will cause severe avalanches around Denver, burying the defensive positions under tons of snow and ice. Best estimate is that they will make their approach up the 106 super freeway. It is the widest path through the mountains still passable. The remains of the US 64th and 37th armored still clutter the lanes, but their front ranks, according to satellite imagery, are made up of modified Rampage assault tanks with dozer blades on the front. It will allow them to clear the snow, ice, and dead vehicles for the rest of them." A map overlay appeared above them, showing the super freeway the United States built at the beginning of the century in red. It was supposed to allow quick and easy travel from Los Angeles to New York without the worry of congestion. Now it could spell the end of America all together. The imagery showed hundreds of boxy shapes, covered in snow, littering all twelve lanes. They became congested as they neared the pass cut into a mountain, the high walls of rock giving way to the natural slope at the top. Johnny stared at those slopes as an idea began to form.

"Your primary mission will be to slow down the advance of this assault any way you can," Odin continued. "We passed our Intel up, and the pentagon is moving on it, but the arrival of the joint armored task force is estimated three hours after the Tiger companies begin their assault. That's where you come in. We need to stall them for three hours, at least. Your standing orders are, of course, to kill these three commanders as well."

"Their crimes?" Johnny asked curious. Odin looked at him, contemplating his answer. "Torture, murder of five hundred civilians, slavery, and rape. The two older ones like to force all women they capture into their personal harems," Odin said, anger laced his words. "According to our intel, Tajiko likes them really young. Ken, the youngest, has an affinity for torture. Gets off on it."

Johnny felt his anger flare up at the list of charges. It no longer mattered that they were enemy commanders. Their removal from existence would be a blessing upon the world.

"Let's get going then," Johnny said calmly. Odin nodded.

"From here, Junker will take you to the air field. Your armor and an assortment of available equipment will be in the hangar. Our pilot will take you to this spot, two miles up the freeway from the pass." Odin explained, pointing to Johnny's drop off point. "Our best estimates is that you will have six hours to prepare your ambush. You'll be alone out there, so be careful. Once your objectives are complete, make your way to the extraction here, five miles to the south east. We'll pick you up on your signal."

"How will I know when it is time to bug out?" Johnny asked.

"We'll send a transmission once the task force has arrived. Then you'll know. Any other questions?" Odin asked. Johnny shook his head. "Ok then, good luck and we'll see you when you get back." He walked around the holo-table and held out his hand. Johnny took it and gave it a short, but firm shake. He turned to Ben and nodded, then headed for the door. Ben waited until the door was fully closed before speaking.

"Think he's going to make it back?" Ben asked. Odin turned to his longtime friend and gave a rare smile.

"I think our fortunes in the war have just turned to our favor," Odin said, turning back to the door, and the young man he just sent to kill a whole lot of enemy soldiers.

Johnny was silent as he left the Barracks and climbed into Junker's HMMV. He simply stared out the window, running all the available intel the Minutemen had through his vision. Maps, weather models, enemy disposition and numbers, vehicle types and armaments, and the time table for the task force. He noted that his three targets always rode in the same three vehicles during every engagement: A customized Rampage heavy tank, a customized Spider light assault vehicle, and a heavily modified Niu, or Ox, Command Vehicle. The Rampage tank had been modified with a third cannon and a mark six Hammer rocket pod system. The Spider had three mark fourteen Heavy Storm 34milimeter auto cannons and two mark eight railguns. The Ox Command Vehicle had a communication scrambler antenna on it, as well as an experimental reflective armor covering, making it nearly invisible to scanning devices and immune to laser guided weapons. Johnny brought up known and estimated schematics of the three vehicles. He highlighted specific details and weak spots in each one.

Junker pulled through the gate, accessing the airfield. A pair of soldiers saluted them as they passed. Johnny looked forward out the windshield, watching helicopters and VTOLs take off and land. Troops moved between the aircraft, some carrying tools, others geared for combat missions. Junker maneuvered around corners and parked vehicles, closing in on a lone hangar at the back of the field. He pulled around to the side and put the armored vehicle in park. He motioned, silently, for Johnny to follow. Johnny opened the door and stepped out into the cold air. He felt the wind blow by him, the smell of fresh snow carried by it. Johnny stepped around the HMMV and walked toward the door to the hangar. Junker stopped and opened the door, waiting for Johnny to step in first. Johnny stepped in and his eyes adjusted automatically. The hangar contained four separate aircraft: a Viper fast attack helicopter, a Wildcat interceptor, an Imperial Typhoon fast attack helicopter, and a Twister VTOL assault craft. Junker stepped in beside Johnny.

"Your armor is in there," Junker said, pointing toward a small building ten feet to their right. Johnny nodded and headed toward the door to it. He opened it and a grinned formed on his face. His armor sat on a table in the small room, laid out nice and neat for him. His helmet sat in the center, its facemask toward him. The mask's face was no longer blank. A pair of eyes had been painted over the visor slots. A thin line had been drawn through the right eye. Johnny stepped up to the table and looked closer at the eyes. He had thought they were different, and he had been right. Instead of a pair of normal, human eyes or even the eyes of a devilish creature, they were the eyes of one of the world's most perfect hunters. They were the eyes of a wolf, their amber green irises fading in and out in the light. Johnny turned from the table and began to undress. He folded the utilities and set them neatly on the table beside his armor. He quickly dressed in his armor, sliding his gloves on, feeling them tighten against his skin. He flexed his fingers, feeling the under armor against him. He picked up his helmet, staring into the eyes for a moment. He turned the helmet over and slid it over his head, surrendering his identity to the Hunter he was to become. Johnny felt the under armor seal around his neck and turned from the table, feeling invulnerable and complete. He left the room, finding Glitch standing outside waiting on him.

"Ready to arm up?" Glitch asked. Johnny nodded. Glitch waved at him to follow and turned toward the center of the hangar. Johnny and Glitch passed Haywire and the others as they moved about, carrying equipment or loading magazines. Johnny nodded to them as they greeted him. Glitch stepped up to a stack of weapons crates and turned toward Johnny. "Each crate holds a variety of weapons you can use, basically every weapon we have access to that is. Choose what you want or can carry. I'll get you anything that isn't here. Choose wisely."

Glitch stepped to the side and watched as Johnny stepped forward. The next hour was spent going through each crate. Johnny chose his modified hunting rifle, both of his modified pistols, a MXB-566 battle rifle, and a next generation Arc-1226 double barreled repeating shotgun with the barrels cut down to eight inches, mimicking his old side by side double barreled shotgun. As he made his choices, Glitch retrieved magazines of ammo for each. Johnny set the weapons on a nearby crate and began to place the magazines on his armor. He felt a little bit of the weight pulling him down. He picked up the first pistol and loaded a full magazine into the well. He pulled the slide back and racked the first round. He placed it against his right thigh and heard the clamps engage, holding it in place. He repeated the process with the second pistol, placing it against his left thigh until the clamps engaged. He picked up the shotgun and loaded eight of the stubby rounds into the well under the barrels. He pulled the hammers back, loading the first two rounds into the barrels. He engaged the safety between the hammers and the firing pins and swung the weapon behind his back. He held the side of the weapon against the armor on his back and felt the clamps engage. He loaded his hunting rifle and swung it over his shoulder, letting the clamps lock it into place over his left shoulder. He picked up the battle rifle and a fresh magazine. He slid it into the well with a satisfying click. He pulled the charging handle back, letting the bolt slam forward, inserting the first round into the chamber.

"Got everything?" Glitch asked, watching. Johnny looked at the rifle, then at Glitch as a thought crossed his mind.

"I could use thirty of your most powerful explosive charges," Johnny replied. Glitch chuckled as he stood up and walked a few feet away. He picked up a small crate and carried it over to where Johnny had loaded up his weapons. He set it down and pulled the lid off.

"Here ya go. Fifty packs of HXC456. Combination of high explosives in a small pack. Two of these will drop just about any normal three story building. These are the brain child of another one of our Minutemen," Glitch explained, pulling what looked to be a hockey puck from the crate. "Press the center here, twist clockwise, each click is five minutes, or press the button a second time to set the charge to remote. A third press of the button shuts the charge down." He handed the charge to Johnny, then cocked his head to the side. "What are you planning on doing with these?" Johnny grinned behind his facemask as he looked from the charge to Glitch.

"They want me to stall the enemy advance…I'm going to stall their advance," Johnny replied. He pulled thirty of the charges out and stacked them next to the crate. "Gonna need a bag."

"Here," a voice said from behind him. Johnny turned to see Haywire and Wildkat standing there. Haywire was holding out the pack he was wearing before he ended up in the hospital. He took the bag from her, hearing pieces of metal bang into each other. He set the battle rifle down and opened the pack. He reached in and felt the familiar grip of his hatchet. He pulled it out and held it up, turning it in front of his face. He reached back and held the bladed weapon against his back. His armor recognized the pressure and engaged a set of clamps, securing it to his back. He pulled the second one out and repeated the process. He looked from Wildkat to Haywire.

"Thanks," He told them, trying to keep the emotion he was feeling out of his voice. He turned back to the crate and loaded up the thirty charges. He closed the pack and slung it over his right shoulder. He felt the armor's clamps snag the strap and back of the pack, holding it in place. He picked up his battle rifle and looked around. The others stood around him, nodding there approval.

"Ready to go, hoss," a twangy voice said from behind the girls. A tall, lanky figure stepped around a stack of missiles and next to Haywire. His armor was the thinnest Johnny had yet seen. His helmet had a full faced visor, a twisted devilish face with spiraling eyes adorned the mask. Johnny looked at the new comer and nodded.

"Hunter, this is Screwball. He's going to be your ride in and out of this mission," Haywire said. "He's a bit...unusual."

"Says who?" Screwball said, looking at the smaller woman. He turned back to Johnny. "Let's go, ride's outside." He turned and walked toward the exit. Johnny looked once more at the Minutemen around him and nodded before following. He was stepping by Haywire when she grabbed his forearm. Johnny looked at her.

"Be careful," She whispered. Johnny nodded and she released his arm. He looked away and continued to the exit. The others stood there for a few moments, watching his retreating form. Johnny pushed the door open and stepped outside behind Screwball. Snow had begun to fall, its flakes were light and airy, but Johnny knew that could change in a moment. Screwball led Johnny around to the front of the hangar, where a Twister VTOL sat on a pad. Its panels and baffles were blank of any identification numbers nor military descriptions. The ramp at the back was down as Johnny and Screwball approached. The cargo area was empty, with the exception of a single seat near the wall separating the cockpit from the rest of the aircraft.

"You'll sit there," Screwball said, motioning to the empty seat. "Sit down, strap in, and switch your freq to one one nine." Johnny nodded and looked at the radio frequency designator at the top left of his vision. He sent the thought to change it to what he was told. He watched as the frequency changed. His ears filled with static as he sat down in the seat. "Can you hear me?"

"Yes," Johnny answered. He looked to the rear of the VTOL as the ramp began to close.

An intense hum began to shake the aircraft as the engines fired up. "Not very talkative are ya?"

"No."

"Fair enough," Screwball chuckled. The humming became higher pitched as the engines reached full power. He felt the rumble through the seat as the high powered engines pushed the craft from the ground. The rumble lessened slightly as they gained altitude. "Flight time is going to be just under ninety minutes. Relax and enjoy the ride."

"Thanks." Johnny replied. He began to run the intel through his vision again, getting lost in his thoughts.

"Prepare to touch down," Screwball said over the radio, jerking Johnny back to reality. He had been inspecting the topographical maps provided in his intelligence brief, finalizing his plans. He gripped his battle rifle as the VTOL shook again. The ramp began to descend, sending a blast of frigid air and loose snow at him. "Annnnnd…touchdown." Johnny felt the solid thud as the VTOL's pads hit the snow. "Screwball has touched down at insertion point Alpha."

Johnny hit the release on the straps holding him in his seat. He slowly stood, rolling his shoulders to loosen them up. He walked slowly toward the ramp, his footfalls unusually loud in the bay, even with the engines running. He reached the back of the ramp and looked out at the terrain. They had landed in a snow covered clearing surrounded by trees. The forest all around were bleak and gray, their tops heavy with already fallen snow. He took a deep breath, feeling the chill in the air through the filters in the facemask. He lifted his foot and took a step off the ramp. His footstep crunched as his weight compacted the snow beneath him. He took a few more steps, feeling the blast of the engines at his back. He looked to the sky, watching the snow heavy clouds crawl across the sky.

"Hunter has entered the field," Johnny said. He hefted his rifle, turned toward the north and set off at a run, heading for the trees.

"Copy, Hunter. Set off your beacon when you get to the extraction point and I'll come get you," Screwball answered. "Good luck and good hunting."

Johnny heard the comm switch off in his ears as he picked up his pace. He determined that the snow was thick and sturdy enough to keep him from getting bogged down. He kept his ears open and his eyes scanning the terrain around him, searching for any sign of life. He made it to the trees as the VTOL cleared the top of the trees and turned east, rocketing back toward the Line. Johnny slowed as he reached the trees, warily casting his gaze about, looking for signs of an ambush. He quickly found a deer path through the snow and decided to take it. He began to run again, hoping to make it to his objective site earlier than anticipated. He was grinning as his blood pumped and a feeling of utter joy passed through him. This was his natural element, and he was going to use that to his advantage. He could feel a larger snow storm coming, smelling it in the wind, spurring him to run faster. Unknown to Johnny, he was being watched from thousands of miles up, a surveillance satellite tracking his progress.

It only took him a little over an hour to cover the few miles to the super freeway. He stayed to the forest as much as he could, only leaving it to cross a small river and a couple of roads. He emerged from the tree line and paused to take in what he was looking at. Hundreds of abandoned and destroyed vehicles littered the freeway in front of him. He saw everything from small cars to massive Kodiak tanks. The only thing to signify their age was the amount of snow covering the dead machines. Johnny slowly stepped over the barrier separating the freeway from the forest next to it and took a knee. He paused and looked around for any sign of movement. He stood and turned toward the pass, looming above him, the tops of each side shining and shimmering in the light of the early day. Johnny began to jog toward it, weaving around the many vehicle husks, getting closer to the walls of the pass. The shadows lengthened as the walls rose to either side of him. Johnny stopped and moved closer to the southern wall, searching for a spot to begin his climb. He finally found a likely spot and placed his battle rifle on his back, releasing it once the clamps engaged.

He gripped the cracks and ledges in the rock as he made his way up the sixty foot wall, hearing the magazines attached to his chest scrape against the rock. He moved quickly, but steadily as he ascended, knowing that one slip up could mean a fall to his death. His hand finally found a flat spot as he reached the top, allowing Johnny to pull himself up. He paused to take a few deep breaths, feeling the lack of oxygen in each. He stood up slowly and reached around for his pack, pulling it free from his back. He brought up the map again in his vision as he opened the pack. He had calculated the approximate spots where he was going to set the charges to effect the action he wanted. He set about placing the charges along the ridge just below the slope, cringing every time he heard the snow above him shift. He placed ten along the five hundred yard ridge evenly. He returned to his climbing spot and began to slowly lower himself back down the face. He paused again once at the bottom, feeling his muscles burn from exertion and lack of oxygen. He crossed the freeway to the northern face.

As he surveyed the wall, he realized his ascent would be more difficult. There were many places for his hands and feet, but then he would have to shuffle a dozen feet to the left to find the next set of hand and foot holds. Johnny popped his knuckles and began his climb, slower this time. It took him nearly twice as long as the first to get to the top. He realized once at the top, he had little time to finish setting up before the first of the Imperial vehicles were within sight. This side, he noticed once he was at the top, had no ridge. It was all one continuous slope. He moved carefully along the edge, placing charges in the snow of the slope, eleven total. He replaced his pack on his back and began his descent, pausing and gripping the cliff tightly as a large gust of wind threatened to pull him from the face. Once it died down, he continued his descent, finally reaching the bottom. He rolled his shoulders and stretched his arms to work out the muscles.

He looked around, trying to figure out the best use of the last nine charges in his bag. He smiled when he remembered the river he crossed earlier. It ran under the east bound part of the freeway. He moved quickly to that section, noticing that several dead tanks created a roadblock at the halfway point. He vaulted over the barrier and made his way down the bank to just where the road left the ground. He moved under the freeway, placing charges in an arc, hoping it would be enough to collapse that section of the road into the frozen river thirty feet below. He focused on the charges and ensured that they were not on the same frequency as those at the top of the cliff faces. He finished his work and made his way back onto the freeway, running his plan through his head one last time. He started jogging toward the western entrance to the pass, trying to get to the firing position he chose earlier. He cleared the pass and moved toward a large outcropping of rock to the south of the freeway and quickly climbed it. It stood twenty feet higher than the freeway itself, giving him an elevated view of the pass. He thought about just setting up at the very top, but decided against it. Choosing, instead, a smaller ledge just below the top. He set his battle rifle down and pulled his hunting rifle off his back, extending the bipod and setting it on the rock. He lowered himself into a prone position and relaxed.

Johnny watched as the snow fell in heavier flakes, the storm he had sensed earlier was rolling in quickly. He was running the images for his three targets and their vehicles through his vision for the umpteenth time, when he heard the rumbling. Loose snow was shaken loose as the ground began to shudder slightly. The wind brought the sounds of engines to his ears, causing him to become alert once more. He looked to the west and saw a massive cloud of exhaust emitting from hundreds of engines. His eyes widened as the first of the convoy broke over the rise. The Rampage tanks were impressive pieces of equipment as they rushed toward him, their blades throwing up streams of snow, clearing much of it away for the rest of the convoy. Every now and then, one of them would hit a hidden vehicle sending the terrible sounds of crashing and tearing metal shrieking on the wind. Johnny narrowed his eyes as he saw the rest of the convoy behind the line of tanks. Johnny's hearing was drowned out as the roar of the engines became overwhelming.

The first line of the convoy moved into the pass, slowing slightly as the pile of snow, ice, and dead vehicles piled up in front of the Rampage tanks. Johnny grinned at the sight. The added weight of the pile would only serve to help his plan. He watched carefully as the Rampage tanks closed in on the far line of explosives. He saw the front line pause as the pile of debris in front of them seemed to be too much for their combined horsepower. They inched forward, passing over the eastern line of explosives. Johnny gave it a heartbeat of a pause before switching his comm unit over to the designated frequency.

Back at Liberty Barracks, Odin and the rest of the Minutemen stationed there watched the satellite images over the holo-table. They saw the convoy approach hours after Johnny had disappeared to the west of the pass. The convoy reached the eastern side of the pass, with the front ranks pausing nearly fifty meters from the opening to the pass, trying to push a massive pile of debris in front of them. The Minutemen looked at each other, looks of worry crossing their faces.

"What's going on?" Wildkat asked.

"I don't—HOLY FUCK!" Glitch yelled. Others cursed out loud too as they watched the footage.

Johnny smiled broadly as he triggered the explosives under the freeway. The road seemed to bend upward slightly, as flames shot through cracks and around the side. The Rampage tanks and the armored vehicles behind them jumped as the shockwave hit the bottom of them, the roar of the explosives blasting through the pass, overpowering the wind itself. They then disappeared in a blinding haze of snow, ash, smoke, and dust as the road collapsed, sending the first three lines of the convoy dropped into the river below. The next two lines fell as well as they tried to stop, only to be slammed and pushed from behind as the following lines were too slow in their reactions. Johnny saw hundreds of troops jump from their vehicles and rush toward the blast site. He grinned again as he heard a new sound over the engines and collapsing road way. The hollow cracks of the ice and snow at the top of the walls began to split and slide, unknown to the imperial troops below. Johnny switched the frequency of his comm to the other lines of explosives. He triggered them all at once, watching a line of fireballs erupt from the top of the cliffs. The shockwaves and force of the explosives completely shattered the fragile bonds keeping the snow and ice on the slopes from falling into the pass. The slopes shifted slowly, at first, picking up both speed and intensity as it turned into a pair of massive avalanches.

The imperial troops in the pass looked up in horror as the faint light they had turned to night as thousands of tons of snow, ice, and rocks poured into the pass.

Vehicles slammed into each other and unfortunate soldiers on the ground as their operators panicked and tried to flee. Johnny watched as the avalanches hit the freeway and rushed outward toward both ends of the pass. Johnny put his eye against his scope and swept his gaze along the convoy until he spotted his first target. Captain Lieutenant Tajiko Myn had opened the hatch to his modified Rampage tank to see what the holdup was. He sat there, frozen in fear and confusion as the mountain devoured his company. Johnny rested his crosshair on the officer and thumbed the safety off. He let out a breath and squeezed the trigger. The rifle bucked against his shoulder as the round flew off toward his target. Johnny watched as Tajiko pitched backward, a spray of blood erupting from his chest, unseen by the fleeing troops around his vehicle. Johnny lost sight of the tank and his dead target as the avalanche slammed into them and subsequently buried them. He cycled the bolt and chambered a new round, readjusting his position slightly to see the rest of the convoy.

Johnny continued his survey of the convoy until he spotted the modified Spider assault vehicle. He peered closely through his scope, zooming in on the vehicle. He could just see Shen Myn in the windshield, horror stitched across his face. Johnny used the connection between his eyes and the electronics in his rifle to up the power being poured into the concentric rings. He began to squeeze the trigger when a soldier ran in front of the vehicle. He eased up on the trigger until his line of sight was clear. He squeezed the trigger just as the soldier blocking his view moved. He watched as the windshield of the vehicle splintered then turn red from blood erupting from Shen's head. He saw the gunner behind Shen drop into the vehicle as the round passed through Shen and into his leg. Johnny shifted his aim and cycled the bolt, chambering a new round. He looked toward the back of the convoy and spotted the command vehicle. He caught sight of Ken Myn just as he ducked behind his vehicle. Johnny sighed angrily as he realized he would have to get up close and personal. He rose to a kneeling position, picking up his rifle. He closed the bipod and placed the rifle on his back, feeling the clamps engage.

He picked up his battle rifle and prepared to do the most dangerous thing he had ever contemplated. He grinned maniacally as he realized he was about to run into an avalanche that was still falling. He held his battle rifle tightly as he dropped from his ledge, sliding against the rocky slope toward the freeway. The edge of the avalanche was just starting to reach his position as Johnny came to his feet and jumped the barrier, touching down on the icy pavement.

He thumbed the safety of his battle rifle off and put it against his shoulder as he took off at a run. He squeezed the trigger, feeling the rifle buck against his shoulder five times, sending the burst into a trio of camouflaged troopers, cutting them down in sprays of crimson. The roar of the avalanche was deafening as it chased him. He weaved through the vehicles, firing on only those troops that tried to stop or take shots at him. He burned through half the magazine as he fired a burst nearly point blank into a heavy set trooper holding a shotgun. He kept his pace up as he jumped and slid across the hood of an armored vehicle. His feet touched the ground as the front of the avalanche slammed into the other side of the vehicle. Johnny heard the crack and zip of a dozen rounds as a handful of imperial soldiers tried to cut him down. Johnny fired the rest of his magazine into the group, cutting all but two down. He barely checked his run as he placed his battle rifle on his back, feeling the clamps engage and tug the weapon out of his hand. He pulled both pistols, thumbing the safeties off. He pointed them both at the two remaining soldiers and pulling the trigger. The pistols bucked as their heads practically exploded from the large caliber rounds. Johnny refocused his attention to the back of the convoy, trying to urge his legs to move faster. His muscles and lungs burned as he sprinted for all he was worth. He fired the pistol in his right hand dry as he shot down a pair of soldiers that were trying to get a heavy machine gun firing. Unable to stop and reload, Johnny checked his sprint long enough to holster the weapon, then moved again. That split second was long enough for the haze from the avalanche to start enveloping him.

Johnny spotted the command vehicle as he neared the end. His vision zoomed in to the back corner for a moment, bringing Ken Myn's face into full view as he peered around his vehicle. Johnny blinked and his vision returned to normal. He saw what appeared to be an officer ahead of him try to organize a handful of soldiers into a firing line, berating and beating them into submission. A few of them spotted Johnny's running form in the haze of the snow. Johnny heard the rounds zip by him, ricocheting off vehicles around him, and hitting their unfortunate comrades who wandered into their lines of fire. Johnny's left shoulder pitched backward suddenly as a round found him. His armor stopped the round, but it still stung like crazy. He lifted his pistol and let off an entire magazine of rounds into the firing line. The officer was the first to die, getting thrown backward into the snow as two or three round hit him. A few more dropped as more rounds found them, causing the others to take cover behind the vehicles next to them.

Johnny took advantage of their fear and rushed by them in a blur. He pressed the spent pistol against his thigh, hearing a few of the clamps engage. He reached back and pulled on the pistol grip of the shotgun, disengaging the clamps. He brought the shotgun around and then reached back with his right hand, gripping the handle of his hatchet. He pulled it free and swung it into the body of a soldier as they rounded the back of a vehicle in front of him. His forward momentum increased the force of the blow, causing the blade to bite deep and then get pulled free, throwing the unfortunate man into the vehicle behind him. Johnny was slowed by the hit and felt chunks of ice and snow pelt his back, warning him to move faster. He saw the end of the convoy and readied himself. His instincts screamed at him suddenly. Johnny dropped into a slide as he passed the command vehicle, avoiding the pair of soldiers that swung around it and opened fire. He twisted his body as he slid past them, bringing up his shotgun and thumbing the safeties off. He squeezed the trigger halfway back, firing the right barrel into the soldier to his left. He quickly shifted his aim and pulled the trigger fully, unloading the remaining barrel into the second soldier. They were both thrown against the vehicles they stood behind in a spray of blood. He used the momentum of the slide to come back to his feet, turning just in time to block a rifle strike from Major Captain Ken

Myn with his shotgun. Johnny pushed the officer away and swung his right arm around. The look in Myn's eyes showed shock and fear as the blade of Johnny's hatchet buried in his chest. Johnny pulled the blade free, blood dripping from it and watched the officer fall, the blood draining from his face, his eyes glazing over. Johnny looked up, his eyes narrowing, just as the avalanche slammed into the last line of the convoy.

The Minutemen watched in horror and amazement as the avalanched buried the convoy, the dust and debris being thrown up by it obscured the pass and immediate area around it. The had watched a figure they knew to be Johnny sprinting just ahead of the avalanche and then be swallowed by it as he finished fighting someone at the end.

"Liberty Barracks to Hunter, come in over…Liberty Barracks to Hunter, come in over," Odin said, keeping his voice steady and calm, even though at that moment he wanted to nothing more than rage. He watched as the reality of Johnny's fate set in on the faces of those around him. "Liberty Barracks to Hunter, come in over…Liberty Barracks to Hunter, come in please."

Broken static answered their hails. They watched as the debris settled, showing massive devastation.

"Liberty Barracks to Hunter, please respond," Odin repeated. His face fell as he realized they had lost another one. He reached over to shut down the comm channel, when the static broke, causing him to pause.

"Liberty Barracks, this is Hunter, over. Looks like I'm going to need a new extraction point," Johnny's voice broke through the static. A massive cheer erupted from the throats of those around him, causing him to smile. They watched as a signal beacon began transmitting, marking Johnny's position nearly thirty meters from where they had last seen him. It was moving steadily to the south into the dense forest nearby. Odin waved everyone to be silent as he answered.

Johnny was rattled back to consciousness by his radio screeching in his ear. His vision was black, yet he knew his night vision wouldn't help. He began to move his arms and legs, trying to claw his way out of the snow that had buried him. He had taken a chance to flee, hoping to outrun the worst of the avalanche. He had barely made it twenty meters when the full force of the avalanche had slammed into him, throwing him over the barrier of the freeway and into the ditch on the other side. With any luck, he was only a couple feet down as he clawed harder. The static in his ears became more pronounced. He spotted lighter sections of snow as he finally reached the surface. He burst through the top layer in an explosion of ice, worming the rest of his way out of the ditch.

"...Liberty Barracks, please respond," his radio crackled in his ears. He couldn't help but grin as he bent over double to catch his breath. He activated his microphone and spoke.

"Liberty Barracks, this is Hunter, over. Looks like I'm going to need a new extraction point," Johnny said. He heard cheers explode from the other end of the comm channel. He activated his beacon and looked around him. He saw a few Imperial soldiers climbing from the snow and decided it was a good time to become scarce. He stowed his hatchet and his shotgun, before turning to the south and heading for the trees.

"Copy, Hunter, alternate extraction coordinates sent. Get home safe," Odin responded. A set of coordinates scrolled through his vision, indicating a location three miles to the south. Johnny set off at a walk, feeling slightly exhausted. He smiled though as a thought came to mind. He opened his comm channel again.

"Think that 'delayed' them any?" Johnny said, a slight laugh in his voice. He heard several different laughs from the other end as Odin responded.

"I think it may have, just a little," Odin said. "Now get back here as soon as you can." Johnny nodded to himself.

"Yea, got a lot of work ahead of me," he responded, mostly to himself, looking toward the horizon to the west. Mostly to himself.

CPSIA information can be obtained
at www.ICGtesting.com
Printed in the USA
LVHW021209070423
743749LV00004B/53